ANOTHER DAWN

Deb Stover

Zebra Books
Kensington Publishing Corp.

http://www.zebrabooks.com

ZEBRA BOOKS are published by

Kensington Publishing Corp.
850 Third Avenue
New York, NY 10022

First Printing: January, 1999
10 9 8 7 6 5 4 3 2 1

Printed in the United States of America

For my family—Dave, Barbi, Bonnie, Ben, and Kookie-Dog, who never question my ongoing conversations with imaginary people and animals. Thanks for not sending out a search party to find me in my office while I finished this book.

As always, my undying appreciation to all the WYRD Sisters for brainstorming without a net or hazardous-duty pay. Special thanks to Karen, Paula, Carol, and Cindy for critiquing above and beyond the call of duty, and to Karen Harbaugh for a huge vote of confidence.

"*The current flows along a restricted path . . . in the meantime the vital organs may be preserved; and pain, too great for us to imagine, is induced . . . For the sufferer, time stands still; and the excruciating torture seems to last for an eternity.*"

—Nicola Tesla

Chapter One

The heavy thud of Luke Nolan's heart played a funeral dirge. Footsteps echoed through the tunnel, keeping time with his pulse, as if the entire proceeding were meticulously choreographed.

Music to fry by.

His hands were cuffed, and chains linked his ankles, their rhythmic *chink, chink, chink* punctuating his death march. Everything seemed magnified, in slow motion. Surreal neon lighting provided the finishing touch.

Looking around, he counted one woman—the prison doctor who would pronounce him dead—and eight men. *How many assholes does it take to execute Luke Nolan?*

He almost laughed. Hell, he should laugh. Eleven years rotting on death row should give him that right. So much for the Court of Appeals and a pitiful excuse for a public defender.

How do you plead?

Not guilty.

And no one had believed him, including his so-called attorney.

The prison chaplain appeared at Luke's side, an open Bible clutched in his hands as they continued the long walk to the execution chamber. Luke was beyond prayer, but it couldn't hurt. Maybe, just maybe . . .

Get over it. You're dead meat, Nolan.

He banished hope from his mind and heart as the heavy doors opened before them. It was freezing cold, in absolute contrast to what he'd soon feel.

Luke swallowed the lump in his throat, commanding himself not to reveal his fear. These sons of bitches wanted him to fry, and there wasn't a frigging thing he could do to prevent it, but he'd be damned before he'd give them the satisfaction of seeing his terror. No matter how real . . .

"Would you like last rites, Luke?" the chaplain asked.

For a moment, Luke met the man's gaze. The expression in the priest's aging eyes left no doubt he disapproved of these proceedings. "Nah, that's all right, Father. Too late for me."

"I've always believed in your innocence," he whispered. "I'll pray for your soul, my son. Is there anyone you'd like me to call?"

"No thanks, Father." So there was one person in the whole world who actually believed him. One. "Tell my grandma . . ."

"Yes?"

"Never mind." Luke released a long sigh. "She wouldn't even believe you. Thanks just the same, Father."

Raised by his devoutly Catholic grandparents, Luke Nolan had been a kid from Denver, in the wrong place at the wrong time. Tough, cool, cocky as hell . . .

And gullible.

Eleven years ago, he'd followed Ricky—a punk from nowhere with no last name—into that liquor store, believing they were after a fresh six-pack. One minute they were joking around. A few seconds later, Ricky pulled a gun on the old man behind the counter.

The crotchety old fart triggered an alarm before Ricky could clean out the register. Enraged by the man's nerve, Ricky shot the clerk between the eyes and ran, leaving both his gun and Luke behind.

Luke was a wild kid, but not a killer. He'd never even owned a piece, for Christ's sake. But when the cops rushed in and found him on his knees with a rag pressed to the man's bloody forehead, it was a done deal.

No witnesses and no prints on the gun—just an eighteen-year-old punk who'd already found plenty of trouble in his young life. Luke was arrested, tried, and convicted practically before the victim drew his last breath.

Eleven years. Luke sighed and looked around the room—anything to keep him from fixating on the *chair*. Public outrage over capital punishment had delayed his execution countless times. With so many idle hours on his hands, he'd even managed to earn his college degree.

After the raging hormones of adolescence had loosed their grip on his sanity, Luke discovered a new side to himself. If his appeal had ever came through, he'd intended to complete his Master's and teach high school. Hell, maybe be could've prevented a few punks from ending up like him.

Idealistic bastard.

Bitterness settled in his gut like acid, and he swallowed the bile that burned his throat. Hell, at least getting his degree had kept him busy.

"I have something for you," the priest said, jerking Luke back to the present. "Your grandfather wrote a—"

"My grandfather *died* three years ago." Disbelief and the pain of remembrance sliced through Luke. His pulse escalated to a jarring thud in his ears as he recalled his grandmother's words when she'd phoned with the news. She'd accused him of murdering the old man with shame.

The priest lowered his gaze for a moment, then drew a deep breath, reached into his pocket, and withdrew an envelope. "Your grandmother sent this yesterday. Your grandfather left instructions that you were to have it if—"

Luke gnashed his teeth, hoping the noise might blot out the memory of his last visit from his grandfather. Albert Nolan was the only man in the world Luke had ever truly respected. That respect had given the old man power— too damned much power.

With shaking fingers, Luke took the envelope, swallowing the lump in his throat. "Thanks, Father." It wasn't the priest's fault that Luke had once cared enough for someone to make himself vulnerable to this kind of pain.

"What's that?" Warden Graham stopped in front of Luke and snatched the envelope.

"It's only a letter from the boy's grandfather," the priest explained, sighing.

With a smirk, Graham looked at the envelope, then returned it to Luke. "Make it quick."

Luke refused to meet the warden's gaze, knowing he'd find a malicious gleam in those accusing eyes. After the warden turned and walked away, Luke opened the envelope and unfolded the single page to view his grandfather's spidery scrawl. His vision blurred, but he blinked several times to clear it, then noted the ten-year-old date at the top of the page—the same day Luke's death sentence was handed down.

You shamed me. I will go to my grave grieving the end of the Nolan name. I hereby disown you. Albert Nolan.

Neatly, Luke refolded the page and returned it to the envelope. "Will you destroy this for me later, Father?" He cleared his throat and tried not to see the pity so obvious in the priest's faded gray eyes.

"Of course, my son." He sighed. "I'm sorry."

"Don't be, Father," Luke said, looking beyond the priest's white hair to the stark walls of the chamber. "Don't be."

Then a prickling sensation on the back of his neck told him someone was watching him. He looked up and met the doctor's anxious gaze. She looked nervous as hell as she tucked a dark curl behind one ear. Something sparkled on her cheek, and she brushed it away with the back of her hand. Tears? *Fat chance.* No one would cry for him.

"It's time," a rough voice said from behind the priest.

"I hate this," the woman said loud enough for everyone to hear. "Why won't you let me ex—"

"Too late now, *Doctor,*" the warden said, rubbing his chest.

"But you can't do—"

"All you have to do is tell us when it's over and sign the death certificate." The warden turned his back on the doctor and approached Luke again. "Now I can retire knowing I did my job right," he said, his eyes glinting with malicious victory before he walked away.

Luke drew a deep breath, deciding not to waste it on a response. The warden's wishes had been obvious for years. Swift justice. *Yeah, right. Justice.*

"Go with God, my son," the chaplain said quietly. As he backed away murmuring in outdated Latin, he made the sign of the cross toward Luke. A blessing.

Once upon a time, Luke would've understood the words. Now, too late, he wished he could remember their meaning. He wished so damned many things, but he dared not think of his grandfather again. Anything but that.

Defeated, he pushed away thoughts of the priest and all things religious. This was the end—he had to face it. Resolutely, he forced his gaze back to the vehicle for his one-way trip to hell. It looked like something from Dr. Frankenstein's lab. A moment later, two men led him to the chair, replaced the chains and handcuffs with automatic restraints, then placed electrodes on his shaved head and one leg.

The sick part of him had wanted—needed—to know exactly what would happen today, so he'd researched the fine art of electrocution in preparation for the big event. These innocuous little electrodes would send two thousand volts of current blasting through his body. Nineteen hundred degrees Fahrenheit. His eyeballs would pop out of their sockets, and his face and appendages would become hideously contorted and disfigured. The stench of his burning flesh—inside and out—would permeate the chamber.

The burning flesh of an innocent man . . .

The condemned usually defecated and urinated after the current had done its job. Pity he'd be too far gone by then to witness his executioners' gagging and retching. They'd know soon enough why Luke Nolan had requested a hot and nasty burrito for his last meal.

Another man rushed into the room, his face flushed and his breathing labored. Luke couldn't prevent a surge of hope, and he exchanged a questioning glance with the priest. Could this be a last-minute reprieve?

"We got a bomb threat and we're evacuating," the man said.

"Not a chance. We'll be finished in a few minutes," the warden said. "Those bleeding hearts don't see a damn thing wrong with blowing us to hell and back, but they cry cruelty at simple justice."

Last year, when a particularly aggressive activist organization had threatened to prevent Luke's execution by any means necessary, the authorities had transferred him to a brand-new underground facility far up in the mountains. He didn't even know exactly where they were—some new prison with high-tech equipment for ridding the world of scum like him. The maximum security facility was built into a mountain like NORAD. It wasn't even officially open yet, and as far as he knew, he was the one and only prisoner.

Soon, there would be none.

Compassion filled the priest's eyes, and Luke jerked his gaze away, hating himself for hoping, even for a moment. "Just get it over with," he muttered, grinding his teeth. He refused to beg for his miserable life.

The doctor stood beside the priest, more tears trickling unheeded down her cheeks. Everyone deserved at least one mourner when they died, and now Luke had two more than he'd expected.

Except for the doctor's murmuring to the priest, an obscene silence fell over the room as the head fry cook pulled a black hood over Luke's face. The mournful wail of sirens sounded in the distance as thunder rumbled to a roar, then faded, only to return even louder. Closer. Not thunder, Luke realized. Explosions.

The first searing jolt tore through his body and he screamed. Unbearable pain . . . If the current failed to kill him, insanity would finish the job. No human could endure such pain and live.

The chaplain reverted to English and Luke clung to the familiar words above the boom of another explosion. Pandemonium erupted around him just as the next surge plundered through him.

This time he didn't scream. Instead, he could've sworn he heard his own desperate voice join the priest's.

Our Father, who art in Heaven . . .

Something heavy pressed down on Luke's chest, pinning him beneath its oppressive weight. He had to breathe. He clawed the hood from his face, but even without it only darkness greeted his gaze.

His arms and legs were free. Strange. When had they released the automatic restraints? Or maybe he was already dead, and this was hell.

He drew the deepest breath possible as he ran his hands down his chest until he found something cool and rough. Jagged edges scraped his burned fingers, and he realized the weight was a pile of pieces, rather than one large object.

His heart slammed against his chest as the truth emerged from his fried brain. No, not quite fried—only singed. The explosions had saved him.

I'm alive.

Joy and fear rushed through him as he shoved the crumbled stones from his chest. Little by little, the weight eased until he could breathe. His ribs were intact—a miracle.

Luke closed his eyes and sighed. A miracle, yes.

He remembered the prison chaplain and the doctor. Were they alive, too? Then another thought made his gut wrench into a tight fist against his heart.

Escape was his only hope. If anyone found him, they'd only try again. Hell, they'd probably pin the bombing on him, too. But wasn't there something in the law about men who survived execution? No, he couldn't be sure of that. Warden Graham would find a way.

But Luke Nolan would commit suicide before he allowed them to strap him into that chair again. The pain . . .

Sweat popped from every pore and his skin stung. He felt sunburned. Yes, his skin was burned all right. No telling how much internal damage all that electricity might have inflicted. He could still die.

The hell I will.

Determinedly, Luke freed himself from the rubble and sat upright. His head throbbed and he rubbed his temples, struggling with his memory. They'd brought him down one or two floors in an elevator, then through a long tunnel. The building must have collapsed during the explosions. Now all he had to do was find his way to the surface.

To freedom.

At least he wasn't completely buried. A few more small rocks fell, as if to remind him how quickly that could change. Shielding the top of his head with his folded arms, he rose. The entire mountain could come down at any moment. He had to get out fast, for more reasons than one.

The air was thick with dust and smoke. With gas and electric lines, the place could go up without warning. Resisting the urge to cough, he took a step just as a beam of light appeared in front of him. Instinctively, he ducked, bumping his knee against something hard and smooth. Somehow, he knew it was the electric chair, and he swallowed convulsively.

The light grew brighter, dragging Luke's gaze to it again. At first, he'd thought it was a flashlight, but now he realized it was the sun. *Of course.* His execution had been scheduled to occur before dawn.

Another dawn he was never meant to see.

"God, I'm alive," he whispered, his parched throat stinging as his eyes filled with tears. This sunrise was a gift, a sign. A new beginning. Drawing a deep breath, he took a step toward the light, praying it would lead him outside.

A sharp pain shot through his knee and he stumbled, barely preventing a fall. His injuries were minor compared to electrocution and being buried alive.

Alive.

Limping, Luke continued his slow trek through the debris, picking his way blindly over piles of rubble. If only he had shoes . . .

A sudden sound made him freeze. Despite the thud of his pulse, he listened. There it was again, a low moan. Someone else was alive in this mess. But who? More importantly, did it matter?

An icy chill raced down his spine. Whoever it was could

very well cost him his freedom. Nothing—*nothing*—was worth that price.

He pushed his foot forward to continue his escape, but the moan came again. Closer. *Keep going, Nolan.* He slid his other foot forward, but it stopped against something solid and warm.

A body.

Warm and alive, the body trembled, and Luke jerked his foot back. *God, no. Please, no.*

"Help me."

The voice was so weak he'd barely heard it. Maybe he hadn't.

"Help," it came again, barely more than a strangled whisper.

He mentally kicked himself for not running. What made him pause? His conscience? Fat lot of good that had done him the night he tried to help a dying liquor store clerk.

Remembering the injustice, the past eleven years of living hell, and the horrors of the electric chair, he started to walk away just as icy fingers clamped around his bare ankle. Luke's gasp sounded more like a shout in the deathly silence. He struggled to free himself, but the person's fingernails gouged his singed flesh.

A death grip.

Terror plucked at his sanity as he remembered the pain of the electric chair. No, he couldn't go through that again. He'd rather die here and now by any other means.

Panic strengthened him as he freed his foot and lunged forward, falling headfirst over another body. A strangely still body. Cold like death.

He eased back on hands and knees. The sun was higher now, glinting off something on the dead man's chest. With shaking fingers, Luke reached out to touch the object, knowing without seeing. The crucifix felt cool and smooth beneath his burned fingers.

"Go with God, my son." His memory of the priest's words filled Luke's head even as another moan reached his ears.

The only man who'd believed in his innocence was dead. Luke was supposed to have died this morning, but for some reason he was alive and this man wasn't. He eased the crucifix over the priest's head and slipped it over his own, holding its weight in his palm before releasing it.

It's a sign.

The sun now filled the chamber with enough light to allow Luke to see the dead man. His injuries must've been internal, because there wasn't a mark on him.

As Luke stood, he remembered his state of dress. How far would he get wearing something similar to a hospital gown and no shoes? The priest's robe was intact, and he wouldn't need his shoes anymore.

Without another thought, he took the man's black robe and slacks, tugging them on over his tender flesh. He needed shoes, too, and as he slipped on the chaplain's roomy wingtips, Luke was thankful for his smaller feet. The priest's Bible lay to one side, and Luke took that, too, justifying the act as part of his disguise.

"Thank you, Father," Luke whispered, then moved again toward the light.

"Please help me." This time, no doubt remained—the voice was female.

Damn. If it had been anyone else he'd be out of here by now, but he couldn't leave her. The least he could do was help her outside where someone might find her. Hell, for all he knew a rescue team was already digging for them and would drag him back to prison until another execution could be arranged.

Gritting his teeth, he picked his way back to the woman and knelt beside her. Pain pierced his kneecap, but he allowed himself nothing more than a wince. If he and the doctor were alive, then someone else could be, too. Someone like the warden from hell . . .

He could see her face now. Blood soaked one side of her head and neck, but her eyes were open, pleading. With strangers, his disguise might have worked long enough to permit his escape. Why was he such a sucker?

"We have to get out of here," he said quietly. "Can you walk?"

She licked her lips. "I—I'm not sure."

Luke refrained from telling her she could either walk or stay. Instead, he leaned closer, noting her legs and body seemed unharmed. "I'll help you stand."

She groaned as he eased her to a sitting position. Blood seeped from the wound at her temple, and he fished through his pockets until he found a handkerchief. Pressing it against the flow of blood, he helped her to her feet. She wavered slightly and gripped his arm for support.

"Let's go." He kept one arm wrapped around her waist while she continued to cling to him. Cursing every second's delay, he finally found the opening. He'd never appreciated the sun before, but everything was different now. Every breath was precious.

"My head," she said, leaning more heavily against his arm.

"Look, we're getting out of here now." Luke propped her against a pile of rocks, then turned to examine the opening. It might be wide enough for her to squeeze through, but he'd never fit. Loose bricks hung like broken teeth on either side. Carefully, he knocked them away until the space was wide enough.

"C'mon." He practically dragged her through the narrow opening, ignoring the searing pain of his burned flesh scraping against jagged bricks.

Luke paused to look back once. Sunlight glinted off something metal. *The chair.* A cold lump formed in his gut, followed by a flash of heat, as if he needed reminding . . .

With renewed resolve, he turned away and led the doctor outside. A sheer wall of granite hid the opening from the outside world. They were lucky even a little sunlight had managed to find its way into the chamber.

Outside, Luke shaded his eyes and looked around. They were far out in the wilderness. To put it simply, he had no idea where they were, other than somewhere in the Rocky Mountains.

Where would he go? He glanced at the doctor, knowing he could travel much faster without her. Besides, she needed medical attention. "Someone will find you here," he said, easing her to the ground where she leaned against a rock.

"Don't leave me." Tears trickled down her cheeks when she looked up at him. "I . . ."

"Trust me, lady," he said quietly, "you don't want to go where I'm going."

Her pleading expression tore at him, but Luke forced himself to remember everything. The injustice, the pain, the betrayal . . . No, he wasn't willing to sacrifice his freedom for anyone or anything. Never again.

"Please, I—"

"No. I'm outta here." He pushed her hands away and took several steps, that nagging voice in the back of his head tormenting him. She was hurt—he shouldn't leave her here like this. What if she died?

She cried for me.

No one had ever shed a tear on his behalf before. No one. Hell, he knew she hadn't been crying for him specifically, but still . . .

"Please?"

He barely heard her as a brisk wind whistled through the trees. Clouds gathered and blocked the sun, promising either rain or snow. There were no roads, no parking lot, no sign of civilization at all. Something wasn't right. He stopped and turned in a full circle, trying not to look at her, yet knowing she still followed.

He reached into his pocket and found the priest's car

keys. A small crucifix dangled from the key ring. With a sigh, Luke looked directly at the woman. "Come on, let's find the car that goes with these keys."

Ignoring her expression of relief, he waited for her to catch up with him. She seemed more stable now. Maybe her injury wasn't as serious as he'd feared. "I'll drive you to the nearest hospital, then you're on your own."

She nodded, gingerly touching the ugly gash at her temple. "I think the bleeding's stopped."

"Yeah, looks like it." Luke looked around, trying not to dwell on the woman's vulnerability. She didn't reach his shoulder, and he doubted she weighed more than a hundred pounds, if that.

"Where are we going?"

Luke looked at her and shook his head. "Away. Who gives a shit?"

She gave him a look of disbelief. "I didn't know p—"

"Enough talk." He'd wasted too much precious time already, though every indication told him there was no reason to hurry. None at all. "Weird."

"What's weird?"

"Nothing." He took her hand and started downhill, though there wasn't even a trail to follow. All he could do was hope he'd find a parking lot soon with a Chevy to match the priest's keys.

The altitude stole his breath, and sweat did nothing to ease the sting of his skin, but he kept walking. Somehow, miraculously, the woman kept up with him, though he knew she must be even worse off than him. She'd lost a lot of blood.

"How much farther?" she asked at the base of the hill.

Luke shot her a side glance and noticed her flushed face and rapid breathing. He probably looked even worse, especially with his head shaved and his skin fried. "You okay?"

She nodded. "But how much farther to the car?"

"How the hell should I know?" Why hadn't he left her behind? She would've been all right.

"You don't know where you parked your car?"

"*My* car?" He chuckled in disbelief. "Lady, I've never owned a car."

Furrowing her brow, she looked beyond him. "Maybe we should go up that hill and have a look."

That made sense. If he could find a highway to follow . . . Of course, he'd have to be more careful about staying hidden once they reached civilization.

Without comment, he started up the hill, dragging her by the hand. By the time they reached the summit, they were both gasping for breath, and they collapsed at the base of a tall pine.

After a few minutes, Luke managed to stand, using the tree for assistance. When he looked down, he saw the doctor holding her hand out toward him in a silent plea for help.

"God, I'm such a fool," he muttered in disgust, even as he pulled her to her feet.

The clouds were thicker now, covering the tops of the higher peaks in the distance. He shivered as the air cooled his skin.

"Over there."

Luke looked where the woman still pointed, squinting to see. "What?"

"I saw some buildings, but the clouds moved again."

Shaking his head, Luke slowly surveyed their surroundings. He released her hand and walked around the tree, looking as far as possible in every direction. Trees, mountains, and one stream. No roads, cars, or buildings.

"Where the hell are we?"

"There, I told you so," she said, drawing Luke's attention back to where she'd pointed earlier. "See?"

The clouds at this altitude were more like fog, shrouding mountains and trees in white. He looked where she continued to point, waiting as the clouds grew more dense, then gradually parted.

"See?" she repeated. "Over there."

"Yeah." Several buildings were clustered on the side of a mountain.

"It must be a town," she said.

Luke nodded, then looked back from where they'd come. There was no evidence that a prison had ever existed. None at all. "I don't get this." He remembered being escorted into a brand-new facility, with every possible convenience. Where the hell was it now?

Government buildings didn't just vanish. There should be tons of rescue equipment up here now, digging for survivors.

What building?

"Come on, let's go," she said, tugging on his sleeve.

The woman didn't seem the least bit concerned about their peculiar situation. "All right." So much for the priest's car, wherever it was.

After they'd walked for what seemed like miles, she stopped and looked at him. "You look tired, Father, and my feet are killing me."

Father? Luke froze in mid-step to stare at her. "What'd you call me?"

"Father. You are a priest, aren't you?" The look on her face screamed sincerity. "Should I call you something else?"

"Uh . . ." Luke remembered the priest's Bible in the pouch at his waist. The robe. The crucifix. *Go with God.* "Father is fine." He swallowed hard. If she didn't remember who he was, then . . .

She didn't know he was a condemned man. Luke's heart slammed into his bruised ribs, and he drew a deep breath. "We'll stop and rest here."

She sat cross-legged on the ground, only a few feet away.

The expression on her face was one of complete innocence. Bewilderment. Forgetfulness?

Thank God.

Still, just because she didn't know who he was didn't mean others wouldn't. He had to put some distance between himself and the law. Maybe he'd go to Central America.

"Ready?" he asked, suddenly eager to start his new life. Her memory lapse was a gift. Another one.

They both stood and looked toward the town. It didn't seem nearly as far now, and the clouds had thinned somewhat, enabling Luke to make out the definite shapes of a few buildings. None of them looked big enough to be a hospital, though.

Once he knew she was safe and being cared for, he could walk away with a clear conscience. At last.

"Father, before we go . . ."

"What is it?" Luke tried to hide his impatience, reminding himself that she thought he was a real priest. With any luck, she wouldn't remember his true identity until he was hundreds of miles from here.

"Could you answer one question for me?"

"I'll try." Did she remember watching them strap him into that horrible chair? Did she remember his screams of agony? He closed his eyes and swallowed hard. Her tug on his sleeve made him open his eyes to meet her gaze.

Her eyes were large pools of blue, their intensity rivaled only by the purpling at the side of her head. "What is it?" he asked. They needed to keep walking. "Your question, I mean."

"Father," she said quietly, "who am I?"

Chapter Two

A gray veil shrouded her mind and words came to her disjointedly. Her thoughts were incomplete, as if someone had taken a giant eraser to part of her brain.

"You remember *nothing?*" He gripped her upper arms and stared into her eyes. "Nothing at all?" His voice fell to a harsh whisper. "Not even your name . . . or mine?"

She shook her head, and sharp pain stabbed through her skull. "Oh." She pressed the bloodied handkerchief to her temple, then removed it, relieved to find it dry.

"The bleeding's stopped, but you must have one helluva headache." His voice gentler now, he dropped his hands to his sides.

Immediately, she missed the warmth of his touch. *Bereft.* Yes, that was how she felt. If she could remember vocabulary, then why couldn't she remember her own name? "Please tell me what happened and who you are. Who I am . . ."

"Try very hard to remember." His nostrils flared, and

the expression in his gray eyes grew even more intense. "Please, just try."

"I *am* trying, but there's nothing." She watched him standing there, his black robe fluttering in the chilly wind. Every inch of his exposed skin was fiery red, and his sunburned head was almost comical. He certainly didn't look like a priest. Then again, how would she know? "I really don't remember anything," she said again.

"*Try.*"

Why was he pushing so hard for her to remember? It would be so much simpler if he would just *tell* her everything. Biting her lower lip, she drew a calming breath. This man was a priest, and he was obviously trying to help her. His insistence was for her own good—maybe he knew something about head injuries. Besides, she had no choice but to trust him.

She closed her eyes. Words and images flew by, barely eluding her, indistinguishable. The unexpected touch of his fingertips on her wrist surprised her, and she jerked her eyes open to watch him. He turned her hand over in his, then slipped his finger under a shiny, silver bracelet dangling from her wrist.

"This says your name is Sofie," he said quietly, looking at her with an intensity that stole her breath. "You still can't remember?"

"No, nothing. Sofie," she whispered, testing the sound of it on her lips. It felt right, sounded right. "What about my last name?" She squinted, trying to focus on the bracelet, but her vision blurred.

His brow furrowed and he drew a deep breath. "No last name here." He turned the silver rectangle over until the chain pulled the fine hairs on her forearm.

"Ouch."

Instantly, he dropped the bracelet. "Sorry." His voice seemed harsher now and he leaned toward her, peering into her eyes as if probing for something. "How do you spell it?" he asked, his gaze narrowing. "S-O-P-H-I-E?"

"No, with an F," she corrected, wondering how she could be so certain.

Several seconds of silence passed as he continued to stare, broadcasting accusation and suspicion. His extreme scrutiny made her feel as if she were on trial. This trust thing definitely wasn't reciprocal.

"Tell me, Sofie," he began, gripping her upper arms again, "if you remember the unusual spelling for your name, why can't you remember anything else?"

Bewildered, she licked her lips and wished her head would stop pounding. "I . . . I don't know." He obviously didn't believe her, yet why would she lie about losing her memory? Why would *anyone*? He didn't trust her. Was she a bad person? "I only remember opening my eyes in that cave—was it a cave?"

His eyes closed and he released her again. As he straightened and reopened his eyes, the lines on his sunburned forehead smoothed. "Yes, sort of," he said. His Adam's apple worked up and down in his throat.

At least he seemed to believe her now, though she couldn't imagine why he hadn't earlier.

He made a snorting sound and opened the leather pouch at his waist. "Well, look here." He withdrew a small white vial. "Aspirin for your headache." After tipping two white pills into his hand, he passed them to her and continued to search through his belongings.

He acted as if he didn't know what the pouch contained. How odd. Of course, who was she to question anyone's memory? Maybe she would remember more later. The correct spelling of her first name had come to her, after all. Eventually, other things would follow. Wouldn't they?

But since she'd remembered something on her own, perhaps now he would tell her. "Will you please tell me my last name now?'' Maybe hearing it would jar the rest of her memory.

He shook his head slowly, and something resembling compassion softened his expression. ''I really don't know. I'm sorry.''

Frustrated, she sighed, staring at the aspirin in her open palm. She remembered aspirin was for pain and fever, but she needed water to swallow it. With a sigh, she dropped it into her pocket for later.

She looked at him, wishing he would suddenly reveal this was all nothing more than a cruel hoax, and that he really did know her name. ''I guess if you don't know my name, then you don't know where I live either.''

''Nope.'' He turned away and looked toward the town again. A fine mist started to fall from the heavy clouds and the temperature dropped a few more degrees. ''We'd better get moving,'' he said, then looked at her again. ''Did you take the aspirin?''

''No water.''

''Oh, yeah. That's right.'' He looked up at the sky and sighed. ''This is lousy hiking weather, and I've known it to snow in the high country this time of year.''

''Snow?'' Had they survived one disaster only to fall victim to another? ''I guess we'd better hurry.''

''Yeah, that *was* my plan,'' he muttered, offering her his hand. ''Let's go.''

Sofie looked at his hand—a hand belonging to the man who had saved her from certain death in that cave. ''You may not know my name, but you must know yours.'' She made a halfhearted effort to smile as she placed her hand in his and met his gaze.

His breaths came in rapid succession, filling the air around them with white vapor. ''Father Salazar,'' he finally said in a strained voice. Thunder rumbled overhead as if to punctuate his introduction, then the sky burst open with a deluge. Without another word, he started up the rocky incline, dragging her along.

She struggled to keep pace, stumbling several times before they reached the top. The wind drove the rain harder now, whipping it into their faces.

"How much farther?" she shouted into the wind.

He paused, and she saw the dark shape of his head through the rain as he turned to look down at her. His expression was blurred by the watery curtain, but she figured he probably didn't appreciate her stopping at this point, even for a moment.

Without bothering to answer her question, he picked his way along, never releasing her hand. The sky darkened even more and the storm worsened, shrouding Father Salazar's dark shape—so close, yet so far. She clung to his wet hand, praying his status as a priest would grant them a miracle.

Like sand, the raindrops stung her icy cheeks until they felt like raw meat. Her feet had long since turned numb, as had the tip of her nose. Only her hands still had feeling—one tucked trustingly into Father Salazar's, and the other shoved deep into the pocket of her dirty white blazer.

Their pace slowed and Sofie's fear mounted. With visibility practically zero, they could be moving farther away from the town, rather than toward it. God, they were going to die and she couldn't even remember her name. Did she have a family? Would anyone miss her?

Scalding tears pricked her eyelids, but she blinked them away. The last thing she needed now was any more water on her skin.

Weariness pressed down on her and her head felt as if it would explode. *Explode* . . . Then she remembered the loud, thundering noises in the cave where she'd been injured. What was that place, and why had she been there?

A wave of dizziness gripped her and she lost her savior's hand. What little she could see turned to blackness, and she felt herself falling. She slid down a slope and hard gravel ground into her already raw face, but she was too weak to struggle. No more. She couldn't take another step.

This was the end. She would die up here in the wilderness without even knowing her name.

Luke felt her hand slip from his grasp and he stopped to look back. Rain fell so hard he could barely see his own hand, let alone Sofie. She could have tumbled down the mountainside without his knowing, the sound of her cries muffled by the raging storm.

And why should he care? Why should he continue to risk his own life for hers?

"Damn." Why didn't matter, because he couldn't leave her out here in this. No one deserved to be left alone to die in the wilderness.

Or in the electric chair.

Luke swallowed. Hard. It didn't help. Despite the frigid rain, the heat of electrocution flashed through him again. He shivered as hot and cold swept through him intermittently.

His breath came in rapid bursts as he stared back through the rain, hoping for, yet fearing a glimpse of Sofie. The thought of her name brought a pang of regret and he closed his eyes. He couldn't leave her here. She was almost as much a victim in this mess as he.

And she cried for me.

"Shit." He lowered his chin to his chest and forced his eyes open. *Wimp.* Gritting his teeth, he dropped to the ground and felt his way back a few feet. At first, the rain had stung his raw scalp and face like fire, but all he felt now were the flames of remorse in his gut.

If he didn't find her within a few minutes, he'd have to go on without her. At least by trying to find her, he might appease his guilt later. Still, he knew the memory of her tears would haunt him forever.

Unless the cops found him and saved him the trouble of forever.

He brushed against something rough. A rock. The wind and rain weren't as bad here, partially blocked by the rocky wall. Good news and bad news, since he couldn't remember passing this before. Where was Sofie?

Carefully, he turned until his feet were against the rock, then he crawled straight out from it, slowly picking his way. He blinked several times when he realized the ground took a slight drop. How far down? After a moment, he determined it was only a slight incline—just enough to hide Sofie in the storm. As he drew closer, he made out the shape of her dark hair and scrambled toward her.

Leaning close, he felt her neck for a pulse. She was alive, but unconscious. He slid one arm behind her shoulders and the other under her knees and lifted. Her weight made him stagger as he pushed to his feet. They'd both been through hell today, and he was ready to pass out right beside her.

But he couldn't, dammit. He had to keep going until he found help for her and freedom for himself. *Freedom.* The mere thought of it gave him strength, and he trudged back toward the rock wall.

He moved carefully, hoping they wouldn't end up tumbling all the way down the mountain. When he found the wall again, it brought welcome shelter from the wind and some of the rain. He adjusted his burden and turned his back against the cliff, inching his way along, tentatively testing the ground with his foot for any sudden drops.

The wall ended, but the ground didn't. Squinting through the rain, he saw a small opening in the side of the cliff. He eased through far enough to provide shelter. Like a womb, the rock closed in around them, shutting out the storm. The silence inside was startling, compared to the howling wind and deluge outside. As he lowered himself to the cold but dry stone floor, all Luke heard was their heavy breathing and the steady thud of his heart against the woman in his arms.

Incredible. Here he was alone in the wilderness with a beautiful woman—an unconscious woman who might very well cost him his freedom. And his life.

If he left her here out of the rain, she might regain consciousness and find her own way to civilization. Then again, she might die.

Which was more important, a clear conscience or his escape? He looked at her pale face in the dim light and his throat constricted. Yes, helping her would appease his guilt, but at what price?

Fool. Even as he argued with himself, he knew he wouldn't—couldn't—leave her. Like that night he'd tried to save a liquor store clerk's life . . .

Luke Nolan was no killer, and he wasn't about to start now.

He brushed her dark curls away from the bruise at her temple. At least her wound hadn't started to bleed again.

She looked young for a doctor. Young and vulnerable. She shivered and he pulled her closer. If only there were some way to get dry.

Her sodden lab coat gaped open, revealing small firm breasts, clearly outlined against her wet T-shirt. Running for his life or not, he couldn't prevent his hungry male gaze from seeking and finding her nipples. It had been so long since he'd touched a woman . . . And the last time, he'd been nothing but a horny teenager.

Now he was a man. A man who'd spent all his adult life behind bars. On death row. In isolation.

Oblivious to their predicament and his burned skin, Luke's body responded to her softness filling his lap. At least everything seemed to be in working order—amazing, considering. She was a beautiful woman, though a little on the skinny side. If only their situation were different . . .

"Oh," she moaned, shifting in his lap.

Luke tensed as her bottom pressed against his thrusting anatomy. *Some priest.* Holding his breath, he forced aside thoughts of sex and raging hormones and watched her closely. Her inky lashes fluttered a few times, then she opened her eyes and stared up at him.

"What . . . what happened?" She tried to push herself to a sitting position, but abandoned her efforts when he pressed his hand gently against her shoulder. "Where are we?"

"I think it might be an old mine," he said, watching her face closely. Had she remembered anything more? "How's your head?"

She touched her temple uncertainly. "Better, I think." She sighed and said, "But I still can't remember anything."

"I'm sorry." Of course, that was a lie. He was relieved she couldn't remember his true identity. Her expression of trust would undergo an immediate reversal if she realized who he was—a convicted felon.

Again, he was reminded that only a miracle had saved him. If not for that series of perfectly timed explosions, he would be dead by now. And this woman—this doctor— would have signed his death certificate.

"I must have fainted." She gave him a weak smile. "I'd like to try sitting up now."

"Take it easy." He helped her into a sitting position, which brought their bodies into even more intimate contact. But if she'd noticed his arousal, she didn't show it. *Yeah, some priest, Nolan.*

Luke winced as she slid across him. Bracing herself with her hand, she eased off his lap and onto the floor at his side. Now, maybe, he could get his ill-timed and ill-mannered cravings under control. He had far more urgent matters to attend.

"You okay?" he asked. His voice sounded hoarse. Strained. Had she noticed?

"Yes, I think so." She drew a deep breath and smiled. "Thank you again, Father."

He could grow to hate that title, except it might save his life yet. "You're welcome." Clearing his throat, he brought his knees up to chin level. "We'll rest here until the storm passes."

"Yes, maybe when the rain stops, we'll be able to see the town again."

"If we've been heading in the right direction." Luke tried to keep impatience from his voice, but this delay could cost him plenty. "From what I saw before the rain started, we still have to go down this mountain and up another."

She sighed and scooted against the stone wall beside him, her thigh barely touching his. Following his example, she pulled her knees against her chest.

Luke couldn't prevent himself from remembering what she'd felt like in his lap. His pulse escalated and his heart pressed against his constricting throat, just as his erection pressed against the zipper of Father Salazar's trousers.

Shame filled him. The real priest was dead and Luke was alive. The least he could do was keep himself from getting a boner every time a woman brushed against him. But how?

By planning his future. Now that he had one . . .

He'd take Sofie to the town, then head south. There wasn't much money in Father Salazar's wallet, but there was probably enough for a bus ticket. Distance was the key.

Distance . . . and speed.

* * *

Sofie tried not to remember Father Salazar's erection, but she couldn't help it. A priest had responded to her sexually.

A priest! She swallowed hard and bit her lower lip. Of course, she shouldn't even have noticed, and it was wrong of her to think about it now.

What kind of person was she? She had no idea. Sofie was a stranger to herself. For all she knew, maybe she was the kind of woman who would encourage such attention from a man. Even from a priest . . . ?

No. It had been a simple quirk of nature. Nothing more. The sooner she forgot about the incident, the better. Right now, survival took precedence.

And regaining her memory.

Her clothing was soaked through, but at least they were out of the storm. She sniffled and wiped her nose with her sleeve. Her shivering stilled somewhat, becoming intermittent, rather than continuous.

"Do you know what time it is?" she finally asked.

"Beats me." His voice was warm and vibrant. Alive. "My stomach thinks it's lunchtime, though. Especially since I didn't get breakfast."

Sofie nodded, amazed that her head no longer pounded. Nearly freezing to death seemed to have helped. Gingerly, she touched her temple and sensed Father Salazar's gaze on her.

"How's your head?" he asked again. "Really?"

"Better. Really." She sniffled again. "I wonder how long the storm will last."

"Hard to say, but it's early enough in the season that even if it changes to snow, it shouldn't be too bad." He gave a derisive laugh. "But it sure seemed bad enough while we were out there."

"Yes." She looked down at her thin white blazer, worn over a pair of jeans and a dark green T-shirt. At least she was wearing hiking boots. Still, even to her frazzled mind, her clothing seemed mismatched. Wrong, somehow. "What's this jacket I'm wearing? Some kind of uniform?"

"A lab coat, I suppose." The harsh edge had returned to his voice. "You're a doctor."

"A *doctor?*" Sofie stared at him for several seconds. The intensity of his gaze was riveting yet disturbing. He watched her as if he expected something. "Are you serious? I'm a doctor?"

"Yeah." He released his breath in a loud *whoosh* and looked down at his hands, draped over his knees. "Are you still cold?" he asked without looking at her.

"Yes." A draft infiltrated their cocoon and she shivered violently. "If only we could get d-dry."

"Dumb question, huh? We're both wet and cold." He scooted closer and put his arms around her shoulders. "I can't think of any other way," he said in a somewhat apologetic tone.

The warmth of his embrace stopped her shivering. Maybe their combined body heat would keep them from freezing. At any rate, it made her feel safe and warm. Neither of them spoke, and despite the cold, his sunburned skin radiated heat through his wet clothing. She drew comfort against the solidness of his shoulder.

"I can't be a doctor," she said finally, breaking the silence. "I would remember something about medicine, wouldn't I?"

His arms tensed around her and she heard his teeth grinding. "Believe me, you're a doctor."

"How do you know? Where were we and what were we doing? For that matter, what happened back there?"

"What do you think happened?"

"I . . . I'm not sure." She lifted her head and looked up at his face through the dimness. "Something exploded."

He nodded. "That's right. Something exploded."

She had so many more questions to ask, but he pulled

away and poked his head through the narrow opening to the outside.

"It's stopped." He turned to face her with an urgent expression. "We have to go now, or we'll end up spending the night in this cave."

Alone. Priest or no priest, Sofie didn't feel right about being here alone with him all night. Not after what she'd noticed earlier. In fact, it was *because* she'd noticed that made her wary. But why? There was nothing even remotely attractive about a bald, sunburned priest.

"I'm ready to try," she said. "Let's go."

He rose to a half-crouch beneath the low ceiling and held out his hand. Trusting him with her life yet again, she placed her hand in his and followed him outside.

Patches of blue showed through the clouds now, and she shaded her eyes to look into the distance. They both scanned the landscape several times before he pointed and said, "There it is."

Without waiting for her response, Father Salazar started walking. How many more mountains? She tried to remember what she'd seen earlier from a higher vantage point, before the storm. Down this one and up one more?

Her wet clothes chafed her skin as she struggled to keep pace. She understood and shared his urgency, but her body protested every jarring step.

At the bottom, she pulled her hand free. "Please, I need a minute."

He turned to look back at her, his eyes blazing with impatience . . . and something more. He looked frantic. But maybe it was the thought of being stranded in the wilderness overnight that made him seem that way.

Or maybe he shared her concern about the two of them being stranded out here alone.

"I'm sorry," she said quietly. "I'm ready now."

Grunting in acknowledgment, he started up the mountain, then paused to take her hand. His shaved head glistened fiery red in the filtered sunlight.

How had he been sunburned so badly? And who was she, and why had she been way up here in the mountains with a priest in the first place? And why didn't he know her name if he knew she was a doctor? None of this made sense.

And what had caused the explosion she barely remembered? In fact, that was the very last thing she remembered before Father Salazar had saved her from certain death. She owed him her life.

Regret slithered through her as she struggled against her clinging wet jeans to keep pace with the priest. She should never have distrusted him, or given his physical reaction to her a second thought. How ridiculous.

Enough of this. It was time for her to concentrate on survival and recovery. Someone somewhere would know who she was. Wouldn't they? She hoped so, because a thorough search of her pockets had netted nothing but a couple of dissolved aspirin. No identification at all.

"Here we are." Father Salazar's voice broke through Sofie's thoughts. "It's not much of a town, but it's better than nothing."

Sofie mopped perspiration from her brow with her damp sleeve and nodded. Soon this nightmare would be over, and someone would tell her who she was.

"Let's go find you a doctor or hospital."

A few wood-framed buildings skirted the edge of town, as well as a couple of log cabins. They emerged from the trees and onto a dirt road that led to the town. Sofie looked down the mountain, where the road twisted and turned, then vanished into the trees.

"Civilization, such as it is," Father Salazar muttered, and started toward town.

Sofie took two steps for every one of his to keep pace, but she was as eager as he to end their adventure. A crude wooden sign at the edge of town read, "Redemption, Colorado, Population 247."

He chuckled, but she didn't ask why. Nothing mattered now except finding help. She hadn't realized how frightened she'd been of dying in the wilderness until now. A tear trickled down her cheek unheeded.

"Stop right there," a gruff voice said as two men emerged from the nearest cabin.

"Oh, God, no." Father Salazar squeezed her hand hard, then released it. He took a backward step as the two men aimed their long rifles.

And cocked the triggers.

Chapter Three

Terror seized Luke. Panic spread from his gut and into his chest. It flowered through his veins like molten lava from an erupting volcano.

He stared at the rifle barrels aimed at his chest. His blood turned icy, as memories of the electric chair's merciless, blazing pain returned to torment and torture him.

The mountains seemed to close in as he scanned the area for a means of escape. He took two backward steps. The men advanced on him, their rifles unwavering.

Again, he tried to swallow, but his throat felt as if he'd been drinking battery acid. His eyes burned and his vision blurred and cleared repeatedly, as his tear ducts tried to replenish the moisture two thousand volts had zapped from them. Despite all the rain, his body was parched inside and out.

The men took another step.

They won't take me back alive. Never.

But even as he made his vow, a slight movement at his side reminded him that he wasn't alone. What about Sofie?

He had to make sure she'd be all right here before he escaped—assuming he *could* escape. *But why do I have to?* He'd already lost most of the day trying to get her to safety.

He shot her a sideways glance. *Damn.* She looked terrified. Why shouldn't she be? She'd lost her memory, been stranded in the wilderness with the likes of him, and now she faced a pair of armed bullies who could have just stepped off the set of *Deliverance.*

Even so, he should run. Let the bastards shoot him in the back and end this nightmare. Anything was better than facing that chair again.

Yes, he *should* run . . . but he didn't. Why?

Think. These guys didn't look like prison guards, or any other branch of law enforcement, for that matter. Dressed in dirty jeans with many-colored patches, they looked like good ol' boys or ranchers with hunting rifles.

Drawing a deep breath, Luke forced himself to meet the taller man's gaze. The man's expression left no doubt he meant business but he appeared almost apologetic, as if he didn't approve of his own actions.

"What do you want?" Luke asked finally, his tongue sticking to the roof of his mouth. He was so thirsty he could barely talk, but all he wanted was to be free . . . and to leave Sofie somewhere safe. Nothing more. He didn't even want food or water, if they'd just let him walk—run—away. "I don't have much money."

His gaze unwavering, the taller man spat tobacco juice on the ground near Luke's stolen shoes. "Nah, you got it all wrong, *Padre.* We're here to protect you."

"Yeah, sure. See, I'm not used to having guns pointed at me for my own protection." Luke made a feeble attempt at a smile, but the corner of his lip cracked in protest, and he felt blood trickle down his chin.

Sofie moved closer to Luke and took his hand again. He didn't *want* to be responsible for her. Hadn't he suffered enough already, without having this woman's safety on his conscience, too?

"Protect us from what?" Sofie asked, her voice surprisingly steady, and her gaze riveted on the rifles. "I really don't like guns."

The short, bald man lowered his rifle, allowing the barrel to point harmlessly toward the ground. "She's right, Zeke. We don't need no guns for these two, but we sure in tarnation could use us a priest."

Luke wanted to tell them he was no priest, but that would be counterproductive. Stupid. After all, if his disguise was going to save his ass, he had to play the role. "What's going on here? Why do you need a priest? And . . . and guns?"

Zeke lowered his rifle, too. "Reckon we don't need the rifles at that. Beg pardon." He drew a deep breath, then exhaled slowly, obviously prone to dramatics. "We're here to keep folks outta Redemption. Got us a epidemic."

Epidemic? Luke had to put some serious distance between himself and the law, but that obviously wasn't an option. Of course, options were luxuries condemned men didn't have. When was the last time he'd had any at all?

How do you plead? Yeah, right, some option.

Silence stretched between them, making him realize how quiet the town was. Deathly quiet. Maybe they really did have an epidemic. Looking beyond the armed men, he saw a wide dirt street. A deserted dirt street. The place looked like a frigging ghost town.

He quickly noted the lack of cars and power lines. Of course, they could have underground utilities, but at this altitude that was very unlikely. And judging from the modest architecture—mostly logs and native stone—he doubted the town could afford utilities at all.

Then he remembered Sofie's profession. Maybe the men would be more willing to help her if they realized she could offer medical assistance in return.

And, even more importantly, he could leave without her welfare on his conscience.

"Epidemic?" Luke asked, trying to remain calm.

"Yeah, an epidemic. Doc Taylor says nobody gets in or out of town who ain't already ee—what was that word?" He ran his hand through his greasy hair. "Eemmune. That's it."

"What *kind* of epidemic?" Getting information out of this guy was like pulling teeth. Luke aimed his thumb at Sofie, determined to end this nightmare. Fast. "You know, she's a doctor."

"No, I—"

Luke squeezed Sofie's hand tightly and she fell silent. Still, he felt the heat of her angry gaze as she gouged his palm with her fingernails.

The men exchanged surprised expressions. "Well, I'll be. Maybe that's why she's wearin' britches," the short one said. "I heard tell of a lady sawbones once, but I ain't never met one myself."

She gouged Luke's hand again, but he didn't even flinch. This was for her own good and his survival. Besides, she really was a doctor, even if she didn't remember. Her medical degree wasn't his doing, nor was it his fault that the only town they'd come across looked like a prototype for something out of a Zane Grey novel.

"What kind of epidemic?" Luke asked again, shifting his weight from one foot to the other. It would be dark within a few hours. He *had* to get the hell out of here. Soon.

"Pox." The shorter man scratched his bald head, his expression haggard. Exhaustion etched every crevice on his craggy face, and seemed to tug downward at the corners of his rheumy eyes. "It started with the miners over to the Last Chance Mine, but now the whole blamed town's been exposed." He heaved a tired sigh.

"Pox?" Luke shot them a questioning glance, though

every minute's delay ticked through his head like a sledge-hammer on a bass drum. "I had the chicken pox when I was four. That's a disease for kids. Why are you quarantined for something like that?"

"Ain't chicken pox. Got us smallpox, *Padre*." Zeke slowly shook his head. "My missus come down with it, but I had it nigh on thirteen years ago. Ab here's had 'em, too. We was both a lot luckier than most. Got only a few scars left between us. But my missus . . ." He looked down at the ground.

"But there's no such thing as smallpox anymore," Luke finally said. "They don't even require immunization now, so whatever the people here have can't be smallpox."

Zeke scowled. "I don't know who *they* be, but we defi-nitely got us smallpox here. More'n twenty cases as of this mornin'." He waved the barrel of his gun toward the woods. "Why don't you two just skedaddle if'n you ain't gonna help?"

Damn. Luke had to leave Sofie here. He had no choice. He'd lost too much precious time already, and all because of her. "Show them your arm, Sofie," he said quietly, hoping his desperation didn't reveal itself in his voice.

Seeming to understand, she slipped off her lab coat and pulled up her sleeve, displaying the small puckered mark that proved her immunity to smallpox. Assuming, of course, there really was smallpox here . . .

"You see this?" Luke slipped his hand under her arm, surprised he'd never noticed before how soft a woman's skin could be in that particular spot.

"I seen one of them before. It keeps folks from gettin' smallpox, just like they'd done had 'em before, like me." Zeke nodded in approval. "You got one of them there marks, too, *Padre*?"

Luke released Sofie's arm and rolled up his left sleeve. "Satisfied?"

The men exchanged glances, obviously in nonverbal

consultation. After a moment, they seemed to reach an agreement, and they leveled their guns at Sofie and Luke again. "Yeah," Zeke said. "We'll be satisfied right fine if'n you two just march yourselves on ahead of us now."

"No, I—"

A hammer clicked.

"I don't cotton to usin' guns on nobody, and especially not on a priest and a woman," Zeke explained quietly, "but my missus is doin' poorly." He looked at Sofie, his faded eyes glistening with unshed tears. "Maybe you can help the doc save her and the others." He turned to face Luke. "And if they cain't, then *you* can give her a proper buryin'. She's always set a powerful store in things like that, even if we be Baptists."

Luke's disguise had backfired. He swallowed hard, looking down the long, cold barrel of Zeke's rifle. Luke had no choice but to agree to their demands. For now. Once night fell and he assured himself of Sofie's safety, he'd sneak away. It was his only hope.

And if a bullet finished the job the electric chair had started . . . so be it.

Better than frying.

Sofie shivered, acutely aware of Father Salazar's anxiety. Veins bulged on his neck and sunburned scalp and perspiration trickled down the sides of his face, disappearing into his soiled white collar.

Bewildered, she looked from the priest to their captors, resigned. Guns gave them an indisputable advantage, though she didn't really believe they meant any harm. Zeke's pain regarding his wife's illness was too raw, too real, to be feigned.

She and Father Salazar could be courting serious illness, or even death, by entering Redemption. Was that what worried Father Salazar?

Slowly, she began walking in the direction Zeke's rifle pointed. Father Salazar released her hand and followed a few steps behind.

This morning at the cave, he'd threatened to leave her behind. His actions had belied his words repeatedly throughout this harrowing day. Thank God.

She glanced back at him again, ignoring the throbbing in her temple which had returned with a vengeance, undoubtedly aggravated by hunger and exhaustion. The priest's gaze darted back and forth and his lips were set in a grim line. He had the look of a desperate man, a caged lion. Again, she asked herself *why*.

Yet another mystery, reminding her of his persistence concerning her profession, even while maintaining they'd never met before today. No matter how she tried to understand how that was possible, it made no sense. How could he be so sure, and why should she believe him, even if he was a priest?

Intensity burned in his eyes—a trait contrary to his calling? Though she couldn't remember any other priests she'd ever met, she thought she understood what it meant to be one. Father Salazar should be holy and good, better than the average man. More giving. Well, he'd saved her life, hadn't he? *Yes, he saved me.*

Why did general definitions of everyday things remain in her thoughts, while everything personal had vanished completely? She had no idea whether or not she was even Catholic, though Sofie knew without a doubt that Father Salazar was one weird priest.

In fact, the term weird summed him up in many ways. And hero. *My weird hero.* A smile tugged at the corners of her mouth, surprising her.

"Giddyup, *Padre*," Zeke prodded, nudging Father Salazar with the barrel of his rifle. "Don't got all day, and I feel a powerful need to check on my missus."

Father Salazar stumbled and almost fell, catching himself with a stagger and a lurch. Sofie stopped, reaching out to assist him, but he shook his head as if to clear it, then wavered only once more before regaining his footing. He drew a deep breath and looked at her.

The expression in his eyes stole her breath. Desperate was an understatement. Father Salazar looked like a man whose immortal soul was on the line. Frantic.

"Don't worry yourself none, *Padre,*" Zeke said quietly. "Folks in Redemption'll treat you right kindly. I dunno where you was headed before, but my missus would say the Almighty brung you to us. I reckon it ain't my place— or your'n—to question His way."

Had God brought them here? Why? If she was here to save lives with her medical training, then why hadn't the "Almighty" seen fit to spare her memory?

Sofie tried not to dwell on the fact that Zeke expected her to save his wife's life. She tried to conjure something— anything medical—from the black void that was now her brain. Nothing. The only memories she had were of today, beginning with the sound of an explosion. *The Big Bang? Yeah, right.*

Tears of frustration welled in her eyes and she swiped them away angrily. Drawing a deep breath, she turned her attention to the silent little town. Redemption's deathly calm was eerie and disturbing, like an abandoned western movie set—*why can I remember something like that?*—complete with hitching posts and watering troughs. Most of the buildings were weathered planks or split logs, with stone foundations and wooden shutters instead of windows.

Other than their captors, the only other face she saw was that of a young man behind a window with iron bars. He couldn't have been much over twenty, if that, yet the sign in front of the building clearly identified the small stone structure as the local jail. *Definitely a western movie.*

Sofie swallowed hard and looked back over her shoulder

again at the young prisoner's forlorn expression and shaggy blond hair. He should be in college, playing football and joining a fraternity.

Even allowing for her amnesia, nothing about Redemption seemed logical. And she suspected it still wouldn't, even if her memory returned this very instant.

She was tired and hungry, and her head ached. The aspirin in her pocket had melted hours ago from the drenching rain. Maybe Father Salazar had more.

But her physical woes were the least of her problems. She was frightened. Terrified. She didn't know herself, or anyone else in the world. She didn't even know what she looked like. And unfortunately, no one here knew her.

"The doc's house couldn't hold all the patients, so we took over the schoolhouse," Zeke said, as he and Ab paused before a long, low building. "Doc Taylor'll be pleased to have some help." He inclined his head toward the door.

Sighing, Sofie summoned every ounce of strength she could muster. Ab opened the door and she hesitated for only a moment, then walked into the dim, stifling interior. She felt, rather than saw, Father Salazar's presence behind her.

A tall slender man wearing a vest with his shirtsleeves rolled up to his elbows quickly approached them. His expression was stern as he stopped before them, glared at their escort, and yanked off his glasses. "I told you not to let anyone into town."

"I know, Doc, but they both got the mark on their arm like the Widow Fleming." Ab ducked his head and his face turned bright red.

" 'Sides, he be a priest and she be a sawbones," Zeke added matter-of-factly.

The physician turned his gaze on Sofie and curiosity replaced his earlier anger. "You're a doctor?"

Uncertain, Sofie shrugged. "So I'm told."

"I'm sorry, but either you are or you aren't." The doctor sighed and shook his head. "People are dying here, and I could really use the help." Clearing his throat, he wiped his hands on a towel. "By the way, I'm Roman Taylor, Redemption's only, very inadequate, doctor."

"Now you have one more doctor." Father Salazar's calm tone took Sofie by surprise. "We were in an accident this morning, and she got hit on the head. Doesn't remember anything before that. All we know is her first name is Sofie. I'm Father Salazar." He thrust out his right hand.

After shaking hands, the doctor said, "Father, I wish we could welcome you under better circumstances, but I'm glad to hear you've both been inoculated against smallpox."

Dr. Taylor turned to Sofie and touched her chin with gentle fingers, tilting her head slightly to examine her injury. "Nasty bruise." He dropped his hand to his side and met her gaze again, his expression gentle and filled with concern. "Any dizziness or blurred vision?"

"A little earlier, but not now. Just a turbo-headache."

"Turbo?" Dr. Taylor shook his head. "I have some headache powders in my bag." He turned to face Zeke. "I was about to send for you, Zeke."

"She's worse?" Zeke bowed his head at the doctor's nod. "I was afeared of that."

The doctor placed his hand on Zeke's coat sleeve. "Go to her. Now."

Zeke rushed away, disappearing into the bowels of the huge, dim room. Real-life drama. Sofie felt Zeke's pain, absorbing it until her knees buckled beneath her.

Father Salazar and Dr. Taylor both grabbed her. With a man on each arm, she couldn't possibly fall, but her stomach lurched and burned ominously. Any moment, she'd double over with dry heaves. She needed food and some cool water.

"Dizzy?" Dr. Taylor asked, still holding her arm.

She shook her head. "Just hungry, I think."

Father Salazar released her arm and stepped back, allowing Dr. Taylor to support her alone. For some reason, Sofie always felt lost when Father Salazar moved away. Perhaps because he'd saved her life this morning. If not for him, she'd still be buried in that pile of rubble. He was her only link to her past.

"I'd best get back to my post," Ab said, leaving so quickly the door slammed shut behind him.

"We have soup and bread in the back room." Dr. Taylor steadied Sofie. "Can you walk?"

"Yes." Sofie drew a deep breath, dreading going any farther into the building. It seemed like a tomb—dark and airless. But keeping patients somewhat cool made more sense. Didn't it? "It's so hot in here."

"Sweating the fevers." Dr. Taylor shrugged. "I'm afraid that's about all we can do at this point. It makes me feel so useless. If only . . ."

"How many cases do you have?" Father Salazar mopped his head with a handkerchief.

"Too many. Eleven have died and twenty-three more are in here. Dying." The doctor lowered his chin, then looked up at Sofie, his expression pleading. "Tell me, is there anything new about the treatment of smallpox that I should know?"

"I . . . I really don't remember." Sofie choked back a sob, wishing she could somehow resurrect her memory from the worthless black hole of her brain. "I'll try to help as best I can, but please—"

"I'm sorry. I forgot. Please forgive me." Dr. Taylor appeared resigned. "Well, at least you've both been inoculated, as have I."

Sofie looked at Father Salazar, noting he appeared as confused as she. Tilting his head to one side, he said, "Dr. Taylor, I don't understand any of this. Smallpox has been nonexistent for so long they don't even require immunization anymore.''

"Nonexistent? *Nonexistent?*" Dr. Taylor's nostrils flared and he shoved his glasses back onto his nose. "Allow me to show you nonexistent, Father."

Before either of them could protest, Dr. Taylor started weaving his way through the building, leading Sofie by the elbow. She had no choice but to follow, though she looked back several times to assure herself that Father Salazar still followed.

The stench of disease and death permeated the air and Sofie's stomach lurched again. They stopped beside a low cot, where a young man lay dying. Oozing sores covered his body, and he thrashed around in obvious agony.

"Dear God," Sofie whispered. Suddenly, she knew what she had to do. Maybe she didn't remember medical school, but something told her the stifling heat and foul air couldn't possibly be good for anyone. Without a word, she pulled her elbow from Dr. Taylor's grasp and marched to a nearby window. She released the latch and swung open the shutters partway.

"We must keep them warm," Dr. Taylor argued. "You'll kill them all."

Sofie put her fist on her hip, feeling stronger than she had all day. Maybe her medical training was surfacing at last, or it could be intuition or simple common sense. Either way, she knew without question that fresh air was better than foul. "No," she said quietly but firmly. "Every living thing needs fresh air to heal."

Dr. Taylor studied her in silence for a few minutes, then nodded in surrender. "Very well. At this point, I'm willing to try anything. We'll try it your way for a while and see if there's any change, either good or bad."

Sofie bit the inside of her lower lip and hoped she wasn't making a terrible mistake. Father Salazar's frantic look remained, and he looked toward the partly open window with a hunger that stunned her.

Still, he seemed to battle his internal demons and recognize her self-doubt. He came to her side, offering her his arm for support. His touch comforted her and she leaned against him, grateful for his continued presence.

"We'd better get some of that soup," he said quietly. "It looks like we have a lot of work here."

For the first time since this morning when she'd awakened battered and bruised, Father Salazar actually sounded like a priest. She met his gray gaze and blinked, wondering why that didn't exactly please her. His behavior throughout the day had been so unpriestlike, she'd forgotten for long stretches of time who and what he was.

Heat flooded her face as she also remembered the feel of his aroused male body pressing against her. Her pulse quickened and she struggled against the urge to throw her arms around him for support and comfort.

And something more?

Luke weighed his options. He could probably walk away while the doctor was busy talking to Sofie, but he couldn't bring himself to do it yet. Why?

Because he felt like hell? Because no matter what he'd thought earlier, he needed a hot meal and some cold water before he hit the road again? Because he was so exhausted from the longest day of his life, he could crawl in a hole and sleep for a year?

Yes and no.

Sofie held him here as sure as Warden Graham had held him prisoner. For some stupid reason, he felt responsible for her. Hell, he'd brought her this far, it only made sense to ensure she'd be all right here before he left. Besides, he'd seen no evidence to indicate he was being hunted.

Yet. Still, the thought of hanging around here didn't exactly give him a warm fuzzy.

And Sofie herself . . . Who was she? The way she'd rallied and thrown open those shutters had caught him by surprise. She had balls, so to speak. Dr. Sofie What's-Her-Name was a woman he would have liked to meet at another time and place.

In another life.

Regret slithered through him again, but he forcibly quelled it. *No time for that.* Of course, there would never be enough time for that in his life. The moment he'd decided to leave that execution chamber, his fate was determined.

Luke Nolan was a man on the run. A fugitive. A man on a life-or-death quest for freedom.

Focus. He drew a deep breath of the fresh mountain air wafting through the partially open window. *Yeah, focus.* He could play this game until dark—he had no choice. Then he would run fast and hard.

To freedom.

When Sofie leaned into him for support, the urge to wrap his arms around her and cradle her against his chest hit him like a two-by-four between the eyes.

Her softness melded against him and, despite his fatigue and worry, his body responded with intrepid—and infuriating—enthusiasm. He winced, his burned flesh tugging and stretching where nature demanded. But pain did little to suppress his rampant libido.

Eleven celibate years did that to a man.

Dr. Taylor's voice dragged Luke from his half-stupor. "Well, let's get you both something to eat before we put you to work."

Clearing his throat, Luke kept his arm around Sofie for support and followed the doctor through a door at the back of the building. The kitchen, at least, harbored no beds for the sick and dying.

The real Father Salazar wouldn't have thought such a thing. Guilt pressed down on Luke. That old man probably would have been out there praying over each and every patient before allowing himself a bite.

But I'm no priest.

Did it matter? Luke had been raised Catholic, and he knew the routine, so to speak. With Father Salazar's Bible and other paraphernalia, he could manage this gig until he disappeared into the night.

So what if he was a fraud? The people of Redemption needed a priest for comfort. It was the least Luke could do to repay them for a hot meal.

And the *very* least he could do for Father Salazar.

After a bowl of Irish stew as good as any Luke had ever tasted, he felt almost human again. The Widow Fleming he and Sofie'd already heard about looked like Betty Crocker, only older. Dressed in black from chin to foot, she was a tiny but imposing white-haired figure who ran the kitchen—and everyone in the makeshift hospital—with a firm hand.

Dr. Taylor returned to the kitchen with Zeke just as Luke finished the best piece of apple pie he'd had in exactly eleven years. His grandmother and Mrs. Fleming would've enjoyed exchanging recipes.

No, he mustn't think about his grandmother, because she wouldn't want to know her grandson was an escaped convict, rather than an executed murderer.

When Luke saw the expression on Zeke's face, he knew the time had come for him to play priest for real. His captor's long face looked even longer now, and he kept his eyes lowered.

"We've lost Mrs. Judson," Dr. Taylor said quietly, placing his hand on Zeke's shoulder. "But Zeke was at her side when she left us." The doctor heaved a heavy sigh.

Luke pushed away from the table and stood, as did Sofie.

She put her hand on Zeke's shoulder and said, "I'm so sorry."

What would Father Salazar say? Luke swallowed the lump of cold hard fear in his throat and imitated Sofie's behavior. Even with amnesia, her manners were considerably better than his. Of course, prison hadn't required manners.

"I'm sorry," Luke said, feeling his face grow hot; his words seemed so damned inadequate. Zeke had said he and his wife were Baptists, so maybe the new widower wouldn't find fault with Luke's shortcomings as a priest. *I can't believe I'm doing this.*

Zeke nodded, then met Luke's gaze. "Like I done told you, *Padre,* the missus ain't—weren't—Catholic, but I know she'd like for you to speak a few words over her."

"If . . . if you'll show me what you want me to do, and where we need to do it, I'll try my best," Luke said, and meant it. His memory of Father Salazar backing away from him in the execution chamber this morning returned, along with a flash of fire to Luke's gut.

"Go with God, my son," the priest had said.

So far, so good. Luke reached up to drag his fingers through his hair, surprised to find his bald scalp instead. He'd almost forgotten . . .

"Should I go with you?" Sofie asked quietly, meeting Luke's gaze.

They hadn't been separated all day, except for those few terrifying moments after she'd fallen during the storm. "If you want—"

"No, please," Dr. Taylor interrupted. "I'm sorry, but I really need Dr. Sofie here to help." He shot her a pleading look. "Please?"

"Dr. Sofie?" Her face reddened and she turned her gaze on Luke. "Of course, I'll do what I can. If only I could remember . . ."

"I understand." Dr. Taylor faced Zeke. "I'm sorry I can't go with you to the cemetery, but . . ."

"It's okay, Doc. I understand better'n most, I reckon."

Luke gave Sofie's hand a reassuring squeeze, hoping he could pull off this priest thing to Zeke's satisfaction. The old boy might have brought Luke and Sofie here against their will, but he was grieving and deserved whatever comfort any of them could offer.

Then Luke could run for his life.

He faced the grieving man, resigned to do whatever he could. "Let's go."

Without looking back at Sofie, he followed Zeke through the back door. "They took the missus over to the pastor's house for washin' and layin' out."

Luke's blood turned icy. "Zeke, if you have a pastor, and you aren't Catholic, then why do you want me to perform your wife's funeral?"

Zeke paused and shoved his hands into his pockets. Without looking at Luke, he gazed toward the mountains and said, "Pastor died last week, *Padre*, and his wife the next day."

What the hell kind of epidemic was this? Luke remained silent as they started walking again, angry with himself for not demanding more information before endangering Sofie and himself this way. If this was something other than smallpox, entering Redemption could prove as big a mistake as following that punk into a liquor store eleven years ago. Almost.

But Sofie . . .

Dammit, forget Sofie.

When Zeke started walking again, Luke followed in silence. This man's wife was dead, and all he wanted was a few moments of Father Salazar's time. So be it.

But once the funeral was over and darkness fell, all bets were off. Luke Nolan would hit the road again. Fast.

Determined, he kept pace with the lanky widower, until he stopped in front of a modest house built of stone. Zeke knocked once and removed his hat, then pushed open the door and stepped inside.

Candles burned on an upright piano across the room, and a small woman rushed toward them, tears trickling down her cheeks. Her red hair was piled high on her head, and like Mrs. Fleming, she wore an old-fashioned black dress that went to the tops of her shoes. Luke's earlier suspicions about Redemption being some sort of religious cult or retreat returned.

No electricity, no cars, old-fashioned clothes, so many nonimmunized citizens . . . The evidence pointed toward something bizarre.

"I'm so sorry, Mr. Judson," the woman said. "Fanny was one of my favorite people."

"Thanks, Miss Dora." Zeke lowered his gaze as the woman patted his hand reassuringly. "Lots of folks set quite a store by my missus."

"A priest? How fortuitous." Dora turned her attention to Luke and held out her hand. "It was good of you to come, Father. I'm Dora Fleming." She wiped her tears away.

Like mother, like daughter? "I'm . . . I'm Father Salazar," Luke said, still cringing inside each time he uttered the words. He'd never forget the man whose name he'd stolen. Swallowing hard, he shook the woman's small hand. "Zeke asked me to . . . uh . . ."

"Oh, yes, Fanny would want that, Father. Thank you so much." Dora kept his hand and led him across the room. "Mr. Judson probably told you about the pastor and his wife." She paused and placed her hand over her heart with a sigh. "So much tragedy."

"Yes, I'm sorry to hear about the epidemic." *And I'd sure as hell like to know what it* really *is.*

Luke couldn't help but notice the body stretched out on boards across the room. Several women fussed over the dead woman, sniffling and sharing stories about the good things Fanny Judson had done in her life. *Damn waste.*

Dora opened a huge book on a desk near the front door. "This is where Reverend Bodine recorded deaths, marriages, baptisms, and such," she explained. "If you'll enter her name here, and the dates of birth and death here, we'd be much obliged."

Luke looked down at the pages, where his predecessor had written in previous events for the citizens of Redemption. The entire page was filled with deaths—not a single birth or wedding.

All these senseless deaths . . .

Luke paused for a moment to consider the irony. Today, he was supposed to have died. Instead, here he stood trying to comfort the grieving by playing a role for which he was unworthy. More than unworthy.

His eyes focused on the most recent entry, just above where he would record the name of Fanny Judson.

Elizabeth Ann Morton, he read silently. *Born August 19, '86.*

Died September 11, 1891 . . .

The date reverberated through Luke's head, then finally reached his lips.

"*1891?*"

Chapter Four

"Father?"

Luke winced when Dora touched his sleeve, but not from the sudden pressure against his sensitive burned skin.

A loud roar filled his head, rivaling even the explosions that had saved his miserable life this morning. The day's events replayed through his mind at warp speed.

1891. Bizarre. Unbelievable.

Impossible? After this morning, how could he consider anything impossible? By all rights, he was the one who should be dead. Very dead.

"Father, are you all right?" Dora slipped her arm beneath his and guided him toward a chair. "Perhaps you should sit a spell. Did you get caught in that storm we had earlier this afternoon?"

"Storm? Yes, the storm. Yes. Uh, we were caught in the storm."

"It came on so suddenly . . . ." Dora's expression left no doubt she questioned his state of mind.

As did he.

1891? He looked around the room. *Victorian furnishings. Long skirts and upswept hair.* Either he'd really fallen back in time somehow, or Redemption was the Rocky Mountain equivalent to Brigadoon.

Of course, and smallpox. Yes, it all made sense now. Sick sense. But how?

"You must be exhausted." Dora nudged him, urging him to sit. "It may not be very Christian of me to say so, but I'm glad you came to us today. Fanny Judson was one of the kindest women I've ever known. She . . . she deserves a prop . . . proper funeral."

Luke looked up at the woman and saw her lower lip quiver as tears rolled silently down her face. He should offer comfort, as the real Father Salazar certainly would have, but his mind was reeling from other matters.

Like time travel.

"I'm sorry, but if you'll just give me a minute . . . ?" He patted Dora's hand and tried his damnedest to appear pious. Or at least something besides nuts.

"Of course, Father. Please forgive me." Dora dabbed at her tears with a pristine lace handkerchief, then hurried back to the grieving Zeke Judson and his wife's dead body.

Okay, Luke, think. He rubbed the back of his neck and glanced at the items on Reverend Bodine's desk. A calendar with several dates circled—all the Sundays—also proclaimed the year was 1891.

What was he looking for anyway? Another sign? Another miracle? An explanation for all this? He opened the drawer, feeling like a thief, though he had no intention of stealing anything. Escaping from prison would be the last crime Luke Nolan ever committed. And the first . . .

"I'm free," he whispered, perspiration popping from every one of his fried pores. Then a rush of joy swept through him and his heart did a fair imitation of what his grandmother would've called the Snoopy dance.

Could it be true? *Hell, yes.* If time travel was possible,

then Luke Nolan—wrongfully convicted and condemned man—was finally free.

Free!

No more prison, no more running for his life, no more electric chair.

A shudder gripped him and he closed his eyes, willing the moment of remembered terror to pass. There was no electricity here, and no electric chair. More importantly, there was no criminal record for Luke Nolan. He could make a new life for himself. Maybe now he could even become a teacher, as he'd dreamed of in his time.

My time? No, this was his time now. Maybe he could teach Future History. He almost smiled as he closed the desk drawer, leaving its contents untouched.

He stared at his hands, flexing and spreading his reddened fingers against the desk's smooth surface, the open book only a few inches away. Why was he here in this time and place? With these suffering people?

Slowly, he brought the trembling fingers of one hand to the crucifix dangling around his neck, remembering Father Salazar's expression. With his fingertips, he traced the shape of the crucifix, then closed his eyes and swallowed hard. *Was* he here for a reason? His grandparents would've thought so, but despite this morning's miracle, Luke couldn't see himself playing a priest for the rest of his life.

A life that should've ended this morning.

Guilt slammed into him yet again. Yes, guilt was one part of Catholicism he'd learned very well. Father Salazar was dead because of those explosions. Because of Luke. If not for him, the old man wouldn't have been in that execution chamber in the first place.

And what about Sofie?

Luke jerked his eyes open and blinked several times, trying to focus. Sofie was in this mess with him, but she didn't even know it. Still, she'd be safe here in Redemption even after he left to begin his new life. After meeting more of the townspeople, Luke was convinced of that.

But what if she remembers . . . ?

A sinking sensation gripped him. So what if Sofie remembered Luke's true identity and the reason they'd been in that so-called cave this morning? What could she do about it? No one in this time had ever heard of Luke Nolan, or the terrible crime he was to have died for. No one.

Except Sofie.

Of course, no one would believe her if she claimed to have traveled back from the future with a condemned murderer. They'd all think she was crazy, and Luke would still be free. *Free!*

"Father, are you ready now?"

Luke drew a deep breath and stood, clutching Father Salazar's Bible in his hand. "Yes, I'm ready."

No, it wouldn't matter at all if Sofie regained her memory.

To anyone but him.

And he couldn't *let* it matter.

Sofie bent over a cot near the front of the building, her hands trembling and her throat contracting. Self-doubt attacked from all directions. Again.

She *couldn't* be a doctor.

The young patient looked up at her and smiled weakly. Her rash was covered with dry red scabs, and Dr. Taylor wanted Sofie to bathe the girl and check her progress. If all the child's spots were dry, they would consider her on the road to recovery.

Sofie prayed it was so.

"You're pretty. Who are you?" the child asked, her soft brown eyes wide and trusting.

"I'm Sofie, and I think you're pretty, too." She knelt beside the cot and brushed a strand of limp blond hair away from the girl's eyes. The spots looked threatening, though Sofie quickly reminded herself that she was immune.

"Dr. Taylor tells me your name is Jenny and that you're ten," Sofie continued, examining each of the girl's arms. "How do you feel?"

"Just tired, but better than before." A shudder rippled through Jenny's small frame. "I was very sick and my mama was taking care of me. Where is she?"

Sofie bit the inside of her cheek, praying the girl's mother wasn't one of the epidemic's victims. "I'm not sure, but I'll ask after you have your bath. Can you sit up by yourself?"

Nodding, Jenny pushed herself up on her elbows. "I'm dreadful tired of lying in bed."

"I can imagine." Sofie bathed the girl's face and shoulders, then removed her soiled gown and slipped a fresh one over her head. It was huge, obviously intended for an adult. "Dr. Taylor says you're almost well."

Jenny sighed as she laid back against the pillow, a telltale tremor in her lower lip. "Can you please ask someone about my mama?" She gathered a handful of the nightgown's soft fabric and brought it to her cheek. "This is Mama's gown, so she must be here."

Sofie swallowed hard, afraid. She didn't want to learn this child's mother was dead or dying. "Yes, you rest for a while and I'll go ask right now," she promised, filled with an unrelenting sense of dread.

She rose to go in search of Dr. Taylor, surprised when she turned around to find him standing a few feet behind her. From his solemn expression, she knew without asking that this child's mother was dead. Obviously, someone— probably Mrs. Fleming—had taken the mother's belongings and laundered them for Jenny's use.

She shook her head, hoping Dr. Taylor would tell her Jenny's mother was fine and would be along any minute to calm her child's fears, but Sofie knew better. Still, she'd promised to ask, so she bent down to retrieve the basin of dirty water and walked slowly toward the doctor.

"She's old enough to be told where her mother is," Sofie said without preamble.

She couldn't help but wonder about her own mother. Was she still alive? Was she wondering what had happened to her daughter right now? Would she worry? *Was I close to my mother?*

Past tense?

Stop. Think of Jenny.

Mrs. Fleming paused beside the pair and took the basin from Sofie's hands. Then the older woman turned to face the doctor, lifting her chin a notch to meet the physician's gaze.

"My Dora and I will raise this child, and we'll do it right. We understand little girls." Mrs. Fleming sniffled and blinked several times, glancing toward the cot where the girl had, thankfully, fallen asleep. "We'll tell Jenny about her mother as soon as Dora returns from . . . from Fanny's funeral." The older woman's face crumpled and a tear slid quickly down her wrinkled cheek.

Dr. Taylor reached out and touched Mrs. Fleming's shoulder. "You're an angel of mercy, Anna," he said, his voice thick with exhaustion. "I don't know what we'd do without you and Miss Dora. But what about the boy?"

Oh, not another victim. Sofie watched Mrs. Fleming's expression change from pity to anger.

"No matter what we think, the law has already proclaimed that one's fate," the woman whispered, shaking her head.

"So it has." Dr. Taylor's words sounded clipped. Disapproving?

"She has a brother?" Sofie didn't understand any of this. "Is he here, too?"

"No." Mrs. Fleming drew a deep breath. "He's in jail. For now."

No additional information appeared forthcoming, and Sofie sensed any additional questions would be unwelcome. *The boy in the jail.* She remembered mention of a rope, though that still didn't seem possible.

But at least Jenny would have a home. Sofie tried not to think of the boy. Clearing her throat, she faced Mrs. Fleming. "Jenny asked me to find out about her mama. I think she suspects what's happened, so please don't wait too—"

The front door burst open and Ab staggered in, bearing the weight of a much larger man. Without hesitation, Dr. Taylor hurried toward the new arrival, slipped his arm around the taller man, and dragged him toward a freshly made cot.

"My God, what happened?" the doctor asked.

Then Sofie saw the reason for his urgent tone. This patient showed no sign of smallpox, but his face, head, and shoulder were horribly burned. Distorted and disfigured, the new patient barely resembled a man at all.

"Dunno," Ab said, stepping back. "He crawled into town on all fours, more dead than alive. Ain't pox, though. I couldn't very well turn him away, quarantine or no quarantine."

"No, of course not." The doctor immediately pulled away the injured man's tattered jacket and shirt, then looked back at Sofie. "We'll need clean bandages and cool water. Lots of it." Dr. Taylor paused for a moment to sigh. "Dear God, *if* he lives, he's going to wish like hell he hadn't."

Only incoherent groans came from the man's lips— rather, what was left of his lips. Sofie stared in horror at his charred flesh, possibly an earlobe. The stench of his burns stole her breath.

The lower part of his face and neck were practically

gone, and only singed stubble covered his head. When he opened his eyes and looked her way, Sofie saw pain and rage unlike anything she'd ever seen. Covering her mouth, she recoiled and turned away, unable to gaze on the man's hideous injuries a moment longer.

I'm a doctor. She drew huge gulps of air until her trembling ceased and she no longer felt as if she would heave.

Mrs. Fleming returned from the back room with a basin of fresh water and placed it on the floor near the doctor. "Rags and bandages," she said, and hurried away.

Remembering her duties, Sofie followed the older woman, eager for any excuse to escape the pain and dying for even a little while. Mrs. Fleming whirled around to face Sofie the moment the kitchen door closed behind them, her hands on her hips and her expression unreadable.

"Who are you?" she demanded, though not unkindly.

"I . . . I don't remember." Sofie watched Mrs. Fleming's gaze rake the length of her. "Why? What's wrong?"

"You say you're a doctor, but—"

"No, *Father Salazar* says I'm a doctor. *I* have no idea who or what I am." Sofie lifted her hair off the back of her neck and looked up at the ceiling, willing her tears not to come. *Not now.* "I don't remember medical school or even my last name, for that matter. *Why?* Have I done something wrong?" Had she already made a grievous medical error?

"Your clothes, your language, your mannerisms—how can you be a doctor? I believe doctors come from good families with proper upbringings." Disapproval showed clearly in Mrs. Fleming's eyes. "*Ladies* do not wear britches, Sofie, and they certainly do not wear their hair in a state of complete and utter chaos."

Confused, Sofie touched her hair, pulling a dark curl forward to examine it. She took a step back and looked down at her filthy jeans and green T-shirt. At Mrs. Fleming's insistence, her soiled white lab coat had been replaced earlier by a clean, ruffled apron. Strange, but even without her memory, Sofie knew ruffles weren't her thing.

"I just don't get it." She shook her head and shrugged. "I think *you're* the one who's dressed weird, Mrs. Fleming." She took a step toward the back of the kitchen, but paused to look over her shoulder at the woman's shocked expression. "No offense intended."

"Well, I never—"

Trying not to dwell on the woman's bewildering disapproval, Sofie gathered a stack of clean rags from the cupboard and walked toward the kitchen door. "Let me know when you're ready to talk to Jenny," she said. "I'd like to be there, since I promised her I'd ask about her mother."

Mrs. Fleming drew herself up to her full height and nodded, grudging respect showing in her faded eyes. "Please, forgive me for snapping at you so. Worry and exhaustion are my only excuses for such ill manners." She heaved a weary sigh. "You're an enigma, Sofie, but I do admire your . . . uh . . ."

"Sass?" Sofie arched a brow and gave Mrs. Fleming a crooked grin, though she felt more like crying.

The older woman smiled and nodded. "Perhaps."

"And I admire everything about you, Mrs. Fleming," Sofie said with complete sincerity, holding the door open for the older woman, "except your taste in clothes."

Mrs. Fleming shook her head and sighed. "I don't know who you are or where you came from," she said passionately, "but I'm glad you came to us, child. Very glad."

Warmth spread through Sofie as she followed the woman from the kitchen. She knew somehow that Mrs. Fleming's approval mattered to the citizens of Redemption, and to Dr. Taylor.

And, for some reason, it mattered to Sofie, too.

With a little more confidence than she'd felt earlier, Sofie returned to Dr. Taylor's side with the bandages. The burned man thrashed around on the cot until Ab managed to tie him down with leather straps.

"I hate to restrain you, but you're doing yourself more harm than good." Dr. Taylor's voice was soft as he spoke to his patient and washed away some of the mud caked on the side of his head. "All we can do is try to keep you comfortable and pray." Muttering, he added, "Dear God, I haven't seen burns like these since Vicksburg."

Sofie stared at the back of Dr. Taylor's white head, admiring his gentleness and dedication. *Vicksburg*? The vaguely familiar name reverberated around in her mind for several minutes. Something wasn't right. Who was she kidding? Nothing seemed right.

"You look tired," Mrs. Fleming said, touching Sofie's shoulder. "You've had a long day and taken quite a bump on the head, too. You'll do us and yourself more good tomorrow, after you've had some rest."

Sofie sighed and nodded. "Maybe after I sleep, I'll remember something. Anything." She rubbed her throbbing temples.

"There's a nice clean cot in the room off the kitchen, dear." The older woman nudged Sofie in that direction. "Sleep while you can, and I'll bring you some hot water for a bath and clean clothes in the morning."

A bath sounded like heaven. Sofie waited for Dr. Taylor's approval, but he was too busy with his new patient. "All right." She glanced toward Jenny, relieved to find the girl still sleeping quietly.

Sofie had been exhausted for what seemed like forever. All the urgency here in Redemption had kept her so busy since her arrival, her physical needs had taken a back seat until now. Suddenly, her body refused to be ignored another second. She'd eaten earlier, and now she had to sleep.

Her feet and legs were like lead weights as she trudged back through the kitchen and into the quiet room off the pantry. Rubbing the back of her stiff neck, she yawned and stretched, closing the narrow door behind her.

For the first time since she'd awakened this morning in the dark cave, Sofie was alone. Completely alone. She didn't even have herself for company, since she didn't *know* herself.

Tears of frustration stung her eyes as she leaned her head back against the door's cool surface and surveyed her surroundings. A kerosene lamp spilled soft golden light onto the floor and ceiling, leaving the corners dark and unfriendly.

Across the room from the tall window, a narrow bed with a cheerful patchwork quilt beckoned to her. But as she pushed away from the door, something else seized her attention.

A mirror.

Light. She needed more light. With her right hand, she brushed the wall beside the door several times, sensing there should have been a switch there. She knew it, though she didn't know *why* she knew it. Her gaze drifted across the high ceiling, finding no source for additional light, even if she'd found a switch.

Frustrated, she retrieved the lamp from the nightstand and carried it to the low dresser beneath the mirror. Her heart hammered against her ribs as she turned up the wick until the golden light grew somewhat brighter.

Her mouth went dry as she lifted her chin to look into the mirror, fearing who she might find staring back from the silver surface. She gasped, seeing herself for the first time she could remember. The light sent her features into sharp relief, light and shadow contrasting harshly on the stranger's face.

Her face.

"How do you do, Sofie?" she whispered, reaching out to touch her reflection. Wild, dark curls framed her small face and fell to her shoulders in back. So that was what Mrs. Fleming had meant about Sofie's hair being in utter chaos.

Her ears were small and flat against her head, with a gold hoop in one lobe. "I lost an earring." She touched her naked lobe, then noted the purple bruise on that side of her head, spreading toward her eye. Gingerly, she probed her injury, realizing how lucky she was not to have lost something much more significant than an earring.

Like her life.

But in a way she *had* lost her life. At least the life she'd known before today.

She turned down the lamp and placed it back on the nightstand. The bed looked clean and inviting, but her clothes were too filthy to climb between the sheets.

The mere thought of sliding her exhausted body into bed made her shudder with longing. She'd have to sleep in her undies. After all, Mrs. Fleming had promised Sofie a bath and clean clothes in the morning.

She pulled off her soiled clothing and left it in a pile near the door. Again, she looked at the strange woman in the mirror. No bra, small breasts, and white panties with red hearts.

Mrs. Fleming won't approve.

Too exhausted to ponder the possible ramifications of Mrs. Fleming choosing her wardrobe, Sofie left the lamp burning low and climbed beneath the quilt. The clean sheets felt wondrous against her bare skin, and the quilt offered welcome warmth.

"Dear God, what am I going to do?" she prayed.

* * *

Fear and misery had been painful.

Hiding happiness was pure hell.

After playing the role of priest for Fanny Judson's funeral, all Luke wanted was to run through town, shouting to the world that he was free. No one was hunting him, and no one knew about his past.

But even in his state of shock-turned-ecstasy, Luke knew such a display of unadulterated happiness would be bad form in the midst of a smallpox epidemic and countless funerals. Very bad indeed.

Though he truly did feel for Zeke's loss and Fanny's death, Luke struggled to restrain himself. Darkness was nearly upon them by the time he bid Fanny's mourners goodbye and escaped their presence.

No one guarded him now, and no rifles demanded his continued cooperation. He could walk away from Redemption anytime he chose, but even more importantly, he didn't *have* to run or hide ever again.

The possibilities were endless. He could do whatever he wanted, go wherever he wanted, and be anyone he wanted. *Free, free, free!*

Elated, confused, and exhausted, he headed back toward the schoolhouse, wanting to check on Sofie. She alone held the power to tarnish his newfound happiness, but he still couldn't shake that nagging sense of responsibility.

Of course, if he disappeared by morning, it wouldn't matter how much Sofie ever remembered, because he'd be long gone and could even use a new name if he chose. No one would ever know.

He walked behind the schoolhouse and into a pine grove, inhaling the sweet air and looking up at the darkening sky. For the first time in eleven years, he could go anywhere he chose, whenever he wanted. Or not.

Simultaneous joy and terror rippled through him and

the exhaustion he'd battled all day struck without warning. Staggering, he made his way to a fallen log and pulled Father Salazar's robe closer to his half-naked, burned skin.

"Free," he whispered, folding his arms across his chest and trying to concentrate through the fog of fatigue. That meant he had important decisions—real choices—to make.

Stay and help Sofie, satisfying his illogical notion that he was somehow responsible for her? Or leave Redemption, Sofie, and his memories of Father Salazar far behind to begin his life anew?

He could go to Denver, then catch a train somewhere. California, maybe?

An owl hooted overhead as darkness gathered. Stars blanketed the sky, appearing in magical clusters sprinkled across a bed of black velvet.

He drew another deep breath of the rapidly cooling mountain air. The Nolans had lived in Colorado since his great-great-grandparents arrived from Ireland. Still looking at the stars, he wondered if he would meet his ancestors one day. Obviously, he couldn't tell them his true identity—not that they'd believe him—but just to meet them would be an incredible experience.

And Grandpa . . . would Luke live long enough to see him again?

His gut burned as if he'd swallowed battery acid.

"You killed your grandfather with shame, Luke," Grandma had said.

There was nothing he could do to change his past—or future, such as it was. Luke Nolan would follow Ricky-No-Name into that liquor store and be tried and convicted of murder.

Would or had? The paradox was almost comical, though Luke wasn't laughing now.

He mustn't dwell on his past . . . or future past. Whatever. He was alive and he was free. Nothing else mattered.

Struggling to his feet, Luke yawned and stretched, his body protesting the movement. Soon his skin would start to peel and his hair would grow back. Wouldn't it? Sofie would undoubtedly be surprised by his transformation, especially upon learning he wasn't a priest.

Definitely not a priest. Luke Nolan was a man with a man's needs and desires, compounded by more than a decade of total deprivation.

Banishing thoughts of unfulfilled desire, Luke stared through the darkness with narrowed eyes. A square of golden light spilled from a window at the back of the schoolhouse. Sofie was in there somewhere. Was she all right? That bruise on her head was pretty nasty. He should check on her before turning in for the night, assuming he could find a bed somewhere.

Slowly, he trudged toward the back door. He'd ask for a place to sleep, and if the people of Redemption wanted him to perform any other priestlike duties tomorrow, he would. Then he'd begin his new life as a free man.

Soon. Very soon.

Was that his decision? He couldn't be sure. Too much had happened today to permit him to make a rational decision about anything. He'd almost died and been thrown back in time. Enough excitement for one day.

The golden glow of the window next to the back door lured him, and Luke found himself peering between the ruffled lace curtains, even as he reached for the door handle.

Sofie.

Sleeping on her side, her dark hair made a dramatic contrast against the snowy sheet. She was so pale, nearly as white as the bedding. He'd noticed earlier how tiny she was, especially when he'd carried her through the raging storm to shelter.

The memory of how she'd felt in his arms then stole his breath *now*. He could almost feel her again, and he reached up to rub his palm against the rough door as if to remind himself he no longer held her softness in his lap.

But his body responded as hungrily to the memory as it had to the real thing. He wanted to hold her again. Hell, he wanted to do much, much more . . .

The heat of desire created a startling contrast with the brisk night air. Luke's breath came out in a white cloud as he stood there staring. And dreaming.

He swallowed hard and pressed his fist into his palm. Eleven years in prison without a woman, and his first and only had been an inexperienced teenager like himself. Of *course* he wanted a woman. Any woman.

No, not any woman. At least, not yet.

As he watched her sleep, he recognized an invisible bond or force reaching out from Sofie and extending toward him. He wanted to deny it—he *should* deny it.

But he couldn't.

In that moment, Luke knew his path. Part of it anyway. He wouldn't leave town until he knew for certain that Sofie was safe. Never again would he have guilt as his relentless companion. At least, he told himself that was the only reason he felt responsible for Sofie.

She rolled onto her back and the quilt slipped from her shoulder.

Her bare shoulder.

His gaze drifted along the creamy curve of exposed skin to where the side of her breast rose. Tempting. The sheet draped over her nipple, catching and shielding that part of her from his hungry, all-consuming gaze.

Get a grip, man. He closed his eyes for a moment, reminding himself of his temporary role here in Redemption. Voyeur didn't fit his job description.

When he reopened his eyes, he frowned, noticing her bruised temple and the jagged gash that had bled so copiously this morning. She'd almost died.

He'd almost died.

Yet here they both were, alive and in another century. Together. Why?

Go with God, my son.

"Damn."

Chapter Five

Sofie didn't care what kind of clothes Mrs. Fleming brought her to wear this morning. All she wanted was to remain submerged in the tub of warm water in the small room where she'd spent the night.

Hiding from the big bad world.

"Hiding is not allowed, Dr. Sofie." She wrinkled her nose at the sound of her title and sighed, splashing warm water over her bare breasts and abdomen.

Despite the tiny metal tub, the warm water felt luxurious, even if filling it had been a real pain. Carrying hot water to the tub had seemed foreign to her. European maybe. Was it? Or was her loss of memory the only reason the chore seemed odd?

No, she remembered bathing, and showers, too. This *was* weird. She closed her eyes and pictured a large white tub, with shiny knobs that controlled the flow of water. In fact, as the water cooled, she had the urge to reach up and turn on the hot water with her toes, but there was nothing to turn.

Something she'd done many times in her life. Hadn't she?

Using an outhouse was the worst, though. She frowned, remembering the small building behind the schoolhouse, which Dora had pointed to when Sofie asked about the bathroom. A "twoholer." Luxury?

Everything was odd. *She* was odd, according to Mrs. Fleming's daughter Dora. Sofie leaned her head back against the smooth slope of copper that formed the tub's rim.

"Mother, where's she from? I can't believe you're going to let a stranger wear my clothes." Dora's shrill, nasal voice came through the closed door clearly. Unfortunately.

"She doesn't remember who she is, let alone where she's from," Mrs. Fleming answered, her tone strained and clipped. "She arrived with the priest yesterday afternoon. Besides, letting her borrow some of your clothes is the Christian thing to do."

"Well, if you ask me, that priest is every bit as strange as she is."

"Dora," Mrs. Fleming scolded, "you're being unkind. If he seems strange, it's because we're unaccustomed to their ways, child."

Their ways? Sofie sank deeper into the cooling water, immersing her shoulders as far as possible.

"That's true," Dora said.

What's true? Maybe Dora understood her mother's meaning, but Sofie was still baffled. She grabbed the huge bar of soap, which smelled and felt like anything *but* soap, and lathered herself all over, avoiding the tender wound on her temple.

"The Catholic Church has peculiar ways," Mrs. Fleming said. "Your daddy—God rest his soul—always said it was merely a different path to the same place."

"Sounds like a very wise man." Father Salazar's voice sounded just beyond the door.

"Oh, dear. Father, we meant no harm, I was merely explaining—"

"That's all right, Mrs. Fleming."

Sofie cocked her head to one side, listening to every syllable. The sound of his voice eased and reassured her, made her warm from within. Father Salazar sounded different this morning—more relaxed and cheerful. Younger. Perhaps he'd rested, too. *She* certainly felt younger and more cheerful today—black and blue and rosy.

Grimacing, she dumped a pitcher of water over her soapy head. "Ow!" Soapy water and nasty cuts were not friends, and it didn't take a medical degree to know that. "Dummy." Pressing the corner of her towel against her wound, she waited for the stinging to stop.

"Are you all right, Sofie?" Father Salazar called through the closed door.

"Fine." Sofie bolted up, sloshing water onto the floor as she clutched the towel to her bare breasts. The sound of his voice, so comforting a moment ago, sent shivers through her now—shivers she couldn't even begin to blame on the water's temperature. "Just got soap in my eye."

My God, I just lied to a priest.

"All right, I'll see you at breakfast."

Her stomach grumbled in response. Right on cue. She giggled quietly.

"Who's taking care of the patients this morning, Mrs. Fleming?" Father Salazar asked.

A pang of guilt wormed its way through Sofie. She should hurry.

"It's the Browns' turn to nurse this morning," Mrs. Fleming said. "There are six of them—all girls. Luckily for them, their father insisted they all be inoculated for smallpox before they left Kansas City."

"That's good news."

"He learned the hard way," Mrs. Fleming continued.

"Jedediah Brown lost his mother and brother to pox when he was a child."

"*Definitely* another wise man." Father Salazar's voice sounded distant and strained. "I wonder when they started requiring smallpox vaccinations."

"Required?" Dora echoed. "I didn't know that."

"I mean, when *will* they require them."

"Breakfast will be ready shortly, Father," Mrs. Fleming said. "Let me just take Sofie some decent clothes. These don't fit Dora anymore, but I do believe Sofie's a mite *smaller* in places."

"Mother." Dora groaned.

"Fine," Father Salazar said. "Where's Dr. Taylor this morning?"

"Oh, he's out at Zeke Judson's cabin near the creek," Dora explained quickly. "The vaccine arrived this morning."

"Vaccine?" Father Salazar echoed.

"For the inoculations," Mrs. Fleming said. "Dr. Taylor ordered it from back East right after the first miner come down with smallpox."

"Oh, of course."

"Too little, too late, I'm afraid. If only it had come sooner . . ." Mrs. Fleming gave a dramatic sigh. "As I recall, my brother the doctor said it takes weeks for the inoculation to protect a body even after it's been given."

"Oh, I see. Like a flu shot," Father Salazar said.

Sofie nodded. That made sense. "Oh." She brought her hand to her mouth, surprised by her own thoughts. Did this mean she'd finally remembered something from her medical background, or was it common knowledge that flu shots took a couple of weeks to become effective?

"Flu shot?" Dora asked. "I've never heard of such a thing. What is it? Mother?"

"I have no idea, dear."

Carefully, Sofie finished rinsing her hair and body,

avoiding the wound at her temple. She climbed from the tub and dried herself quickly, then wrapped the sheet around her, securing it under one arm.

She went to the mirror to stare at her face again. The bruising at her temple had spread to include her eye this morning. Nothing she could do about that, but her hair was another matter. Damp curls hung in spirals to her shoulders. "Utter chaos," she whispered. Mrs. Fleming had called that one right.

How had Sofie worn her hair before yesterday? Up like the other ladies she'd seen here in Redemption, or down and in utter chaos? Cocking her head to the side, she studied her ebony locks. The utter chaos seemed right for some reason. It was her—whoever that was.

For now, she had to look at this as a new beginning, regardless of how she'd worn her hair or behaved two days ago, or whether or not she'd wanted or needed a fresh start. Of course, there were far more important issues she should take into consideration, like what kind of foods did she like or dislike? Was she allergic to anything? Where had she gone to medical school? What kind of doctor was she—a specialist? Had anybody loved her? Would anyone miss her?

"Who the hell am I?"

A soft knock made her whirl around just as the door opened. Her pulse leapt at the base of her throat as she waited to identify the visitor. Would Father Salazar walk in uninvited? While she was undressed?

She clutched the towel more tightly across her breasts a moment before Mrs. Fleming peered around the corner. "Good, you're finished." She closed the door behind her and walked over to the bed, placing a stack of neatly folded clothing on the bed. She took the pale gray dress hanging over her arm and held it out in front of her. "What do you think?"

Relieved was the first word that popped into Sofie's

mind, because the dress was simple and ruffle-free. *Whew.* And long, but at least it didn't have frills. "Thank you, it's lovely." She crossed the room and touched the soft fabric. "I'm sure this must belong to your daughter." Of course, she knew that only too well, after listening to Dora's whining on this very subject.

"Yes, it's Dora's, but she's gained a few inches through the middle these last couple years." Mrs. Fleming spread the dress out on the patchwork quilt. "Being a spinster hasn't agreed with her, I'm afraid." The woman sighed heavily.

Sofie had only seen Dora briefly yesterday. "A spinster? She doesn't even look twenty."

"Twenty come March." Mrs. Fleming cast Sofie a sober look. "By the way, I'll be speaking to Jenny about her mother right after I take Dr. Taylor his breakfast . . ."

Remembering why they were all here in this building in the first place, Sofie nodded. There were people sick and dying here—people who needed the medical expertise she supposedly possessed. "I'll hurry and get dressed."

"Dr. Taylor might send word for you to come help with the inoculations, if you aren't needed here today."

Give shots? With needles? Shuddering, Sofie made no response as she watched Mrs. Fleming walk toward the door. The woman looked poised and polished, completely together, despite the tragedy awaiting them in the other room.

"I'll do whatever I can to help," Sofie promised, and meant it. Though she knew none of these people, she'd seen enough suffering yesterday to know they needed any help she could offer, medical or otherwise.

"I know you will." Mrs. Fleming looked over her shoulder and smiled. "I'll help Dora finish breakfast, then I'll take a tray over to Dr. Taylor. The man won't even stop to eat if I don't practically spoon-feed him myself. Not only that, but he forgets for days on end that a body needs sleep.''

"He's lucky to have you, Mrs. Fleming." Sofie watched a blush creep from Mrs. Fleming's collar and bloom in her cheeks. The woman was obviously in love with the aging physician. Did Dr. Taylor realize it? Probably not, but she hoped he would eventually, after the epidemic. After hell on earth.

"How many patients do we have this morning?" Sofie wasn't sure she wanted to hear the answer. "Any new cases?" *Any more deaths?*

"No new cases." Mrs. Fleming folded her hands beneath her chin. "And I pray to God there won't *be* any more new cases. As of this morning, we still have fifteen patients, plus the burned stranger."

"Fifteen?" Sofie swayed and sat on the edge of the bed. Hard. "There were twenty-two last night when I went to bed. Does that mean . . . ?"

Mrs. Fleming blinked rapidly and looked down for a few moments, then met Sofie's gaze. "Seven more passed on during the night."

"Oh, God. Oh, no." Sofie brought her knuckle to her mouth and bit down. This was too horrible. Children, mothers, fathers . . . This relentless and insidious disease killed indiscriminately.

The older woman crossed the room again and placed her hand on Sofie's shoulder. "I know it's hard, but it was their time, child."

"No." Sofie shook her head and stared at Mrs. Fleming, who had known and cared about these people. "I can't— I *won't*—believe there's anything ordained about any of this."

"Don't you?" Mrs. Fleming sighed and turned back toward the door. "I can't imagine anything less powerful than God Himself could've brought you and Father Salazar to us through yesterday's storm."

Sofie stared in silence as Mrs. Fleming left the room, closing the door firmly behind her. Alone again, a shudder gripped her.

She didn't even know these people, yet their deaths touched her. Maybe because she was a doctor, death's impact was more powerful. On the other hand, didn't it make more sense for her to be somewhat accustomed to death? Fear, revulsion, and horror rippled through her.

"Enough."

She jumped to her feet and grabbed the underwear Mrs. Fleming had brought. One look at the only thing remotely resembling panties jerked Sofie from her maudlin thoughts. She held the garment out before her to examine, noting its length and bloomerlike shape. These were nothing like the skimpy panties she'd removed this morning.

But she had no choice. At least these clothes were clean. They'd do for now. After pulling on the bloomers and securing the drawstring at her waist—*don't these people believe in elastic?*—she slipped something that looked like a woven cotton tank top over her head. A chemise, she realized, tucking it into the bloomers.

Shaking her head, she went to the mirror to stare at herself. Maybe she couldn't remember what kind of panties were in her dresser drawer at home—wherever home was—but she knew they wouldn't even begin to resemble these.

Resigned, she returned for the slip and stepped into it, tying yet another drawstring at her waist. Glancing down, she found what she'd been dreading.

Rows of ruffles and flounces edged the cotton slip. A petticoat? Yes, that was the word.

"No way." She picked up the gray dress and held it up to the morning light spilling through the lace curtains. If she couldn't see through the dress, she didn't need a slip, let alone a petticoat.

Satisfied no one would be able to see through her

dress—and even if they did, all they'd find would be her baggy bloomers—Sofie finished dressing. However, she was relieved to discover Mrs. Fleming had failed to bring shoes along with the black wool stockings. At least Sofie knew her hiking boots would fit, and they were comfortable, even if they probably weren't intended to be worn with a dress.

And no ruffles.

Luke watched Dora move around the kitchen preparing breakfast, her generous backside bumping into everything in her path of destruction. She placed thick slabs of bacon in an iron skillet, and the savory aroma soon filled the room.

He closed his eyes as a pang of remembrance stabbed through him. His grandmother had prepared bacon almost every morning, until Grandpa's doctor had put them on low-fat diets. Luke's childhood memories were filled with the scents and sounds of his grandparents' old house near Capital Hill, and the shoe repair shop his grandfather had owned in an historic part of downtown Denver.

Blinking several times, he cleared his throat and rose from his seat at the round table near the back door. The few hours he'd slept had been fraught with nightmares of running for his life until he couldn't take another step. And the ending was always the same.

The electric chair.

After thrashing around until he'd awakened drenched with perspiration, he abandoned all hope of real rest. Besides, since he'd been trying to sleep in the front room with the patients, he'd heard Dr. Taylor informing more than one family that their loved ones had died during the night. That dedicated man never seemed to sleep.

Father Salazar had done his duty, performing last rites for one young man, while praying over half a dozen who were beyond that. Luke was repaying the dead priest's kindness to him with interest.

No, not really. Father Salazar had believed in Luke's innocence, and nothing could repay that.

"Careful you don't break the yolks this time, Dora," Mrs. Fleming said as she came back through the kitchen door.

She paused and shook her head, a tear rolling down her cheek. "Oh, Father, I just can't believe we lost so many more patients in one night."

"Yeah, I know." Luke reached up to rake his fingers through his nonexistent hair, grimacing from the pain of his fried scalp instead. What the hell was he doing here?

Then the door opened to the room off the kitchen and Sofie paused in the doorway, staring at him. She looked beautiful. Luke's breath froze as his gaze drifted down the length of her and back again. Shiny black hair curled in spirals around her small face, and her eyes seemed even larger and bluer than—

The bruise on her temple had spread, and now included half her face, including one eye. Regret slashed through him, as he remembered those blue eyes looking up at him yesterday, begging for help.

He'd almost left her to die.

Swallowing the lump in his throat, he remembered that he was free, that they were stranded together in another century, and that she had no memory of the past. She was lost, while he was celebrating a new beginning. He had no regrets about helping her. Not anymore.

"You look lovely," he said, reminding himself that they all considered him a priest, regardless of his thoughts and desires. "I hope you slept well." In his mind, he saw her asleep last night with her full, firm breast half-exposed to his gaze. The mental image knifed through him.

Straight to his groin.

"Yes," she said, still staring at him. "I . . . for a moment,
I . . ."

"Are you all right, Sofie?" Mrs. Fleming went to her
side and took her arm. "You aren't dizzy, are you? Dr.
Taylor said to watch for that."

"No, I just . . . " Her gaze riveted to Luke, she slowly
shook her head. "Nothing. It couldn't be. For a moment,
I thought I remembered something."

His heart hammered his ribs and he held his breath. *God,
please don't let her remember. At least, not yet.* Luke managed a
weak smile and, finally, a breath. "Maybe your memory
will come back a little at a time," he said, though in truth
he hoped she never remembered everything. That made
him selfish and small, but there it was.

"Maybe." Sofie visibly shook herself and dragged her
gaze from Luke. "Dora, thank you for lending me this
dress. I'll return it after I've washed my own clothes."

Mrs. Fleming made a sound of open disapproval. "Sofie,
those rags—"

"Are all I have of my own," Sofie said. "You've been
very kind, Mrs. Fleming, but I hope to regain my memory
and my life as soon as possible. I don't wish to be a burden
to anyone." She shrugged and sighed. "I'm not even sure
where we are."

"High in the Rocky Mountains," Luke said, trying not
to remember the day Warden Graham and company had
escorted him up to the new facility. "Somewhere near the
Continental Divide, I think."

"Redemption is part of the Cripple Creek Mining Dis-
trict," Dora said, lifting pieces of bacon from the skillet
with a fork. "So the miners here stake their claims and
such over to Cripple Creek. Assayer is there, too."

"A city of sin." Mrs. Fleming filled a plate with bacon
and steaming biscuits, then held it while Dora ladled out
a hefty serving of eggs. "I'll just take this out to Dr. Taylor,
and stand there until he eats every bite."

Luke tried not to look at Sofie. She seemed so vulnerable in the oversized gray dress. It swallowed her, made her appear even smaller and more fragile than before. Then he noticed her worn leather hiking boots peeking out from beneath the long dress, and he smiled. Really smiled.

"Cripple Creek," Sofie said. "I wonder why that sounds familiar."

Was she from that infamous mountain town? But most people knew about Cripple Creek, even if they'd never been there. The tune to "Up on Cripple Creek" raced through Luke's mind. Of course it sounded famliar to her.

In fact, he remembered visiting the historic mining town with his grandparents the summer he turned twelve. He'd found the old buildings and living history fascinating then, but the stories of huge gold strikes had been more than compelling. *Age appropriate, no doubt.*

But even at twenty-nine, Luke's palms turned sweaty and his heart rate surged. Could he walk into the mountains now and stake a claim? Might he find a fortune in gold lying just beneath the earth's surface?

Did it matter? Would it change anything?

No, freedom and life were more important. He sighed. Money was merely a means to an end. Of course, train tickets would cost money, and the few dollars in Father Salazar's wallet wouldn't take him far. And he should make sure Sofie had some money, too. Then he remembered that all currency carried a date.

The Denver Mint would have a fit.

Luke caught himself smiling again. That was twice in one morning.

He looked at Sofie as she set plates and silverware on the table. She was so quiet. Why? Was she trying to remember something?

Like seeing him in the electric chair?

The back door opened and Ab shuffled inside, wiping his feet on the mat. "Mornin'," he muttered.

"You're just in time for breakfast, Ab," Dora called over her shoulder, broadcasting a brilliant smile. "As usual."

"Mornin', Miss Dora. Mrs. Fleming." Ab blushed and ducked his head. "Dr. Taylor said he reckons he'll be tied up all day, but to send for him if need be." The short, stocky man looked at Sofie and his face reddened even more beneath his beard. "He said for Miss Dr. Sofie to handle things here until he finishes out at Zeke's place."

"Miss Dr. Sofie?" Mrs. Fleming looked at Sofie and smiled. "I'm going out there now. What shall I tell him?" The woman tied a cape beneath her chin, then lifted the heavy tray. "Can you handle things by yourself for a while?"

Sofie's face paled and her hand trembled as she brought it to her cheek. "Tell him that's fine," she said, though her eyes revealed her uncertainty.

"Very well." Mrs. Fleming nodded in open approval. "I'll be back a little later. Dora, show Sofie where everything is if she has questions."

"Yes, Mother."

"Frank Latimer was first in line for his inoculation," Ab offered, his tone reserved.

"What?" Mrs. Fleming looked back, her eyes wide. "That horrible man?"

"Come for his rightful share of the serum, he *said*." Ab shrugged.

Mrs. Fleming's nostrils flared and she squared her shoulders. "The world would be better off if he'd died and his brother's widow had been spared."

Confused, Luke looked around the room, trying to digest all the names and information. Frank Latimer was obviously not well liked.

"That reminds me, Sofie, I almost forgot that we need to talk to Jenny this morning," Mrs. Fleming said. "I'll come back after—"

"Latimer was askin' about the girl, too," Ab said, looking downward as he spoke. "Said he'd raise his kin."

"Over my dead body." Mrs. Fleming's lips thinned and her eyes snapped. She drew a deep breath, then said, "Jenny Latimer would be better off dead than living with the likes of him, uncle or no uncle."

"I reckon. Seems he's concerned 'bout Charlie's mine." Ab appeared apologetic. "He also asked about the boy— wanted to know when the hangin's supposed to take place."

Hanging? Luke's blood turned to ice as he recalled the kid in the jail. Young and sentenced to die . . .

Like me.

"That horrible event should never take place," Mrs. Fleming said. Then without another word, she took her tray and waited for Ab to open the door for her. She left without even glancing back.

Dora placed a platter of bacon and another of eggs on the table. "Better wash up, Ab," she said, her expression grim. She shook her head. "I still can't believe they plan to hang that boy."

"That *boy* killed a man, Miss Dora." Ab's tone was gentle as he crossed the room to a pitcher and bowl near the huge wood burning stove. "In these parts, the law takes an eye for an eye."

Luke's mouth went dry and he looked at Sofie's furrowed brow. The expression in her eyes was pure confusion as she met his gaze.

Don't remember yet, Sofie, he silently pleaded. *Please, not yet.*

"That man needed killing." Dora slammed the pan of biscuits onto the table and poured steaming coffee into cups.

"I reckon that's a fact." Ab sat at the table and tucked his napkin into his collar.

Luke didn't protest as Dora forked enough bacon onto his plate to send his cholesterol into orbit. A pair of eggs, sunnyside up, slid onto his plate alongside the bacon, everything shining with bacon grease.

His mouth watered in anticipation, though his mind kept replaying Dora's words. *That man needed killing.*

Luke hadn't killed anyone and had been sent to the electric chair. The boy in Redemption's jail had apparently killed someone deserving of such a fate, and he would hang.

Justice, my ass.

He looked up and met Sofie's gaze again. She looked quickly away. *Still staring at me, Sofie?* Was her memory returning? Maybe he should revise his plans and leave today, after all. But what would happen to her after he left Redemption?

"The man Shane Latimer supposedly killed was low and mean." Dora sat at the table with a huff, snapping her napkin before placing it in her lap. "Mother and I *saw* what he did to his wife. Twice."

"Miss Dora," Ab said quietly, pausing with his fork in midair, "the boy killed his own pa."

Sofie gasped, but all Luke could think of was the phone call his grandmother had made to the prison, informing him of his grandfather's death.

You killed your grandpa with shame, Luke Nolan. Shame . . .

Chapter Six

Gently, Sofie unwrapped the burned man's bandages. Dr. Taylor had managed to scrounge up enough laudanum to put the man into a semiconscious state. Thank God. The last thing Sofie wanted was to cause any of the patients additional pain with her bumbling attempts at playing doctor.

But she had no choice. Dr. Taylor's instructions had been explicit. They had to change the bandages twice a day, but he was still busy with the inoculations. If she didn't change them, the cloth could adhere to the man's burns and cause him even greater misery.

If only Father Salazar were here. She sighed softly, knowing she had to stop looking for his support. Someday, she hoped, fate would return her to the life she'd left behind. Then she wouldn't have Father Salazar's reassuring presence in her life anymore.

Besides, he had his own horrendous responsibilities in this epidemic. The poor man had gone to officiate over more funerals, including one for Jenny's mother.

Sofie glanced toward Jenny, wondering when Mrs. Fleming would return to speak to the child. The expression on the girl's face when she'd clutched her mother's nightgown to her cheek ate away at Sofie. This was so unfair.

Her patient groaned, dragging her attention back to her task. *Concentrate, Sofie. Be careful. Don't hurt him.* She hated this, because she simply didn't know what she was doing. Dr. Sofie was incompetent at best.

Carefully, she cut away a soiled bandage and applied the special salve Dr. Taylor had prepared. *Please don't let him wake up now.* She paused. The salve's pungent aroma triggered an image in Sofie's mind. A memory? A dark-haired woman bending over her, pressing her cool hand to Sofie's forehead . . .

"Mother?" she whispered. Sofie's throat convulsed and perspiration coated her face and neck. The woman had to be her mother. "Mother?" she repeated, earning yet another groan from her patient. "I'm sorry."

Wincing in remorse, she jerked her attention back to the present, trying not to look at the man's wounds any more than absolutely necessary. Her stomach felt queasy every time she came near him, though his injuries certainly weren't his fault.

Some caring medical professional she was turning out to be. More guilt. Despite her memory loss, Sofie had learned she was good at guilt. Gifted even.

With a sigh, she completed her task and rose, but the man's hand snaked out to grab her wrist. His eyes were open and wild, glazed with pain, drugs, and something else. Something undefinable. Terror rippled through her and a scream froze in her throat, her gaze imprisoned by his maniacal one.

Screaming is not allowed, Dr. Sofie. This was a hospital, and this man was seriously injured. He was probably as frightened as she.

"It's all right," she said soothingly, fighting the tremor

in her voice. "I'm here to help you. Go back to sleep now. Rest."

The man blinked once. Twice. Then his eyes closed and his fingers relaxed around her wrist. Sofie quickly retreated with the basket of soiled bandages.

Her heart pounded through her chest as she made her way to the kitchen to dispose of the soiled mess. Dr. Taylor had left instructions that they were to be burned, so she opened the stove and used a long stick to shove them onto the hot embers until greedy flames devoured the strips.

After closing the door, she washed her hands thoroughly, trying to remember how and why she knew that was necessary. But she didn't *know* why, and it didn't *matter* why. Cleanliness was necessary around the sick, and that was that.

Again, she saw the woman's face, hovering over her with worry etched across her brow. She had dark hair like Sofie's, and her eyes were blue. The woman had to be Sofie's mother, or a close relative. Didn't she?

"Damn."

"Sofie." The sound of Mrs. Fleming's voice sliced through Sofie's reverie. "Such language." Shaking her head and frowning, the woman stepped into the kitchen and closed the back door behind her.

More guilt. Why didn't the word "damn" seem wrong to Sofie? What kind of woman was she? "I'm sorry."

"Well, you've been through a great deal, but such language from a *lady,* well . . ." Mrs. Fleming's cheeks reddened. "Perhaps the . . . the soiled doves at Miss Lottie's House of Ill Repute, but not you, Sofie. After all, you're a woman with an education, which must mean a proper upbringing."

An education and a proper upbringing again? It must be true, Sofie decided as she dried her hands and paused before Mrs. Fleming. The expression in the woman's eyes reminded Sofie of something more important than her education or questionable upbringing. "You're going to tell Jenny now, aren't you?"

"Yes, right away." Mrs. Fleming untied her bonnet and hung it on a nail near the back door. "Her uncle is making a lot of noise about taking her away, though he won't dare come here until the epidemic is over, thank heavens."

"But she's getting so much better . . ."

The older woman nodded. "And she won't always have this epidemic to protect her." A bitter laugh left Mrs. Fleming's lips. "Amazing to consider this horrible epidemic as a shelter for that sweet little girl."

"The same epidemic that killed her mother." Sofie's lower lip trembled and tears stung her eyes. She blinked them back, determined to be brave for Jenny. "Well, we'd better talk to her now."

"Yes." Mrs. Fleming washed her hands, tied her apron around her waist, then pushed open the kitchen door. "Let's get on with it."

Sofie followed behind Mrs. Fleming until they reached Jenny. Then she stepped around to stand beside the older woman, determined to follow through with her promise to the child. She only wished she had better news.

"Hello, Jenny," Mrs. Fleming said, kneeling beside the cot. "How are you feeling today, child?"

Sofie didn't need a reminder of what a good person Mrs. Fleming was, but now she knew the woman was meant for nothing less than sainthood.

"Better." Jenny looked up at them with big brown eyes. "Where's my mama?"

Sofie knelt beside Mrs. Fleming and took Jenny's hand while the older woman stroked strands of blond hair away from the girl's eyes.

"Your mama was real sick, honey," Mrs. Fleming said quietly, soothingly. "She tried real hard to get well, and she asked after you all the time."

Jenny jerked her gaze away from them and stared up at the ceiling. "Mama's dead." No tears fell from her eyes, though they glittered threateningly.

"Yes." Mrs. Fleming gathered Jenny in her arms, and peered up at Sofie through the child's tangled hair.

Tears spilled from Sofie's eyes, and she reached down to touch Jenny's shoulder. Sofie's heart pressed upward against her throat and she knew her own agonizing pain couldn't possibly equal this little girl's. Children should never have to hurt this way.

This is wrong and cruel and . . . Sofie bit her lower lip as tears soaked her face.

Then she remembered what Ab had said at breakfast. *That boy killed his own pa . . .* Jenny was truly alone. Both her parents were dead, and her brother had been sentenced to hang.

Squeezing her eyes shut, Sofie saw the dark-haired woman again. Though the murmuring she heard was only Mrs. Fleming speaking to Jenny, the face she saw was her mother's. She knew it.

The vision spoke, and Sofie heard the words clearly. Undeniably.

"Your daddy's gone to sleep, sweetheart," her dream mother said, pressing her cool cheek against Sofie's. *"He won't ever wake up this time, but at least he won't hurt anymore."*

Sofie opened her eyes after the image vanished. Her father had died, too. "Daddy," she whispered, knowing somehow that she'd been very young when tragedy struck her family. *My family.* If only she could remember her last name, then she could go to her mother.

She could go home, where she belonged.

"Home."

A gray mist swirled around her and the room swayed. Sofie grappled for something substantial enough to prevent her fall, but all she found was air.

She hit the floor with a jarring thud. Pain stabbed through her skull.

Then there was nothing.

Luke shivered as he walked down Redemption's only street—a wide, muddy, rutted road, lined with haphazard buildings, and crowded by the majestic Rockies on all sides.

A picturesque setting for death.

God, how many funerals? He'd lost count after six. Innocent men, women, and children killed by smallpox—unnecessarily, even in 1891.

From the corner of his eye, he caught sight of the small stone building which served as the jail. Jarred from his return trek to the schoolhouse, he paused to stare at the barred window, wondering about the prisoner inside.

Luke swallowed hard. *Bars.* A chilly breeze chased itself down the pass and encircled him. Father Salazar's black robe flowed around him as he stood there staring. And waiting.

After a moment, the youth appeared at the window, his shaggy blond hair completely concealing one eye. The barest hint of golden stubble covered his chin.

Luke took a step toward the window. The kid seemed oblivious to being watched. Either that, or he was beyond caring.

Luke understood that.

Too damned well.

Slowly, he approached the jail, drawn to seek out the boy. The condemned prisoner. The murderer. Had he really killed his own father? Or, like Luke, had Shane Latimer been wrongly accused, convicted, and sentenced?

Guilty . . . guilty . . . guilty . . .

Luke would never forget the sound of those words coming from the jury foreman's lips. Nor would he forget the judge's condemning words as he'd sentenced Luke to die for a crime he hadn't committed.

And Grandpa . . .

Pain wrenched through Luke's gut and he froze in mid-step. His breathing labored, he stared at the prisoner, whose gaze was directed toward the schoolhouse at the far edge of town. Studying the boy's expression, Luke saw pain, fear, and helplessness etched across the young features.

Father Salazar's words reverberated through Luke's mind yet again: *"Go with God, my son."*

Why now?

Because Father Salazar would've spoken to the boy, just as he'd spoken to Luke. He would've offered comfort and reassurance in the face of death.

You're taking this priest stuff too seriously, Nolan. So what? His impersonation wasn't hurting anyone and, as impossible as it seemed, Luke had actually brought comfort to the citizens of this cursed town. Besides, this kid deserved the same consideration Father Salazar had shown Luke.

Even if he was guilty?

Luke hesitated for only a moment. *Yeah, even then.*

Had anyone told Shane Latimer about his mother's death? Or that his sister would recover? Luke clenched his fists at his sides, making his decision even as he continued toward the window.

The boy must've heard Luke's approach, because he retreated into the dingy cell, his gaze wary as he stared at his uninvited guest. "Who are you?" he asked when Luke stopped outside the window.

"Lu—" He froze and drew a ragged breath. "Father Salazar," he said, wishing more than ever that he could shed his facade.

"I didn't send for any priest. What do you want?" Shane's gaze darted back to the schoolhouse twice before settling again on Luke. "You been over there with the sick folks?"

Though the kid was obviously trying to appear tough, Luke heard pain and worry in his voice. "Yes."

Shane reached up and gripped the bars so tightly his knuckles turned white. His transformation from tough and aloof to frantic and impassioned occurred within a heartbeat. He pressed his face against the iron bars, pretense crumbling away to reveal stark fear. "Please, tell me about my ma and sister. *Please?*"

No trace of the tough veneer remained. Naked emotion filled the imploring eyes. Luke hated being the one to tell the boy about his mother, but it had to be done.

Who better than the local priest? *Get a grip.*

"Shane—your name is Shane?" He had to make sure, and at the boy's nod, he continued. "Your mother and sister have both been very ill with smallpox. Jenny is much better now. Dr. Taylor doesn't think she'll even have bad scars."

Shane lowered his gaze. Hair the color and texture of straw fell across his face, concealing his expression. After a few minutes, he cleared his throat and met Luke's gaze again. "And Ma?"

"I . . . I'm sorry."

The boy's eyes glittered with unshed tears. "I knew she was gone. I just knew it."

This was Luke's cue to lapse into priest mode, but the words wouldn't come. He couldn't mutter a single "It was God's will" or anything else the least bit comforting. This epidemic wasn't God's will, dammit. It was hell on earth. Period.

"Yes," he finally said. "She died—"

"Night before last," Shane finished, a grimace twisting his young face. "A few hours before sunrise." The kid's voice cracked with emotion and he blinked several times.

"Someone told you then." Luke breathed a sigh of relief.

"Yeah, I guess you could say that." Bitterness honed

Shane's voice to a bitter edge. "*She* told me herself. Nancy Latimer always does—did—everything herself. Absolutely everything. She never asked anybody for a blessed thing."

One lone tear trickled down Shane's face, but he swiped it away, then turned his back on Luke and stalked across the dirt floor. "Thanks for telling me," he muttered.

Luke stared helplessly at the young man's back. The shoulders were slumped, but they didn't shake with weeping, nor did Shane make a single sound to reveal his anguish. The kid suffered in silence, and with dignity.

After a moment, Luke drew a deep breath and dropped his hands to his sides. "Your mother must've been one helluva woman to raise fine kids like you and Jenny."

Shane turned slowly to face the window again. He opened his mouth as if to speak, then snapped it shut and nodded. "She . . . she was," he finally whispered.

"If you want to talk, send someone to the schoolhouse for me."

"Wait. Tell my sister . . ." Shane approached the window again.

"Yes?" Luke waited. The tension in the air was so thick he could almost hear it, and he couldn't help remembering almost exactly the same words coming from his lips moments before his trip to the chair. *Tell my grandma . . .*

"I can't raise Jenny like I promised Ma I would if anything ever . . . happened to her." Another tear slid down Shane's cheek. "I won't be here to do it."

That did it. Even when Luke had faced execution over a century in the future, there hadn't been a child depending on him. He'd left no one except a bitter old grandmother who'd written him off years ago. Hardened criminal or not, Luke's heart broke.

"Mrs. Fleming plans to raise Jenny," Luke said, wanting to ease the boy's mind.

"*I'll* raise Jenny," a man called from the middle of the street.

Luke whirled around to find the owner of the voice. A man sat on horseback, his face partially covered by a bandanna.

A roar erupted from the jail cell. Shane's fist shot between the bars, reaching toward the rider. "You stay away from Jenny," the boy shouted. "Stay away!"

"That bald-headed priest ain't gonna help you, boy. You're as good as dead already." The rider tilted his head back and laughed, a wicked, penetrating sound that made Luke shudder.

"Stay away from her!"

Luke knew with absolute certainty that if Shane could have reached the man, he would've killed him with his bare hands. From the information Luke had overheard this morning, he realized the man on horseback was none other than the notorious Frank Latimer.

"Sure hope you've had smallpox," Luke said casually, facing the newcomer. "If not, you're pretty stupid to ride into town this way."

The man looked down the street, then narrowed his gaze on Luke. "Got the inoculation this morning." He pulled the bandanna up higher over the bridge of his nose.

So Frank Latimer thought that piece of cloth would protect him from smallpox. Luke shook his head.

"I hope you *do* get smallpox," Shane said, letting his hand fall limply outside the cell window. "I want you to *suffer* before you burn in hell."

The man laughed again, but he sounded nervous even to Luke. "I'll be back for the hangin'. Wouldn't miss that for nothin'." A moment later, Frank Latimer turned his horse and dug his heels into the animal's sides, leaving Redemption and its epidemic behind.

"Don't let him get Jenny." The urgency in Shane's voice made Luke wary. Very wary.

"Mrs. Fleming will raise Jenny," Luke vowed.

And prayed this was one promise he could keep.

* * *

Chills gripped Sofie. She was burning hot one minute, then freezing the next, floating between a strange dream world and reality. The dream world was much more pleasant, and she welcomed its return.

A blurry shape formed beside her, and she blinked to focus on Dr. Taylor's white head. With his stethoscope, he listened to her chest, then he lifted the lids of her eyes and leaned very close.

"Can't rule out an infection with the fever, but I think she's just worn herself out," he said, then stood and moved away. "Keep her in bed the rest of the day. I'll check on her again later."

"Not smallpox?" Mrs. Fleming asked.

"Definitely not. Besides, she's been inoculated. This is my fault. I shouldn't have put her to work right away after that nasty head wound."

"It isn't your fault, Roman."

"If you say so," he said uncertainly. "You're too good to me. I don't know what we'd do without you."

"This epidemic isn't your fault, and neither is Sofie's condition," Mrs. Fleming repeated, her tone adamant.

"I know better than to argue with you," he said. "Give her a dose of laudanum to help her sleep. I'm sure she'll be all right after a rest, Anna."

Sofie tried to concentrate on their conversation, but only parts of it penetrated the smothering gray veil. It was like being under water, struggling to reach the surface. Weird, staccato music played through her head, and she saw an openmouthed shark coming toward her. A huge one.

The door opened and closed, then she heard Mrs. Fleming's soothing voice, blotting out the strange shark music. "There, there. We didn't let you mend long enough, child. I'm so sorry."

A cool rag soothed Sofie's burning forehead and something cold and metallic pressed against her lips. Too tired
to fight, she took the bittersweet medicine and sighed.

And dreamed.

*Bright lights and people rushing around her. Someone stopped
and powdered her nose, then took her center stage, where a huge
sign spelled out "This is Your Life" in glaring neon lights.*

*A game show? Of course, a television game show. Scenes and
images flew past. She saw birthday parties, family weddings, herself
at various ages, and the dark-haired woman she knew was her
mother. Daddy was there, too, and a little boy whose name she
couldn't remember. He was bigger than Sofie—her older brother?*

*All the faces were nameless, though. Sofie wanted desperately
to know their names. Were they really her family? Were they searching for her? Did they miss her? She saw a casket draped with
flowers, and her mother standing there holding Sofie's hand and
the little boy's. They all looked so sad and lost, but they were
together. A family?*

*She had to remember. "Try, Sofie." It was her mother's voice,
soothing and pleading. "Come home soon."*

*Home. Ruby slippers, heels clicking together, and a soft voice
saying, "There's no place like home . . ."*

Coolness touched her cheek again and Sofie leaned into
it. Gentle fingers brushed her hair away from her face, then
something else touched her. Something soft and warm and
wondrous. Lips? Yes, someone had kissed her forehead.

Fingertips brushed her cheek again, and Sofie knew it
was a man who touched her now. These rough but gentle
fingers couldn't belong to Mrs. Fleming or even Dr. Taylor.
Father Salazar?

"Just rest, Sofie," he said. "You scared the hell out of
me—I mean us—today."

Yes, of course. Definitely Father Salazar. She'd know his
voice anywhere, even under the influence of the potent
drug Mrs. Fleming had given her. It didn't matter, because
her weird hero was here to rescue her again.

She struggled to awaken completely, but her eyelids were too heavy. Everything felt heavy, and she was weak. So weak . . .

He touched her again and she managed to find his hand with her lips, and planted a kiss in his palm. He tasted of salt and man. She inhaled his scent and snuggled against his thigh, where he sat on the edge of her bed. His solid warmth reached something deep inside her, stirring sensations and thoughts probably better left buried.

Another dream? Yes, it had to be. Surrendering to the power of her dream, warmth oozed through her and she kissed his palm again fiercely.

"Sofie," he said, his voice quiet but intense. "Sofie, don't."

Empowered, she nipped his hand playfully with her teeth. Dreams were safe—a place to let it all hang out. She wanted this dream man to keep touching her forever, but in other, more intimate ways.

Everywhere.

She wanted him to kiss her again. *Really* kiss her. "Kiss me," she whispered, trying to reach out to him. "Please, dream man?"

A deep, nervous chuckle rumbled from him, and a smile tugged at her lips. *Only a dream . . .*

"Kiss me," she repeated.

"Then will you go back to sleep?" His whisper was hoarse, strained.

"Yes," she promised, even though she was already very much asleep.

She felt the warmth of his body as he bent toward her. His broad chest brushed against her nipples, and she moaned. Her breasts grew heavy and hard, aching for his touch.

Summoning every ounce of strength she could manage, she lifted her arms and slipped her hands behind his neck, locking her fingers together. Anything to prolong this delicious dream . . .

His mouth was soft and warm on her cheek, but it wasn't enough. Not nearly enough. She turned her face to capture his lips with hers. He tensed, but didn't pull away. Empowered, she drew him closer, her lips parting in invitation.

"Sofie," he whispered against her lips.

She traced the shape of his mouth with the tip of her tongue. He moaned, and the sound rumbled through her, enticing and inciting.

Closer now, his lips finally formed a seal with hers. Liquid warmth surged through her. She was floating, swelling upward, eagerly seeking his hard maleness to complement her own softness.

He tried again to pull away, but she held fast. And when he tried to speak, she took advantage of his parted lips to explore the warmth of his mouth.

Moaning again, he returned her kiss. His hands cupped her face as he tasted her thoroughly. Deeply. Hungrily.

Hot. Sofie was so hot. She wanted to shed her clothing, to press her naked flesh against his, to feel his desire in turn.

But suddenly, he broke their kiss and wrenched himself from her embrace. "No, I can't," he whispered fiercely. "This is wrong. *Wrong.*"

"No, don't leave me." If only she could open her eyes and see him, then, maybe, she could make him stay. *I'll just dream him back.* "Love me."

"God help me."

She heard the door open and close, but before she could protest her dream lover's sudden departure, she slipped into a deeper, dreamless sleep.

Chapter Seven

Behind the schoolhouse, Luke gulped frosty night air into his lungs, struggling to regain control. Mrs. Fleming had warned him earlier that she'd dosed Sofie with laudanum—probably not the best treatment for someone with a head injury, now that he thought about it. Modern medicine, such as it was . . .

Sofie's behavior had been a result of her injury and a dose of opium. *Not* any latent, ardent desire for a sunburned, bald-headed priest.

Yeah, get real.

Luke, on the other hand, had no potent narcotic flowing through his veins as a handy excuse for his behavior. His instantaneous red-hot response to her guileless—and highly effective—attempt at seduction had been totally natural. Unenhanced.

Volatile.

Hell, even a *real* priest would've had trouble walking away from her soft lips, firm breasts, and blatant eagerness.

Yeah, eagerness.

"Man, I'm in sad shape." He unbuttoned the top few buttons of his robe and yanked the stiff collar from around his neck. As a kid, he'd heard some refer to it as a dog collar. He hadn't understood it then, but it made a lot of sense now. Dogs were neutered, and he might as well be at this point.

Merciful and humane? *Yeah, and permanent.* No, not for Luke Nolan. Playing priest could be the death of him yet, but at least it was temporary.

Being so close to a woman like Sofie without being able to . . . to . . .

"No." He wouldn't—couldn't. Mopping perspiration from his forehead with the back of his hand, he looked up at the sky. Last night's stars were totally absent this evening. Only a sliver of moonlight penetrated the total blackness shrouding the mountain town.

Screw the stars.

He was harder than the iron bars on any jail cell. Pacing in the darkness, he punched the palm of his left hand with his right fist. Repeatedly. Rhythmically.

Reminding him of something else. An activity he hadn't experienced nearly enough in his twenty-nine years. Bumping and grinding. Yes, that's what his teenaged mentality would've called what he wanted to do right now.

"Shit." Finding no relief from beating his palm black and blue like his balls, he stopped and stared at the collar still clutched in his fist. *Damn that collar.* One way or another, he'd have some different clothes by morning. Besides, these were filthy. Good excuse to shed his sheep's clothing, especially since he felt a lot more like a wolf . . .

He drew more cold air into his lungs and closed his eyes. Perspiration trickled down his face and neck, despite the chilly night air. He was on fire, and this time he couldn't blame the electric chair. All the heat came from the inside.

Straight from his groin.

"Damn, damn, damn." He needed a woman. Eleven

years of celibacy had caught up with him in a big way. How did priests do it? Sure, he'd heard stories about those who'd strayed, but in his heart, he believed most people who took vows of celibacy kept them. Didn't they?

The throbbing between his legs increased.

Didn't they?

"Of course they do. Don't be an ass. Crap." Grandma would've washed his mouth out with soap about now.

But Luke Nolan was no priest, and he had no intention of going through life without having sex. Frequent sex.

Great sex.

"This isn't helping," he muttered and punched his palm again. Good thing Father Salazar's trousers were baggy, because Luke filled them out much better now than when he'd first pulled them on, and it wasn't from Dora Fleming's good cooking. "I'm weak. I can't do this abstinence stuff." No, that wasn't quite true. He didn't *want* to abstain, and motivation was everything, after all.

Just the thought of indulging himself increased the throbbing between his legs to critical. Thinking about sex definitely wasn't helping, but he couldn't *stop* thinking about it. He'd done all right until Sofie touched him. Now all he could think of was feeding the fire she'd ignited. After spending the best years of his life on death row . . .

In isolation.

No, he'd have to make up for the last decade during the *next* eleven years. What choice did he have? Time travel or not, he couldn't relive those lost years. They were gone forever, regardless of the century.

Sure, he could make up for lost time. But lost sex? "Stop thinking about it, Nolan." Resuming his pacing, he punched his bruised palm again.

This morning, he'd overheard Ab mention something called Miss Lottie's House. Could that be a—what would Grandma have called it?—whorehouse? No, Grandma would've called it a massage parlor or something equally lame.

Grinning despite the enthusiastic state of his libido, Luke released a frustrated sigh. Fat lot of good a prostitute would do a priest—talk about scandal. Besides, realistic or not, he wanted Sofie.

No, he couldn't want Sofie. He couldn't *have* Sofie.

The feel of her lips on his, her breasts against his chest, her hands locked behind his neck . . .

"Cut the crap, Nolan." His words vanished into a cloud of white vapor in the darkness.

He wanted Sofie. Okay, he'd admitted it. Faced it. So, now what? He couldn't do a damned thing about it. She was off limits. The forbidden fruit and then some.

Enough already. He should've left last night, before he'd tasted her lips. *No, don't think about her lips.* He had to get the hell out of Redemption, Colorado, and leave Sofie's lips behind. He *had* to. Her lips, her breasts, that tattoo on her—

No! Don't go there.

But if he left, what would happen to her? What was the significance of the fainting spell she'd suffered today? Would she recover at all? Regain her memory . . . ?

He shook his head, desire waning only slightly in light of his genuine concern and that frigging guilt he couldn't shake no matter what. Sofie had to get well. She *would* get well.

And destroy his clean slate?

"No, don't think about that now." Threat or no threat, he couldn't leave Redemption until he was certain of her recovery. No way. He didn't need any more guilt piled on top of what he already had.

His grandparents, Father Salazar . . . He looked down at the white collar. Moonlight struck the crucifix hanging from his neck. "Damn."

Another sign, Luke?

Hell, he'd seen some kind of subliminal significance in almost everything else since his failed execution, so why stop now? As long as he was at it, what about that kiss? Was that some kind of sign, too? What about Sofie? Another sign? Hell, and what about this boner messing with his head? What kind of sign was that?

"Damn. Shit. Fu—"

"Whooee, Moses. I ain't never heard a priest cuss so fine in all my born days," someone said from the darkness. " 'Course, I ain't had much call to hear priests talk at all, let alone cuss."

"Who's there?" Luke swallowed hard, trying to identify the voice. Not Ab or Dr. Taylor, and definitely not Frank Latimer, thank God. "Is that you, Zeke?"

"Yep, the one and only, in these parts, anyway." The muffled sound of boots striking earth and pine needles signaled the man's approach. "Cold night."

Luke nodded, making out the dark shape of his companion in the inadequate moonlight. "Yeah, but it usually is cold at night up here."

"Sure 'nuff." Zeke lifted a jug to his lips and took a long pull, sighing afterward. "Do priests drink mash, too, or just cuss right fine?"

Luke could use a drink about now. He remembered priests drinking wine. Besides, this priest crap was getting old. *Past tense.* "Yeah, thanks. Some priests do both, I guess, in moments of weakness."

"Well, I reckon this epidemic could make even Matthew, Luke, and John weak. Seems to me the Lord'll forgive anybody a nip 'bout now." Zeke wiped the mouth of the jug with his sleeve, then passed it to Luke. "Have your fill, *Padre.* I got plenty more where that come from."

Imitating Zeke, Luke looped his finger through the jug's handle and let its bulk rest across the back of his hand and wrist. He sniffed the sour stench and almost changed his mind. Liquor was something he had almost as little experience with as sex, after all. He was a neophyte at just about everything, especially by 1891 standards.

Remembering Sofie's kiss, he shuddered and made his decision. The brew tasted even worse than it smelled as it flowed across his tongue and blazed its way down his throat. After three big gulps, he lowered the jug and gasped, hoping to cool the fire the stuff had left behind.

"It'll either cure what ails a man, er kill him." Zeke wiped the jug and tipped it to drink, then he smacked his lips and offered it to Luke again. "Another swig, *Padre?*"

"Don't mind if I do," Luke said, repeating his previous actions. The alcohol didn't burn nearly as badly this time. In fact, he barely tasted it. After another somewhat smaller sip, the inferno in Luke's throat spread to his gut, then oozed through his body. His knees turned to rubber and the night's chill no longer penetrated his bones. "You, uh, make this yourself, Zeke?"

"Well, yeah, but no need to tell Doc Taylor 'bout it." Zeke's teeth flashed in the darkness. "He don't cotton much to spirits, 'cept for medicinal purposes."

"I won't say a word." At least talking and drinking had directed Luke's thoughts away from his crotch.

He returned the jug to its rightful owner, dredging up his priest persona. "I know things can't be easy for you right now. I'm sorry about Mrs. Judson." It surprised Luke to recognize the truth of his own words. "Do you have any other family in Redemption?"

"My kin's all back in Arkansas." Zeke took another drink. "Got me two daughters and seven grandkids on the White River. I weren't no fine planter, see, but that farm's the finest bottom land to ever feel a plow."

"Yours?" Luke paused, waving aside the proffered jug. He'd pushed his luck enough already. Besides, the liquor's potent kick already had him in its grip. "The farm, I mean."

"Was mine." Zeke shoved the cork into the mouth of

his jug. "My great-grandpa settled the land nigh on eighty-five years ago. Judsons been born and died there ever since."

Luke stared at Zeke. He already knew Fanny had been much younger than her husband. Had she lured this man away from his family and ancestral home? Or had it been gold fever? Only one way to find out. "Tell me, what brought you to Colorado?"

A low chuckle drifted through the darkness, along with the stench of sour mash on Zeke's breath. "I come out here with Ab three years back," Zeke explained, staring beyond Luke and into the darkness. "Lookin' for gold and freedom." He cleared his throat loudly. "But I found Fanny instead."

Unspoken words hung in the night air. Luke knew without hearing Zeke say the words, that the love he'd found with Fanny was even more precious than gold. Luke's grandparents had loved each other that much. And they'd loved him, too. Once . . .

"My first wife—my girls' mother—died back in '84," Zeke continued. "I never had much heart to work the land after that, but my sons-in-law did. My girls married better men than their pa."

So Luke didn't have an exclusive on guilt. *Imagine that.* "I suspect your daughters probably chose fine husbands *like* their father." There, that sounded like something a priest would've said.

Zeke sighed. Several moments of silence allowed other night sounds to make their presence known. An owl hooted and scurrying sounds came from the dense forest just beyond the clearing. The sound of rushing water reached Luke's ears, too. Strange, he hadn't even noticed a river or stream before. Of course, he hadn't been in very good shape when he'd first arrived in Redemption.

"Me an' Ab come here to strike it rich," Zeke continued without prompting. "But I'm too durned old and tired now. Still, I owe Ab for savin' my hide, even if I cain't go home.''

Luke wondered about Zeke's age. The man could be anywhere from fifty to eighty. ''So why can't you go home to your family now?'' *Don't spend your life wallowing in guilt, Zeke. I've got enough for us both.*

''Cain't go home, *Padre.*'' Zeke cleared his throat and turned to face the trees, his profile silhouetted against a light shining from the schoolhouse.

From Sofie's room.

Pay attention to Zeke, dammit.

Luke shoved the white collar into his pocket, then clenched and unclenched his fists. ''Why not, Zeke? I'm sure your family would—''

''Cain't go home,'' Zeke repeated, his voice strained and filled with regret, ''unless I'm ready to meet the biz'ness end of a rope.''

Oh, no, not that. Luke rubbed his temples, trying not to see another sign in this. Yet how could he not? He'd been a condemned man, and he'd fallen into a nest of others here in Redemption. Why?

''I see,'' Luke said, not asking the obvious questions. He didn't want the gory details. Zeke's past was none of his business, and neither was Shane Latimer's.

What about their futures?

Knock it off, Nolan.

''Yeah, I reckon you do see.'' Zeke turned toward Luke and chuckled. ''And in case you're wonderin', I'm guilty as sin, *Padre.* I killed them two sidewinders, and if I had it to do over again, I'd still kill 'em.''

I don't want to hear this.

''There's a United States Marshal huntin' me,'' Zeke continued. ''One of them lawmen who always gets his man. I reckon it's only a matter of time.''

''I see,'' Luke said again. What the hell else could he say?

"Matter of fact, with Fanny gone, I prob'ly oughta just turn myself in and get it over with." Zeke uncorked his jug and took another long pull, then offered it to Luke.

"Hell, why not?" Luke took the liquor, but didn't bother wiping the mouth clean this time. The alcohol content would kill any germs anyway. He tipped the jug and swallowed hard and fast, swaying and gasping as he lowered it.

"I hear tell you Catholics confess your sins on a reg'lar basis." Zeke recorked the jug and set it on the ground near his feet. "You reckon that'll help a sinner like me make it into heaven with Fanny?"

Luke swallowed hard, trying to focus on Zeke's shape in the darkness. He shouldn't have taken that last drink, but he couldn't give it back now, regardless of how much his gut protested.

"I believe," Luke said quietly, trying to ignore the slight slur of his words, "you're destined for heaven, Zeke. Even if this lawman catches up with you."

"Then I'll hang."

"You called those two men sidewinders, and I assume that means they weren't exactly good men."

"*Good?*" Zeke's voice sounded low and ominous now. "They raped and murdered at least two women. Prob'ly more."

Luke held his breath and stared, waiting for Zeke to explain, but he didn't. "But why didn't the law arrest and try them for—"

"Hell, *Padre,*" Zeke said, his voice edged with bitterness, "you prob'ly wasn't even born during the War of Northern Aggression. Some of them bluebellies raped and killed whenever and whoever they wanted, and nobody did nothin' 'bout it." He shoved his hands into his pockets. "So *I did.*"

"Who . . . ?" Luke wasn't sure he wanted to hear this,

but he sensed Zeke needed to tell all. "Who were the two women, Zeke?"

"Angels, *Padre*. Angels." Zeke yanked off his battered hat and mangled it in his hands as he continued. "In 1865, I was thirty-three and felt a hundred." The older man's voice sounded distant, as if he'd also traveled through time to relive his own personal hell. "The war was over, and I was the only one of my brothers goin' home alive. Home . . ."

In Luke's mind, his grandparents' house appeared, complete with lilac bushes and a picket fence. He blinked, blotting out his own memories to focus on Zeke's.

"Found two Yankees at the farm when I got there," Zeke said. "I didn't know what they was doin' there in front of the house, and I didn't care until after they rode away and I went in the house."

"Oh, God." Luke's stomach pressed upward against his throat, the sour mash churning and burning.

"Them thievin' bluebellies had . . ." Zeke's chin dropped to his chest. "They raped and murdered my ma and baby sister, *Padre*."

Helplessly, Luke reached out to touch Zeke's shoulder, but the man didn't look up. Still looking toward the ground, Zeke drew a shaky breath.

"Them scalawags bolted when they seen me, but one of 'em dropped some papers." Zeke nodded and lifted his chin. "Had their names right there in my hands. The law didn't do nothin', so I hunted 'em down myself."

"My God." Luke drew a shaky breath.

"Took me twenty-three years." Zeke sighed again. "Sure, I got married and raised a family, but I never forgot. Never forgave . . ."

"Why would the law hang you for that, Zeke?" Luke shook his head. Even in his time, judges had shown leniency to those who'd committed justifiable homicide, though there'd been none for an innocent man like himself. "I don't understand."

"I didn't have no proof, *Padre.*" Zeke laughed with no trace of humor. "My wife had been dead over a year when I heard about two outlaws livin' across the border in Indian Territory. My girls' husbands had the farm well in hand by then, so I did what I had to do."

"You went after them, and . . ."

"Made sure who they was first, then I killed 'em with my bare hands." Zeke's voice trembled with fury even now. "In my mind, it was like that day when I first come home and found . . ."

"So you were arrested, tried, and convicted of murder," Luke said, remembering his own ordeal.

"Yep. Marshal hunted me down near Tahlequah and took me back to stand trial. I told him the whole story." Zeke chuckled and shook his head. "I believe he woulda turned me loose, if not for his oath and all."

"Oath?" Luke closed his eyes for a moment, wondering if a U.S. Marshal's oath was as binding as a priest's vows? "Yeah, right. Justice and retribution."

"Somethin' like that." Zeke seemed calmer now. "Judge Parker let me speak my piece, but the jury said guilty. The war was over, they said. Next thing I knew, they was buildin' the gallows."

Guilty . . . guilty . . . guilty . . .

A shudder rippled through Luke as he remembered being restrained in the electric chair all over again. The terror. The pain.

The injustice.

Zeke exhaled. "I never got a chance to tell my girls the truth. Ab broke me outta the jail there in Ft. Smith, and we run like the devil was on our tails." He slapped his thigh with his crumpled hat. "Ab thought he owed me, 'cuz I saved his hide at Pea Ridge. I shamed my family and turned Ab into a criminal right along with me, though nobody knows who sprung me, 'cept you. Them's my only regrets.''

Shame *and* guilt . . .

Sofie stretched and swung her legs over the edge of the narrow bed. As she sat upright, the floor seemed to rush toward her again. She swayed slightly and grabbed her head. Placing one hand on the bed frame, she assured herself that falling was not imminent.

What had Mrs. Fleming given her? A strange sweetness coated her mouth and she grimaced. She'd kill for her toothbrush and some potent peppermint toothpaste. The corner of a clean, wet rag wrapped around her fingertip just wasn't the same.

Feeling more stable, she searched her mind for information. She'd fainted, but why?

Her mother. She'd remembered her parents. Hearing Mrs. Fleming tell Jenny about her mother had triggered a painful childhood memory. Would more memories follow?

Then she'd had a bizarre dream about a television game show. That memory made her look around the room, wondering again why there were no electric lights, phones, or televisions in Redemption. She shivered. Or a wall thermostat that would produce instant warm air.

She *remembered* those things. They were *real.*

Weren't they?

She shivered again, but not from cold this time. How could she remember things that couldn't possibly exist? Why had she been wearing men's clothing upon her arrival in Redemption? What was the significance of the tattoo on the side of her breast? No amount of scrubbing had made it fade, and she felt certain it never would.

Rising, she walked over to the mirror and pulled down the neckline of Dora Fleming's voluminous flannel nightgown. There it was, the circle with lines drawn through it, and a butterfly beneath it. The word peace appeared just beneath the symbol.

Mrs. Fleming had said Sofie was branded like a steer, and she'd said it with extreme disapproval.

Then another memory intruded. Following the strange game show dream, she'd had another, much more pleasant one. Redness crept up her neck and flamed in her cheeks. Warm lips, a heated embrace, her breasts swollen and—

My God, she'd kissed Father Salazar. A priest!

No, no. Only a dream.

Her breath froze in her throat as she remembered the sound of his voice when she'd begged him to kiss her.

"Then will you go back to sleep?"

Had it been a dream? Uncertain, she watched her blush intensify. Her ears felt as if they'd blow off the sides of her head any minute. How could she be sure without asking Father Salazar?

Instantly, she shook her head and regretted it. Pain stabbed through her skull and she made her way back to bed. Of course it was a dream. A priest would never have kissed her that way.

So thoroughly. Deeply. Hungrily.

Trembling, she sat on the edge of the bed again and stared across the room at the lace curtains. *A dream, Sofie. Nothing but a dream. Get it straight and don't forget it again.*

A soft knock sounded at the door, thankfully interrupting her disturbing memories. "Come in."

The door opened and Mrs. Fleming walked in carrying a tray and smiling. "My, you look much better this morning." She closed the door behind her and crossed the room. "I brought some tea and toast. Dr. Taylor didn't want you to have anything else until we're sure you're all right."

"I feel a little woozy, but I'm okay." Sofie watched Mrs. Fleming place the tray on the bureau. When the older woman turned around, she saw a frown crease her brow. "Is something wrong? More smallpox?"

"No, not that, thank the Lord. Roman—Dr. Taylor— thinks we may be near the end of this. I pray he's right." Mrs. Fleming gave a weak smile and took a few steps toward the bed, then paused.

Though Sofie was relieved to hear there were no more cases of smallpox, she knew there was more the woman wasn't saying. "What is it, Mrs. Fleming? What's wrong?"

"Well, it's just . . ."

"I can tell something's wrong." Sofie rose and waited for an explanation. Had she bumbled someone's care so badly they'd died? *Please, not that.* "What?"

"I know you don't remember why you were with Father Salazar when you came here, but . . ." Mrs. Fleming sighed, then thrust her hands outward in a gesture of helplessness. "I guess there's nothing to do but just say it."

"All right." Sofie's sense of dread increased with each beat of her heart. "I'm listening."

"Late last night, I saw Father Salazar running out of your room . . ."

Chapter Eight

At the town's insistence, Luke moved into the vacant parsonage. More guilt, yes, but as long as he was playing religious leader, he might as well enjoy the perk of having a bed. At least now he could finally bathe regularly—six more days a week than Zeke thought necessary.

Thanks to Mrs. Fleming's donation of her late husband's wardrobe, Luke now had clean clothes, too. Pure luxury at this point.

However, despite his return to daily grooming, he hadn't attempted to shave yet. Not only would he have to use an ominous-looking straight razor, but his skin wasn't exactly in prime condition.

He looked like a molting bird or a snake shedding its skin. It had started gradually, less than a week after his date with the electric chair. A few days later, he'd been a hideous sight, with dead peeling skin and stubble growing back on his face, scalp, and other areas he couldn't even scratch in polite company.

Now, weeks later, he looked like a displaced lifeguard

at summer's end. Well, he was definitely displaced and it was September—two out of three—though he was no longer the color of a boiled lobster.

Mrs. Fleming had laundered and returned Father Salazar's robe and collar, despite Luke's insistence that they were beyond repair and their return was unnecessary. Well, he'd tried . . . But now he only wore the robe and collar for funerals, which had, thankfully, grown far less frequent.

Dr. Taylor had announced that if they made it until today with no new cases of smallpox, he would declare the epidemic officially at an end and lift the quarantine. *Thank God.*

Luke looked at himself in the warped mirror and stroked his scruffy chin. Weeks' growth of beard mingled with dead flakes of skin. "This mess will keep babes from falling at my feet, priest or no priest," he muttered.

Even Sofie?

He closed his eyes, remembering that night in her room, when she'd performed a pseudotonsillectomy on him in her laudanum-induced state. Fire flashed to his groin, his face, and his gut.

In that order.

Did she remember? Though he couldn't be certain, he had to wonder why she'd avoided him since. Or had she remembered much more than merely a stolen kiss?

Like who he was and where—when—they were from?

Opening his eyes, he leaned on the dresser with the heels of both hands. At least she hadn't experienced any more fainting spells, and other than a scar he hoped would fade over time, she appeared fully recovered from her injury. Except for her amnesia . . .

But he couldn't be sure without talking to her. Drawing a deep breath, he made his decision and reached for the late Reverend Bodine's straight razor and strap.

He would accomplish three things today. Shave his fuzzy, peeling mug without slitting his throat, talk to Sofie and determine whether or not she'd regained her memory, and make a decision about his future. Whether he wanted to admit it or not, number three would be more than a little dependent on the results of number two.

It wouldn't be easy, but he had to get on with his life. He couldn't stay in Redemption pretending to be a priest forever. Sooner or later, someone was bound to notice Father Salazar's shortcomings as a priest—not to mention his frequent hard-on—and see him for the fraud he truly was. Then Luke's fresh start would be tarnished big-time.

Hell, playing priest was probably illegal on several levels, and Luke Nolan wasn't going back to jail in any century. As soon as he made sure Sofie would be all right, he was out of here. Anyone from Redemption searching for Father Salazar later would never find Luke.

Unless Sofie told them his real name.

He swallowed hard and lathered his face and neck, then clutched the handle of the sharpened blade with trembling fingers. Whether she wanted to see him or not, one way or another, he would talk to her today. That was the only way to find out how much she might have remembered.

He'd considered changing his name after leaving Redemption. In fact, it might save a lot of confusion later on, when future generations of the Nolan family traced their family tree. But what about his pride? Dammit, couldn't he keep his name, his dignity, *and* his pride in this new life?

He winced as he scraped the razor across his tender skin. Though he hadn't felt any pain from his near-electrocution for over a week, other than itching like mad, shaving would take a fair amount of dead skin along with his whiskers.

"Ouch." And a little O positive blood, too. He grabbed a handkerchief and pressed it to his chin. After a few moments, he resumed shaving, nicking himself only twice more before he called his task a success.

"There." After wiping the remaining lather from his face, he leaned closer to examine his handiwork. "Not bad, Nolan." A definite improvement, if he did say so himself. Right now, his hair looked like an incredibly short spike any punk would've envied, but eventually the Nolan curls would kick in and take care of that problem.

And his disposition was *infinitely* better. He smiled, rubbing mineral oil on his face and neck. It helped settle the flakes somewhat, and, thankfully, it didn't smell like the bear grease Ab had offered.

Amazing what feeling safe and free could do for a guy's mood. Well, almost safe. Would he ever completely lose that nagging feeling that someone was still after him? That at any moment he could be swept back to his own time and an electric chair with his name on it?

There'd been several other people in that execution chamber, yet only he and Sofie had come through alive. His heart trounced against his ribs. He'd never forget finding Father Salazar's body. Luke touched the crucifix he'd continued to wear even when not in character, so to speak.

But he hadn't actually *seen* the others. In retrospect, he'd realized running for his life hadn't been necessary, he should've stayed and buried the dead.

Buried Warden Graham?

A shudder rippled through Luke; he wiped his hands on a rag and cleared his throat. After all this time, he wasn't about to go back to that mountain—assuming he could find it at all. The bodies would be decomposing by now. The execution chamber had become their tomb.

A time-traveling tomb.

No, he couldn't go back there. *Forget it, Nolan.* Those explosions hadn't been his fault, nor were the deaths of those who'd gathered for his execution.

Justice? No. He couldn't wish that on anyone, including the warden.

"Well, maybe . . ." He put on the hat Mrs. Fleming had insisted he wear to prevent another sunburn and walked to the door, pausing with his hand on the knob. "Nah, live and let live." Easy enough for him to say now. Sighing, he opened the door and stepped into the crisp autumn air.

Immediately, he zeroed in on the schoolhouse. Sofie was in there, toiling over the sick, and behaving like a proper Victorian lady. Being a twentieth-century doctor, she was undoubtedly a liberated woman, who'd be shocked by her own behavior once she—

No, she can't remember. She won't *remember.*

Luke rubbed his temples, trying to banish that damned guilt. Again. Sofie had a right to her life and to her past. But at what price to him?

He had to stop treating her amnesia as if it was his fault. It wasn't. Furthermore, he had no power over whether or not she ever remembered anything at all. Still, couldn't he help her by telling her all he knew? Would knowing she was from another century trigger other memories, or maybe help her understand why she was different from the other women here in Redemption?

Get real. Anyone who hadn't experienced time travel firsthand—or didn't remember experiencing it—couldn't possibly believe his story. *Strike that idea.* He had to keep what he knew to himself and see what she remembered on her own.

If only *he* could forget . . .

No bump on the head could erase the pain and injustice he'd suffered. Of that he was certain. He'd never forget, no matter what.

Concentrate, Nolan. Right now, he needed to know if she'd remembered anything more.

"Ready or not, Sofie . . ."

*   *   *

"Mother says you have a brand like a steer on your, uh . . ." Dora ducked her chin and blushed.

Sighing, Sofie straightened from folding the last of the boiled linens. Only two patients remained in the school-house—the burned stranger and Jenny, who'd been more helper than patient for weeks. In fact, she'd taken it upon herself to read to the burned man, who still hadn't been able to speak. The child's presence seemed to comfort the man, though every time he saw Sofie, he became agitated.

The stranger was a mystery. At least Sofie knew her first name, though if not for her small silver bracelet, she might not even know that. Still, she suspected he knew his name, but simply couldn't speak. Later in the day, Dr. Taylor planned to move his patient to his home, and Jenny would go with Sofie to the Fleming house.

So, despite Dora's badgering, this was a good day. At last, Dr. Taylor had declared the epidemic over and lifted the quarantine. *Hurray.*

"Did you hear me, Sofie?"

Still trying to ignore Dora's fingernails-on-a-chalkboard voice, Sofie concentrated on the last of the bedding. Soon they would turn the building over to the teacher for school again. The walls, ceiling, and floor were being scrubbed with strong lye soap, and Dr. Taylor had insisted the chil-dren not return to school until the building sat empty for another week.

However, those who hadn't contracted smallpox had received the inoculation. Sofie sighed, satisfied there would be no more new cases in Redemption.

"Did you *hear* me, Sofie?" Dora's whisper seemed louder than a shout right now.

"Yes, I heard you." Obviously, the only way to shut Dora up was to answer. Sofie smoothed her apron and tugged at the ruffled neckline. Despite her pleading, Mrs. Fleming had refused to return her jeans and T-shirt. "Yes, I have a mark—I believe it's called a *tattoo,* not a brand—on the side of my breast. It won't wash off. Satisfied?" Straightening, she shot Dora a challenging look.

Dora's mouth fell open, then she giggled like a schoolgirl hearing her first dirty joke. "Can I see it?"

"No." Sofie turned and retrieved the stack of folded sheets and towels. "I have no idea what it means or why it's there, but I'm not showing it to you or anyone else."

"Mother saw it," Dora pouted, her eyes gleaming maliciously as she leaned against the wall. "She said it's some kind of circle with a butterfly under it."

"And the word peace," Sofie added, "is printed under the butterfly." She shrugged and pushed open the swinging door to the kitchen with her back. "Peace is a nice word, so how could the circle be anything bad, Dora? And the only reason your mother has seen it is because she took care of me while I was sick. Now will you just drop it?"

"I will if you let me see." A nasty smirk split Dora's round face.

"You don't really think I'll fall for that, do you?" Sofie couldn't prevent her grin as she proceeded into the kitchen, despite the fallout from Dora's indignant gasp.

"Well, Miss Uppity," Dora chided, pushing her way into the kitchen on Sofie's heels, "Mother says you'll be staying at our house until you can remember who you are, so I guess I'll see your brand for myself sooner or lat—"

"Brand?"

Father Salazar's voice startled Sofie, and she juggled the stack of clean linens to keep them from falling to the floor. He rushed forward and grabbed for the stack, his hand brushing against her rib cage.

His innocent touch sent shock waves through her and she froze, the linens safely clutched to her chest as he stepped away. Her breath caught as she struggled against the onslaught of desire.

Again, she remembered the night he'd come to her room and she'd kissed him. No, she 'd *dreamed* the kiss. *Get it straight and don't forget it.* Even though Mrs. Fleming had confirmed Father Salazar's presence that night, Sofie had to believe the kiss had been a dream.

She *had* to.

"Thank you," she mumbled, trying to avoid his gaze as she hurried to the basket on the table and deposited the linens. The temperature in the room had skyrocketed the moment he'd touched her, deliberately or not.

Not.

"Well, this is a great day," Father Salazar said with a sigh. "The epidemic is really over."

"Yes, praise the Lord," Dora murmured.

Miraculously, Father Salazar's arrival had stopped Dora's whining. "Yes, it's finally over," Sofie said, not voicing her concerns regarding her own future.

Concern was a major understatement. Now what? That summed her situation up pretty well. She still couldn't remember her last name or where she was from, and every day that passed made her realize how different she was from the other women of Redemption. Where would she go, what would she do? Surely she fit in somewhere. Belonged somewhere . . . Besides, she couldn't very well mooch off Mrs. Fleming forever. Gads, she and Dora would be almost sisters. *Perish the thought.*

She should talk to Father Salazar again, and insist he tell her everything he could possibly remember about the morning of the explosion. Maybe there was a clue some- where that would lead her back to the life she'd left behind. Home. She wanted to go home. Didn't she? Yes, of course she did.

But the prospect of having a private conversation with him made her face flash with heat and her hands tremble.

Perspiration trickled down her neck and between her breasts. She had to do this. Her future was at stake.

Nervously, she rearranged the linens in the basket. Twice. Her memory of that dream kiss was so vivid. So provocative. So . . . stimulating.

Deep in her core, she clenched and pulsed with life. It didn't take a medical degree or a memory to diagnose what ailed her. She was horny. *Horny?* Yet another word she felt certain would shock Mrs. Fleming and Dr. Taylor. To her it seemed a little naughty—as were her thoughts— but not scandalous or shocking.

Unlike that shockingly disturbing dream . . .

Mrs. Fleming's words returned to torment her: *"Late last night, I saw Father Salazar running out of your room . . ."*

My God, her memory of that dream was so real, and he *had* been in her room. How could she face him alone without knowing the truth? Yet, if there was any chance he might be able to tell her something to help her determine her identity, how could she not?

"What were you saying when I came in?" Father Salazar asked quietly. "Something about a brand?"

Dora snickered and Sofie looked up sharply from the basket. Her face grew even hotter, and her throat was so dry she couldn't swallow the lump threatening to choke her. Dora wouldn't . . .

"Well, Father Salazar, Sofie has some kind of mark with a butterfly on her . . . her . . ."

Sofie shot Dora a scathing look, somewhat comforted by the other woman's obvious distress. *Good, I hope she gets a ferocious case of heartburn.* "It's nothing," Sofie said. "Nothing at all."

"A mark? A butterfly, you said?" Father Salazar removed his hat and held it in front of him. "You mean a tattoo. Oh, uh . . ."

His gray eyes suddenly widened, and a blush crept upward from his open collar. The sunburn he'd had when they first came to Redemption had faded to tan, but at this moment, he was almost as red as that first day.

Why?

No one had mentioned the location of Sofie's tattoo, so why was he blushing? Surely he hadn't . . . seen it?

He couldn't have. She closed her eyes for a moment, trying to remember the dream. Even if it had actually happened—which it hadn't—all she remembered was the kiss. Nothing else.

Nothing except red hot, molten desire . . .

Miss Dr. Sofie What's-Her-Name had a priest fetish.

My God. Flustered, she reopened her eyes and met Father Salazar's gaze again. A mischievous twinkle danced in the gray depths and one corner of his mouth curved upward, just so.

The man was laughing at her.

Not a man—a priest.

"Well, since Sofie won't show me her brand, I'm going to check on Jenny and see if Mr. Smith needs anything," Dora announced.

"Mr. Smith?" Father Salazar echoed, looking beyond Sofie at the other woman. "Not another—"

"No, no." Dora paused and shook her head, her hand resting on the swinging door. "There's no more smallpox, Father, but we needed to call the stranger something, so Jenny named him Mr. Smith."

"Oh, of course." He sighed again. "And Jenny will go home with you and your mother today?"

"Absolutely."

Dora's adamancy on this topic almost made up for her shortcomings, Sofie decided. Almost.

"If that low-down Frank Latimer so much as shows his face, I'll use Papa's shotgun on him. Both barrels." In a flourish of ruffles and skirt, Dora left the kitchen.

Sofie stared at the door as it swung toward them, then back and forth twice more before coming to a stop. They were alone now. Completely alone. She licked her lips and turned to look at Father Salazar again.

He smiled openly this time, and she became acutely aware of his transformation. The sunburn and baldness had made him seem homely and undesirable, but that hadn't stopped her from dreaming about kissing him. His priest's robe and collar should have helped prevent her dreams and shameless desires, but they hadn't done the job either.

And now she didn't have even that flimsy deterrent to her apparently wanton nature. He didn't resemble a priest at all now, with a pair of worn jeans and a chambray shirt. A leather belt encircled his trim waist, where he held his hat in front of him right where she should never even think about looking.

But she *had* looked, and the memory of the day he'd held her in his lap during that storm returned with a vengeance. Had his reaction to her that day been the catalyst for her dream?

"Sofie?" He took a step toward her and reached out to touch her cheek with the backs of his fingers.

She closed her eyes, remembering the feel of his hands on her face in her dream. She shouldn't feel this way about a priest, but she couldn't help herself. Maybe it was because he'd saved her life.

She had to get a grip on this rampant libido. Ladies didn't think these things, did they? Ladies shouldn't want these things, should they? And she *was* a lady, wasn't she?

She opened her eyes and tried to smile. "I was just remembering the day we came here," she said—a lie of omission only.

"Remembering?" His voice had a brittle edge to it. "How . . . how much have you remembered?"

"About life before Redemption?" She sighed. "Nothing really." How could she ask him about her dream? There had to be a way. "Father, I was wondering . . ."

He winced and dropped his hand to his side.

"What's wrong?" Sofie reached for his hand, immediately regretting her impulsiveness. The warm, rough feel of his hand had the same impact as gasoline on a flame. She had to regain control of herself. This was crazy. "Are you ill?"

"No, I just wish . . ." He smiled and shrugged, raking his other hand over his new growth of dark brown hair.

"Wish what?" Was there a subliminal message beneath his words, or was it merely wishful thinking on her part? Gads, she was worse off than she'd realized.

"Nothing important." He squeezed her hand, then released it, a mask falling into place over his handsome face.

Handsome? Yes, now that his burn had faded and his hair was growing back, Father Salazar qualified as handsome. A lean, muscular body, soft gray eyes, dark hair, tall . . . Definitely hunk material in her book.

Obviously. Grimacing, she wiped her sweaty palms on her apron and tucked a wayward curl behind her ear.

"That's what you were doing the first time I saw you," he said, chuckling. "Tucking that wild hair behind your ears, as if that would make a difference." He reached toward her hair, then seemed to think better of it. "Forgive me."

Forgive you? She was the one who needed forgiveness, but she also needed information. "Father, I need to hear everything you might know about me, about the explosions, and about whatever we were doing in that cave."

"So you really haven't remembered anything else?"

"No, but I want to." She stepped closer and gazed into his soft gray eyes. "I want to desperately," she whispered. "Please help me remember."

* * *

Please help me remember . . . Luke winced, torn between his own needs and hers. He cared about Sofie, and he was her only link to her life. But there was no way back—not that he knew of anyway—so maybe her amnesia really was for the best.

She couldn't remember anyone to miss, or any burdens of guilt to fester in her gut. Luke knew all about that. Big time.

"I . . ." He ached to touch her. The palm of his hand actually itched with the need to cup her soft cheek and tilt her chin upward to make her lips more accessible.

Her lips . . . His groin tightened and throbbed, and he was grateful for the hat he'd positioned to hide his blatant desire. Yes, he wanted to kiss Sofie again and again and again. More than that, he wanted to touch her. All of her.

Closing his eyes momentarily, he recalled their first night in Redemption, when he'd seen the tattoo on the side of her breast. He'd known then how much he wanted her, and he knew now that no other woman could satisfy his growing hunger.

Only Sofie.

It was much more than hunger that surged through him. Sofie had become an obsession, haunting every waking moment and taunting him in his dreams.

"Please?" she repeated, jerking him back to the present.

And the guilt. She was here in 1891 because of him. He was the only link to the life she'd left behind, and all she wanted was information that might lead her home.

All she wanted was the one thing he couldn't give her.

If he told her all he knew—which really wasn't much— that wouldn't really help her. He didn't know her last name or address, and he sure as hell couldn't undo their quantum leap.

So get over it, Nolan. "I'm sorry," he said, reaching for her hand again. Wouldn't Father Salazar have held her hand? Such a soft hand, warm and small . . . *Get a grip*. A grip was precisely what he'd like to get right now. Of her.

"I wish I could help you," he said, justifying the lie with the reassurance that he really couldn't help her. "The first time I saw you was the morning of the explosions."

Her blue eyes widened and she took a step closer. "Tell me about that place and those explosions, Father. Please?"

Luke struggled against the memories. The pain. The terror. In many ways, Sofie was the lucky one. Without her memory, there was no pain to remember, and nothing to miss.

What had he told her before? He had a vague memory of their conversation the morning of the explosions, when he'd made up some lame excuse for where they were and why. *Damn*. His lies were so numerous, he needed a guide to keep them straight. *Sick, really sick.*

"I remembered my mother," Sofie said suddenly, her expression wistful. "And an older brother, I think."

A chill rippled through Luke. "I . . . I thought you said you couldn't remember anything." His words sounded like an accusation even to him, but he had to know. Was she lying to him, too? If so, why?

"Only that little bit." She sighed and tucked a curl behind her ear again. "I was there when Mrs. Fleming told Jenny about her mother. That's when I saw the woman in my mind. My mother."

"You're sure it was your mother?" Luke swallowed the lump in his throat and dragged the toe of his boot along a seam in the floor. "How can you be so sure?"

Sofie shrugged and looked away. Guiltily? "I just know somehow." After a moment, she locked her gaze on his. "And I know I need to go home to her."

How could he tell her? She'd never believe they'd been thrown back in time together. Why should she? If the situation were reversed, *he* wouldn't believe it.

"We were never even introduced, Sofie," he said truthfully, remembering when he'd first laid eyes on her. She'd cried for him. His pulse thundered through his veins. "We'd barely arrived when the explosions started."

"Arrived where?" She took another step toward him, so close now he could smell her clean, soapy scent. "Where were we that morning? What were we doing?"

He didn't want to think about that morning, about the horrendous pain or the fear. His fear. "I . . . I . . ."

"Where were we, Father?" Her voice rose and tears glistened in her eyes; one trickled down her cheek. "Please?"

Luke reached out to capture her tear on his fingertip, holding it out between them. It sparkled like a diamond dream in the early morning light spilling through the kitchen window.

He wanted to bury his fingers in her shiny black curls, to cup her small face between his hands and cover her lips with his. She had such a beautiful mouth, full and tempting.

"Please, Father?" she repeated.

Luke resisted being dragged back to the topic. Instead, he focused on her lips, moist and slightly parted. Another tear slid down her cheek, and she reached up to wipe it away.

Angry with himself, and with her for asking the impossible of him, he dropped her hand and watched her wipe tears from her face. He wanted to kiss away her tears, to touch every inch of her, to gaze on her naked flesh without shame.

God help him, but he wanted to have sex with Sofie.

Sex. Great sex. Lots of sex.

His breathing became shallow and his body suffused with fire—a far more pleasant burning than that inflicted by the electric chair. Yes, he burned with need, with hunger, with desire.

"You can't help me, Father?" she asked. "Or won't?"

"Can't." *And won't.* Both were equally true. Luke licked his lips and wished the late Mr. Fleming's jeans were a bit roomier through the crotch about now. "I didn't know you before that morning, Sofie. Honest."

"You're a priest," she whispered, "so you can't lie to me."

Her words knifed through him and Luke tried to drag his guilty gaze from hers, but she held him prisoner with the intensity of her voice and eyes. "I'm not lying." He would avoid the truth at all costs, but he would try not to lie to her. "We were part of a team sent to a government site to witness an . . . an experiment." Since it was the first time the site had been put through its heinous paces, experiment seemed like the right word.

"What kind of experiment?" She tilted her head to one side, her tongue slipping between her lips to moisten them, leaving a silken pink sheen behind.

Fueled by his memory, Luke's need to kiss those lips skyrocketed. "It was, uh, top secret." He shrugged. "We were brought in from various places, and most of us didn't know each other before." *True statement.*

She shook her head. "A government experiment?"

"I really don't know anything more, except that you're a doctor, and we were in the wrong place at the wrong time." *My life story.*

"Maybe we'll both remember more later."

Good, she was dropping the subject. Luke resisted the urge to sigh in relief.

"Remember when I was ill?" she continued, her nervous gaze darting to the door and back again.

"Yes, but you're all right now." He would never forget that night. Never. So much for his short-lived relief.

"Yes, I'm fine now, but . . . but something bothers me about that night."

"*Bothers* you?" he repeated, finding that word choice far short of accurate.

"Y-yes." Again, she looked nervously toward the door, then back. With a sigh, she lifted her chin a notch and met his gaze steadily. "Mrs. Fleming said she saw you coming out of my room that night."

A roar echoed through Luke's brain as he tried to read her tone. Accusation, curiosity, or something else? "Yes, I, uh . . ." He hesitated, wondering how much of that night she remembered. She'd been pretty out of it. "I stopped to check on you."

Her cheeks reddened, but her steady stare held. "Did you . . . did I . . ." She sighed again and held her hands out to her sides in a gesture of helplessness. "Father, did I—"

The back door swung open and the jingle of spurs made them both look that way. *Saved by the bell,* Luke thought, though he knew Sofie would question him again, and he knew exactly what she wanted to know. Had she really kissed him?

And had he kissed her back?

Oh, yeah, I sure as hell did.

Ab came through the door, removing his battered hat and looking down at the floor. A taller man loomed in the doorway behind him, drawing Luke's attention.

"Doc Taylor here?" Ab asked, jabbing his thumb over his shoulder at the stranger. "United States Marshal's here, and he wants to see the mayor."

Marshal? Luke stared long and hard at the lawman, the epitome of every John Wayne western he'd ever seen. The man's weathered face was tanned, his eyes narrowed as if still squinting into the sun. Dark hair curled around his collar, where a bandanna sat off-kilter, and his faded jeans and shirt were coated with a fine layer of dust. A pair of guns hung in a leather holster at the man's narrow hips, and a silver star twinkled through the dust on his chest.

"Sam Weathers," the man said in a voice that could've

been the biological equivalent to Dolby. "United States Marshal out of Ft. Smith."

Ft. Smith? Where had Luke heard that before, and why was it important?

"Dr. Taylor should return shortly." Sofie moved away from Luke and turned her attention on the newcomer.

A surge of jealousy swept through Luke as he watched her give the Marshal the once-over. Did Sofie find the lawman attractive? Of course, if she fell in love and forgot about Luke, that would be for the best. Wouldn't it?

Damn straight. Luke jerked his attention back to the marshal. "You may have heard about our epidemic."

The stranger nodded once and removed his leather cowboy hat. "Need to speak to the mayor—Doc Taylor?—right away."

Ab shifted uncomfortably, fidgeting with the hat clutched in both hands. "What for?" he asked. "You didn't say."

"I'm lookin' for a man by the name of Zeke Judson."

Yes, that was where Luke had heard of Ft. Smith. How could he have forgotten Zeke's confession? *Some priest.* Of course, his shortcomings in that department had been well established by now.

Ab's face reddened and sweat coated his brow. "What do you want Zeke for?"

Luke knew Ab was fully aware of why his friend was a wanted man.

"Judge Parker sentenced Judson to hang, and I'm here to take him back."

"Zeke's wife just died of smallpox," Sofie said, taking a step toward the marshal.

"Well, I'm right sorry to hear that, ma'am," the marshal said, "but I'm only here to see justice done."

Justice? The scorch of anger crept through Luke as he remembered Warden Graham's countless taunts about seeing justice done.

"Zeke was the one carrying out justice." Luke's voice trembled with barely controlled rage. "Are you familiar with the case, Marshal?"

The man's eyes narrowed even more as he studied Luke with an intensity that rivaled an MRI. "You been hidin' Judson here? That makes you as guilty as him."

Luke straightened, praying his uncertainty didn't show. Maybe he didn't know much about the Code of the West or anything like that, but he knew a little something about truth and honor. Not that it had ever done him much good . . .

"Zeke confessed to me."

"Confessed?"

"He's a priest," Ab interjected.

The lawman's gaze raked Luke, then shot to Sofie. "My mama raised me to believe a man of the cloth." He shrugged and gave her a crooked grin that made Luke's blood run Vulcan green. "He tellin' the truth, ma'am?"

Sofie nodded. "Yes, this is Father Salazar, and I'm Sofie."

"Pleased to make your acquaintance, Miss Sofie." The marshal inclined his head politely, then faced Luke again. "Father, you know where I can find Zeke Judson now?"

Helplessly, Luke shot Ab a questioning glance. The last thing Luke wanted was to betray Zeke, yet the Marshal's presence in Redemption pretty well settled things once and for all. "I'm not sure," Luke said truthfully.

"Well, I'll call at the mayor's house again then."

"No need."

The figure looming in the doorway behind Marshal Weathers stood tall and proud.

"Zeke, no . . ." Ab's voice broke as he faced his old friend. "I won't let—"

"Too late, Ab." Zeke didn't even flinch while the marshal stared at him. "I figgered you'd catch up with me sooner or later, Sam. Well, here I be."

"Zeke, it's been a few years." The marshal had his back

to Luke and Sofie now, but he was still an imposing figure, especially with those guns strapped to his hips. "I'm sorry I have to do this, but . . ."

"Yep, I know." Zeke gave the marshal a sad smile. "Like I done told the *Padre,* I'm ready to turn myself in now anyway, with the missus gone."

The lawman nodded. "I'm sorry to hear about your loss, Zeke."

"When do we leave?"

Silence filled the room until the swinging door signaled Dora's return. To her credit, the woman waited quietly.

"Breakin' in a new mount, and he bruised a hoof comin' up the pass," Marshal Weathers said in a slow drawl. "Lucifer's gonna need a few days, maybe a week, to mend."

"Fair 'nuff."

"You ain't gonna run this time," the marshal stated, rather than asked.

"Nope."

"Why?"

Luke held his breath. Zeke didn't deserve this.

"I seen justice done to them two killers, and now that Fanny's gone, I just got no cause to run."

"But *this* isn't justice." Luke couldn't keep quiet a minute longer, even when the lawman turned to stare at him again. "You call it justice when a man is sentenced to hang for avenging the deaths of his own mother and sister?" *Or wrongfully convicted of killing a liquor store clerk?*

"A jury and Judge Parker saw it otherwise." The marshal's voice was low, ominous. "Ain't my job to say, and it ain't yours either."

"How can you call this justice?" Luke's voice rose and he clenched his fists at his sides. "Turn your back and let Zeke walk away. *That* would be justice."

"No, not entirely." They all turned to face Mrs. Fleming, who'd come in behind Dora from the front of the building.

"That will only be justice if Shane Latimer walks away, too."

"Now that's a fact." Zeke nodded, a sly twinkle showing in his faded eyes. "I reckon there might be another job here for you, Marshal."

"Well, I ain't goin' nowhere until Lucifer's good and ready." Marshal Weathers pulled a chair out from the table and looked around the room at them all, his gaze coming to rest on Mrs. Fleming. "Speak your piece, ma'am."

Chapter Nine

Who is this guy? Sofie was more than a little impressed with Marshal Sam Weathers. He had *man* written all over him. Virile, fearless, larger than life.

"Your timing couldn't be better, Marshal," Dora said, urging her mother to take a chair at the table. "There's a town meeting tomorrow evening. We're going to elect a new sheriff."

Sofie couldn't stop staring at him. He was easily the tallest man she'd ever seen—at least, that she remembered seeing. His badge, his hat, his guns . . .

"John Wayne," she said. *Where did that come from?* Her childhood? Movies. Television. Westerns. Things that didn't exist here, yet she remembered them with a sort of vague certainty that made her question her sanity daily.

"Can't say I ever met up with this John Wayne fella." Marshal Weathers pulled out a chair for her. "Is he a lawman, too?"

Father Salazar's chuckle dragged Sofie's attention from the marshal. His eyes twinkled with a mixture of wry amusement and something totally opposite. Anger? Resentment? Then he arched one brow questioningly, as if expecting Sofie to understand his laughter.

"John Wayne is just a name I remember from . . . somewhere," she explained, flustered and more confused than ever. Why did she remember that name so clearly, when she couldn't remember her own last name? John Wayne must've been someone important. She could see him in her mind, on the big screen. Though in Redemption there were no such things as movies and television.

But somewhere there were such things—electric lights, telephones, and cars, too. Airplanes? Yes, there had to be. Either that or Sofie's imagination was even more dangerous than she'd realized. Redemption seemed to be in its own little world. *Weird.*

"It doesn't matter right now," she added quickly, realizing they were all staring at her. "There are more important things to discuss."

The marshal nodded and flashed her a heart-stopping smile, his eyes crinkling at the corners. "That's a fact." He turned to face Mrs. Fleming. "Sam Weathers, ma'am. United States Marshal outta Ft. Smith."

"Pleased to meet you, Marshal. I'm Anna Fleming." She waved toward the others. "My daughter Dora, Father Salazar, and this is Sofie. I guess you already know everybody else."

Marshal Weathers nodded and leaned back in the chair, his narrowed gaze settling on Zeke. "Well, if you really ain't plannin' to run, Zeke, then my job here just got a whole lot simpler."

"I ain't got no more call to run." Zeke's expression revealed only resignation. But to what?

"I can't imagine why you've come for Zeke," Sofie said, trying to avoid Father Salazar's probing gaze. Why was he staring at her so?

Zeke sighed. "It's true, Miss Sofie. The marshal's gotta

take me back to Ft. Smith." He lowered his gaze. "To hang."

"No." Mrs. Fleming's voice was clear and strong. "This is wrong, Marshal. Surely you realize that."

Marshal Weathers placed his hat on the table before him, staring at it as if all the answers were there in its soiled brim. After a few moments, he met Mrs. Fleming's gaze. "I don't make the laws, ma'am," he said slowly, "but I'm sworn to uphold 'em, just the same."

"I understand that." Dora gripped her mother's hand, her face reddening. "But couldn't you just leave and forget you ever saw Zeke?"

"Marshal cain't do that, Miss Dora," Zeke said. "It'd be wrong."

"No, what's *wrong* is hanging men and boys for doing what had to be done." Dora's voice cracked.

"Do you *know* what happened?" Father Salazar came to the table and he gripped the back of the chair so tightly his knuckles turned white. "Do you know *why* Zeke killed those two men, Marshal?"

Sam Weathers blinked once and met Father Salazar's gaze. The tension between the two men crackled through the room like lightning. Sofie held her breath, waiting for the marshal to answer.

"I do." Sam Weathers sighed slowly and shook his head. "And I would've done the same, considerin'."

"Then you realize it was *justifiable* homicide," Father Salazar said, his nostrils flaring and his jaw twitching. "Zeke Judson killed the men who raped and murdered his own mother and sister. How can the law condemn any man for that?"

Marshal Weathers didn't even flinch, but Sofie was mesmerized by the passion in Father Salazar's voice. At this moment, he was the most magnificent man she could imagine.

But he's a priest.

Why couldn't she seem to remember that fact? Looking at Father Salazar like a *man* wasn't allowed. He was off limits, yet knowing that didn't prevent her gaze from devouring the length of him again. Her cheeks—and other regions—warmed at the sight. He was quite impressive in civilian clothes. Too impressive.

She closed her eyes and forced her attention back to the marshal. Though he was every inch a hunk, Sofie's tastes leaned more toward men like Father—

No! Besides, how did she know what her tastes in men were? She couldn't remember any of the men in her life.

"Like I said, Father, I don't make the laws." Marshal Weathers turned to face Mrs. Fleming again. "Now, tell me about this Shane Latimer, ma'am."

Mrs. Fleming blinked rapidly, but a tear trickled down her cheek despite her efforts. "His father was a horrible man," she said, her voice quivering. "Shane and Jenny's mother came to us on two separate occasions, after her husband had—after he had . . ."

Dora took her mother's hand in hers and met the marshal's gaze. "Charlie Latimer was a drunk, and he beat his wife nearly to death." She paused to draw a fortifying breath. *"Twice* that we know of, though Lord only knows what happened before they moved to Redemption."

Mrs. Fleming nodded and met the marshal's gaze again. "Both times, Shane brought his mother and Jenny to us afterward."

"Jenny is Shane's sister?"

"Yes." Mrs. Fleming cleared her throat and drew a deep breath. "The first time, Dr. Taylor talked Shane out of going after his father, though the boy wanted to. Understandably, of course."

The marshal leaned back in his chair, his expression unreadable. "And the second time?"

Mrs. Fleming and Dora exchanged glances and Sofie

held her breath. Waiting. She'd known there was more to this than a simple case of Shane killing his father.

A noise sounded from the pantry, and Ab jumped up to open the door. Jenny stared out at them, trembling.

Mrs. Fleming rushed over to take the child's hand and led her from the large closet. "What on earth . . . ?"

"I . . . I was scared," Jenny said, her gaze darting around the room. "I saw the bad man."

"What bad man, honey?" Mrs. Fleming smoothed the child's hair gently. "Only good men are here now. What's wrong, child? Don't be frightened."

"My pa . . . papa was a very bad man."

Mrs. Fleming tried to gather Jenny in her arms, but Jenny pulled free and approached the table. "My brother carried Mama to Mrs. Fleming's house," the girl explained, her voice quivering. "There was so much . . . so much blood." Her voice fell to a whisper. "Her face . . ."

She stood erect, her blond braids hanging neatly in front of her shoulders, her hands clasped before her. "Papa hit Mama all the time, and sometimes he hit me, too."

"Oh, God," Father Salazar whispered, followed by something too faint to identify, though it sounded a great deal like "bastard."

"I'm sorry," Marshal Weathers said softly. Expectantly.

"I remember him hitting Shane, too, but that was be— before my brother got big." Jenny blinked once. Twice. "That last time, my brother went back after he made sure Mama was all right."

Sofie couldn't breathe. She was terrified to hear the rest of the story, yet she sensed Jenny needed to tell it at least once. All of it. Sofie glanced anxiously at Father Salazar to find his gray eyes wide and his mouth drawn into a thin line.

"While Mrs. Fleming and Dora were helping Dr. Taylor with Mama," Jenny continued, her expression distant as if she were in a trance, "I followed Shane."

"Jenny, no." Mrs. Fleming stepped behind the girl and gathered her back against her. "Don't do this to yourself, child."

"I got to." The child's adamancy made even Mrs. Fleming fall silent. "My brother went back in the cabin, and Papa hit him. He hit him so hard Shane fell down and didn't get up."

Several moments of silence stretched between them as they all waited for the child to finish her morbid tale. Sofie wanted to tell Jenny not to torment herself this way, but by the same token, she had to know what happened. Every sordid detail.

"I thought maybe he never would get up again. Maybe Papa'd killed him." Jenny sniffled and reached up to hold Mrs. Fleming's hand at her shoulder. "But he finally did. I seen him through the window. There was blood all over his face, just like Mama's."

She sniffled and hiccupped. No one said a word.

"Papa hit him again, and Shane fell again." She looked down for a moment, then aimed her gaze directly at Marshal Weathers. "Then I heard a horse."

"A horse?" Mrs. Fleming stepped around Jenny and turned the child to face her. "I don't remember you telling this before, Jenny."

"I was afraid," she whispered, her hand trembling as tears slipped unheeded down her cheeks. "Still a . . . afraid."

"What did you see, Jenny?" Marshal Weathers had a voice like raw silk—rough and smooth at the same time.

"I hid behind a bush."

"Who did you see?" Father Salazar's voice was gentle.

"Bad man."

"The same bad man who made you come hide here?" the Marshal asked.

"I can't tell you. He'll hurt me, too."

*   *   *

Luke shuddered. He was supposed to be a priest, for Christ's sake. Surely, he could come up with something comforting enough to convince Jenny to tell them everything.

He remembered Shane's expression when the boy had asked Luke to tell Jenny he couldn't take care of her as he'd promised their mother. Luke's gut clenched and he gripped the back of the chair again so tightly he thought it would break.

His gaze drifted around the table, studying the faces as they all waited for Jenny to stop crying and finish her story. Could she clear her brother and prevent him from being hanged?

Luke wouldn't—couldn't—let Shane hang. Or Zeke either for that matter. He'd been thrown back in time and had his ass saved for a reason. Here it was right in front of him.

Two condemned men, neither who deserved their fate.

He had to stop their executions. *This* was his mission. His purpose. How could he deny it? Swallowing hard, he touched the crucifix, drawing strength from its smooth surface. What would the real Father Salazar have said to these people? To Jenny Latimer in particular?

"I . . ." Luke's voice caught and he cleared his throat. "I won't let anyone hurt you, Jenny," he vowed, praying he knew what the hell he was doing. "Tell Marshal Weathers everything you saw. You have to do it for Shane."

Jenny turned her hopeful gaze on him and his heart broke. Luke drew a deep breath, renewing his vow to protect this child and to save two men from injustice.

"Tell me, Jenny," Marshal Weathers urged quietly. "Puttin' bad men in jail is my job."

And sometimes not-so-bad men, like Zeke.

A tear trickled down Jenny's cheek, and Luke stepped

around the table and reached for her hand. "Tell us, Jenny," he coaxed. "Tell us everything so we can help your brother."

Her lower lip trembled and more tears followed.

"Jenny," Sofie said softly, standing to take the girl's other hand. "Do it for your mama. She'd want you to help your brother."

The big guns. *Do it for your mama.* Luke closed his eyes for a moment, then reopened them to meet Sofie's gaze. Her large blue eyes glistened with unshed tears and sincerity.

Jenny Latimer and Sofie were looking to him for support. He wouldn't fail them like he'd failed his grandparents. No way. And he wouldn't fail Shane and Zeke either, even if he had to break them out of jail himself.

So now you're Superman, Nolan?

Weeping quietly, Mrs. Fleming slumped into the chair vacated by Sofie. Dora reached for her hand, and Ab held Dora's.

This was a regular crying orgy.

"Tell us, Jenny," Luke urged. "No one will hurt you." *Please, help me make it so.*

"I saw the man shoot Papa." Jenny's voice fell to a whisper. "Papa fell and he shot again. Shane was still on the floor, and I thought the second shot . . ."

Tears burst from Jenny's eyes like someone had turned on a faucet, and Sofie dropped to her knees to cradle the girl against her shoulder. "There, there, Jenny," Sofie cooed. "It'll be all right. Father Salazar promised."

Sofie tilted her head just enough to meet Luke's gaze, and he held his breath. She intended to hold him to his promise. *Oh, God.*

Of course, he fully intended to keep his promise, as well. To Shane, to Jenny, to Zeke . . .

And to himself.

"Who's the law around here?" Marshal Weathers asked, jerking Luke's attention away from Sofie and Jenny.

"Sheriff Yates died in the epidemic," Dora said. "Early on."

The marshal rubbed his whiskered chin. "I see. And when's the circuit judge due back?"

"Don't rightly know," Ab said, shooting a side glance in Zeke's direction. "Ain't seen him since Shane's sentencing, 'cuz of the quarantine."

"Well, then." Marshal Weathers twirled his hat in a circle on the table, then looked up to meet Luke's gaze. "I reckon it's up to you and me then."

Uh-oh. Luke swallowed hard. "What is?"

"Justice, Father," the marshal said matter-of-factly. "Justice."

What incredible irony. Luke almost laughed. Hell, he should laugh, after all he'd been through.

"Until Miss Jenny's ready to tell us the killer's name," Weathers continued, "we gotta protect her from harm. It's our duty."

"She's going home with us," Mrs. Fleming said, looking anxiously at the little girl. "Aren't you, dear?"

Jenny only blinked.

"We don't know who we're dealin' with here," Zeke said thoughtfully. "Beg pardon, ma'am, but if I was lookin' for Miss Jenny in this here town, I reckon your house'd be the first place I'd look."

"You have a point." Mrs. Fleming folded her hands and met the marshal's gaze. "But one thing is perfectly clear from what Jenny's told us. Her brother is innocent."

"Yep, that's the way I see it, too." The marshal looked at Luke again. "Father, you new to these parts?"

Luke squeezed Jenny's hand and flashed Sofie what he hoped was a reassuring look before he faced the marshal. "Oh yeah, real new."

"The *Padre* and Miss Sofie come durin' the quarantine," Zeke offered.

"Right." Luke felt Sofie's questioning gaze on him.

"And we didn't waste any time putting you to work, I'm afraid," Mrs. Fleming said, dabbing her eyes with a handkerchief. "I'm convinced God sent Father Salazar and Sofie to us. She's a doctor, you know, and it's clear she has a way with children, too."

"That's a fact. Miss Jenny trusts her, and I trust Miss Jenny." The marshal shot Sofie a curious look. "I only come across a lady doctor once before, and that was down in Indian Territory. Cherokee, she was."

"Indian Territory?" Sofie whispered, renewing Luke's resolve to avoid looking at her right now.

Zeke shook his head. "Well, I'll be."

Marshal Weathers stood and walked toward the window. He stared outside for several moments, then turned to face them again. A strange light glittered in his eyes. "I got a plan."

Luke had a strange feeling he'd live to regret this. "Whatever it takes, Marshal."

A calculating grin split the lawman's face. "I'm glad to hear you say that, Father. Mighty glad."

Oh, boy. "Just what do you have in mind?" Luke could've kicked himself. Still, he meant every word. He would do whatever it took to prevent Shane's hanging, then he'd worry about Zeke.

"Where you stayin', Father?"

"Father Salazar is staying in the parsonage," Dora Fleming said. "Sadly, Reverend Bodine and his wife both perished in the epidemic, too."

Marshal Weathers was silent for several moments, then he returned to the table. "You folks have had more'n your share of grief. That's a fact."

Mrs. Fleming nodded and sniffled. "Yes, it's been hard to lose so many friends and neighbors, Marshal."

Though the man seemed completely sincere, Luke also recognized a slyness to Marshal Weathers that just might manage to save Shane Latimer's hide. The marshal wasn't old by any means—thirtyish—but he had the cunning of a seasoned professional. Yes, he might save the day, but at what cost?

The marshal looked directly at Jenny Latimer, who still whimpered quietly in Sofie's arms. "Miss Jenny, I gotta ask you one more thing now."

Jenny sniffled and looked up at the marshal. "All . . . all right."

"Is the bad man who made you come hide the same one who killed your pa?"

Holy cow, this guy could've been a prototype for the Lone Ranger and Rooster Cogburn. Luke could almost see the tension in the room as every gaze turned toward Jenny.

Finally, the little girl gave Marshal Weathers the most trusting look Luke had ever seen.

And nodded.

"Do you know the man's name?"

Another nod.

The marshal leaned on the back of the chair and maintained his sincere expression, his gaze never wavering. "Are you ready to tell me the fella's name, so I can put him in jail?"

Jenny's lower lip trembled, and she shook her head so violently, her pigtails swung back and forth.

To his credit, Marshal Weathers didn't even blink, though he must've felt the same level of disappointment as Luke. *What's his game?*

"I understand, Miss Jenny." The lawman straightened and released a long sigh. "We gotta protect you, then, until you're ready to tell."

If there was any possibility the killer knew there'd been a witness to his crime, then Jenny was in grave danger. Unless . . .

Too bad the killer hadn't been a smallpox victim. *There really is no justice in this world.*

"Miss Jenny, 'til you're ready to tell us everythin', I got no choice but to keep your brother in jail." The marshal looked down at his hand as if checking his nails for cleanliness. "I'll tell him we know he's innocent, but he's gotta stay put until two things happen."

"Wha . . . what two things?" Jenny sniffled and met the marshal's gaze.

"First, the circuit judge has gotta come set him free."

"Praise God," Mrs. Fleming said, and a bright smile lit Jenny's face.

"But there's another thing."

Sly dog. Luke knew Sam Weathers had left that statement incomplete for impact. Luke's grandfather had loved Westerns, so they'd watched them on television every weekend throughout Luke's childhood. Marshal Weathers was the epitome of the tallest, leanest, meanest, and most honorable cowboy who'd ever graced the silver screen.

No wonder Sofie was still staring.

Damn. Luke had to get his jealousy under control. He'd come here to talk to Sofie, but this situation had cut that short. Maybe for the best. Being alone with her probably wasn't a very good idea at this point.

"What other thing?" Jenny finally asked.

"The man who killed your pa is still in town," the marshal said slowly, "so you and Shane both might be in danger."

Jenny's eyes widened.

"We can protect Shane in jail easy enough . . ."

"Will you put me in jail, too?" The child's pupils dilated and Luke thought she might faint.

Marshal Weathers shook his head. "Nope, I got another idea."

He looked right at Luke. After a moment, his gaze drifted

to Sofie. "I don't reckon that killer would look for you at the parsonage."

"No, of course he wouldn't." Dora stood and went to her mother, squeezing the older woman's hand. "Jenny will be safer there than anywhere for now."

Mrs. Fleming nodded, but Luke just stared at the marshal. He shot Sofie a "save me" look, but she seemed in complete agreement with the plan.

"Someone will have to go with the child to help take care of her, of course," Mrs. Fleming said. "I can—"

"No, you cain't." Zeke stood and folded his arms. "Everybody in town'd notice you bein' gone."

"True." Mrs. Fleming sighed "Dora, then?"

"Beg pardon, since I don't really know you folks," the marshal said quietly, "but seems to me, because of the epidemic, that lots of folks don't know about Miss Sofie." The lawman looked around the room, his expression solemn. "And it's clear Miss Jenny trusts her. She's the logical choice to go with the girl."

A dull roar began in Luke's head and the skin around his mouth tingled. Slowly, he turned his head until he met Sofie's gaze. The marshal wanted him to hide Sofie and Jenny in the parsonage. All day. Every day.

And night.

"But that would be unseemly," Mrs. Fleming said, looking at the marshal as if she thought him insane.

You tell them, Mrs. Fleming. Luke held his breath.

Zeke slapped the table's surface and snorted. "Beg pardon again, ma'am, but the man's a priest."

Oh, God.

Mrs. Fleming's face reddened and she opened her mouth several times. Finally, she drew a deep breath and looked right at Luke. "Father, forgive me, but . . ." She sighed and closed her eyes for a moment, then leveled her gaze on him. "I saw you coming out of Sofie's room the other night. Late."

Sofie gasped, then a powerful silence filled the room; the temperature of Luke's face hit the flash point. He looked around the room. They were all staring at Mrs. Fleming as if she'd lost her mind. Relief struck in waves, though he didn't dare look at Sofie yet.

So he'd been seen leaving her room that night. Did Sofie remember what happened? The fire from his face redirected itself along with his blood flow. He'd never forget her lips, her softness, her—

"Well, *Padre?*" Zeke winked as Luke met his gaze.

Drawing a deep breath, Luke faced his accuser. He knew Mrs. Fleming didn't mean to cast blame. In fact, she was closer to the truth than anyone.

"I was checking on her after that fainting spell." He gave a nervous laugh and shrugged. "I guess I've felt sort of responsible for Sofie since that explosion." *That's no lie.*

Mrs. Fleming's expression waffled from suspicion to self-condemnation. Good old guilt—Luke knew it well. As a matter of fact, watching Mrs. Fleming struggle with her own intensified his. She had no reason to feel guilty, but he couldn't help her without destroying everything. "But if Mrs. Fleming feels it isn't, uh, proper for—"

"Tarnation, *Padre,*" Zeke interrupted. "I reckon God's the only chaperon you and Miss Dr. Sofie needs."

Luke looked at Mrs. Fleming again. She looked absolutely miserable and it was all his fault. Grandma would've put him in the corner for a week for this.

The woman's eyes glittered with tears, then she threw her hands up in surrender. "You're right, of course. Forgive me, Father, Sofie."

Oh, God.

"Good, now we got that settled," the marshal continued, "I'll snoop around and drop a few hints that we got us a witness to the killin', and that young Latimer ain't gonna hang after all."

"A trap?" Ab asked.

"Somethin' like that." Marshal Weathers looked around the room. "I'll sleep in the jail 'til the judge comes 'round."

"You reckon the killer'll make a move," Zeke said, rather than asked.

"Yep." The marshal aimed his piercing gaze at Luke. "This all settin' right with you, Father?"

Luke tried to ignore the conflicting voices in the back of his mind. He wanted Sofie. And now he was being asked to sleep under the same roof with her, albeit, for a good cause.

Still, the thought of Sofie sleeping in another room of the same house, without Mrs. Fleming to play watchdog . . .

"Yeah," Luke said, his voice hoarse. He cleared his throat and felt someone's gaze on him. Instinctively, he met Mrs. Fleming's accusing glare. She still didn't completely buy his story. *Smart woman.*

Perspiration trickled down the sides of his neck and into the open collar of his shirt. Did the woman know his secret? Did she know that he wanted Sofie with a fierceness that made him awaken every night, shaking and drenched with sweat?

Did she know who he was?

And wasn't?

Sofie was going to shack up with the same man who'd haunted her dreams for weeks.

A man of God.

She gathered the few articles of clothing Dora had reluctantly given her, trying to control her breathing and her thoughts with every passing moment. Why couldn't she shake her foolish desire for Father Salazar?

Sure, at first she'd blamed the fact that he'd saved her life. *My weird hero.* But that excuse didn't wash after all these weeks. If only he'd remained sunburned and bald, and, most importantly, garbed in attire befitting a priest.

In jeans and an open-collared shirt, Redemption's only priest was a drop-dead gorgeous hunk of man who would turn any woman's head. More than her head, Sofie decided. Father Salazar was turning her hormones inside out and bass ackwards. In fact, mutation was an increasingly plausible possibility.

"Mutation?" Her vocabulary amazed even her. If only her memory would follow.

She finished packing and opened the door. Sadly, this room was the only home she could remember. How strange. With a sigh, she lifted the borrowed carpetbag and walked into the kitchen.

Only Marshal Weathers and Dr. Taylor sat at the table now. She glanced toward the window. Within the hour, it would be totally dark.

"Miss Sofie, there you are." Dr. Taylor stood along with Marshal Weathers.

"Good evening." Sofie allowed Marshal Weathers to take her bag and place it near the back door. She murmured her gratitude, still surprised by the way men in Redemption treated women. Of course, the marshal wasn't from here, yet the same chivalry was part of his makeup as well. Somehow, she doubted such behavior had been a typical part of her life before now. It seemed . . .

Old-fashioned. Yes, that was it. She paused to ponder that as Dr. Taylor pulled out a chair for her at the table. Was she regaining her memory at last? John Wayne this afternoon, and now realizing that these people were old-fashioned?

"Miss Dora does know her way around the kitchen," Marshal Weathers said, returning to his chair. "That's the finest meal I've had since Ft. Smith."

"Mrs. Fleming and her daughter are both fine cooks,"

Dr. Taylor agreed. "Best watch yourself though, Marshal. Dora can smell an eligible bachelor a mile away."

Sofie remained silent while the men chuckled. Poor Dora. Though the young woman had pissed her off more than once, Sofie couldn't help feeling sorry for her. Not even twenty, and Dora considered herself a spinster. And a good cook? Well, yes, but only a man could truly appreciate several courses of fried everything.

"Well, I'm flattered, but I'm afraid she'll have to keep sniffin'," Marshal Weathers said, smiling. "I got me a brand-new bride at home in a family way."

In a family way? Sofie cleared her throat daintily to avoid laughing out loud.

"Congratulations." Dr. Taylor patted the marshal on the back. "I hope you make it home before the birth."

"Without Zeke," Sofie added and smiled prettily, trying to play the role these men seemed to think she should.

"Amen." Dr. Taylor lifted his coffee cup to his lips.

"Trust me, Miss Sofie, I'd like nothin' better." The marshal took a sip of coffee, then met her gaze, his expression solemn. "Takin' Zeke Judson back to hang leaves a bad taste in my mouth that'll follow me to my grave."

"Good." Sofie shifted her attention to Dr. Taylor. "Where is everyone?"

"Gone to get the parsonage ready, and Jenny's reading to Mr. Smith again." The doctor covered Sofie's hand with his. "You're a good woman, Miss Sofie. Thank you for doing this."

"I want Jenny to be safe and happy."

"We all do." The doctor faced Marshal Weathers again. "I sure hope your plan works."

"Yep, so do I."

"I'm still not real clear on this plan of yours," Sofie said, choosing her words carefully. "Just exactly what is it you hope to achieve by hiding Jenny?" *Besides putting me into dangerous proximity with a man I have the hots for?*

Marshal Weathers took another sip of coffee, prolonging his answer. The guy was definitely prone to dramatics.

"Draw the killer out." Marshal Weathers set down his cup and leaned back in his chair. "If he knows somebody saw him, then he'll panic. Panickin' makes a man careless." He looked around the table, his expression ominous. "And I'll be waitin'."

A shudder rippled through Sofie. She knew one thing for certain. She'd hate to be on the other side of the law from Marshal Sam Weathers.

Time to change the subject. "Now that the epidemic is over, this building will become a school again soon," she said.

"Yes, thank God." Dr. Taylor raked his fingers through his thick, white hair.

"I was in a quarantine once, but it was for measles." The marshal shook his head slowly. "Indian Territory, up near the Kansas border. Sorry business."

No one spoke for several minutes, then Sofie remembered the one remaining patient. "Did I hear Dora say you're taking Mr. Smith to your house, Dr. Taylor?"

"Yes, it's a miracle he's alive." Dr. Taylor raised his coffee cup. "Here's to miracles."

"I'll drink to that." Marshal Weathers raised his cup, too.

"Do you think he'll ever be able to talk?" Sofie asked. "Or maybe he'll be able to write."

Dr. Taylor drew a deep breath and said, "I don't think he'll ever regain full use of his right arm, but the left is in pretty good shape. Talking remains to be seen."

"Is this the fella you mentioned earlier?" Marshal Weathers asked. "With the burns?"

Nodding, Dr. Taylor set his cup aside. "He wandered into town during the epidemic. Miracle he didn't contract smallpox, too."

Sofie shuddered. The thought of anyone suffering smallpox in addition to such serious burns made her stomach lurch. "Maybe someone will come looking for him."

"Could even be wanted." Marshal Weathers rubbed his chin with thumb and forefinger, his whiskers making a rasping sound in the quiet room. "Just wandered in here from nowhere and all, eh?"

Dr. Taylor drummed his fingers on the table. "I suppose anything is possible, Marshal, but he's suffered enough for any crime he might have committed."

"Like they say, the Lord works in mysterious ways."

"Jenny seems to calm him," Sofie said. "For some reason, though, he doesn't like me."

"Well, I wouldn't say that," Dr. Taylor said, "but he does seem to get agitated whenever you're around."

"Probably 'cuz you're such a pretty gal," the marshal said, grinning.

Sofie blushed, actually *blushed.* "Thank you, Marshal, but I hardly think Mr. Smith is in any shape to . . . to . . ." Her cheeks blazed with fire and she averted her gaze. *This is ridiculous.*

When she looked up, Father Salazar was standing in the doorway, twilight filling the sky at his back. Her gaze was drawn to his as if by homing device.

Even beside an impressive side of beef like Sam Weathers, *she* was drawn to Father Salazar. As the weeks went by, she'd realized more and more that her attraction was based on much more than merely the fact that he'd saved her life.

The memory of his lips on hers—dream lips, that is— confirmed her greatest fear.

Dr. Sofie was in love with a priest.

Chapter Ten

A pretty gal? What an incredible understatement.

Luke stood in the doorway without saying a word, just staring at Sofie. She was gorgeous. Only a pale scar remained as evidence of her injuries, and all the bruising had faded long ago.

Now in the soft glow of lamplight, her skin appeared flawless. Luminous. *I'm turning into a frigging poet.*

Still, it was true. Ebony curls framed her small face, contrasting dramatically against her fair skin. Her blue eyes were probably too large for the rest of her face, but to Luke they were the most beautiful eyes he'd ever seen.

Don't do this. Why did he continue to torture himself this way? He wanted her, but he'd learned at an early age he couldn't have everything he wanted. *Get over it.*

But he didn't want to get over it. He wanted to savor every glance, every accidental touch, and each and every one of his erotic fantasies.

About Sofie.

His gut clenched and his groin tightened, aching and

demanding attention. If only it *was* just about sex. Only a fool could continue to ignore the other stuff—the ache in his heart and his very soul.

He couldn't admit it even to himself, because his feelings for Sofie were futile. Wasted energy. A dead end, just like his appeal. His physical desire for her was much easier to consider, though also a waste of time.

The expression in her eyes didn't help matters. She looked at him the way he'd looked at age eight, staring through the toy store window at a train set. God, did that mean *she* wanted *him* that much?

Then he remembered that kiss. Of course, she did. At least subconsciously.

And she was moving in with him. Tonight.

He was in deep shit. Really deep shit.

Yes, she wanted him as much as he'd wanted that toy train. He'd been afraid to ask Santa for that train set, believing he didn't deserve anything nearly that cool. Only the very rich and the very good received toys as awesome as that train.

But on Christmas morning . . . Luke's eyes burned as he remembered the thrill of finding that very same train circling their Christmas tree, his grandparents looking on, their faces glowing with pride.

Pride, dammit. For him.

No, not now, Nolan. Not now.

Drawing a deep breath, he cleared his throat to alert the others of his presence, before he made love to Sofie with his eyes. Right here. Right now. She must've sensed his thoughts, because her cheeks reddened and she looked quickly away, down at her small hands clasped on the table before her.

"Evenin', Father." Sam Weathers stood and indicated a chair at the table. "Soon as it gets a bit darker, we'll mosey over to the parsonage. I gotta relieve Ab at the jail soon, too."

Mosey? Luke suppressed a smile and took a seat at the table. "Where's Jenny?"

"With Mr. Smith." Dr. Taylor rose and pushed in his chair. "Which is where I should be. It's time to change his dressings."

"How's he doing?" Luke hadn't seen the burned stranger for over a week.

"It's a miracle he's alive at all. In fact, he's doing so well, I've eliminated some of his bandages," Dr. Taylor said. "Though I doubt even his own mother would recognize him now."

"Sad." Luke raked his fingers across his new growth of hair.

"Would you mind trying to talk to him, Father?" Dr. Taylor asked, pausing near the kitchen door. "It might help. I'm hoping he'll find a way to communicate, to tell us who he is, so we can contact his next of kin."

Luke shrugged. "I'm willing to try." He didn't feel like playing priest tonight, but maybe that would take his mind off toy trains and Sofie. And sex.

Keeping his gaze away from her, Luke followed Dr. Taylor through the kitchen door. Sam Weathers followed them, making Luke more than a little uncomfortable. After eleven years in prison, it was hard to feel comfortable with a lawman. Any lawman.

Jenny looked up from the book in her lap as they approached. "Are you going to change his bandages again?" she asked, looking at Dr. Taylor.

"Yes, it's time." Dr. Taylor sat on the stool near the man's cot, beside a basket of clean bandages. "How are you feeling this evening, Mr. Smith?"

The man's eyes seemed more alert now than when Luke had last seen him. He looked at Dr. Taylor and Jenny, then his gaze came to rest on Luke.

Mr. Smith's expression shifted during one blink to the next, from placid acceptance to some kind of mania. He came off the bed like a man who'd suffered no injury, like a mummy from a low-grade horror flick. He lunged toward his intended victim—in this case, Luke. Lurching and staggering, Mr. Smith charged, his outstretched hands falling short of their target.

Luke's blood turned to ice water.

"My *God.*" Dr. Taylor and Marshal Weathers both grabbed the man before he fell, and subdued him.

A roar erupted from the stranger's throat as they eased him back onto the bed, his lips unmoving. The hatred in his eyes and the rage in his voice made Luke cringe. He put a protective arm around Jenny's shoulders and the child buried her face against his side.

"What's all this about?" the marshal asked after they had the man quieted.

"I have no idea." Dr. Taylor gave his patient a dose of laudanum. He examined the man's eyes and listened carefully to his chest, then shook his head. "Everything seems all right, though."

Marshal Weathers straightened and faced Luke. "You know him?"

"No, I don't know anyone from around here." That was the truth.

"Mighty peculiar."

Dr. Taylor shook his head and rose. "He's dozing off now. His behavior could be from all the medication, though I've been reducing it little by little."

Luke nodded, though he couldn't shake the image of the stranger's eyes when he'd locked gazes with him. Disturbing? Yes, but much more than that. Almost fanatical.

Anytime his grandma had been frightened, she'd claimed someone had walked over her grave. That was precisely how Luke felt right now. Despite the warmth radiating from the potbellied stove in the center of the room, a chill raced through him.

"I think you'd all better leave while I change his dress-ings."

That sounded like the best idea Luke had heard today. He guided Jenny through the kitchen door, sensing that Marshal Weathers was right behind them.

Sofie stood in the center of the kitchen, staring toward the door. He wanted her, but he also feared her. Maybe the stranger's reaction to him had triggered that reminder. Luke's future—the future he wanted for himself—could be destroyed by this woman who made his libido spring to life every time he saw or thought about her.

More than his libido, dammit. She made his heart swell with—

No!

He'd known leaving Redemption was the wisest course of action, but now he'd fiddle-farted around until he was trapped. He'd promised to protect Jenny until the circuit judge came to town.

Yes, he was trapped all right. With Sofie.

And with himself.

"I heard some kind of wild animal," she said, standing. "But I don't think the sound came from outside."

"It was Mr. Smith," Jenny said, taking Sofie's hand. "He came clear up off the bed and tried to attack Father Salazar."

Sofie jerked her head up to stare at Luke. "What? Why would he do such a thing?"

Luke shook his head. "I don't know, but I'll never forget the look in his eyes." Another chill rippled through him.

"That man had murder in his eyes," Marshal Weathers said from behind Luke. "I've seen it before. Many times. Make no mistake."

Luke met the marshal's gaze and nodded. "I won't."

Marshal Weathers inclined his head toward Jenny. "I reckon it's dark enough now. You ready, young lady?"

Jenny's eyes were large and trusting. Luke's gut clenched

again. He'd promised to protect her, and to prevent Shane and Zeke from being hanged.

A promise is a promise.

"Can I go see Shane first?" Jenny asked. "Please?"

Sam Weathers knelt in front of Jenny and patted her shoulder. "You gotta understand, Miss Jenny, that we're tryin' to protect you and your brother."

"I know."

"I'm powerful sorry, but the only place you're goin' is the parsonage," he continued, " 'til you're ready to tell the bad man's name."

Her lower lip trembled and Sofie put a hand on her shoulder. "You can send a message to your brother, though."

"Sure, that'd be right fine, but first you gotta climb into this." The marshal aimed his thumb toward an oak barrel sitting near the back door. "Can you do that?"

Jenny's eyes widened again, but she nodded and went to look inside. "Oh, it smells dreadful." She wrinkled her nose and turned to face them, a scandalized expression on her young face. "It smells of whiskey."

Chuckling, Marshal Weathers lifted her and set her down inside the rancid-smelling barrel. "Well that's 'cuz it *is* a whiskey barrel. The storekeeper was clear outta empty cracker barrels."

Luke shared a smile with Sofie, fighting the urge to take her hand. Soon they'd be at the parsonage with Jenny, and Mrs. Fleming and Dora would go home. The marshal would sleep at the jail to guard Shane. Then Jenny would go to sleep, and Sofie would be there with Luke.

Alone.

He shifted his weight, hoping to create more room in his jeans for his responsive body. This was getting old— he had to find relief soon. He'd hoped to avoid resorting to the only sexual solace he'd had in prison—what his grandfather had called "Rosie Palm and her five sisters."

The marshal put the top on the barrel loosely. Several holes had been drilled in the sides for ventilation, and a rope fashioned a handle for both sides.

"Pee-yew," came a muffled voice from deep in the barrel.

They all chuckled, then the marshal said, "Quiet in there. Whiskey ain't supposed to talk." He grinned at Luke and Sofie. "Now if you'll grab one side, Father, I'll take the other."

"Sure." Luke avoided looking at Sofie again as he followed the marshal's instructions.

Sofie opened the door and stood back for them to exit. Luke brushed against her as he edged by with his half of the barrel. His gaze locked with hers and she licked her lips, her expression revealing the one thing he'd both feared and hoped to see.

Desire.

Carrying her carpetbag, Sofie followed the men, relieved that Jenny remained silent. Though Redemption's only street was deserted now, her wary gaze darted around to ensure no one was watching them make their way to the parsonage at the far edge of town.

A town that had taken her in without knowing anything about her. They trusted her enough to charge her with the safety of one of their own.

Could she make Redemption her permanent home, assuming, of course, she never regained her memory? Though the people here had been good to her, it still didn't *feel* like home. And there was still the issue of her bizarre memories of things which couldn't possibly exist.

Eventually, she'd have to make some kind of decision about her future. But right now there were more pressing matters, like moving into a safe house with a little girl and a man of God.

The man she loved.

No, not a *man*—a *priest*. She had to keep reminding herself of that, and ignore the impudent voice of reason that insisted priests *were* men. That was dangerous territory—no gray areas allowed here. She couldn't handle it right now.

The stone and log parsonage looked warm and friendly, drawing Sofie's thoughts away from Father Salazar and her irrational feelings. She had to concentrate on protecting Jenny. Nothing else mattered now.

Mrs. Fleming opened the door and, within a few minutes, they were all inside, the shutters closed against the chilly night and prying eyes. A warm fire blazed in the hearth, making Sofie's heart ache. It was cozy and inviting, like a real home.

Like the home she couldn't remember?

She blinked back her scalding tears, determined not to dwell on anything else this evening that would make her cry.

Once the door was closed and bolted, Marshal Weathers lifted the lid off the barrel and peered inside. "Whooee. You been drinkin' whiskey in there, Miss Jenny?"

A little-girl giggle wafted up from the barrel, followed by the top of Jenny's head as she popped up like a Jack-in-the-box and waited for Sam Weathers to lift her out.

Mrs. Fleming rushed forward and wrinkled her nose. "Couldn't you have found something that didn't reek of whiskey, Marshal?" She sniffed the top of Jenny's head. "The child smells like a saloon."

"With all due respect, ma'am, I'd be willing to bet you ain't never smelled a saloon." The marshal's eyes twinkled mischievously. "Besides, she'll wash."

Sofie hid a smile behind her hand, though she noticed Father Salazar didn't bother hiding his. Even Dora's lips twitched a little.

After a moment of stunned silence, Mrs. Fleming laughed quietly. "Yes, she'll wash, Marshal."

"Thank you for thinking of this," Dora said, stroking Jenny's hair. "I'll be glad when this is all over and Jenny can come home with us."

"You're welcome, ma'am." Marshal Weathers gave Jenny a patient look that was all business. "As soon as Miss Jenny understands we ain't gonna let nobody hurt her, she'll tell us what needs tellin'."

Jenny looked down and Mrs. Fleming cleared her throat. "Yes, well . . ." She turned to Sofie. "I brought you some of my sourdough starter, and a few other things I thought you might need."

Sourdough starter? Sofie'd gone from incompetent physician to Martha Stewart. *Who's Martha Stewart, and why did I think of her now?* And if she could remember this Martha Stewart, why couldn't she remember her own last name?

"Thank you," she murmured, realizing she had to say something.

"Well, I reckon we'd best be goin', before the whole town knows we're here and wonders why." The marshal tweaked Jenny's nose. "You be good."

"I will." Jenny looked up—way up—at the marshal, hero worship shining in her eyes.

Who could blame her? Marshal Weathers sounded like Sam Elliot, looked like Magnum—though Sofie couldn't remember Magnum's first name, she had no difficulty picturing him—and acted like John Wayne. She was practically a trivia queen, with all the tidbits surfacing.

But what about the important things? With a sigh, she felt someone watching her, and she looked around to find Father Salazar's gaze fixed on her. Intense.

Hungry.

She warmed from deep in her core, and her limbs felt loose and languid beneath his scrutiny. Priest or no priest, Father Salazar had noticed her as a woman.

She should feel shame—in fact, did to some extent—but she couldn't deny the surge of joy in her heart. And *that*, she reminded herself, should make her even more ashamed.

With great effort, she looked away from his intense gray eyes and right into a pair of equally intense ones. Disapproving ones.

Mrs. Fleming's lips were pinched and her eyes narrowed as she stared at Sofie. The woman was like a saint, and disapproval displayed itself plainly on her face right now. And it was all for Sofie.

That shame she'd been unable to summon a few moments ago now surfaced with a vengeance. Only a harlot—wasn't that what Mrs. Fleming had called Miss Lottie's girls?—would harbor sexual fantasies about a priest. It didn't matter that Sofie's feelings for Father Salazar were more than merely sexual. All that mattered was that her obsession with him was wrong, wrong, *wrong*.

Marshal Weathers strolled toward the door, his spurs jingling with every step. He paused and looked back over his shoulder. ''I think it's best we all go, ma'am.'' His comment was directed at Mrs. Fleming, who hadn't budged, even though Dora was tying her bonnet beneath her chin and pulling her shawl around her shoulders. ''So no one wonders what's goin' on here,'' he added.

Sofie suspected that what *might* go on here was exactly what was playing through Mrs. Fleming's mind right now. And it had nothing to do with protecting Jenny.

''I . . .'' Mrs. Fleming shook her head and reached for her cape, shooting glances in Sofie's direction every few seconds. ''I'm worried about—''

A quiet knock at the front door silenced Mrs. Fleming's words and prompted her to usher Jenny into the kitchen. Dora followed, pulling the door closed behind them. Then Marshal Weathers stepped back and allowed Father Salazar to open it just a crack.

Sofie noticed the lawman's hand poised above one of his guns, and her heart lurched. There was danger here. Danger for Jenny. She had to stop thinking of Father Salazar and her stupid infatuation.

"Dr. Taylor." Father Salazar opened the door wide, admitting the doctor. The physician stepped through, removing his hat while his host closed and latched the door.

"Everything all right?" the doctor asked, looking around the room. "I don't see Jenny."

"In the kitchen," Marshal Weathers said. "Can't be too careful."

"Of course. Please, forgive me for calling so late." Dr. Taylor actually appeared nervous. "Father Salazar, do you have a moment?"

"Sure, have a seat."

"Well, I'm gonna mosey on over to the jail now." Marshal Weathers nodded. "You know to keep the front and back doors bolted."

Father Salazar threw the bolt home after Marshal Weathers had disappeared into the night, then turned his attention to Dr. Taylor. He returned to the fire and sat in a straight-backed chair, facing the doctor.

Sofie admired Luke's profile, firelight bathing his face in light and shadow. He had strong features, accentuated by his extremely short hair. Again, the only word that came to her mind to describe him was magnificent.

"The epidemic has made me come to a decision, Father," Dr. Taylor began, holding his hat in his lap.

He glanced at Sofie, who suddenly realized she was just standing there like a piece of furniture. "Oh, forgive me, I'll just go see Jen—"

"No, stay." Dr. Taylor gave a nervous chuckle. "I might need a witness later, in case I turn chicken."

"Witness?" Father Salazar leaned back in his chair. "This sounds serious."

"It is." Dr. Taylor cleared his throat. "And please call me Roman. After all we've been through, formalities seem ridiculous."

"I agree." Father Salazar smiled. "My first name is Luke."

Luke. She hadn't known, but now she realized the name suited him well. Much better than Father Salazar. Of course, she had other reasons for disliking his formal title.

Dr. Taylor arched a brow. "Is it permitted?" Chuckling, he shrugged. "I've never addressed a priest by his first name before."

"Sure, why not?" Father Salazar laughed, too. "Now what is it you wanted to talk to me about?"

"All right, Luke." Dr. Taylor steepled his fingers beneath his chin. "During the war, I was very young, and even with all the dying around me, I couldn't see *then* what this epidemic has taught me *now.* "

"Go on," Father Salazar—Luke—urged.

"Life is too short and too precious to waste."

"Amen," Father Salazar said in a fierce whisper, his expression fervent.

"So I've come to a decision I should've made over a year ago." The doctor raked his fingers through his thick, white hair and sighed. "In the morning, I'm going to ask Anna Fleming to marry me, and—"

A gasp sounded from the kitchen and Dr. Taylor shot to his feet. Father Salazar joined him and they all stared at the woman none of them had heard open the kitchen door.

"Anna," Dr. Taylor said, his face reddening. After a moment, he smiled. "I meant this to be more romantic, but . . ."

"Roman Taylor, it's the most romantic thing I've ever heard." Mrs. Fleming walked slowly toward him and took his hands in hers. "But before I give you my answer, I have a question for you."

Dr. Taylor's face paled several shades and he cleared his throat again. "What . . . what is it?"

Sofie saw Dora and Jenny peeking through the kitchen door, and she raised her finger to her lips. They both nodded and slipped into the room.

"What in heaven's name took you so long?" Mrs. Fleming's face crumpled and she burst into tears as Dr. Taylor caught her in his embrace.

"God only knows, Anna," he whispered fiercely. "All I know is I love you more than life itself."

Sofie stared openmouthed, tolerating Dora's impromptu embrace, and Jenny's jumping up and down. The child kept saying, "A wedding, a wedding," over and over again.

After a few moments, Dora and Jenny rushed over to congratulate the newly engaged couple. Sofie moved toward them slowly, hanging back while they celebrated. This was, after all, a moment for family, and she was an outsider.

She felt Father Salazar's gaze on her and looked up—a mistake. The naked emotion blazing in his gray eyes stole her breath. It took several minutes for her to recover, drawing deep breaths into her oxygen-starved lungs.

"Wait, wait," Dr. Taylor said, laughing joyously with his bride-to-be. "There's more, if it's all right with you, Anna?" The doctor looked lovingly into Mrs. Fleming's eyes.

"What is it, Roman?"

"I know neither of us is Catholic, but I'd like very much for Father Salazar to perform the ceremony."

"I think that's a splendid idea," Mrs. Fleming agreed.

"Yes, so do I," Dora said, dabbing her eyes with a handkerchief. "It seems just perfect, after all we've been through together."

"Yes, and it also means we don't have to wait for the judge," Dr. Taylor added, his eyes twinkling when he winked at Mrs. Fleming. "I'm finished waiting."

Mrs. Fleming blushed and nodded. "Yes, please, Father?"

Like the others, Sofie turned her attention to Father Salazar, stunned by the panic in his eyes. He reached up to loosen another button on his already open-collared shirt. Perspiration trickled down the sides of his face, and his eyes were wide.

"Why, Father," Dora said, laughing, "you look as if you've never performed a wedding before."

Father Salazar tried to smile, but failed. After a moment, he shrugged and said, "Actually, I haven't." He chuckled, his face turning crimson. "I'm sort of new at this. Maybe you should wait for—"

"Nonsense, Father." Dr. Taylor clapped him on the back, beaming. "I've never been married before, so the two of us will learn together. Besides"—the doctor's voice grew serious—"even if there were someone else here to perform the ceremony, I'd still want you to do it."

"As would I." Mrs. Fleming moved closer and kissed Father Salazar on the cheek. "Please, Father?"

"I guess I don't have any choice." Father Salazar smiled, but it didn't reach his eyes.

He looked over Mrs. Fleming's head and met Sofie's gaze. What she detected in his eyes made her shudder. Fear. He was terrified of something.

And, just for a moment, she saw an image of him with that same look in his eyes, but it was from before, when he'd had no hair. A wave of dizziness shot through her and she gripped the back of a chair for support as the image became clearer.

They were in a stark, cold room with several other men, all murmuring in low voices and moving around performing various tasks. Some of them wore uniforms. There was a priest, too, but this one was much older. He was talking in earnest with Father Salazar, who was wearing something that looked like a hospital gown.

A hospital? Cold steel, low voices, a priest, the hospital gown, and Sofie a doctor . . . An operating room?

And her patient had been Father Salazar himself.

A loud explosion sounded, and Sofie's daydream vanished like a popping soap bubble. Explosions like the morning she'd been hurt and Father Salazar brought her here?

Then another explosion sounded, and Dr. Taylor rushed toward the door.

"Gunshots."

Chapter Eleven

Luke stood frozen, listening to the staccato echo of the gunshots. Vaguely aware of Dr. Taylor rushing out the door, he didn't stir from his state of shock until Sofie grabbed his arm and shook him back to reality.

"Father Salazar, are you all right?" She shook him again.

He was far from all right, but he nodded. "Gunshots," he said, then he looked into her eyes. Big mistake. He wasn't even close to all right. "I'd better go help."

The gunshots gave him an excuse to run away, a handy escape hatch from an impossible situation. *Coward.*

"Stay with them?" he asked Mrs. Fleming, and she nodded.

Running into the dark night to discern the source of gunshots could hardly be considered cowardly behavior, but in this instance, it was just that. He heard the bolt slide into place behind him as he darted into the cold and raced toward the jail. Somehow, he knew that's where he'd find trouble.

Of course, he had far more serious trouble back at the parsonage.

Spurred to action, he ran like he should have that first morning. *Alone and free*—his heart pounded the words over and over in his head.

But he wasn't free.

Comprehension dawned with all the pH balance of drain cleaner. Right in his gut.

Despite everything, he wasn't free at all. Now he was trapped by circumstances of his own creation. *Damn.* He ran faster, not caring whether he fell on his face or ran into a tree in the darkness.

Breathing took every ounce of strength he could muster as he maintained his pace. The boom box pounding in his head rumbled through his bones, made his blood quiver like the lime Jell-O he'd learned to hate over the years.

Anger aimed at himself—at the past and present, at his stupidity—fueled him until he flew down the dirt road. Working out in prison had been a balm, but now his endorphins failed. Hell, even Valium couldn't soothe his nerves at this point.

He was screwed.

He either had to commit the ultimate act of fraud, or run away from Redemption right now and never look back. His steps faltered and he staggered to a halt.

Run, run, run. The word played over and over again in his head, and he looked around frantically, almost as if he expected to find another source for the voice. But there was no one.

The jail was just ahead. He had to decide now. Would he listen to the voice of reason and run . . . or would he remain in this new prison he'd created for himself?

A horse galloped toward him full-out, and he saw the flash of a gun before he heard it explode into the night. Rolling toward the nearest tree, Luke took cover and watched the rider roar past, still shooting into the night sky.

Roman. Shane.

He couldn't leave them like this, and—*dammit*—he couldn't leave Jenny and Sofie. His decision made, he bolted for the jail. Marshal Weathers stood on the porch, his still-smoking pistol clutched in his fist. Light from inside the jail flooded out around him, bathing his face in shadow.

"Where's Dr. Taylor?" Luke asked, gasping for air. "Where—"

"I'm right here." The doctor emerged from beside the building.

Marshal Weathers was still staring in the direction the rider had taken. "That fella ain't comin' back tonight."

"How can you be so sure?" Roman asked, following the lawman into the lighted jail.

"My gut." Sam Weathers put the paper down on the small, battered desk in the corner, and read, *"Get on with the hangin'."*

"Short and sweet." Dr. Taylor's voice dripped with sarcasm. "I'm glad he doesn't know where Jenny is."

"Yeah." Luke mopped his sweaty forehead with his sleeve. Despite the frosty night air, he felt as if he'd gone one-on-one against Michael Jordan.

"I don't know what I thought to accomplish, running down here without a gun." Roman shook his head. "Is Shane all right?"

Weathers quirked an eyebrow. "See for yourself."

Roman went through the unlocked door into an area beyond the bars. "Shane," he called. "Father, bring the lamp in here."

Luke couldn't move. The sight of those bars made him shudder. There was no way he was going into that cell. He'd rather die than set foot behind bars again.

"You look like you seen a ghost," Marshal Weathers

said, taking the lamp to the doctor. "Look all you want, Doc, but he ain't there."

"Wha . . ."

Luke stepped closer, watching as the marshal unlocked the cell and admitted the other man. Roman rushed to the bunk and threw back the blanket.

Nothing but straw bunched into a mound occupied the bunk.

"What—where?" Roman picked up the blanket with both hands and held it up to the light. "My God."

The tattered wool blanket was full of holes. Bullet holes. "How . . . how did you know?" Luke whispered, more in awe of the lawman than before.

"My gut again." Sam Weathers merely shrugged. "Pesky thing, but I reckon it's come in handy a time or two."

"Where's Shane?" Roman dropped the blanket and approached Marshal Weathers.

"I ain't sayin'."

Luke moved closer to the bars, feeling their coldness even from a distance of several feet. "You trusted us with Jenny," he said. "Why not Shane?"

"It ain't a matter of trust." The lawman moved back into the main room, taking the lamp with him.

"We have a right to know where you've hidden—"

"Nope."

"But—"

"Look, you can see here I was right about hidin' the boy," the marshal said. "You just gotta trust me and stop askin' so durn many questions."

Roman looked at Luke, his eyes filled with questions. "I guess we don't have any other choice."

"That's the way I see it." The lawman turned his gaze on Luke. "Father?"

Luke sighed and shook his head. "Like the doctor said, we have no choice." When was the last time Luke had a choice about anything? He should've kept running. *Yeah, right.* Running would only add more guilt to his already overcrowded portfolio.

"I trust y'all to keep Miss Jenny safe, and I'll keep her brother safe. Deal?"

Roman extended his hand to the marshal and they shook on it. "Deal." The doctor looked toward Luke. "That reminds me, Marshal," he said, smiling. "How do you feel about weddings?"

"As long as there ain't no shotgun involved, I'm in favor of 'em." The marshal chuckled. "Why you askin'?"

"I'd like to invite you to one. Mine."

"Well, I'll be." Marshal Weathers pumped Roman's hand again. "I reckon Mrs. Fleming's the bride."

"Well, yes, how did you know?"

"I'd have to be blind not to know that." Marshal Weathers chuckled.

"Consider yourself invited, Marshal."

"Call me Sam and I'll be there."

"Fine, Sam it is, but only if you call me Roman."

"When and where's the weddin'?"

Roman looked at Luke with a baffled expression. "Tomorrow night after the town meeting?"

"Town meeting?" Sam scratched his whiskery chin. "Reckon I'd best get me a bath and shave before then, even if it ain't Saturday."

"Well, we'd better tell the bride, eh, Father?" Roman chuckled and slapped Luke on the back.

God, why didn't I keep running?

Sofie owed Dr. Taylor more than he would ever realize. His timely proposal had distracted Mrs. Fleming enough that she seemed to have forgotten all about Sofie and Father Salazar.

Sofie and Luke . . .

After tucking Jenny in bed upstairs, Sofie sat in the

rocker vacated earlier by Luke, but she kept jumping up and pacing the room. Several times, she went to the door, itching to go find out what was happening. If only she could look out the window . . .

"Sit down, Sofie," Mrs. Fleming urged. "They're fine."

"How do you know?" Sofie raked her fingers through her hair, which had crawled free of the bun Mrs. Fleming had insisted she wear. "Aren't you worried?"

"Of course, but I know in my heart that God will protect them." Mrs. Fleming's smile was downright sublime. "Sit."

Dora flashed Sofie a grin and rolled her eyes. "Trust me, Sofie, Mother has a gift for knowing when to worry" —she patted her mother's hand—"and when not to."

"Thank you, dear." Mrs. Fleming gave her daughter's hand a squeeze, then pointed to the rocker. "This is not a time to worry, so sit. Trust me, there will be plenty of times in your life for real worry. It's woman's lot, you know."

Sofie wanted to shout that everybody in Redemption was nuts, that the only way to make sure Luke and Dr. Taylor were all right was to go see for themselves, but she didn't. Instead, she returned to the rocking chair, surprised by the exhaustion that pressed down on her.

Mrs. Fleming was a wise woman, and if she didn't see a need to worry, then Sofie wouldn't. Well, at least she'd try not to. Resigned, she pushed her feet against the floor, sending the old rocker into slow, silent motion. Mrs. Fleming and Dora sat a few feet away on something they called a settee, and Sofie wanted to call a loveseat. They were making plans to send out wedding announcements, and discussing how all their relatives would react to the news.

Despite Mrs. Fleming's assurances, every few minutes the older woman's gaze darted to the door, worry etched across her soft features. Then she would sigh and smile, and that infuriatingly serene expression would return.

The woman obviously had a hotline straight to the Big Guy.

All right, so Sofie would let Mrs. Fleming and God worry. Besides, she was so tired. So very, very tired . . .

She closed her eyes and leaned into the afghan draped across the chair. The fire crackled nearby, and there hadn't been any additional gunshots since she'd heard a horse gallop through town almost an hour ago.

Fatigue and the warmth of the fire made her drowsy. Though she tried to stay awake, the chair was too comfortable and the silence too seductive. Soon, she no longer heard the women's voices. All she heard was the rhythm of her breathing and the steady thud of her heart as sleep overtook her.

Images filled her mind as her dream world beckoned and she fell willingly into a deeper slumber . . .

The man stared at Sofie with an intensity that stole her breath. She was chest-deep in water—a pond?—looking up at the tall figure standing on the bank. Sunlight filtered through the trees, playing games of light and shadow across his familiar features.

"You're beautiful," Luke whispered, his voice flowing over her like warm honey.

Hesitantly, she slid her hand down the curve of her hip, confirming her suspicion—skinny-dipping. Her gaze followed her hands downward, where her bare breasts seemed to float on the water's sparkling surface; her rigid nipples playing peek-a-boo as the ripples caressed her naked skin.

He stepped closer, his gray eyes glittering in the dappled sunlight. Warmth swelled within Sofie, filling her with the heat of desire, contrasting brilliantly with the cool water. Deep inside, she throbbed and ached, barren and sobbing for . . . something.

For him.

God help her, but she wanted this man with a fierceness she couldn't deny. She was weak and her need powerful.

"I want you," he said, reaching for the buttons on his shirt. Those three simple words said it all. Sofie held her breath as he

slowly unbuttoned his shirt and slid it from his broad shoulders. He held her prisoner with his gaze, never releasing her for even a moment.

Hungrily, her gaze drifted over his newly exposed skin. Well-defined muscles played across his chest and arms, and his abdomen was taut. Her hands tingled with the need to touch him as she looked lower, following his long, sensuous fingers to the fly of his jeans. She heard the snap's pop in the awesome silence, and she held her breath. Then he grasped the zipper with his thumb and forefinger.

Liquid fire shot through her and she pulsed with life and longing. Every muscle in her contracted as she grew increasingly aware of her need. This man could fill the emptiness in her heart and soul, and only he could assuage her feminine longing.

Never breaking eye contact, he hooked his thumbs inside his waistband and lowered his jeans. Inch by devastating inch, more bare flesh appeared, making her breathing quicken and her body tremble.

She wanted him. Needed him. Loved him.

Within moments, he stood before her naked, his magnificent form exposed to her greedy gaze. As he walked into the water, she took a wary step backward. Then another. His progress was slow, determined—her retreat feeble, halfhearted.

Because running away from Luke would deny her heart.

She stopped and waited, swallowing the lump in her throat as he came closer and closer. The water surrounding her seemed to warm with his approach, as did she.

Her breasts grew heavy and her feminine core clenched into a coil of longing.

"I want you," he whispered again, pausing less than a foot away.

Sofie trembled and banished the voice at the back of her mind that tried to convince her this was wrong. What could be wrong with something she wanted this desperately?

How could love be wrong?

"I want you, too," she said, her voice quivering as she waited. And wanted.

One step. That's all it took to bring him so close her nipples grazed the crisp dark hair on his chest. Something warm and hard brushed against her hip, sending her libido into overdrive.

"Oh, yes," she whispered, dismissing all doubt as he moved closer still.

"Sofie. My beautiful Sofie."

His breath fanned her face and she moaned, her lips parting to breathe in his essence. She couldn't wait any longer, and as she brought her hand up to caress his face, his palm cupped the fullness of her breast, lifting it from the water.

"Perfect." He brushed his thumb across her damp nipple, sending her spiraling higher. Then he lowered his face toward hers, his full lips seeking and taking hers in a kiss so exquisite, she thought she might die from the want of more.

Much more.

He placed his hands at her waist and lifted her up and against him. Sofie gasped at the intimate contact, but craved it even more than she feared it.

His hard, pulsing maleness pressed against her tender woman's flesh. Hungry for all of him, she wrapped her legs around his waist, but he held her so his erection merely teased her.

Sofie gasped as his lips left hers to kiss her throat and the curve of her shoulder. He lifted her higher and kissed the hollow between her breasts.

"Sweet," he murmured. Tenderly, he brought his mouth to the peak of her breast, taking her with a savage gentleness that sent rivulets of desire cascading through her shocked and pliant body. She moaned, looking down between them to watch his tanned face against her milky white breast.

The sight of Luke's mouth devouring her was shocking at first, but as her pleasure mounted, Sofie found it . . . erotic. She locked her hands behind his neck, holding him against her, relishing every tug of his lips and brush of his tongue.

She ached and throbbed, beyond ready for him to fill her so

completely, she'd never want again. Though it seemed impossible that she'd never want him again after this.

"Now, Luke," she whispered. "Now."

A noise dragged Sofie from her exquisite dream. *No, not yet,* she pleaded, but the sound came again and her dream vanished as she opened her eyes.

Startled, she looked around the room. Mrs. Fleming and Dora were gone, but the fire still crackled merrily. A grandfather clock ticked steadily from across the room, but not loudly enough to have disturbed her sleep.

And destroyed her beautiful dream.

Guilt rushed through her as she recalled that dream with a rush of fire to her cheeks . . . and lower regions. *Talk about sexual frustration.*

Then she again heard the sound that must have awakened her—a man clearing his throat. Warily, Sofie shifted her gaze. Her skin prickled before she saw him, knowing she was being watched.

By her dream lover.

Luke didn't want to wake her, but watching and hearing her dream was driving him nuts. Her parted lips, flushed cheeks, and occasional moans made him wonder if she was dreaming about sex. Did women have wet dreams?

He cleared his throat loudly, and she whispered, "Now, Luke. Now."

Oh, God. A bolt of lightning struck right between his legs. Whatever she was dreaming, he wished he could join her. Was he the Luke in her dream? *Oh, God.*

He cleared his throat again, and her eyes fluttered open. Silently, he watched her look around the room, until her gaze came to rest on him, seated at Reverend Bodine's desk. She blinked several times and her cheeks turned even redder than before.

Yes, of course he'd been the Luke in her dream. Swallowing the lump in his throat, he clenched and unclenched his fists, trying to control the insistent thrum through his veins. Every beat of his heart seemed to shout, "Sex, sex, sex, sex, sex!"

He drew another deep breath, shifting his weight in the appropriately hard, wooden chair. The settee looked one hell of a lot more comfortable, but that was too close to Sofie.

Yet not close enough.

"Now, Luke?" he repeated, grinning. He simply couldn't resist the impulse to tease. She looked away, making him immediately regret his words. Just because he was hornier than a mutt after a French poodle in heat didn't mean he had to take it out on Sofie. "I'm sorry."

She looked at him again, and he saw tears glistening in the depths of her gorgeous blue eyes. How he ached to kiss away her tears, and to fulfill her every dream. Adjusting himself inside his jeans—discreetly, he hoped—Luke went to the ottoman in front of her rocker and straddled it.

Big mistake.

Wincing, he swung both legs in front of him and leaned toward her, taking her hand. Sofie's skin was so soft. He traced a line from her palm to her wrist, then he looked up to meet her gaze.

Her cheeks still flushed, her breath shallow, she stared at him with wide, frightened eyes. Scaring her was the last thing he wanted to do, but if she felt for him a fraction of what he felt for her, they were both in big trouble.

"Did . . . did everybody leave?" she asked, her voice shaky.

Luke nodded. "They didn't want to wake you, and it's awfully late."

"The shooting." Sofie sat up straighter and gripped his hand. "What happened? Was anybody hurt?"

"No, everything's fine now." He looked at their hands joined on the arm of the chair, their fingers intertwined.

Intimately.

If only it were their legs.

Holy shit. He bolted off the ottoman and walked toward the fire. The flames danced and crackled, their warmth seeping through his bones. He drew a deep breath and looked upward at the ceiling.

Something had to give soon. He couldn't take much more of this pretense. And tomorrow, to top it all off, he had to marry two people he respected and cared about.

Illegally.

Dr. Taylor and Mrs. Fleming would live in sin, but they wouldn't realize it. Did that make it all right? Not really, but at least they'd be together, and that made it sort of all right.

Luke straightened and turned to face Sofie again. He wanted desperately to confide in her, to tell her he wasn't a priest, and that he wanted nothing more than to take her to bed and make mad, passionate love to her.

All night. Every night.

His gut clenched and burned. It was the *every* night part that worried him. All night was perfectly understandable, after all, but every night was dangerous as hell.

Terrifying.

She rose from the chair and took a tentative step toward him, her heart shining in her eyes.

Oh, God. She wanted every night, too. At least he knew he wasn't a priest, but she didn't. Having the hots for a supposed priest must be giving her a mountain of guilt.

He could tell her the truth, then he could jump her bones and—

Man, what was he thinking? Here he'd spent weeks masquerading as a priest to protect his identity from the only person who could ever reveal his past, and now he was ready to throw it all away for . . .

His gaze drifted down the slender column of her throat, where the loose-fitting, borrowed dress gaped open at the collar. Remembering the night he'd watched her through the window at the schoolhouse, Luke's mouth went dry. She had the most beautiful breasts. Even lying flat on her back that night, they'd been full and round. Tempting.

And that tattoo . . . What he wouldn't give to kiss her butterfly.

Kiss her butterfly? You're losing it, Nolan.

She paused a few feet away and stared at him, her lips parted enticingly, her hair curling wildly around her small face. The love he saw in her eyes stole his breath, even more shattering than the desire he'd seen earlier.

Sofie was falling in love with him, and his feelings for her could very well be—

No.

"I had a dream," she whispered, clasping her hands in front of her. "A very . . . vivid dream."

Oh, God. He was as good as nuked. "A dream?" Though he shouldn't ask, he wanted to hear every delicious detail. Then he'd march upstairs and throw himself out a second-story window. All right, so he wouldn't do that, but he had to do something to relieve this sexual frustration.

"Um-hmm." Her voice fell to a husky whisper, inciting hormonal Armageddon in Luke's body.

"Do you"—he cleared his throat—"want to tell me about your dream, Sofie?"

She nodded, and the pain that stabbed through Luke might as well have been a sword cleaving him in two. "Tell me," he urged, knowing he should run upstairs, but he couldn't. "Confession is good for the soul." *Bad boy.*

"I was swimming," she said, taking another step toward him. "Skinny-dipping."

Oh, shit. Oh, damn. Oh, man. Luke shouldn't encourage her to share this dream, but he wasn't about to stop her at this point. "I see," he said, his voice cracking.

She tilted her head back and a small smile curved her lips. "Yes, it was a . . . a naughty dream, I suppose."

"We all have those." Luke wanted to share her naughty dream more than anything he'd *ever* wanted. Even more than he'd wanted that toy train for Christmas.

Even more than he wanted his freedom?

There was no reason he couldn't have both, to a certain extent. No reason he couldn't fantasize about the impossible. "I'm listening," he whispered, clenching his fists to resist the urge to touch her again.

She gave a nervous laugh and looked away for a moment, then met his gaze again. "I wasn't alone in my dream," she confessed, biting her lower lip. "Like I said, it was naughty. *I* was naughty."

"Not alone?" Luke repeated, struggling for a deep breath. He needed to move away from the fire, though the fire in his groin would follow him. "Who . . . ?"

Her tongue slipped out to moisten her lips, sending shock waves of longing through Luke. To taste those lips again would be pure heaven. He'd never forget that night in her room, when she'd kissed him the way a woman kisses a man she wants.

Kiss me . . .

Now, Luke. Now.

"There was a man in my dream," she said, jerking Luke's attention back to the present. "A very handsome man."

"Someone you remember?" He prayed that wasn't the case. After all, she'd called *his* name.

"Someone I know," she said, smiling sadly. "Someone I want to know better, but that's impossible."

Yes, impossible.

"Do . . . do I know this man?" Luke was fishing, but he couldn't stop himself.

She nodded slowly and gazed deeply into his eyes. "Yes," she whispered. "God forgive me, but the man in my dream . . . was you."

"Oh." He tried to swallow, but failed.

Her lower lip trembled and she brought her fingertips

to her mouth. "I must be bad. Mrs. Fleming said nice women don't think about . . . about that."

Luke drew a deep breath. "About . . . sex?" His voice squeaked. Actually *squeaked.*

She nodded vigorously, one lone tear trickling down her face. "It's wrong to want a . . . a priest," she whispered, covering her face with both hands.

Her misery struck a chord deep inside Luke. Only wanting to comfort her—*really*—he reached out and drew her against him. She came willingly, throwing her arms around his waist as her tears fell against his shirt. Her entire body trembled with the force of her crying.

He stroked her hair and held her tightly against his chest, savoring the close contact with a woman he'd grown to care about more than he dared. Much more.

Her firm breasts pressed into his chest, and the feel of her slender body against his made him burn. His need to comfort her waned in light of a far less noble urge.

Lust. Plain, old-fashioned lust.

She hiccuped and sniffled, then tilted her face up to meet his gaze. Her lips were swollen from crying, and so close . . .

"Sofie," he whispered, pulling her even more tightly against him. "Sofie."

She brought her hand to his cheek and brushed her thumb across his lower lip. "Tell me how I can feel this way about you?" Shaking her head, she added, "And why I can't convince my heart that it's wrong? It doesn't *feel* wrong to . . . to . . ."

Luke rubbed her back with the flat of his palm, afraid to answer. Fire burned in his gut, flared in his groin, and threatened to incinerate him on the spot. He should pull away from her, rush up the stairs, and forget about her dream, about touching her, about kissing her, about making love to her.

But he couldn't. God help him, he just couldn't.

She dropped her hand to his shoulder and rested her head beside it. Gazing down at the top of her head, he thought nothing could feel as right as Sofie in his arms. *Nothing*.

Was his fate not only to save Zeke and Shane from hanging, but also to love Sofie? There was that word again. *Love*.

He couldn't escape it any more than he could stop wanting her. Needing her.

She was in his blood, under his skin, and every other cliché he could think of. She was the balm to soothe him, and the weapon to destroy him. Sofie was everything, rolled up in a sexy little package that would be the death of him yet.

"Luke?"

And now she was using his real name. Even that flimsy barrier was gone. He swallowed the lump in his throat. "Yes?"

"Why can't—don't—priests . . ."

He stopped breathing and cupped her face in both hands, bringing her gaze up to meet his. Right or wrong, this *thing* between them would not be denied.

But it wasn't wrong. Not really. And it wasn't fair not to tell her the truth.

"I'm a man, Sofie," he whispered, inching closer to her lips. "You're a woman and I'm a man."

"But—"

Unwilling to hear her protests, Luke silenced her with his lips. Gentle at first, then harder, he kissed her completely, thoroughly.

She moaned, drawing his tongue into her warm mouth. Through their multiple layers of clothing, she pressed her hips against his, and Luke came unhinged.

Like a wild animal released from its cage, he crushed her to him. Deepening their kiss, he cupped her sweet bottom in his hands and lifted her up and against him.

The urge to sample the treasure hidden within the folds of her Victorian skirt shattered his self-control.

Recklessly, he urged her down to the rug before the fire, never breaking their kiss. He covered her slim body with his own, devouring her sweet lips, stroking her warm tongue in a parody of what he wanted to do with the rest of his body.

Once buried deep inside her, he would find the release he so desperately needed. She whimpered against him and pulled him closer still, encouraging him to follow through with what they both wanted.

Desire. Hot, molten, controlling. It washed through him in wave after wave, increasing with every breath, every stroke of her tongue against his, every beat of his heart.

Pulsing and merging as one, they strained against each other, their mouths committing the act their fully clothed bodies craved. He maneuvered his hand between them and released the endless row of tiny buttons at the front of her dress.

Skin. He wanted skin. Her skin.

A drawstring held her archaic undergarment closed. Impatient, he jerked it free and eased his hand inside, savoring the feel of her satiny flesh against his palm at last.

He maneuvered his lips from hers and across the delicate slant of her jaw, then down her silken throat. Holding his breath, he rested his mouth against her pulse, doing the Macarena in the side of her neck, mimicking the frantic beat of his own heart.

Slowly, he slid his hand along her exposed skin, stroking the soft slope of her breast, trembling with the need to taste where he touched. Though she was a tiny thing, her breasts were full. Tempting.

With shaking fingers, he found her rigid nipple, gently stroking, then rolling it between his thumb and index finger. Her moan incited and enticed him and he suckled the tender skin at the side of her throat, wishing it were her breast pressed against his mouth.

"Oh, Luke," she whispered, stroking his back and cupping his buns in her hands.

The need to taste her was nearly his undoing. Hurriedly, he pushed aside her gaping dress and cupped her breast. When he lifted his face from her neck and gazed down at her beauty, his breath caught and his hunger swelled to something with a life all its own.

But she was too beautiful, too special to rush. Slowly, he lowered his mouth to her breast, circling her nipple with his tongue. A moan rumbled from his diaphragm as she locked her fingers behind his neck and urged him closer still.

Then, trembling, he closed his lips over her and drew her nipple deeply into his mouth. Ambrosia. The nectar of the gods.

This was heaven.

Then a little girl's scream of terror turned heaven into hell.

Chapter Twelve

Sofie's blood froze in her veins at the sound of Jenny's scream. Was the killer in the house? After the little girl? *No, please no.*

Luke lurched to his feet, abandoning Sofie on the rug before the fire. She sat up too quickly and a wave of dizziness assailed her, but soon she was rushing up the stairs behind Luke.

Jenny had to be all right. Sofie would never forgive herself if anything had happened to the little girl while her protectors wallowed on the floor downstairs.

Another scream rent the air. Luke flew down the hall and threw open the door. Sofie followed him into the room, both reaching the little girl at almost the same time.

Luke dropped to his knees beside the bed and grabbed Jenny's shoulders, but the child only screamed again and he jerked back as if stung. Her eyes were closed. She was asleep.

"She's having a nightmare," Sofie said, sitting on the

other side of the bed and placing a firm but gentle hand on the girl's shoulder.

Luke met her gaze from across the bed, his expression wretched. Guilt, of course. Sofie knew it well.

"I'll check the window, just in case."

Sofie merely nodded, knowing the windows and doors of the house were secure. No one was here but them. No one but Jenny to stop a priest and a fallen woman from a roll in the hay.

Jenny tensed and whimpered, and Sofie gently shook her, prepared for her to awaken terrified. Where had Sofie learned about nightmares and about children? From her mother? From medical school? From personal experience?

Except her most recent dreams had been anything but nightmares.

"Noooooo," Jenny moaned, bolting upright in the bed, her eyes wide with terror.

"Shh, it's all right." Sofie held her at arm's length so Jenny could see her face. "I'm here, Jenny. No one will hurt you. It was just a bad dream."

"I'm here, too, Jenny," Luke said from behind Sofie.

"Yes, sweetie." Sofie bit her lower lip. "Father Salazar is here, too."

Father Salazar, not Luke. And don't forget it again.

She felt his gaze on her but didn't dare turn around to face him. Besides, she needed to make sure Jenny was all right.

The little girl blinked several times in the dim light, looking from one to the other of them. Luke went to the nightstand and turned up the flame on the lamp until a cheerful golden glow chased away the shadows.

"I'm sorry," Jenny said, drawing a shaky breath. "Were you in bed?"

"Not yet," Luke said, and Sofie looked up at him sharply, noticing the crimson stain creeping up from his open collar. "Er, no."

"Did I scream?" Jenny trembled and Sofie gathered her in her arms.

The child didn't shed a tear, though Sofie felt her misery and her terror. "You know, Jenny," she said quietly, "after you tell us the man's name, you won't have any reason to be afraid anymore."

"That's right." Luke sat on the edge of the bed. "Marshal Weathers will put him in jail and you'll never have to be afraid again."

Jenny shook her head and pulled back slightly, her gaze dropping to Sofie's gaping bodice. "You're undone."

"Undone?" Sofie frowned, then noticed the direction of Jenny's gaze. Unfortunately, she also felt Luke's gaze on her exposed flesh as she quickly tucked herself inside and buttoned her dress. "I was, uh, getting ready for bed."

Getting ready for bed . . . ?

Luke cleared his throat, but Sofie refused to look at him again. Shame slithered through her. "Are you all right now, Jenny?" she asked, hoping her voice didn't reveal her own terror. "Do you want me to stay with you?"

Jenny appeared thoughtful, then shook her head. "No, I'm a big girl."

"You certainly are," Luke whispered, stroking the top of the child's head, then he planted a kiss on her forehead as he stood. "You're a very *good* girl, too, but you yell if you need anything during the night. We'll be just down the hall."

In separate rooms. Sofie ignored the pang of regret that stabbed through her. How she would love to spend the night making love with Luke, then sleep in his arms, sated and exhausted.

With Luke, *not* with Father Salazar. But they were one and the same man.

Don't do this. She should be thankful for Jenny's nightmare, though she couldn't wish such terror on the child.

Still, if not for Jenny's scream, by now she and Luke probably would have—

Oh, my God.

Heat suffused her as she stood beside Jenny's bed. The
little girl settled back against the snowy pillow, her blond
hair hanging over her shoulder in a single braid.

"Thank you," Jenny said sleepily, then yawned. "I'm
fine now."

"Pleasant dreams, sweetheart." Sofie kissed the child's
cheek.

Luke stooped to tuck the quilt more securely around
Jenny's shoulders, then turned down the lamp and followed Sofie into the hall. He pulled the door shut behind
them, and she decided to make a break for it. Hurriedly,
she took several steps down the hall before Luke grabbed
her shoulder.

"We have to talk," he said, halting her escape. "We
can't just—"

"No." Tears blurred her vision and her heart swelled,
pushing upward against her throat. "No, we mustn't talk
about . . . about . . ."

"Sofie, I . . ." His hands fell limply to his sides and
the sorrow in his voice cleaved into her. "I'm sorry," he
whispered, shaking his head slowly. "So very sorry."

Scalding tears welled up in her eyes and spilled down
her cheeks. She didn't bother to blink them back, or to
wipe them away, because there were far too many.

Tears for forbidden love.

Tears for the past she couldn't remember.

Tears for the future that could never be.

Luke watched Sofie run away, scurrying into her room
across the hall as if he were the devil himself. In many
ways, he was much worse than that.

Exhaustion ebbed through him and he stood in the

hallway for several moments, helplessness settling over him with every tick of the grandfather clock downstairs. When it struck one o'clock, he forced himself to trudge down the stairs to check the doors, and to bank the fire.

He stood for several moments at the base of the stairs, gripping the bannister with all his strength. The woman he loved—yes, *loved*—was up there, and in his gut, he knew she loved him, too. He could ease her guilt over wanting a priest by telling her the simple truth.

And, just maybe, they could be together. *Really* together.

But what if hearing the truth triggered her memory? How would she feel about him then? Which was worse? Loving a priest or a convicted murderer?

His feet felt like lead weights as Luke climbed the stairs. He had to pass Sofie's closed door on his way to his room at the far end of the hall. His heart thudded loud and strong as he paused and placed his hand on the crystal doorknob.

Resting his forehead against the cool wood, he remembered the warmth of her lips, the softness of her breast filling his hand, the taste of her on his tongue . . .

Then a sound drifted through the door, and he turned to press his ear to the panel. She was crying.

Damn. Luke tightened his grip on the doorknob, visualizing himself entering her room and taking her in his arms. He would tell her everything, and make her tears stop. He could ease her guilt, and confess his love, and—

Risk losing everything, including her.

Closing his eyes, he summoned memories of the electric chair to strengthen his decision. Then he remembered his grandfather's shame, and pushed away from the door.

Luke Nolan had a job to finish in Redemption, then he had to walk away from the town and from Sofie.

No matter how much it hurt.

She'd get over him eventually and start a new life for herself here. Even if she did remember Luke Nolan's true identity one day and how they'd come to be here in 1891, it wouldn't matter.

He'd be long gone.

Doggedly, he went to his room and pulled off his clothes, leaving them in a pile beside the bed. He needed sleep, but the cool night air encircling his body revived him.

Swallowing hard, Luke looked down at his throbbing erection. Sweat burst from every pore as he closed his eyes and remembered the feel of Sofie pressing her hips ardently against him. Again, he pondered how it would feel to peel away her voluminous skirts and hold her that way again.

He shuddered. Raw, primal hunger coursed through him.

His blood flow concentrated itself in one part of his body, with one goal in mind. Dizzy with desire, Luke staggered to bed and climbed beneath the covers. Curled onto his side, he clenched his legs together and gnashed his teeth, praying the insistent throb would pass and that sleep would send him into oblivion.

Soon.

Instead, when he closed his eyes, he saw his hand against her bare breast, the peace sign tattoo winking at him. He tasted the petal-like nub of her nipple against his tongue. And he heard her moans of pleasure.

"Now, Luke. Now."

"I was naughty . . . skinny-dipping."

"Skinny-dipping . . ." Fatigue won at last and he fell into a troubled sleep.

Sofie awakened early, determined to get her thoughts and her behavior back on track today. She'd lain awake for hours, considering what had almost happened with Father Salazar.

In the light of day, she knew one thing for certain. She would not be a party to any priest breaking his holy vows.

Even though he'd been a willing and *very* active participant in their tumble on the floor?

Yes, even so.

She pulled her wet hair back in a tight bun at the nape of her neck, determined to make herself as unattractive as possible. Dora's baggy dress went a long way toward achieving that. Sofie's breasts were practically indiscernible beneath the loose fabric.

But as she buttoned the front of her dress, the inside of her wrist brushed against her nipple, reminding her of Luke's caresses. And his mouth. *Oh, God, his mouth.*

"No," she whispered, setting her lips in a thin line of determination. He wasn't Luke. She mustn't think of him as anyone other than Father Salazar—a Catholic priest who'd taken a vow of celibacy.

She paused to stare in the mirror, a question ricocheting around in her frazzled mind. Shaking her head, she decided it was a question better left unasked, even of herself.

However, it refused to remain silent. She had to wonder, though she doubted she'd ever know the answer.

Had Father Salazar broken his vows before?

She groaned and leaned on the nightstand with the palms of both hands, staring deeply into her own guilty gaze. Blinking, she jerked away from the mirror and smoothed her skirt.

It didn't matter whether or not he'd broken his vows before, because she wouldn't be a party to him breaking them again, even if it wasn't the first time. "So there."

As she opened her bedroom door and peered down the hall, she ignored the voice in the back of her mind reminding her of his kisses, his touch, the impressive and undeniable evidence of his desire at the front of his jeans . . .

A priest. He was a priest.

Squaring her shoulders, she turned her back on his bedroom door and went downstairs to start breakfast. Mrs. Fleming had left her something called sourdough, and it was time Sofie made friends with it.

At the bottom of the stairs, her gaze zeroed in on the square of carpet before the now cold hearth, where she'd lain in his arms. Her breath froze in her throat and she stood paralyzed, visualizing herself on the floor beneath Luke's passionate kisses.

She swallowed, trying to drag her gaze from that spot, and her thoughts from those memories. She had to stop thinking about him, and about *that*. Especially about that . . .

A tremor chased itself through her body and she drew a deep, fortifying breath. Determined, she marched into the kitchen.

Her heart leapt upward, pressing against her throat, and she swayed, grabbing the door frame for support. There stood Luke, an apron tied around his waist and singing a familiar tune—"Knights in White Satin"—as he kneaded dough.

"Good morning," he called over his shoulder. "I don't know what I'm doing in here, you know."

Sofie shook her head. "Neither do I." That was a major understatement.

"There was a cookbook, so I thought I'd try." He shrugged and gave her a boyish grin.

Her knees grew weak, but she quickly reminded herself what he was, and about his vows. She would not be a participant in breaking those vows. No way.

"I made coffee." He inclined his head toward a pot on the stove. "It isn't too bad."

Deciding to keep herself busy, she poured herself a cup of coffee and took a sip. It was scalding hot, so she set it on the table to cool.

Sunlight streamed into the kitchen, triggering another

memory of the dark-haired woman. Her mother. As the weeks went by, Sofie had become more and more convinced of the woman's identity.

She saw her mother hurrying around the kitchen, pushing buttons and flipping switches. They'd had a microwave oven, an electric range, and automatic everything. She remembered a well-stocked refrigerator, and she could see herself going there after school and getting a can of soda.

These memories were *real,* and those appliances *existed.* She looked around the kitchen again. Why was Redemption so backward?

And Luke—Father Salazar—had answers. He had to.

"Mrs. Fleming left a ham wrapped in a cloth here," he said, placing his biscuits in a baking pan. "I guess it's all right, though I'd feel better if it had come from the supermarket."

Yes, the supermarket. "Luke," she said, grateful to have something besides her hormones to occupy her thoughts. "I mean, Father Salazar . . ."

"Luke," he corrected, placing his pan of biscuits in the oven.

Deciding not to comment on his name, Sofie said, "I remember so many things that don't exist here."

He stared at her for several minutes, then turned his attention to the ham on the counter. He looked worried. "Like what?" he finally asked.

Sofie went to the table, where Luke sawed off thin slices of ham and placed them in an iron skillet. "Like electricity, telephones, TV, cars, airplanes, and all kinds of stuff. Music and movies, too. That song you were singing when I came in—I remember that, too. The Moody Blues. Right?"

He looked at her quickly, his mouth set in a thin line. Yes, he definitely looked worried, but why? "You remember those things, too," she stated, rather than asked. "Otherwise, how could you have been singing that song?"

Pausing, he stood there staring at the ham, then looked

up at her with an unreadable expression. "I guess Redemption seems sort of . . . old-fashioned." He shrugged unconvincingly. "It's no biggie, though."

"*We're* different." She grabbed his wrist, already breaking her promise not to touch him. "We talk different, act different, think different. Why?"

He sliced more ham—enough to feed several grown men. It didn't take a rocket scientist to realize he was avoiding her question.

"Answer me," she whispered, now completely convinced he was hiding something. "You know more about me than you've admitted. Don't you?"

Still not looking at her, he asked, "What have you remembered?"

"Not much." She released his wrist and sat at the table, wrapping her hands around her coffee cup. "My mother, I think, and like I told you before, music and things that seem so . . . so normal. Kitchen things. Appliances. Light switches."

He looked at her, and she saw his Adam's apple run up and down his throat. "That's all?"

"And you," she admitted, her voice growing husky. "I saw an image of you in a cold place, with steel and lots of people rushing around."

His face blanched, and his knuckles turned white from his death grip on the knife.

"I was there, too," she continued, though he stared past her at something she suspected only he could see. "I think you were a patient and I was your doctor. Is that true?"

His eyes widened and he met her gaze. "What gave you that idea?"

"The place I remembered was so sterile and cold, and you were wearing what I think was a hospital gown." She shook her head in frustration. "If only I could remember more."

"Trust me, Sofie, you don't *want* to remember."

An intense undercurrent flowed through his words, enough to make her decide to temporarily postpone her interrogation. She would save her questions for now, but she would ask them later.

And somehow, she knew this man—this *priest*—had all the answers. Including the solution to her sexual frustration.

Why couldn't she get it through her head that he was off limits as a lover? Simple. Because last night he'd taken her in his arms and treated her the way a man treats a woman he wants to know in the biblical sense.

Willingly.

"I think we need to talk about last night," he said, setting his knife aside and carrying the heavy skillet to the hot stove. "About what happened."

Heat flashed in her face and she clenched her fists in her lap. Staying here in this house with him would be the death of her yet. If only Jenny would tell Marshal Weathers the killer's name. "No, I don't want to talk about . . . that."

He wrapped the ham in a cloth, then took it to the pantry at the far end of the room, away from the stove's heat. When he returned, he slipped off the apron and hung it over the back of a chair before taking a seat at the table.

"What happened between us last night," he began, avoiding her gaze as he spoke, "mustn't happen again."

Sofie stared at him in shock. Though she agreed with him, she hadn't expected to hear him say it. "I . . . I know." Her stomach lurched and she took a sip of the bitter coffee, trying not to swallow any grounds. "And it won't happen again."

"No, it won't."

He sounded disappointed, and Sofie looked directly at him, stunned to find him watching her now. His expression was sincere, and regret showed itself plainly across his handsome face.

Even though they were both determined to deny themselves, knowing he regretted that sent a thrill through Sofie. She really was bad. Well, that was something she would change. The new Dr. Sofie What's-Her-Name would be good, even by Mrs. Fleming's standards.

She swallowed hard and looked at his hands, resting on the table. Those same hands had touched her last night and made her want him.

But the new Dr. Sofie What's-Her-Name *would* be good. Even if it killed her.

Chapter Thirteen

Luke needed to keep as much distance from Sofie as possible. Not an easy task, considering they were living together. Jenny Latimer didn't make much of a chaperon, though her nightmare had been perfectly timed. Another few minutes . . .

Damn. He had to stop thinking about what had almost happened. But they'd come so close. *Cut the crap, Nolan.*

Sweat trickled down the sides of his face as he made his way through town. The weather was unseasonably mild for early October at this altitude, but he knew winter would soon arrive in earnest. The few morning snows they'd seen so far were nothing compared to what nature could bring in the coming weeks.

And Luke had to get the hell out of town before he found himself snowed in for the longest winter of his life.

Last night's near miss with Sofie had convinced him that his days as a priest were numbered. The sooner he could leave and resume life as a red-blooded male unfettered by vows of celibacy, the better. He'd forgotten how soft a woman's skin could—

"Jeez, Nolan." He kicked at a rock alongside the road, banishing the image of Sofie and her soft skin from his mind. He had to.

Besides, he had a wedding to postpone.

He'd never visited Dr. Taylor at his office before, which was located in the rear of his small house in the center of town. Luke paused near the sign at the back door, indicating the doctor was in.

He knocked lightly and the door swung open. Roman's sleeves were rolled up to his elbows and his thick white hair stood on end. He looked like the crazy "Doc" from *Back to the Future*.

"Come in." Roman stepped aside and started to roll down his sleeves. "I don't know what's come over me this morning. I overslept for the first time in years, and I can't seem to keep my mind on anything at all."

Prewedding jitters, Luke decided. Well, as far as he was concerned, there would be no wedding in Redemption today. That would put an end to the groom's anxiety.

"Nervous?" he asked, then smiled when the doctor rolled his eyes toward the ceiling.

"Nervous?" Roman dropped his comb, then bent to retrieve it. He dropped it twice more before managing to run it through his hair. "Beyond nervous. I'm more terrified today than I ever was during the war."

Luke grew solemn, considering the impact of his decision not to perform the ceremony. Would Roman change his mind completely? Would he and Mrs. Fleming ever marry if Luke refused to do the deed?

Just what he needed—more guilt. Dr. Taylor and Mrs. Fleming belonged together, and Luke really saw nothing wrong with people who loved each other living as man and wife, legally or not. Of course, he also realized that

Roman Taylor and Anna Fleming would never willingly "live in sin."

"It's a good thing you're here now," Roman said, fumbling with some instruments on a tray near the window. "If I had too much time to think about this, I'm afraid I'd turn yellow and run for the hills."

Talk about twisting the knife. "No, you wouldn't." If Dr. Taylor had been able to read Luke's mind, he couldn't have done any better at echoing his thoughts. "But you love Mrs. Fleming."

"More than my own life." Dr. Taylor dropped an instrument and stooped to retrieve it. "But I've been single all my life, Luke. The thought of getting married at my age . . ."

Luke swallowed the lump in his throat, mentally watching his arguments against the wedding crumble. If he didn't marry Roman and Anna tonight, they might never go through with it.

And if ever two people belonged together . . .

Like me and Sofie?

No, that was dangerous territory. Shoving thoughts of Sofie from his mind, Luke crossed the room and placed his hand on the doctor's shoulder. A sense of defeat washed through him, and he sighed. "You're doing the right thing."

And I'm screwed.

"Thanks. I really needed that reassurance." Roman gave him a weak smile.

"No problem." Luke had enough problems for the whole frigging town.

Dr. Taylor visibly relaxed and finished arranging his instruments. "I've been wondering about your plans, now that the epidemic is over."

"Plans?" Luke wasn't sure he wanted to go there.

"Well, surely you and Sofie were going somewhere else originally."

Flustered, Luke ran his hand across his hair and

searched his mind for answers. For lies, rather. "Right, of course. I was due in Denver weeks ago."

"Ah, Denver." Roman looked in a small book and frowned. "Winter will be here before we know it. I suppose you'll want to be on your way before then."

"Yes, that's true." Luke sat in a chair beside the doctor's desk, trying to ignore the burning in his gut.

"And what about Sofie?" Dr. Taylor sat down at his desk and leaned back, tapping a pencil against his knuckles. "What do you know about her, other than her profession?"

"Not much." Except that she had the most perfect breasts Luke had ever seen, and her skin was as soft and smooth as—

He swallowed hard and mentally kicked himself. "We were in an explosion, which is how she got her head injury." *That's no lie.*

"And her memory loss," Dr. Taylor added.

Yes, thank God. Guilt pressed down on Luke again. All these weeks of feeling thankful for Sofie's amnesia were wearing. Even so, he was still relieved she hadn't remembered who or what he was.

Though this morning she'd mentioned a scrap of memory that could build into something much more significant. The cold, sterile room she'd described could only have been the execution chamber.

With the electric chair.

A chill swept through him and Luke suppressed a shiver. However, remembering the electric chair always helped him get his priorities straight. *Freedom.* He didn't dare let anything matter more than that.

Yet he had. Repeatedly. The town, the people, his new friends . . . and Sofie. They all mattered.

Damn.

"That explosion," the doctor said thoughtfully, "must've been a mining accident of some kind."

Luke shrugged, *definitely* not wanting to go there.

"I appreciate you and Sofie staying on until this matter with Jenny and Shane is settled." The doctor shook his head and sighed. "Between the quarantine and this mess, I think Anna may be right about you both being sent here by God Himself. And what about Sam Weathers? Amazing, him showing up when he did."

Luke nodded. "Yeah." His voice sounded strained, even to himself. Time for him to make some sort of announcement, rather than leave things indefinite, as they had been. After all, Dr. Taylor had already given him an opening. "As soon as this is resolved, though, I have to get to Denver."

"Of course, I understand." Roman appeared thoughtful. "We'll miss you and Sofie."

Me and *Sofie?*

"And I know a doctor in Denver who might be able to help her."

"But . . . why would she want to go with me?" Luke gave a nervous laugh. Too nervous?

Roman arched a bushy white eyebrow. "I just assumed, since you arrived together, that you'd leave together."

"Oh, well, that would be her decision." *Liar.* Luke had no intention of taking Sofie with him when he left. And after last night, chances were she wouldn't want to go anywhere with him anyway.

After all, he was nothing more than a libidinous priest.

"I have to check Mr. Smith's wounds." Roman stood and grabbed a small box off a shelf. "Dora made a soft hood for him. I'm not sure how he'll feel about wearing it, but I imagine once he gets a look at himself . . ."

Luke grimaced. "You mean he hasn't seen himself yet?"

"No." The doctor sighed and lifted the gray hood from the box. "He's healed enough to discontinue the dressings, but I doubt he'll want anyone to see his face."

Luke had to agree. He'd seen enough of Mr. Smith's burns to realize how hideous his scars were. "Has he given you any information yet?"

"He tried to talk some last night."

"And?"

"Nothing I could understand, but I'm going to see if he can write something now."

"Good idea."

Dr. Taylor tucked a small slate under his arm and dropped a piece of chalk into his pocket. "Business is slow this morning, thank God."

"No kidding." Luke stood and shoved his hands in his pockets, concerned that he'd left too much unresolved with Dr. Taylor. "Like you said before, once things are settled with Shane and Jenny, I'll be on my way."

"I hope Sofie will want to see Dr. Bowen in Denver." Roman walked across the room, toward an adjoining doorway. "He's the only man I know who might be able to help her."

Help Sofie? In his heart, Luke wanted only the best for her, but as long as she was stranded in this time, maybe not remembering was the most merciful thing. And he knew it was best for him, but he tried not to dwell on that.

"Maybe Smith will be able to write his real name for me soon, so I can send word to his family." Dr. Taylor moved toward the adjoining room.

Luke couldn't help remembering the maniacal look on Smith's face last night. It made no sense. It must have been a fluke, or a reaction to the drugs.

"That man had murder in his eyes . . . make no mistake," Marshal Weathers had said.

"I guess I'll see you tonight then." Roman paused and exhaled in a loud *whoosh*. "If I live that long."

Luke chuckled, though he felt more like crying. "You'll do fine," he said quietly. "I'd better go back to the parsonage and practice this wedding stuff."

Dr. Taylor gave a nervous laugh and pushed open the door. "Thanks." He slipped through the doorway.

Luke stared at the door for several moments, gathering

his resolve. By God, this would be his final act as a priest. Enough was enough.

"*Go with God, my son,*" the real Father Salazar had said.

Luke was certain joining unsuspecting people in less-than-holy matrimony wasn't quite what the old man had intended.

Sofie spent the rest of the day in the kitchen with Jenny. At ten, the little girl knew how to cook everything, including sourdough biscuits.

When Sofie'd first looked into the crock containing Mrs. Fleming's "starter," she'd almost dumped the mess out the back door. Gross was the only word to describe the fermented, bubbling *stuff*. However, Jenny assured her it was supposed to look and smell rotten.

Besides, learning to cook helped keep Sofie's mind off Luke, and gave her another opportunity to gain Jenny's trust. She hoped the child would confess the name of her father's killer soon. Their isolation for Jenny's protection had just begun, and already they had to miss a wedding.

"Where's Father Salazar?" Jenny asked late in the afternoon. The child stood at the table, stirring flour into cake batter. "I haven't seen him since this morning."

Thank goodness. Sofie's hormones needed the reprieve. "He's practicing the wedding ceremony."

"I wish we could go."

"Well, we can't." Sofie sighed dramatically, but didn't remind Jenny why they couldn't go to the wedding. That was far from necessary.

Jenny made a face but kept stirring. After a while, she poured the batter into pans and slid them into the oven. "We'll make frosting after these come out," she said. "They have to cool first anyway."

Sofie stuck her finger in the bowl and tasted the remaining batter. "Mmm, you're pretty good at this, kid."

With flour on the tip of her nose, Jenny smiled, then her expression grew solemn. "My mama taught me."

Sofie gave Jenny a hug. "I know, and you'll always have the things she taught you. Nobody can ever take those from you."

"But you don't remember."

Sofie shook her head and sighed. "Nothing before the day I came here." But that wasn't exactly true. She had begun to recall disjointed fragments of her past. Maybe someday there'd be enough scraps to piece into something as substantial as a lifetime. She could only hope.

"Can't Father Salazar help you remember stuff?"

Sofie shook her head and bit the inside of her cheek to silence what she really wanted to say. How could she continue to want him sexually, knowing he might very well be withholding information about her past? Maybe if she kept reminding herself of that fact, she'd have better luck managing her libido.

But his lips. His hands. She swallowed hard.

A knock at the back door jerked Sofie's thoughts into a safer zone. "Saved by the bell," she said, earning a curious frown from her cooking instructor. She peeked through the curtain first, then opened the door for Dr. Taylor.

Removing his hat, he sniffed the air appreciatively, while Sofie closed and bolted the door behind him. "Mmm, something smells wonderful in here."

"Wedding cake," Jenny announced with a grin.

Dr. Taylor blushed a bright shade of crimson against his white hair. "That's nice of you, Miss Jenny. Thank you."

"You're welcome." Jenny sighed dramatically. "I wish I could go."

"I wish you could, too." Dr. Taylor turned to Sofie. "I tried the front door first, but no one answered."

"Someone is practicing the wedding ceremony."

Dr. Taylor's blush deepened, and he cleared his throat. "Do you have a few minutes?"

Sofie nodded and offered the doctor a chair at the table. She should probably have taken him to the other room, where they'd be more comfortable, but she didn't want to interrupt or face Luke just yet. This would do.

"I mentioned this to Luke this morning, but I thought maybe I should discuss it with you, too, while it's on my mind."

What could Dr. Taylor possibly have to discuss with both Luke and Sofie? Taking a chair at the table, she folded her hands in her lap and said, "I'm listening."

Jenny went to the pantry to search for something, and Dr. Taylor leaned toward Sofie. "I know a doctor in Denver who specializes in head injuries, especially involving amnesia," he said quietly, pulling an envelope from his jacket pocket. "Here's a letter of introduction. If anyone can help you, Sofie, it's George Bowen."

Sofie stared at the white envelope bearing Dr. Bowen's name and address in Dr. Taylor's sprawling script. "Denver?" Hesitantly, she took the envelope, then met Dr. Taylor's gaze.

"But how will I get to Denver?" There were no trains or planes, or even cars in Redemption. And she certainly didn't know how to ride a horse. Did she? "Of course, I can't go anywhere until after Jenny . . ."

"No, of course not, and we're very thankful for that." Dr. Taylor glanced toward the pantry, then back at Sofie, his expression sincere and eager. "You're a fine woman and a wonderful doctor. Regaining your memory is important to you and to those you might help with your skills."

Tears scalded her eyes as she met his gaze. "Thank you." She sniffled and dabbed at her tears, then asked, "Are you planning a trip to Denver?" She couldn't very well take off across the mountains alone.

"No, but Luke told me this morning that he was headed there before you two ended up here."

Before the explosion. If only she could remember more about how and why she and Luke were in that cave when it exploded. She knew there was an important clue there somewhere.

Then Sofie realized exactly what Dr. Taylor had meant. He expected her to leave Redemption with Luke. "Why would Father Salazar want to be burdened with me when he leaves for Denver?" Would he truly leave her? A heaviness descended over her entire body at the thought of never seeing Luke again. Then again, no matter how much it hurt, she knew it would probably be for the best.

"Well, that's for the two of you to discuss, but I believe he wants to go before winter really sets in." Dr. Taylor pulled out his watch and popped open the cover, then snapped it closed again. "I'd better go shave and put on my good suit before the meeting."

Sofie forced a smile and rose with Dr. Taylor, trying not to look at the envelope or think about Luke. "So the wedding will be after the town meeting?"

"Yes, and I'm not a bit nervous," he said, winking. "Actually, but don't tell anybody, I'm terrified."

Sofie laughed and walked him to the door. After he'd gone, she rebolted the door and sighed. She would miss the people she'd met here in Redemption.

But that made it seem like she really was planning to leave. She sat at the table again and exhaustion seeped through her, making her feel twice her age—not that she actually knew her age.

Jenny approached the table slowly. When Sofie looked up at the little girl, she saw a worried expression in her dark eyes.

"What is it, Jenny?" She took the child's hand. "Are you all right?"

Jenny nodded. "Are you leaving?" Her lower lip trembled, and a tear trickled down her cheek.

"I . . . I'm not sure, Jenny." And that was the truth. "Dr.

Taylor thinks I should see this doctor in Denver who might be able to help me remember."

Jenny nodded and her tears ceased. "That's good. Everybody should remember their ma . . . mama."

"Yes." Sofie squeezed Jenny's hand and smiled, though she felt more like crying. "And you cherish your memories, sweetie. They're so precious."

Jenny nodded and sat in the chair closest to Sofie. "After I tell . . . who . . ."

Sofie held her breath, waiting for Jenny to finish her statement.

"After that," the child continued, "I'll get to live with Shane?"

"Yes." Sofie knew Sam Weathers was hiding Jenny's brother somewhere safe, and that there should be more than enough evidence to prevent the boy's execution. *Thank God.* "Yes, you will."

Jenny appeared thoughtful, and sat in silence for several moments, resting her chin in her hand. Finally, she lifted her face and looked pointedly at Sofie. "I want you to go . . . go see that doctor in Denver."

"Yes, I suppose I should." Sofie waited, hoping Jenny would say more, but also knowing she shouldn't push too hard. At least now she believed Jenny would eventually tell the killer's name, because then the little girl could be with her brother.

"Maybe that doctor can help you remember *your* mama." Jenny sighed, then squeezed Sofie's hand.

Well, that settled it. Sofie would definitely go to Denver once Jenny was safe.

The pain slashed through her again, and she identified it at last. Sadness and loss. Yes, she'd be leaving Redemption, the only home she could remember.

Sorrow poured over her at the thought of leaving, but she knew the town and its citizens weren't all she would miss. *Luke.* He was her rescuer, her friend, and her weird hero. She smiled sadly. But friendship wasn't all she wanted with him, and that was why she *had* to move forward with her life. She blinked back her tears, vowing to see the doctor in Denver, no matter what.

With or without the man she loved.

The population of Redemption must've tripled for the town meeting and the added bonus of a wedding. About half the people squeezed into the church looked like miners, and a small cluster of women garbed in garish clothing occupied one pew near the front. Luke suspected they were the infamous "Miss Lottie's girls" he'd heard mentioned.

He stood at the back of the small church with Sam Weathers, listening to the citizens offer their thanks to Dr. Taylor, Mrs. Fleming, and the others who'd nursed the epidemic's victims. Then Dr. Taylor the mayor took the podium and thanked Father Salazar and the absent Dr. Sofie, announcing the donation of a bag of gold for them both for their tireless service.

Luke could use the money for his fresh start, but he sure hoped there was a bag of gold somewhere with Dr. Taylor's name on it, too. The man had earned a thousand bags of gold by now.

Roman reiterated what his bride-to-be had said more than once about the two newcomers having been sent by God.

Of course, Luke knew how false that was. He'd come to Redemption straight from hell's clutches. And as a fake priest, he could hardly be considered a servant of God. Maybe Sofie, though . . .

The thought of her sequestered next door with Jenny made his throat tighten. He couldn't get her off his mind or out of his heart, no matter how he tried. Even keeping busy trying to learn the wedding ceremony he would perform tonight hadn't helped much.

Sofie filled his thoughts, triggered his libido, and broke his heart with no effort whatsoever. She was a goddess, a temptress, and a tormentor, in one foxy little bundle.

The townspeople unanimously elected Ab Johnson as their new sheriff. Luke smelled a plant but, in this case, manipulating politics was probably a good thing. Between Ab and Marshal Weathers, they might save Zeke as well as Shane.

"Pay close attention here," Sam whispered. "Unless I miss my guess, all hell's gonna break loose after tonight."

Uh-oh. Luke turned his attention to the podium again, where the mayor swore in the new sheriff. After Ab was officially made sheriff, he faced the townspeople with a solemn expression.

"My first job as your new sheriff is to let y'all know we got us a witness to Charlie Latimer's murder."

A low buzz rippled through the crowd, and Luke realized this was all part of Sam's plan to make the real killer nervous. "Very clever," he whispered, peeking at the marshal.

But Sam Weathers was otherwise occupied, his narrowed gaze sweeping the crowd with an inborn savvy that impressed the hell out of Luke. The lawman obviously knew what, if not who, he was looking for.

Luke just hoped Sam found the killer before the killer found Jenny.

"The witness proves Shane Latimer didn't kill his pa," Ab continued. "So *we* ain't gonna be hangin' that boy, and that's that."

Gasps, applause, and cheers erupted from the crowd, and suddenly Luke knew what Sam Weathers was looking for. Someone would be *very* unhappy about this news.

The real killer.

A movement near the door drew Luke's attention. Shoving his way through the crowd, Frank Latimer looked over his shoulder with an ominous scowl.

"You know that fella," Sam asked, his voice low.

"I know who he is." Luke swallowed hard when Latimer's penetrating gaze fell on him. The man's scowl deepened, then he put on his hat and left. "His name's Frank . . . Latimer."

Sam jerked his attention from the door and pinned Luke with a look that meant business. "Another Latimer?"

Luke nodded. "Shane and Jenny's uncle."

"Well, well." Sam clicked his tongue and shook his head. "You'd think the man'd be happier than a hog in a mud hole about his nephew's neck bein' saved."

A chill raced through Luke as he recalled Shane's reaction to his uncle that day at the jail. "Yeah, you'd think."

"Imagine that."

"Where do you suppose he's headed?"

Sam gave Luke a knowing smile. "The jail." The lawman slapped his Stetson against his thigh. "I'll be back shortly."

Luke tapped the marshal's shoulder. "What about Jenny and Sofie? Will they be safe?"

Sam nodded. "I reckon." He looked beyond Luke, at something it seemed only he could see. After a moment, he patted one of the pistols at his hips. "And I intend to make damn sure they stay that way."

Sam Weathers was one of those men of Western legend. A man of honor, who saw no compromise between right and wrong, and who possessed an uncanny instinct about human nature.

And I sure as hell hope he can't see through me.

"I'll try to get back before the weddin'." Towering over the crowd, Marshal Weathers maneuvered his way through the mass of humanity and out the same door Frank Latimer had used.

Envy and admiration flashed through Luke as he watched the lawman slip through the door and disappear into the night. Sam Weathers had hero written all over him. No wonder Sofie had thought of John Wayne when she first met him.

"Wow," Luke whispered, returning his attention to the podium.

Mayor Taylor banged the gavel on the wood until the crowd quieted and he had their attention. "I think most of us are in agreement about the Latimer boy, so let's move on."

Uh-oh. For a little while, Luke had almost forgotten about the fraud he had to perform this evening. His throat tightened, and he clutched Father Salazar's Bible in his hands. Sweat burst from his pores and his mouth went dry.

God, he didn't want to do this.

"I imagine most of you have heard about the, uh, ceremony we're going to have here tonight."

The crowd roared.

Luke's lips went numb.

"This is sort of informal," Roman continued, "but after what we've all been through these last weeks . . ."

"Get on with the weddin', Doc," someone shouted from the heart of the gathering. A chuckle followed, along with several more shouts of encouragement.

"All right, all right." Redness crept up from the groom-to-be's starched collar until it reached his hairline. "Father Salazar?"

The only time in Luke's life when he'd been more terrified was the morning of his scheduled execution. Breathing became increasingly difficult as faces turned toward him.

Expectantly.

As Grandpa would've said, he'd made his bed, so go lie in it. Slowly, Luke headed toward the podium, the crowd parting before him like the Red Sea.

Get a grip, Nolan.

Someone had made a wreath of pine cones and autumn leaves, which miraculously appeared on the front of the podium. Several additional candles were lit, and by the time Luke reached the front of the church, the place looked ready for a wedding.

A lot more ready than he was.

He was doing the right thing. These people belonged together, and they would accept the marriage as genuine. That was all that mattered. He had to remain focused on that fact. Otherwise, he would fail.

Another promise broken? More guilt?

No way.

He took his place facing the congregation, with the groom to his left. The parting in the Red Sea widened even more, and organ music filled the building. Luke shot a glance toward the far wall, stunned to see one of Miss Lottie's girls playing the church organ. But he didn't have time for a chuckle, because Dora Fleming started toward him, sans bouquet.

After Dora took her place the music grew louder and Mrs. Fleming started toward them. She looked years younger in a light blue dress, her white hair pulled into its usual bun, but with a few tight curls framing her face. Her eyes shone with happiness when she looked at her groom.

Yes, Luke was doing the right thing—the only thing.

The music faded as the bride took her place and slipped her hand into the groom's.

Luke cleared his throat, ignoring the funeral dirge playing through his veins, much like the morning of his failed execution. He cleared his throat again and drew a deep, fortifying breath.

"Dearly beloved . . ."

Chapter Fourteen

Following orders to stay inside with the doors bolted, Sofie listened with a heavy heart to the cheers and applause from the church next door. Though she was thrilled for Dr. Taylor and Mrs. Fleming—Mrs. Taylor, now—she longed to join the celebration. She knew Jenny did, too.

"I wish we could go," Jenny said, echoing Sofie's thoughts.

"I know, sweetheart." Sighing, Sofie poured Jenny a glass of milk and staunchly resisted the urge to look outside. Marshal Weathers had cautioned them to stay away from the windows, because someone—the killer—might see them. If only Jenny would tell . . .

By now the wedding would be over, and the crowd would descend on Miss Lottie's—made temporarily respectable—for the reception. There'd be dancing. Sofie closed her eyes for a moment, picturing herself in Luke's arms, swaying to the rhythm of soft jazz or rock. Of course, Redemption probably only allowed country music and square dancing.

She smiled despite her melancholy. The town might be backward, but it was still a special place. Her smile faded as she considered why it was special to her. Redemption was the only home she'd ever known.

She pulled out a chair at the kitchen table across from Jenny, and stared toward the shuttered window near the back door. Determination welled within her as she sat down. Somehow, she would find a way to see the specialist in Denver. She *would* regain her memory.

And her home.

"Everybody oughta remember their mama," Jenny had said.

Truer words were never spoken. Resigned, Sofie scooped up a spoonful of the soup she had helped Jenny prepare. "Mmm, not bad, kid."

Jenny smiled, though it didn't reach her eyes. She sighed and looked longingly toward the door. "It isn't fair."

Sofie remained silent, telling herself not to remind Jenny why they couldn't attend the wedding. That would be cruel, and she felt certain it was unnecessary as well. "Eat your soup before it gets cold."

"Yes'm." Jenny ate several slurpy spoonfuls of soup, then took a biscuit from the basket on the table. After smearing molasses on it, she took a bite. "Mama made the very best biscuits."

Sofie smiled again, glad to hear Jenny speak of her mother. The child mentioned her less often than she had initially, and Sofie suspected this was all part of the grieving process. "She must've been a wonderful mother, to have raised such a great daughter."

A tear trickled down Jenny's cheek, and she swiped it away with the back of her hand. "I'm . . . I'm sorry."

"Don't be." Sofie reached across the table and covered Jenny's hand with her own. "You're allowed to cry. It would be strange if you didn't cry."

Jenny nodded, then took another, far less enthusiastic,

bite of biscuit. Her gaze darted to the door several more times. "Do you think the wedding is over now?"

Sofie nodded. "I think folks are on their way to the reception now." *Will Luke dance with anyone?* Jealousy gnawed at her insides.

"I hope they like the cake I baked."

"What's not to like? The batter alone would make angels give up heaven for a taste."

Jenny gasped and her eyes widened. "Mama would've washed my mouth out with lye soap for saying something like that."

Sofie laughed and apologized at the same time. The difference between Jenny's morals and hers was huge, yet Sofie had no idea where or how she'd become who she was. At least Jenny knew her mother had been initially responsible for her value system.

"You're pretty smart for a kid," she said quietly, taking a sip of tea.

"Everybody knows it's blasphemous to talk about angels leaving heaven." Jenny fidgeted, then took another spoonful of soup. "That doesn't make me smart."

"Maybe, but what you said earlier about everybody remembering their mama. Now *that* was smart."

Jenny's lower lip trembled and she looked down at her half-empty bowl. "I remember my mama real good."

Sofie patted the child's hand. "Always remember. Don't ever forget her, Jenny." Passion crept into her voice, surprising even herself. "Your mama will live forever if you and Shane remember, and tell your children about her someday."

Brightening, Jenny nodded and sniffled. "Yes, she will." The child finished her milk, leaving a white mustache on her upper lip. "I wish I could see Shane."

More regret. Soon Jenny would crack and reveal Charlie Latimer's killer, then they could all get on with their lives. Sofie's stomach lurched at the thought of leaving Redemption and venturing into the big, bad world alone, but she'd do whatever she had to. She couldn't impose on the hospitality of strangers forever, nor could she lean on Luke— Father Salazar—indefinitely. He had responsibilities to his church and to God.

Not to her.

Sighing, Sofie rose and took her bowl to the slop pail near the back door. She was a doctor, and a woman of— what had Mrs. Fleming said?—good upbringing. Someone somewhere missed her and was searching for her. She had a life of her own, and it was time she found her way home.

Home . . .

A warm glow commenced in her chest and spread outward, reaching every filament of her spirit, body, and soul. With a certainty that stunned her, she knew her path.

And, just maybe, her destiny.

Miss Lottie's House of Ill Repute was like a blast from the past—rather, Luke's future-past. At the age of nine, his grandparents had taken him to Southern California, where he'd found little-boy-heaven at Disneyland. The saloon was The Golden Horseshoe—no doubt about it.

Except tonight there were no girls dancing on the bar, flashing their colorful petticoats for the audience's entertainment. No, tonight Miss Lottie's had been transformed to host a wedding reception for two of Redemption's most respected citizens.

Who'd just been married by a flim-flam priest.

Oh, God.

The establishment was on the edge of town, at the farthest end of the road that had led Luke and Sofie to Redemption. Only mountain trails continued beyond the three-story building, where Luke imagined miners came down from their claims for a night of refreshment and entertainment.

"Roman, I've never been in a place like . . . a saloon . . ."
The new and red-faced Mrs. Taylor tugged on her husband's sleeve.

"Anna, Miss Lottie wants to do something nice for us
after the epidemic," Dr. Taylor whispered. "Remember,
some of our patients were her, uh, employees."

Mrs. Taylor's blush deepened, but she nodded. "Very
well," she said. "I suppose it will be all right."

"Of course, just ask Father Salazar."

Luke looked up at the intricate scrollwork on the banis-
ter, hoping he could pretend he hadn't heard the question,
but Roman and his bride moved closer. He had no choice
but to acknowledge their presence and the question.

"Right, Luke?" Roman elbowed him so subtly, no one
else could have noticed.

"Uh, yeah, right." Luke nodded, trying not to laugh at
the irony of this latest fiasco. Anna Taylor was worried
about the scandal of venturing into a saloon, unaware
she'd just entered into a sham marriage.

Not funny, Nolan.

Dora Fleming followed her mother through the swinging doors, her eyes wide and her mouth set in a thin line
of disapproval. "I can't believe we're doing this," she said
quietly, shaking her head. "Of all the places for a wedding
reception . . ."

The perfect place for this particular wedding reception.

"Remember your manners, Dora," Mrs. Taylor said,
drawing a deep breath. "We will be gracious to our . . .
our hostess, and that is that."

"I'm proud of you both," Dr. Taylor said, kissing his
bride on the cheek. Tinny music filled the room from an
old piano, and the doctor smiled at his bride. "I think
they're waiting for us to lead the dancing."

Luke sighed, reminding himself that he'd done the right
thing by performing the marriage ceremony. These two

people loved each other and belonged together. Nothing else mattered.

As the doctor and his bride began to waltz, other couples joined them. Soon, the tension in the room waned as the crowd seemed to forget where they were and what sort of activity typically commenced on the upper floors.

Luke glanced up the stairs again, then tugged at the stiff, white collar at his throat. He hadn't worn it in days, and now he had a rash where it chafed his neck. Hives caused by guilt, no doubt.

Forcibly banishing such thoughts, he pulled the collar free and shoved it into his pocket. As he scratched his now-naked throat, he looked around the room. Miss Lottie's girls were easy to spot, though he suspected they'd toned down their usual attire as well as their behavior for tonight.

"That was a fine wedding, Father," a woman said with a Mae West voice, jerking his attention from the dancers.

Luke met Miss Lottie's gaze and nodded, feeling warmth creep up his neck and into his cheeks. Here he stood talking to a notorious prostitute, blushing like a teenager. Well, sexually speaking, he was a teenager. It had been *that* long since . . .

He swallowed hard.

"Thank you," he said, wincing as his voice cracked. He cleared his throat and tried again. "And thank you for hosting this reception. It was very kind of you."

"Pshaw." Miss Lottie gripped his arm and gave it a squeeze. Though she wore a simple blue dress, her breasts spilled from the neckline, leaving only her nipples concealed. Heady perfume wafted up from her deep cleavage.

And Luke couldn't stop staring.

His throat went dry and, for some inexplicable reason, the sight of Miss Lottie's awe-inspiring anatomy made his thoughts shift to another woman. A much smaller woman, with a tattoo on the side of her breast.

Miss Lottie leaned closer. "Well, Father, if I didn't know better," she whispered, "I might think you was peeking at my bosom."

Luke peeled his gaze from her soft, powdered, perfumed flesh and looked into her laughing eyes. Her hair was a garish shade of red, her lips painted the color of wine, and a beauty mark had been pasted to her cheek. She was the consummate hooker. The only thing missing was a feather of some sort.

Her laughter made his face grow hotter, but rather than concern him, he realized his blush probably enhanced his disguise. To all present, he must have appeared the perfect blushing priest, gawking at women's cleavages and barely able to speak in a coherent sentence.

If only they knew the truth.

Standing in their midst was a horny ex-con whose rampant hormones had long since declared chemical warfare on what remained of his sanity.

"Well, help yourself to some punch, Father," Miss Lottie suggested, moving away from him at last.

There is a God.

The woman made him think of sex in a big way, but not of sex with her, just sex in general. No, that was a lie. Miss Lottie made him think about very specific sex.

With Sofie.

He loosened another button at the top of his shirt. Of course, everything made him think of sex with Sofie. Absolutely everything. Food, drink, scents, sounds, sleep . . . Perspiration trickled down the sides of his face, and he headed toward the cider bowl. Soft cider, no doubt. Pity. He could use some of Zeke's corn liquor about now.

Luke ladled cider into a dainty cup and lifted it to his lips. Even before he tasted it, a familiar scent alerted him the punch had more *punch* to it than he'd anticipated. After he took a sip and confirmed it had been spiked, he looked behind the bar, where Zeke Judson stood. Grinning.

"Evenin', *Padre*."

Luke returned Zeke's grin and drained his cup. After refilling it, he looked at Zeke again and realized who was missing from these festivities besides Sofie and Jenny.

Where was Sam Weathers?

Worry oozed through him as he searched the crowd. Dancers whirled by, doing some kind of reel, and other merrymakers stood on the perimeter, clapping and smiling. Dora Fleming occupied the far side of the punch bowl, sipping steadily, her eyes overly bright. Ab took her empty cup and offered her a full one.

Luke smiled again, despite his concern. *Ab and Dora— imagine that.* Ab said something and Dora laughed, taking the refilled cup and lifting it to her lips. So the good old boy was trying to get the spinster drunk. *Interesting.*

However, if Ab managed to seduce the prudish Dora, Luke had no doubt he'd be called upon to perform another wedding ceremony. He had nothing against Dora and Ab hopping in the sack together, but he had no intention of marrying anybody else, anywhere, anytime. *No way.*

He moved closer and tapped Ab on the shoulder. "Marriage first, Ab," he whispered, knowing he actually sounded like a priest. The other man reddened, tugged on his collar, then gave Luke a sheepish grin.

Luke figured by the time Ab wooed and courted Dora, he'd be long gone from Redemption. The circuit judge or new pastor could perform the ceremony.

As he moved away from a still blushing Ab and slightly tipsy Dora, something silver flashed from Ab's vest, reminding Luke why he'd been so worried a few minutes ago. *Sam.*

The marshal had followed Frank Latimer from the church over an hour ago and hadn't returned. Where were they?

Cold fear shot through Luke. He had to check on Sofie and Jenny. What if Frank—

Luke suddenly knew what he should've realized the day he'd witnessed Shane's reaction to his uncle. "Oh, my God."

Frank Latimer was the killer, and Sam Weathers had known that immediately. Luke had only known that he didn't trust Frank, but he didn't realize exactly why until now.

He had to get out of here. Panic thundered through his veins, but he maintained a calm facade as he placed his cup on the bar and nodded to Zeke.

Though he wanted to tear through the crowd and into the frosty night, Luke maneuvered around the crowded dance floor until he found the bride and groom. After offering his apologies for leaving early, he walked out the door at a casual pace, praying his terror didn't reveal itself on his face or in his demeanor. He didn't want to make a scene and spoil the Taylors' wedding reception.

Once outside, his mask crumbled, and Luke raced toward the jail, his heart pumping wildly. The small stone building was empty and dark.

Where was Marshal Weathers? His breath coming in rapid bursts of white fog, Luke stood in the center of the dark town and looked toward the church.

And the parsonage.

Only two buildings in the entire town had lights burning. The lights in the parsonage windows were a dead giveaway. Every man, woman, and child in town was at the wedding reception.

Except for Sofie, Jenny, Sam Weathers . . .

And a man who'd murdered his own brother.

Damn. Why didn't they just post a billboard pointing the killer to his target? Cold penetrated Father Salazar's black robe and Luke's shirt. He shivered as his breathing slowed and he moved across the dark, deserted street. Stealthily, he slipped from building to building and house to house, until he was at the side of the now empty church.

The killer could be in the parsonage now, with Jenny and Sofie. Luke swallowed hard, resisting the impulse to charge through the front door, though that's precisely what he wanted to do. He had to protect Sofie and Jenny. He *had* to.

They should've warned Sofie and Jenny to keep the lights low and the shutters closed tightly. Why hadn't he and Marshal Weathers thought of—

Oh, no. Of course Luke hadn't considered this, but the marshal must have. The wise and savvy lawman knew exactly what he was doing and had everything under control.

Yes, Sam had a plan all right, and that obviously included using Sofie and Jenny as bait for a deadly trap.

I'll kill him.

Luke bolted from the side of the church to the nearest wall of the parsonage. He used both hands to feel his way along the cold stone, toward the back door.

Please, don't let me be too late.

His pulse pounded, echoing through his head as he strained to hear anything and everything. He paused at the kitchen window nearest the pantry and peered inside. The room was dark, except for a small sliver of light spilling under the closed door from the parlor.

Sofie and Jenny were probably in front of the fire, reading a story. *God, please let them be safe.*

Luke had prayed more since the morning of his failed execution than he had in his entire life. But none of those other prayers had been as important as this one—not even the one begging for his miserable hide in that frigging electric chair.

And he knew why, dammit. Because if anything happened to Sofie and Jenny, he wouldn't care if he lived or died. His life would be worthless without Sofie.

Picked one helluva time to fall in love, Nolan.

And only *he* would fall in love with the only other person in this century who knew who—and what—he really was. But he didn't have time to sort through that now. All that mattered was saving the life of the woman he loved and an innocent child.

He crept around the corner of the house, certain the temperature had fallen well below freezing. Even the threat of frostbite didn't matter, as long as he kept going until he saved Sofie and Jenny . . .

Holding his breath, he reached for the doorknob, knowing if he found it unlocked, that would mean the killer was already inside. *Please, let it be locked.*

The knob turned easily, and the door squeaked slightly as he pulled it open. The killer was already in there—Luke had to hurry, but he also had to use his head.

Quickly, he slipped inside and closed the door behind him. Hoping his heavy breathing wouldn't give him away, he paused until it slowed and quieted. He flexed his nearly frozen fingers and started across the kitchen toward the parlor door.

Luke took another step, then another. He put his hand out to feel any obstacle in his path. What should he do? Just waltz through the door like nothing was wrong? He didn't even have a gun, not that he'd know how to use one.

He froze halfway across the dark room. A prickly sensation crept up the back of his neck and danced across his scalp. Instinct screamed.

Someone else was in the kitchen.

Whoever it was had to have seen Luke, so hiding again was pointless. He held his breath and turned toward the back door. Pale moonlight now spilled through the window he'd peeked through earlier, bathing the room in a silver glow that reminded him of a blacklight.

A shadow shifted near the back door and Luke flattened

himself against the wall next to the kitchen door. His gaze roamed the room, waiting for the intruder to make another move. He had to do something to stop the killer. Whatever it took.

Even kill?

He suppressed a shudder and knew if it came to that, he would kill to protect Sofie and Jenny. God help him.

The silver light wasn't enough. Whoever was in here with him, was obviously being as cautious as Luke about remaining hidden. Then a cloud drifted across the moon and the room went black again.

Shit.

The only sound Luke heard was the thunder of his own heart, but he took comfort in the knowledge that the other man wouldn't be able to see him either. All things were equal in the dark. It didn't matter who was bigger or faster or stronger. Even a gun wouldn't do much good in the dark.

Luke pressed his ear to the door, trying to hear any sounds from the parlor. All he heard were muffled, unidentifiable voices. They could've been male, female, or both.

Resuming his position flat against the wall, he remained totally still, figuring his only chance was to outwait the other guy. Sooner or later . . .

A shuffling sound jerked Luke's attention to the other side of the closed door. He still couldn't see anything, except that sliver of light spilling under the door.

Carefully, he looked across the patch of light to the far edge, sweat trickling down his forehead and stinging his eyes. He blinked, then looked again to make certain he wasn't imagining things.

The patch of light was almost a square, with straight lines on three sides. However, the fourth side—directly across from Luke—wasn't quite straight. Something on the floor marred the line. Something unmistakable. Luke's blood turned the consistency of a slurpee.

Ten human toes.

Sofie tried to stop her trembling as she pulled Jenny closer. Huddled together on the settee, they stared at the crazed man standing a few feet away, firelight gleaming off the barrel of his gun. She knew the back door had been bolted, but Frank Latimer had still found a way into the house.

And his intentions were clear.

"So you was there when your daddy got killed," Latimer said rather than asked. His gaze narrowed as he took a step closer, then stopped again. "Tell Uncle Frank what you seen, girl. A man's gotta right to know who killed his own kin."

A convulsive wave went through Jenny, and Sofie wrapped her arms even more tightly around the child. No one had to tell her who had killed Charlie Latimer. Though she'd suspected before, now she knew for certain. What kind of man would murder his own brother?

Frank took another step, raising his gun higher. "C'mon, girl, what'd you see?" he barked, brandishing his heavy weapon as if it weighed nothing. "I ain't got all night."

Jenny shook her head, and Frank's face darkened. He shook the gun toward her. "How am I gonna help Shane if you don't tell me, girl? How?"

The child shook her head again and Sofie prayed.

"Just go away and leave her be," she said, pushing Jenny behind her as she stood. Determined to protect Jenny no matter what, Sofie lifted her chin a notch and met Latimer's gaze. "She's a child, so just *go*."

"I ain't goin' nowhere, see?" Frank's eyes glazed and

he circled toward the fire, never lowering his gun. "She's gonna ruin it all, and I can't let that happen."

Sofie swallowed, aware of Jenny clutching handfuls of her voluminous skirt. She rotated slightly to keep herself completely between Frank Latimer and his niece.

Of course, if he killed her, she wouldn't be here to protect Jenny at all. Where was Luke? Marshal Weathers? Ab? Dr. Taylor? Anyone?

But she knew very well that everyone in town was at the wedding reception. With music and dancing, no one would hear the sound of Frank Latimer's gun. She trembled again but refused to lower her gaze.

"We . . . we don't know what you're talking about," she said, realizing from the wild look in his eyes that the man was desperate, if not crazy.

Desperate people did desperate things.

Crazy and desperate was even more dangerous.

"She knows. The sheriff said there was a witness, and I seen her that night."

Please, just shut up. If he told them what he thought they already knew, they were both as good as dead. "We don't know anything, and you're frightening Jenny." Sofie didn't budge, though he took another menacing step.

"Charlie was a loser anyway," Frank continued, his expression growing distant. "Always was. Couldn't stay sober most of the time, so every time he made a dime, he lost it."

Sofie didn't want to hear this. She kept her hands at her sides and slightly behind her, with Jenny's shoulders firmly between them. *God, please help us.*

"When he found that rich vein . . ." Frank shook his head and made a snorting sound. "Well, I knew then what had to be done."

He moved sideways toward the back of the settee, and Sofie rotated with him, keeping Jenny behind her. The settee was now between them and the killer, though it offered little reassurance.

A slight movement startled her, then she realized the kitchen door was pushed open partway. She drew a deep breath, willing herself not to turn toward the door. Drawing Frank's attention to their possible rescuer would be foolish.

Whoever it was, she hoped he was armed.

"Please, stop," she said, hoping to buy time. "You're frightening Jenny, and we really don't know what you're talking about."

A look of confusion crossed his face, and his gun lowered ever so slightly. Maybe he didn't really want to kill his niece. Maybe there was hope.

"Of course you know," he said, raising his gun up to its previous level. "Charlie was a loser, but he always had all the luck. Got a good wife, won at poker, then minin'." Frank sighed, then chuckled without a trace of humor. "Stupid bastard couldn't keep nothin'."

The man sneaking through the kitchen door wasn't alone. Though she didn't dare turn enough to discover their identity, Sofie made out two distinct shapes moving toward Frank.

Thank you, God.

"But Jenny's just a child," Sofie said quietly, hoping to keep Frank's attention diverted. "I don't know why you think she's a threat to you."

" 'Cuz I seen her runnin' away that night." He shook the gun and his eyes blazed with fury. "If there was a witness, she's it. That little snot-nosed kid's gonna cost me. I thought Shane was taken care of, but thanks to Jenny, now that ain't even true no more."

Jenny whimpered behind her just as the room went berserk. Luke grabbed Frank around the throat from behind as someone else—someone naked!—dove from the end of the settee for the gun. The men struggled, but the gun discharged as it flew from Frank's hand.

Pain blasted through Sofie's shoulder. Another explosion sounded from across the room. She was vaguely aware of two things as she hit the floor.

Jenny's screams.

And blood.

Chapter Fifteen

Luke shoved Frank Latimer's body off himself and leapt to his feet. *Sofie.* His gaze zeroed in on Sofie's crumpled form lying in a pool of blood, and his heart skipped a beat. No, several.

He stepped over Latimer, not caring if the creep was dead or alive, and dropped to his knees beside the woman he loved. Her face was so pale—deathly pale. Gently, he rolled her onto her back and found the source of all the blood.

"The shoulder ain't as bad as it looks." Sam Weathers holstered his still smoking gun and stooped beside Luke. He removed his bandanna and pressed it against Sofie's wound. "She'll come 'round in a minute, but that bullet's gotta come out. You keep pressin' on that, and I'll fetch the doc."

"Go now. Hurry."

"I'm gone. Shane, get Jenny upstairs. This ain't no place for a kid." The door slammed behind the lawman.

Luke had to believe Sam. If he said Sofie would recover,

then she would. She had to. He willed himself to breathe, determined to be strong for her.

"He's dead," someone announced from behind them.

Then Luke remembered his accomplice. Maintaining the pressure on Sofie's wound, he glanced over his shoulder at Shane. The boy—no, the *man*—wore nothing but a burlap sack tucked between his legs and tied at his waist.

Hence, the naked toes in the kitchen.

"You run on upstairs, Jenny," Shane said.

The little girl snapped out of her state of terror when she finally noticed her brother. "You're . . . naked."

"Jenny, show him my room, please," Luke said. "Find him some clothes." That would get Jenny out of here, away from all the blood and—

He squeezed his eyes shut, struggling against his rising fear.

Jenny paused at his side, looking down at Sofie. "But what about Miss So—"

"You heard Marshal Weathers," Luke said, as much for himself as for Jenny. "Sofie's going to be just fine." He looked up and saw Jenny's tears, then shook his head. "She isn't going to die, Jenny."

Because *he* wouldn't let Sofie die.

Luke blinked back his tears—the suckers were multiplying in droves. He swallowed convulsively as Jenny and Shane started up the stairs. Relief that Latimer was dead and Shane wouldn't hang didn't come. All he could think about was the woman lying here on the floor.

He leaned closer and brushed her forehead with his lips, lingering a moment before he pulled back. "I love you, Sofie," he whispered. "Wake up. Open your eyes."

On cue, her eyes fluttered open and she stared up at him, confusion etched across her features. "I . . ." She tensed and reached for her shoulder. "Shot?"

Luke caught her hand before it found her wound. Had she heard his declaration of love? "Yes, Latimer—"

"Jenny." Sofie struggled to rise.

"She's fine, and you aren't moving until Roman Taylor says you can." Luke brushed her hair from her face and she sighed.

"What happened?"

"Well, Frank Latimer is dead," Luke said, "so Jenny's safe now, thanks to you."

"Thank God." She relaxed some, inclining her head toward her shoulder again. "How bad is it?"

"Sam says you'll be fine, and I'll bet he's had more than a little experience with gunshot wounds."

Sofie nodded and gave him a weak smile. "Thank you." She reached up with her uninjured arm and cupped his cheek.

For a moment, her heart revealed itself in her eyes, and Luke ached to tell her again how much he loved her. He wanted to laugh with her, cry with her, and make love with her for the rest of his life.

A plan slowly unfolded in his mind. When he left Redemption, Sofie would go with him. He would announce his intention to leave the Church—a lie on top of a lie— and ask her to marry him. He prayed she wouldn't insist on seeing the specialist in Denver, because if she regained her memory after this, she'd know about *all* his lies. How would he ever convince her he was wrongfully convicted of murder, when he'd continued to lie to her?

And now he had much more to lose than merely his pride and his freedom. Sofie was far more important than everything else, and he would do anything to keep the love shining in her eyes when she looked at him. *Anything*.

Even if it meant living a lie for the rest of his life.

But marriage would bind them. Shame slithered through him, but Luke was determined to follow through with his plan.

The front door burst open and Roman appeared, his

trusty black bag in tow. "She's awake now," Luke said, stating the obvious. "Bleeding's almost stopped."

The doctor merely grunted and pulled away the bandanna. With a pair of blunt-tipped scissors, he carefully cut the stained dress until he exposed the angry wound.

"This is going to hurt," he warned, then probed her shoulder with his fingers. She flinched and bit her lower lip. "Sorry about that. Bullet missed the bone. That's good." Lifting her slightly, he pulled the damaged dress over her shoulder and looked at her back. "Aha, and here's the best news of all."

The back of her dress was soaked with blood, and Luke couldn't imagine anything good about this situation. "What?" he asked.

"That's damn good news, and I'll betcha . . ." Sam chuckled and pulled the afghan from the back of the rocking chair. "Yep, see for yourself." He pointed at the rocker's high back, where a jagged crack marred the golden wood. "There's the bullet."

Luke stood and looked closer as Sam used a knife to dig a piece of mangled lead from the wood. Jenny and her brother returned, both staring at the object that could've killed any of them. The bullet was misshapen from the impact, but at least it wasn't embedded in Sofie's shoulder.

"That *is* good news." Relief flooded Luke's chest with warmth as he smiled down at Sofie.

"Let's get her upstairs, where I can clean and dress this properly," Roman said. "I'll need two helpers, to make sure we don't twist her too much."

Shane and Jenny thundered down the stairs and went to Sofie's side. "Tell me how to do this, Doc, so I don't hurt her."

"You were naked," Sofie said weakly, and they all laughed, more from relief than anything else.

"Yes, ma'am." Shane grinned, and Luke knew he was

a good young man who would now have a chance for a long life. "The marshal stole my clothes."

"But it didn't stop you none, did it? And I thought I told you to take Miss Jenny up—"

"She wouldn't stay."

Jenny lifted her chin a notch and folded her arms across her abdomen.

"Women," Sam muttered, then went to Frank Latimer's body. "I'd best wait here for the sheriff."

Taking Sofie's other side, Luke followed Roman's instructions on how to lift their patient. Jenny followed them upstairs, and once they had Sofie in bed she ordered Luke and Shane from the room.

"I'll help Dr. Taylor until Mrs. Fleming—I mean, Mrs. Taylor—gets here," she said. Jenny was like a different person, full of confidence and downright bossy. Luke smiled, though he wanted desperately to remain at Sofie's side.

Shane followed Luke from the room and closed the door behind them, then they made their way back downstairs just in time to see Sam covering Frank Latimer's body with the damaged afghan. Good. Luke was sure Jenny wouldn't want to see it again when she came downstairs. Neither did he, for that matter. Sam and Ab were discussing the case, and Zeke stood nearby.

"Best get him outta here," Sam said.

"Wait." Shane bent down and pulled the afghan aside, then reached into his uncle's vest pocket. The young man pulled a watch from the dead man's pocket and flipped it open. "This was Grandpa's."

Grandpa. The word echoed through Luke's head.

"The watch wasn't in Pa's pocket when I woke up that night," Shane said quietly. "I knew the killer had it, and I figured that was Uncle Frank." He sighed.

Seeing Zeke reminded Luke that there was one more

man here in Redemption who'd been sentenced to die unjustly. *Damn.*

"Well, Shane," Ab said quietly, "you're a free man now."

"Hallelujah," Zeke said.

Though his thoughts continued to drift upstairs to Sofie, Luke pounded Shane on the back and shook his hand. "Congratulations."

"Guess I'll help Ab with his report to the circuit judge, then I'll head home," Sam said, looping his thumbs through his holster. "Got me a young 'un on the way, and I reckon Lucifer oughta be mended by week's end."

Luke watched Zeke's face. Though the old coot said he didn't care about going back to hang, his face drooped like a hound dog's. What could Luke do to stop this? His gut burned and his pulse played "Wipe-Out" on his temples. In stereo.

"Let me know when," Zeke said, sighing in resignation. "I'll be ready."

"Ready for what?" Sam shifted his weight and gave Zeke a bland look that could've meant anything or nothing. "Oh, did I forget to mention that wanted poster I been carryin'?"

The man was being sly again, but Luke couldn't prevent "High Hopes" from drowning out "Wipe-Out." He cleared his throat, deciding someone had to play the marshal's game. "What poster?"

Sam looked at Luke, then turned to face Zeke again as he pulled a badly creased paper from his vest pocket. He chuckled as he unfolded the paper and held it out toward Zeke. "It's the darnedest thing. This here poster looks just like you, but it ain't you."

Zeke's brow furrowed as he looked at the paper. "Well, it sure as hell—"

"No, it ain't."

Luke couldn't stand the suspense anymore, and he stepped around the bloodstained carpet to look at the document for himself. The drawing was of a much younger Zeke Judson. Confused, he read the words beneath the picture.

"*Zachariah* Judson?" He grabbed Zeke and thumped his back, laughing in relief.

Shane looked over Luke's shoulder. "Yep, that's what it says all right."

"I can read 'nuff to tell that there don't say Ezekiel, but . . ." Zeke scratched his head and flashed a gap-toothed smile. "I'll be gol-durned. I'm happier'n a pup with two peters."

"Wahoo!" Ab threw his hat into the air and grabbed Zeke in a bear hug. "You're free, Zeke. Free."

Free. Luke swallowed hard, watching Sam for the punch line. There had to be more to this.

"If I was you, though," Sam said thoughtfully, "I wouldn't go back to Arkansas or even Indian Territory for a good long spell. I reckon this here's what Judge Parker'd call a technicality." He chuckled and rubbed his whiskered chin. "The judge gets right testy when things ain't done proper-like, and that's what I aim to do."

"What does tech-nee-cality mean, Marshal?" Ab asked.

"Means I can't arrest him, but . . ."

"But if'n I was to go home, somebody else prob'ly could."

"If it turns out this is really a misprint, and Zachariah Judson is really Zeke Judson."

Of course, they all knew the man on the wanted poster was Zeke, but Sam Weathers had found a way to see justice done. Real justice.

Luke thrust out his hand and Sam took it. "God bless you, Marshal." He might as well take advantage of playing priest while it lasted. "Not only did you shoot Frank Latimer from clear across the room, but now you've performed a miracle. A real miracle."

"Pshaw, the shootin' part's easy, though you and young

Shane was gettin' in my way." The marshal chuckled. "But I'll leave the miracles to the Almighty."

"Like *not* shooting me or Shane by mistake."

Everybody in the room chuckled, but Sam just grinned and shook his head. "Luke, I don't make them kinda mistakes."

"Thank God."

"I already did." Sam laughed quietly. "Several times, as a matter of fact."

The front door opened, admitting Anna Taylor and her daughter. Dora only swayed slightly as she maneuvered herself across the room behind her mother.

"Oh, that's blood on the floor," Dora said, barely slurring her words. She hiccupped loudly, earning a glare from her mother. "Pardon."

"Where's Sofie?" Mrs. Taylor's expression and tone were urgent. "Is she . . . ?"

"She's fine." Sighing, Luke moved away from the men and told the newcomers everything that had happened.

"Shane?" Mrs. Taylor smiled. "You're free now. Praise the Lord."

"Yes'm."

"And Frank Latimer's dead, ma'am," Sam said. "It's all over."

"Then justice has truly been well served. I'm going up to Sofie now." Mrs. Taylor crossed the room, but turned at the base of the staircase to glower at Dora. "Father, I believe my daughter could use a *very strong* cup of coffee. Or perhaps more than one."

"But Mother, I don't like coffee," Dora whined.

"You do tonight." Mrs. Taylor turned and climbed the stairs.

Dora hiccupped again.

*   *   *

He loves me.

Sofie's heart did a somersault as Dr. Taylor finished bandaging her shoulder. She barely heard his admonitions about staying in bed and sending for him if certain symptoms arose.

All she could think of was that Luke loved her. It couldn't have been her imagination, because she'd been struggling to open her eyes for a while before he kissed her forehead and said, "I love you, Sofie."

He really loves me.

Then she remembered why he couldn't—shouldn't— love her. For a few glorious moments, she'd forgotten about churches and vows and celibacy.

But he can't love me.

"Let me give you some laudanum for the pain," Dr. Taylor said, reaching into his bag of tricks.

"No, please. I'm fine." She really didn't want anything to dull her senses until she'd sorted through everything.

Especially Luke.

"I'll leave some here in case you change your mind."

"Sofie, you had us all so worried," Mrs. Taylor said, drawing Sofie's attention to the other side of the bed. "I'm so relieved this nightmare is over."

"Yes." Sofie swallowed hard, hoping she wouldn't cry in front of them. If she shed a single tear, she knew she'd be dosed with laudanum, despite her protests.

But there was no medicine in the world to ease the pain of her broken heart. Luke loved her, yet they could do nothing about it. He *couldn't* give her his heart, because the Church owned him.

God owned him.

And who was she to usurp that relationship? "I'm tired now," she said quietly, desperately in need of privacy. "Besides, this is your wedding night."

The bride blushed and Dr. Taylor cleared his throat. "Yes, so it is." He winked at his bride.

"Yes, well . . ." Mrs. Taylor straightened Sofie's covers for the hundredth time. "Jenny and Shane will be staying here for now," she said. "Until they decide whether or not to return to Texas."

A chaperon, of course. Sofie nodded and let her eyes close, though she was far from asleep. Her ruse worked, and she waited until she heard the door click shut before reopening her eyes.

She listened for the sounds from downstairs. Zeke, Sam Weathers, Ab, Dora, and the Taylors said their good nights and departed. The house grew quiet until she heard floorboards creak in the hall as someone paused at her door.

The knob turned slowly and the door opened. Dr. Taylor had left her bedside lamp burning low, and she saw Luke's face framed in the doorway. Her heart swelled with love.

She smiled in invitation, and he pushed open the door and walked in with Jenny right behind him. A taller figure loomed behind them, and she remembered Shane.

"We just wanted to check on you before we say good night," Jenny said, as they gathered around her bed. "Does it hurt awful bad, Miss Sofie?"

Sofie shook her head and smiled. "Not too bad."

"Good." Jenny looked up at her brother. "Me and Shane can be together like a family again. Mama'd . . . like that."

"Yes, and I'm glad," Sofie said. She looked up at Shane. "Will you stay here in Redemption, or go back to Texas?"

He lifted one shoulder quickly and flashed her a boyish grin. "I don't rightly know yet, ma'am. Me'n Jenny'll talk about that tomorrow."

"Grandma and Aunt Mary are in Texas." Jenny looked at her brother.

"I reckon that's something to think about, too." Shane nodded and added, "We'd best turn in now, ma'am. I just wanted to thank you for looking after my sister." He turned to Luke. "Both of you."

Luke patted Shane's shoulder and cleared his throat. "I'm just glad everything's all right now."

The passion in his voice was unmistakable. *Just like a priest?* Sofie couldn't prevent the jealousy that surged through her. Disgraceful or not, right now she resented Luke's conviction and his faith.

Really sick, Sofie.

Guilt battled emotion, but there was no victor. Maybe if she could remember her upbringing, the life she'd left behind, and whatever path she'd chosen for herself in that life, she'd be better equipped to handle this mess. She was incomplete at best, and though she had a good idea of right and wrong, when it came to more complex issues she was at a loss. Her value system had a black hole in it the size of Colorado.

What kind of woman was she? What kind of woman had her mother and grandmothers been?

"Everybody should remember their mama," Jenny had said.

Yes, everybody *should.* But in addition to her mother, Sofie needed to remember herself. Desperately. She had to regain her past, to learn who and what she was and had been, to give her the strength and convictions to face truth . . .

And consequences.

"Good night, Miss Sofie." Jenny leaned over and kissed her cheek.

"I don't know how to ever thank you for all you've done for my sister," Shane said, his tone solemn now. "If you ever need anything, you just ask. Hear?"

Sofie smiled and blinked back her tears, but one of the liquid turncoats slid down her cheek and into her ear. "I love Jenny as if she were my own sister," she whispered. "And I'm glad she has such a fine brother to look after her."

Shane ducked his head and blushed; Jenny beamed up

at him. This situation, at least, was as it should be. Sofie took comfort in that, though she was far from content.

She remembered her dream about her father's funeral, and the young boy who'd stood there with her mother, holding Sofie's hand. *Her* brother. What was his name? Where was he? Had they been close like Jenny and Shane? Was her brother searching for her right now? Wondering what had happened to her . . . ?

Shane and Jenny left the room, leaving Sofie alone with Luke. Considering her injury, they hardly needed a chaperon.

Besides, Luke was a man of God.

Her throat clogged with unshed tears as she looked from the closed door to Luke. He stood silently beside her bed, his shirt partially unbuttoned and the priest's robe and collar gone again. Faded jeans hugged his slim hips and long legs. He stood with one hip cocked, a thumb hooked through his belt loop.

Her gaze traveled up his taut abdomen to the open V of his shirt. Swallowing hard, she followed a vein along the side of his neck to his strong jaw, now covered with a day's growth of beard. His skin had stopped peeling and the redness was gone, leaving behind a man any woman would want. Even his dark hair had grown out enough to curl softly, rather than stand straight up.

Virile. Yes, he was that and so much more. Father Luke Salazar was a man of conviction, a man with principles, and a man off-limits to the likes of her . . . or any woman.

He gave her a crooked smile and reached down to cover her hand with his. "Tired?" he asked quietly, his deep voice rumbling through her.

"A little." Her voice cracked. It was a miracle she didn't drown in her own misery.

"I'd better leave so you can rest," he said, but didn't budge from her side. He squeezed her hand and drew a deep breath. "There's so much I want to say to you, but I know now isn't the time."

Say it, her wanton, selfish side silently pleaded. "I . . . I'm not sure there will ever be a right time."

His gaze possessed hers with a tenacity which stunned her. "Yes," he said in a fierce whisper, "there will be a time, Sofie. I promise you this."

If only she could say the words, ask the questions left unspoken between them. The air crackled with tension.

And desire.

No matter what happened now, Sofie knew Luke wanted her the way a man wants a woman. There was nothing priestlike about the way he'd held her, kissed her, touched her that night on the parlor floor. Not even close.

She opened her mouth to speak, but no words came forth. What could she say? This was the proverbial damned-if-you-do-and-damned-if-you-don't scenario.

"Dr. Taylor left laudanum." He reached for the bottle on the nightstand. "It might help you sleep."

The ache in her heart made the one in her shoulder seem trivial, and she knew laudanum wouldn't help that. Exhausted, she shook her head and closed her eyes, feigning sleep.

She felt the bed shift slightly beneath his weight as he leaned down to kiss her forehead. The warmth of his breath enveloped her, and the brush of his lips sent a shiver of excitement plundering through her. Too soon—much too soon—he straightened.

Though she knew he waited beside her bed, she willed her eyes to remain closed, her breathing steady. If she gazed into his soft gray eyes again tonight, she'd break. That would do neither of them any good.

Tomorrow, she'd be stronger, and she would ask him to take her to Denver with him. Once there, she would set her weird, beloved hero free at last.

Then, perhaps, she could find her family.
And herself.

Restless, Luke shrugged into the wool coat Mrs. Taylor had given him and went out into the cold night air. The stillness of midnight was magical as he gazed up at the vivid stars.

He drew a deep breath and released it very slowly, watching its steam appear, then dissipate in the darkness. Tucking his hands into his pockets, he walked toward the clearing behind the schoolhouse and stood beside a fallen log.

He would miss Redemption—the people, the peace. Remembering the first day, when he and Sofie'd been escorted at gunpoint to the makeshift hospital, Luke smiled. So much had changed since then.

He'd changed.

"Well, it 'pears we always meet up here, *Padre.*" Zeke strolled over to stand beside Luke, then looked up at the stars. "I'm gonna miss this place."

The lanky hillbilly's sudden appearance didn't startle Luke as it had the first time. On the contrary, it seemed quite normal. "You're leaving, too?"

"Yep." Zeke took the cork out of his jug and lifted it to his lips. After a long drink, he offered the jug to Luke.

"No thanks, Zeke." Luke didn't want anything to affect his judgment tonight. He had plans to make. Important plans.

Zeke shoved the cork back into place and sighed. "Had me a long talk with the marshal," he said, bending down to set the jug near his feet. "Some miner jawin' in a saloon 'bout Redemption is what brung Weathers out here huntin' me."

"Ah." Luke had wondered how Sam Weathers knew to find Zeke here.

"So I reckon it'd be best if'n I ain't here to find, in case somebody else comes lookin' for either Zeke or Zach Judson." He chuckled quietly.

"Sam Weathers is quite a piece of work."

"That's a fact."

"So where will you go?"

"Fanny's folks need to be told what happened to her," Zeke said thoughtfully, tucking his hands in his armpits. "They got a spread out in Oregon, so I figgered I'd mosey out there and tell 'em myself."

"I'm sure they'll appreciate hearing about Fanny from you personally," he said quietly. "When will you leave?"

"Spring, I reckon."

Zeke looked up and Luke followed the direction of his gaze. A shooting star arced across the sky, reminding Luke of his grandma's vow to always make wishes at such times. "Make a wish, Zeke," he said, squeezing his eyes shut.

"I already got my wish, *Padre.*"

Luke swallowed the lump in his throat and released a long, slow breath. He wished for serenity, freedom, respectability, a life free of guilt and shame.

But mostly . . . he wished for love.

Remembering the expression in Sofie's eyes when he'd made his promise, he prayed she would understand and accept his decision to break his alleged vows. She had to. Nothing else mattered without her. Nothing.

"I been wonderin' somethin', *Padre.*"

Zeke's words startled Luke, and he jerked his eyes open and turned to face the other man. "What?"

"Well, no offense intended, hear?"

Curious, Luke chuckled. "I hear. What's on your mind?"

"I reckon you know by now I ain't what you'd call a big-city feller like you," he said slowly, seeming to choose his words carefully. "But I be a flesh and blood man all the same, who knows what it's like to have a hankerin'."

"Hankering?"

"For a woman, *Padre.*" Zeke wasn't laughing now. "I never could understand how some folks go all their lives without a poke now and again. Beats tar outta me."

"I, uh . . ." Far from cold now, Luke tugged open the top button of his heavy coat. "What's your question, Zeke?" His voice sounded strained. Nervous.

Zeke turned to fully face him, his expression solemn in the moonlight. "A body'd have to be blind not to see your hankerin'." The man shrugged, but didn't look away. "I seen the way you git 'round Miss Sofie, *Padre.*"

"Oh?" Luke broke into a cold sweat and shifted his weight from one foot to the other. Zeke had proven himself intelligent far beyond the image he presented to the world, and he'd seen through at least part of Luke's facade.

" 'Course, this ain't none o' my biz'ness . . ."

Luke didn't—couldn't—say anything. All he could do was stand there in the freezing cold and hear what the man had to say. How much did Zeke know? What had he figured out about the fictitious Father Salazar? About Luke? *Besides that I'm a horny bastard?*

"But I cain't help wonderin' how you stand it, *Padre.*" Zeke chuckled again and shook his head slowly. "If'n I was you, I'd be harder'n a year-old hotcake all the durned time."

A hotcake sizzling on the griddle summed things up pretty well. "It isn't easy," Luke said, trying not to think about how long he still had to wait before he could make love to Sofie. Of course, if she decided she didn't want him after all . . .

"Like I said 'afore," Zeke continued, "I seen the way you look at Miss Sofie, an' doggone it if she don't make moon eyes at you, too."

I sure as hell hope so. Luke drew another fortifying breath and released it in a loud *whoosh.* "Zeke, I can't answer for anyone but myself," *and all I can do on that score is lie, lie,*

lie, "but the, uh, cravings of the flesh are pretty powerful stuff. Temptation is everywhere."

"Ain't that the truth?" Zeke chuckled again and looked toward town. "I reckon the doc is givin' in to temptation 'bout now. Looked to me like old Ab was sniffin' 'round after Miss Dora, too."

Luke cleared his throat loudly—his only defense against uncontrolled laughter. After a moment, he rescued his dignity from his sense of humor and said, "I, uh, warned Ab about that already."

Zeke threw his head back and roared. "Well, I'll be seein' you, *Padre*," he said, reeling in his laughter. "Get some shut-eye."

"You, too."

Luke walked slowly back through town, hoping no one had been out visiting their outhouse and overheard Zeke's pointed questions and observations. Man, Luke was even starting to act like a priest. He had to get out of this mess fast, and for more reasons than one.

Soon. The minute Roman said Sofie was able to travel . . . Once they were away from Redemption, Luke would shed his sheep's clothing. His blood warmed at the thought of shedding clothing, baring skin, and *touching* Sofie.

He looked around once more, then threw his head back and howled.

Chapter Sixteen

Sofie eased her healing shoulder into her dress and closed the buttons. Dr. Taylor hadn't wanted her to get out of bed yet, but it had been almost a week and she had plans to make about her future. More determined than ever to regain her memory and her life, she tied a scarf on as a sling and made her way downstairs.

At the base of the stairs, she paused to look toward the hearth, where a low fire now burned. The dark stains on the carpet made her shudder, until she looked beyond that to the area where she'd lain on the floor in Luke's arms.

Her face warmed as memory filled in every delicious detail. She closed her eyes, savoring the flood of love and longing that pervaded her.

After a few moments, she opened her eyes and jerked herself back to the present. There was nothing wrong with certain parts of her memory. A pity she couldn't fill in all the other missing details of her life. With a sigh, she banished the stimulating thoughts of Luke's kisses and caresses and headed for the kitchen.

"Miss Sofie!" Jenny hugged her. "I was fixing a tray to bring up to your room. You shouldn't be out of bed yet. Dr. Taylor said—"

"I feel fine. Just a little weak from being in bed too long." Sofie stroked Jenny's neatly braided hair and smiled down at her. "I'm so happy for you. For you and Shane both." She looked at Jenny's brother, as he bolted from his chair, abandoning a plate of ham and eggs. "I swear, the men in Redemption are too polite for their own good. Sit and eat, Shane."

Grinning, the young man returned to a breakfast large enough for three grown men. Of course, he was nearly as big as three men, Sofie decided, remembering how he'd looked the night he came to their rescue wearing that diaperlike getup. He'd looked like a pro wrestler.

In fact, Shane Latimer could easily give any Hollywood hunk a run for his money. *Trivia Queen strikes again.* Thank goodness he'd live to break a few hearts.

"Dr. Taylor will be mad," Jenny said, shaking her head as she went to the stove. "I think he's coming back with Father Salazar to check on you."

Sofie smoothed nonexistent wrinkles from her skirt and poured herself a cup of coffee. "Father Salazar isn't here?" she asked casually. Too casually.

"Doc Taylor sent for him early this morning," Shane said between shovelfuls. "Some fella named Mr. Smith wanted to see him."

"Maybe he's Catholic," she thought aloud. "Mr. Smith is one of Dr. Taylor's patients."

"You hungry, Miss Sofie?" Jenny asked, bending to take a pan of biscuits from the oven. With a huge hot pad, she carried it to the table. "I found some honey in the pantry. I like biscuits with honey even better than with gravy."

"Unless that's redeye gravy." Shane plucked a biscuit

from the pan, earning a slap on the forearm from his sister. With a sheepish grin, he grabbed a second biscuit.

A yearning need for her own family spread through Sofie as she watched the loving, casual manner the pair had with each other. *Jealous, Sofie?* Yes, without a doubt. She ached to find her own mother and brother, and even if she couldn't be with them physically—after all, she didn't even know if they were living—she at least wanted the memories.

She could just imagine what her mother—what any mother—would think of her daughter falling in love with a priest. Though her concerns seemed more like a teenager's than a doctor's, Sofie couldn't shake the need for her mystery mother's approval. Maybe not knowing her true age augmented this need. In many ways, she was like a newborn discovering the world for the first time.

Taking her coffee and philosophy to the table, she sat across from Shane, accepting the plate of biscuits and honey Jenny pushed toward her. Though she wasn't really hungry, she was eager to recover and get on with her life; maintaining her physical stamina was part of that.

"Jenny's been telling me about you not being able to remember anything. I'm sorry about your troubles, ma'am," Shane said with genuine sincerity, lifting his coffee cup to his lips.

"Yes, an explosion caused it." Sofie nibbled on a biscuit, wondering how soon she could get to Denver. What if Luke refused to take her there? But he wouldn't. Somehow, she knew he'd do anything she asked of him.

Anything? Biscuit caught in her throat and she washed it down with scalding coffee. She reached for the cream pitcher and poured some into her cup, watching the caramel-colored swirls. "I'm going to see a specialist in Denver. Dr. Taylor thinks he can help me regain my memory." She took another bite of biscuit.

"Oh, good." Jenny ate scrambled eggs and biscuits with honey, her appetite much improved since the danger from her evil uncle had passed. "I'm glad you'll get to remember being little, Miss Sofie."

"And I have you to thank for convincing me." Sofie sipped her coffee. "Ah, that's much better." She forced a smile, determined to remain positive and upbeat today. Soon, she would leave this town and these people she'd grown to care for, and she wanted to take happy memories along.

Her vague knowledge of the world she'd once known intruded again. Travel. She remembered flying and cars and . . .

"Do you—either of you—know where the nearest airport is?"

Jenny and Shane exchanged looks, then he cleared his throat. "Ma'am, I ain't ever even *heard* of such a place. Do they make air there?"

"Uh . . ." Sofie's face flashed with heat and she shook her head. "Never mind. Not important."

"Whatever you say, ma'am." Shane looked at Jenny again.

They must think I'm nuts. Then again, maybe she was. Why did she remember airports and planes so clearly if they didn't exist? *I hate this.*

"Me and Jenny been talking a lot about this," Shane said, seeming older this morning than Sofie'd originally thought. "And we've decided to go home to Texas."

"Shane wants to be a Texas Ranger," Jenny said, and her brother blushed.

"Really?" Sofie truly believed Shane Latimer could be anything he wanted, including a Denver Bronco. "What about college?"

"Pshaw." Shane chuckled and reddened even more. "No Latimer ever made it to college, ma'am."

Sofie set her half-empty cup on the table and folded her hands in front of her. "Why not be the first?"

"Well . . ."

"I believe I heard your uncle saying something about your father's mine being of some value?" Sofie hated to bring up either man's name again, but if money was an issue, it needed to be discussed. "Why not sell the claim, settle Jenny with her grandmother, and go to college? You can become a Texas Ranger *after* college."

Jenny's grin was infectious, and Sofie returned it with a wink. "I think you fixed him good, Miss Sofie," the child said. "Now he doesn't got an excuse."

"Jenny Latimer, I swear . . ." Shane folded his muscular arms across his abdomen and leaned back in the chair. After a moment, his eyes softened. "Ma always talked about me going to college one day."

"Yes, she did." Jenny gave a wistful sigh and took a halfhearted sip of milk. "If you go, I'll go."

"Girls don't go to college, half-pint." Shane appeared openly shocked, then looked at Sofie as if expecting support. "Well, most girls don't." His face reddened again.

"You do that very well, Shane," Sofie teased.

"What?"

"Blush."

Jenny laughed with such little-girl glee, Sofie couldn't help but join her. Her shoulder ached and she held her hand over the wound until her laughter subsided.

"Miss Sofie went to college, silly Shane." Jenny wrinkled her nose at her brother. "She's a doctor."

"A doctor?" Shane grew solemn. "Well, I never met a lady doctor before. That's really something."

"She helped take care of me while I was sick." Jenny's lower lip trembled. "After Mama died."

"I owe you a lot more than I realized, ma'am," Shane said, reaching across the table to take his sister's hand. "Thank you again."

"Jenny's very special." And Sofie meant every word, though she still yearned for her own family. If they were out there somewhere, she'd find them.

Jenny suddenly brightened. "I know. You can come with us to Texas."

"No, I couldn't." Sofie brushed crumbs from her loose bodice and pushed her plate away. "Really."

"But we need doctors in Texas, too," Jenny argued, looking toward her brother.

"Ma'am, you're welcome to come home with us," Shane said, sincerity unmistakable in his tone and expression. "Grandma would like to meet you, and you could stay with us as long as you wanted."

Surprise rippled through Sofie. So, the woman without a past suddenly had options. She could stay here in Redemption, she could go to Denver and see the specialist, or she could go to Texas with the Latimers.

Somehow, she sensed she'd find her answers here in Colorado. After all, she'd been here at the time of the explosions, so it made sense for her to begin her search here, too.

"Thank you for the invitation, but I really have to see that doctor in Denver."

"Could we go with her, Shane?" Jenny begged, looking at her brother. "Then take her back with us to Texas from there? Could we?"

"I'm afraid not, Jenny." Shane shook his head sadly. "Marshal Weathers has offered to take us the whole way, but we gotta go when he says. I could probably find the way myself, but why risk it if we don't have to?"

"Oh."

"Shane's right." Sofie leaned forward. "You have to go with Marshal Weathers, and I have to go find my memories of being a little girl. Remember? You said so."

The girl sighed and nodded. "Yes, I remember." She blinked as she met Sofie's gaze. "Maybe after you find your memory, you can bring your mama with you to Texas."

"Maybe." Sofie wasn't burning any bridges. Options

were good. "You give me an address where I can write to you, and I'll let *you* know as soon as *I* know."

"All right." Jenny rose and carried dishes to the sideboard.

"When is Marshal Weathers planning to leave?" Sofie asked Shane.

"Tomorrow morning at first light." Shane buried his hand in his shoulder-length hair. "Reckon I'd better visit the barber first."

Sofie nodded, thinking it a shame to cut off such beautiful golden hair. "I suppose he wants to go before we get any more snow."

"There's only one pass down that I know of," Shane said. "It'll be blocked 'til spring after one really big snow. It's late already."

A shiver skittered along Sofie's spine. Though spending the winter in Redemption wasn't a distasteful idea, the thought of postponing the quest for her memory was. She simply couldn't bear it. Nor would she.

"I guess I'd better make arrangements to get to Denver soon."

"Yes'm." Shane nodded and rose. "And I already got an offer for Pa's mining claim from Miss Lottie, so I'd best go settle that this morning."

"Miss Lottie?" Jenny's eyes grew round, as did her mouth.

"Yes, Miss Lottie." Shane scowled at his sister. "She wants the mine and she's got the money for it. That's all there is to it."

The child shrugged, obviously ready to drop the subject. "We really have to go tomorrow?" Jenny walked back to stand beside her brother. "Couldn't we wait and leave when Miss Sofie goes?"

Shane shook his head. "I can't turn down the marshal's offer to take us home, Jenny. You know that. And I'm not about to ask him to wait." He patted her hand on his shoulder. "If it was just me, I wouldn't worry about going alone, but Grandma'll skin me if I risk it with you."

"I suppose you're right." Jenny looked at Sofie, her large brown eyes glistening with unshed tears. "I'll miss you, Miss Sofie."

Realizing she might never see Jenny and Shane again, Sofie nodded and stood as Jenny ran to her. She hugged the child, vaguely aware of the back door opening.

"How will you get to Denver?" Jenny asked, looking up at her.

"With me."

Sofie lifted her gaze from the top of Jenny's head to the man filling the back door. So Luke still planned to take her to Denver. Relief and terror swept through her simultaneously.

Alone in the mountains with Luke?

A tremor raced through her as she met his intense gaze. It stole her breath and made her heart swell with longing.

"Yes," she said quietly. "Luke—Father Salazar will take me to Denver."

"Well, I'm going to see Miss Lottie now." Blushing again, Shane left the house as Luke stepped inside, closing the door behind him.

Sofie couldn't stop staring at the man she loved and feared more than any other. He had so much power over her right now. That vulnerability frightened her, though she trusted him with her life.

But could she trust him with her heart?

His expression reminded her of their first night in this house, when he'd awakened her from an exquisitely erotic dream. What had he said? His words returned to haunt and tantalize.

"I'm a man, Sofie," he'd whispered. *"You're a woman and I'm a man."*

A man of God, she reminded herself, swallowing hard.

But still a man.

* * *

"I thought you were supposed to stay in bed today," Luke said, struggling to recover from the jolt of love and desire that ambushed him every time he saw Sofie. And often when she wasn't even around.

"I feel fine." She smiled at Jenny as the girl returned to the task of clearing the table. "Really."

"Roman will be by in a few minutes to check on you." Luke walked slowly toward her, wishing he could take her in his arms and carry her back to bed. Of course, his motives were questionable, though he did have her well-being in mind. Among other things . . .

She gripped the back of the chair and her face paled. Luke was at her side in less than a second. "Are you all right?"

"Just a little . . . dizzy. Weak from being in bed too long." She drew a deep breath and her cheeks pinkened again. She gave him a watery smile. "There I feel better now, but maybe I'll go sit in the parlor until Dr. Taylor gets here."

Luke reached out and scooped her off her feet, earning a giggle from Jenny and a gasp from Sofie. "Fine, we'll get you settled in the parlor right now." He ignored the flash of anger in her beautiful blue eyes. God, she was gorgeous. "Jenny, hold the door for me, please?"

Still giggling, the child obeyed, then returned to the kitchen and her chores. "It's a good thing one of us likes housework," Luke muttered, carrying Sofie to the settee, davenport, or whatever the hell they'd decided to call it. Still looked like a loveseat to him.

Of course, that term gave him even more ideas, and *that* was dangerous territory.

He put her down in a reclining position, but she pushed herself upright the moment he released her. "Sofie, Sofie, Sofie." Sighing, he went to the hearth and poked at the dying embers, placing another log on the hot coals. Within a matter of seconds, it flared to life and the fire's warmth drove away the autumn chill.

"Shane said you went to see Mr. Smith." Sofie smoothed her skirt and met his gaze as he sat on the ottoman in front of her. "How is he doing?"

Luke didn't want to go there. That guy gave him the creeps. "He was asleep, but Roman asked me to come back later." He shrugged. "Last night the guy wrote the word priest on the slate. Guess I'm the only one in town."

"Maybe he'll be able to tell you his name."

"Roman said he wrote another word besides priest, but he couldn't make it out." Luke drew a deep breath and leaned slightly forward. "You're determined to go to Denver then?" He had to talk her out of seeing the specialist before they reached Denver. Maybe when he proposed to her she'd forget about regaining her memory. He hoped.

"Of course," she said quietly.

How could he really expect her to abandon hope of regaining her memory forever? Simple, he couldn't. However, he might be able to distract her for a while.

Actually, distracting Sofie held a great deal of appeal. He shifted his position, but it didn't help much. In his condition, he should've remembered how uncomfortable sitting astride anything could be.

Making himself as comfortable as possible, Luke searched her expression, knowing as he did that she loved him, too. Somehow, he'd make this work. He had to. Thank God she wasn't the kind of woman who could hide her feelings, because knowing how she felt helped him remain focused.

She jerked her gaze from his and said, "I'm very anxious to see the specialist." Tugging at the cuff of her sleeve, she looked up to meet his gaze again. "Luke, this is very important to me."

"I understand," he said, and that was the truth. He did understand her need to regain her memory, though he didn't have to like it. With any luck, she'd be married to him before then, though even that didn't guarantee her acceptance of his duplicity. He swallowed hard.

Married. The thought of living with and loving Sofie for the rest of his life brought him more pleasure than he ever could have imagined.

Yes, marriage.

All he had to do was forsake his fictitious priesthood—a sacrifice he couldn't wait to make—and convince Sofie to take the plunge. She had to agree.

"All right, then," he said, rubbing the tendons at the back of his neck. "When Roman gives the okay, we'll leave for Denver."

"Do you . . . know the way?" She shrugged and gave a nervous laugh. "I have no idea."

Well, if Luke could find Highway 24 and Interstate 25, he could make it to Denver in no time. "We'll get directions." He grinned.

"Will we have to ride horses?" she asked. "I'm not sure I know how."

Ouch. Luke hadn't thought of that. "Yeah, I suppose we will. I'll use some of the gold the town gave me to buy horses and supplies." He chuckled. "I can ride a little, but it's been a long time. I'll have to learn all over again."

"Fast." Sofie smiled and the worry lines in her brow eased and smoothed. "I know we have to beat the big snows."

"Yeah, and it's already October." Luke didn't want her to see his worry. He'd lived his entire life in Colorado, and he knew the heavy winter snows could begin any day. If they commenced before their departure, they'd have to wait until spring.

And if they commenced while he and Sofie were traveling . . .

Staying put was the safe thing to do, but Luke couldn't

wait that long, and it was obvious Sofie didn't want to either. They had to leave soon.

"I asked Shane and Jenny about airports . . ." Her brow wrinkled and her obvious confusion tugged at Luke's conscience.

"I . . . I have a lot of things to tell you, Sofie," he said quietly, holding her gaze with his. "But they have to wait until after we leave here. Trust me."

She nodded, but didn't look away. "All right."

She trusts me. Guilt threatened his resolve, but Luke banished it. For now. If only he could permanently exorcise the demons that haunted him, especially guilt.

Once he'd shed his masquerade, Luke vowed to sort through his feelings about his grandparents and his wrongful conviction and near-execution. Suppressing all that stuff wasn't healthy—he knew that. And he wanted to be the best husband he possibly could. That meant having his head screwed on straight.

"Good." He reached out and took her hand, cherishing the petal-like softness of her skin. He wanted her desperately, but he loved her even more than he wanted her.

Miracle of miracles.

He smiled just as someone knocked at the front door. "That'll be Roman." After giving her hand another squeeze, he rose and went to answer the door.

Very soon he'd be able to touch her all over, to kiss her and love her as she deserved to be loved. His heart slammed against his ribs and the renewed tug of desire in his groin nearly drove him to his knees.

Yes, soon.

He opened the door and Roman stepped inside. "Sofie wouldn't stay in bed," Luke explained, closing the door. "She's in the parlor."

Roman sighed as he sat on the settee beside her and placed his black bag on the ottoman. "Sofie, I thought I told you to stay in bed another day."

"You did, but I felt like moving around."

"I never met a soldier or miner who was as stubborn as most of the women I've treated over the years." He asked her a few questions, then said, "I need to check your wound and change the dressing. Would you prefer to do that here or upstairs?"

The implication was clear. Luke could take a hint. "You stay here, and I'll go to the kitchen." He took a few steps, then stopped. "Oh, before I forget, I need to know how soon Sofie will be able to travel."

"She's young and heals fast. If she keeps healing even while disobeying doctor's orders, I'd say any day, if you take it easy." Roman looked up and sighed. "By the way, can you come back to see Smith again this afternoon?"

"Sure." Luke couldn't prevent the tremor of apprehension that raced down his spine. Smith's scars weren't what made him uncomfortable. It was the man's eyes. They gave Luke the creeps. "I'll be in the kitchen if you need me."

"Thank you." Sofie averted her gaze when he looked at her.

Somehow, he had to make this work. His new life would be meaningless without Sofie.

Free or not.

"Smith wrote another word for Anna while I was checking on Sofie," Roman explained, leading Luke through the front door of his small house shortly after noon. Inside, the physician paused and ran his fingers through his white hair. His expression grew pensive. "My job is to serve and to heal, Luke."

Where'd that come from? Sensing his friend needed to talk, Luke merely nodded.

"Smith, or whatever his name is, has recovered enough to get on with his life, such as it is." Roman shook his head and chuckled quietly. "I have a wife now, and having patients here longer than necessary is . . ."

"Unnecessary," Luke finished with a grin. "Seriously, you have a right to your privacy, and the obvious solution is to find out who this guy is and send for his family."

"What if he's wanted by the law?" Roman paced a few steps, then turned and repeated the process, stopping again in front of Luke. "What if he doesn't *want* to be found? Then what? I can't stand the thought of sending him to an institution, but I don't know what else to do."

Luke had experienced more than his fill of institutions. "Yeah, I see your problem." He sighed and gave a shrug. "All we can do is try."

"Thank you." Roman led him down a hall toward the back of the house, next to the office Luke had visited once before. "Anna went to see Dora," he said over his shoulder. "If I don't miss my guess, that young lady is in for another lecture—number ten or twenty, I'd say—about her conduct at our wedding reception."

Luke cleared his throat. Laughing would be inappropriate, though that was precisely what he itched to do. "Yeah, I suppose so."

"Anna planned on letting Dora stay on in their house, but that was when she thought Jenny would be staying there, too." Roman sighed again. "Now that Jenny and Shane have decided to return to Texas . . ."

They paused before a closed door at the end of the hall. "Seems to me, Ab might be more than a little interested in Dora," Luke said thoughtfully. "Maybe they'll get married."

"Now *that's* something I'd like to see."

Luke grabbed the doctor's shoulder before he knocked. "Is he, uh, off the laudanum now?"

"Completely."

Luke needed to make sure he couldn't blame any bizarre behavior on drugs this time. "Good."

Roman knocked, then pushed open the door. "Mr. Smith, Father Salazar is here to see you."

Luke looked beyond the doctor, where the tall man stood before a curtained window. He wore the gray hood Dora had made for him, and a blue shirt and black slacks covered the rest of him. He was only slightly hunched now, and he took a few steps toward them without limping. Of course, the burns had been restricted to his upper body, and only one side of that.

A bell sounded from somewhere nearby. "I have a patient," Roman announced. "I'll be back as quickly as possible. The slate's on the bureau."

Before Luke could object, the doctor was hurrying down the hall. Resigned to face Mr. Smith alone, Luke summoned his priest persona and entered the room.

"Do you think you can write your name for me?" Luke crossed the room and picked up the slate, then faced the hooded man.

"No . . . slate." Mr. Smith's voice sounded hoarse and raspy, barely audible. He took another step toward Luke and paused.

Luke couldn't be sure, but it looked as if the man was smiling beneath his hood. Why did he let Smith get to him this way? "You can talk. That's good."

Smith took another step toward Luke, until he was only a few feet away. The sunlight flowing through the window illuminated the man's eyes. Frenzy gleamed from the twin slits, with nothing less than pure hatred.

"What's your name?" Luke resisted the urge to run. He didn't want to face this guy, and he didn't even know why. "Dr. Taylor wants to notify your family."

Smith made a cackling sound with his singed vocal chords that sounded demonic, though Luke recognized the rhythm as laughter.

"Why won't you tell me your name?" Luke swallowed

hard, trying not to look at the man's insidious eyes. They seemed to look through him.

Knowingly.

"You . . . know."

Cold penetrated Luke's flesh and stole its way into his very soul. The man's eyes grew more fierce, though he didn't move.

"You know," he repeated.

"No . . . I don't know." Luke's pulse roared through his veins as memories assailed him, though he didn't understand why. The electric chair loomed in his mind, threatening and final.

"My name," the man said, still not moving any closer. "Say it."

"I don't know." Luke's voice grew louder, competing against the roar of his own blood.

"I am . . . Justice."

Chapter Seventeen

Luke bolted. He ran like he should have the morning of his execution.

For his life and from the same man.

Smith was Warden Graham. *God help me.* Why else would the bastard have called himself Justice? No wonder those demented eyes had given him the creeps for weeks.

Of course, Graham's definition of justice didn't come close to reality. The man was demented and obsessed.

In any century.

Ignoring the friendly greetings and curious stares of those he passed, Luke ran to the edge of town and stopped. What the hell was he doing?

Sofie. He couldn't leave her here. More importantly, he didn't *want* to leave her.

What a time to fall in love. Why here? Why now? He leaned against a tree, gasping for breath and reason. He had to think. Clearly. Carefully.

His life depended on it.

He doubled up his fist and punched the trunk of the

pine that had been supporting him. "Shit." *Stupid, Nolan.* Flexing his bruised knuckles, he counted to ten and forced himself to regain control.

Why should he be afraid of Warden Graham? That bastard couldn't do anything to him in 1891. Could he? No, Graham didn't have his precious prison system, or court orders for anybody's execution. He had nothing.

He was powerless.

A smug smile tugged at Luke's lips as he turned toward the parsonage. He would complete his plans to leave Redemption with the woman he loved, marry her, then take her away to live somewhere far from Colorado and the warden from hell.

Maybe they'd go to Oregon and look up Zeke Judson again. Wouldn't that old fart be surprised to learn Father Salazar had hung up his collar? Or how about California? Even without Disneyland, it had the Pacific Ocean. That certainly held appeal. They could even invest in California real estate way ahead of the game. Beverly Hills, Rodeo Drive, Malibu.

They could go west, but not until spring. Only a fool would take off across the mountains heading west this time of year. Denver had to come first. The sooner he and Sofie put some serious distance between them and Graham, the better. No, Graham couldn't hurt Luke here and now, unless . . .

Sofie.

She was the soft spot in his armor. His love for her made him vulnerable, just as his need for Grandpa's approval had. But this was worse. More power. More vulnerability.

Warden Graham might not be able to fry Luke's gizzard in 1891, but he could still hurt him if he had the ammunition. Luke had to make sure the bastard didn't get his hands on that ammunition.

On Sofie.

Luke kept walking, not missing a step even when he

realized exactly what Graham *could* do to him here and now.

He could tell Sofie everything.

Pausing outside the back door to the parsonage, Luke ran his fingers down his face, tugging at his lower eyelids as he contemplated this newest mess. Would he never have peace?

Roman had said Sofie could travel any day. Now that Graham had played his hand, any day meant now. Today. Luke might not have a few days. He had to act fast, because it was already past noon.

What if Graham told Roman Taylor who he was? Who Luke was? Still, even if he did, no one would believe him.

No one but Sofie.

Luke slipped quietly through the back door, hoping he would find her alone. What he had to say couldn't be said in front of an audience.

The kitchen was empty, as was the parlor. Jenny must have gone somewhere with Shane. Slowly, Luke climbed the stairs, praying Sofie trusted him enough to leave without asking too many questions.

At the top of the stairs, he paused and listened. The house was quiet. Now he was certain Jenny was either gone or asleep, and he definitely hadn't seen evidence that the girl was a napper before. Allowing himself a smile, he proceeded to Sofie's bedroom door and knocked.

"Come in."

He swallowed the lump in his throat and opened the door. She sat in a chair near the window with a book in her lap, her hair loose and curling wildly as if she'd been asleep.

"Luke." She closed her book and set it aside, then stood, smoothing her skirts. "I was just thinking about you— rather, about our trip to Denver."

"Sofie, I . . ." Where should he start? How could he convince her to leave Redemption with him now?

Today.

"What is it?" She took a step toward him, frowning. "You look as if you've seen a ghost."

Luke gave a humorless laugh and shook his head. "I've seen something much worse than a ghost," he said, no longer laughing. Drawing a deep breath, he banished thoughts of what Mrs. Taylor would think and closed the door.

Sofie arched a brow. "What's wrong?"

"Do you trust me?"

"You know I do. What is it?" She took a step toward him, open concern overshadowing any apprehension she may have had about his presence in her bedroom. "Tell me."

He wanted to reach out and cup her cheek with his hand, to brush his thumb along her upper lip. He *wanted* to say, "I love you, Sofie."

But he couldn't.

"Sofie, go with me today. Now." He *wanted* to weave his fingers through her wild, rich curls, to lower his lips to hers.

Not here. Not yet. They had to leave Redemption and Warden Graham first. Then and only then could he make her his in every sense of the word. He burned with need— physical and emotional—reserved for this woman alone.

She stared at him in silence, worry and confusion furrowing her brow and darkening her eyes from blue to cobalt. "I don't understand," she finally said.

"I need to leave today," he said.

"Why?" She shook her head slowly. "Why, Luke?"

"I have some crucial business to take care of," he said, grasping for any lie that came to mind. He hated lying to her. Desperately. Being vague was his best bet, but still a lie of omission. "The weather will turn on us soon, and if I get stranded here all winter . . ."

I'm dead meat.

"What about Jenny?" Sofie straightened, stiffening. "I need to tell Dr. and Mrs. Taylor good-bye. And what about Dora? I—"

Luke chuckled, though he felt more like crying. "Hmm, what about Dora?"

Sofie gave him an impish grin. "Well, she did loan me some clothes."

"I know." He raked his fingers through his hair, praying he could convince her before Graham took action. "Jenny has Shane now. She'll be fine, thanks to all you've done for her already."

"And you." Sofie gave him a quiet smile. "I couldn't have done any of this without you. You saved me. Without you, I would've died in that explosion."

"The best day's work I've ever done," he whispered, and meant it. "The Taylors will understand. They've always known we wouldn't stay."

"Yes, but . . ."

"Today, Sofie. Please?"

"You're . . . sure about this?"

"Yes." He needed more inducement on his side, but only more lies were available. *Damn.* "I talked to someone at Roman's earlier who convinced me we had to leave now." That was true.

"I still don't . . ."

"The weather, Sofie." He shrugged, hoping this one logical excuse—and the only one that was completely true—would suffice. "We have to be at least nine thousand feet here. It's going to snow, and some of the old-timers around here think that will happen very soon."

She nodded. "Yes, that's probably true, but today?"

He brought his hands to her upper arms, gently touching her before he noticed her sling was gone. "Your shoulder is much better, the weather will be turning any day, and I have important reasons to go now."

She sighed. "I just don't know."

"Trust me, Sofie," he said. *"Please,* just trust me."

"All right, Luke. I trust you more than anyone." The expression in her eyes softened, and she looked down at one of his hands on her arm. Pink crept into her cheeks, and when she met his gaze again, Luke saw what he'd prayed he would see.

What he prayed he would always see in her eyes.

Love.

Luke went to buy horses and supplies, leaving Sofie to suffer her doubts and misgivings alone. She looked in the mirror above her dresser, wishing more than anything that she could come to terms with her feelings for that man.

Later today, she would be alone in the wilderness with a man she loved and wanted desperately. A man who'd kissed her and touched her intimately.

A priest.

She could do this. She *would* do this. Within a matter of days, Luke would return to his church and his vows, and she would see a specialist who might be able to help her regain her memory and her life.

Please, God.

"Enough of this," she whispered. She had work to do.

She couldn't leave without at least leaving a farewell note for Jenny and the Taylors. It would be wrong. Yet Luke had been adamant about not wanting her to go near the Taylors' house. She had no idea why.

"Trust me, Sofie."

She did trust him, and she loved him just as much. Lifting her fingertips to her lips, she remembered his passionate kisses and singular flavor. His forbidden touch . . . A man who should never have responded to her at all had displayed proof of his desire.

And that memory was all she would ever have of him.

She closed her eyes and prayed nothing would steal that precious memory.

A wave of dizziness punched her in the gut, and she grabbed the edge of her dresser to steady herself. Pain stabbed through her temple and into her skull as the dizziness worsened. Her stomach heaved and she broke into a cold sweat.

Shivering, she took two staggering steps to the bed and fell onto it. The room continued to spin and she squeezed her eyes shut, willing the vertigo to pass.

Gradually, the whirling slowed, but she dared not open her eyes. Pressing her hands to both temples, she drew deep breaths until the pain and nausea subsided.

Images floated through her mind, like a slide show against a background of darkness. She saw her mother's face, and the boy who must be her brother again, but older than before.

The dizziness gripped her again and the images rushed by faster, like a tornado with her trapped in its vicious vortex. She wanted to scream, but couldn't summon the strength.

Then the spinning ceased and only blackness remained. She pressed against her temples again, hoping when she opened her eyes the vertigo and pain wouldn't return. But another image stayed her.

Luke. Again they were in that cold, sterile room, with metallic objects and instruments. She saw him with his shaved head, a gray hospital gown covering him only to mid-thigh.

And she was there, wearing the same white lab coat and jeans she'd worn the day of the explosion. She must be remembering the same morning.

Some men led Luke toward a large metal object. She couldn't see all of it, because the men blocked her view. Somehow, she sensed the need to identify the metal thing.

The old priest was there as he had been in her earlier

memory, and another man wearing a dark suit she didn't remember from before. Who was he?

His eyes glittered with excitement and determination, and he paced the cold room in agitation. She was trying to tell him something important, but he wouldn't listen. She needed to stop him.

Stop what? What had she been trying to tell him?

Sofie pressed harder against her temples, but the image vanished, leaving only a misty cloud in its wake. Slowly, she opened her eyes. That mist represented her memory, and she knew now that clearing that mist was the key.

The scene that kept replaying in her mind was important. Critical. She *had* to remember.

And now, more than ever, she knew Luke had been lying to her. The man she loved and trusted had lied to her. He was keeping knowledge and information from her deliberately.

Why?

He'd asked her to trust him unconditionally, to follow him into the wilderness, to believe he would deliver her safely to Denver . . .

And she did.

Yes, despite all the evidence that he was keeping big secrets, she still believed in him and trusted him. The man had saved her life, and he looked at her with adoration. Whatever his secrets, she had to trust him to tell her when the time was right.

She had to.

"Get your butt in gear, Sofie," she said, swinging her legs over the edge of the bed as she eased herself into a sitting position. No dizziness. Whatever had caused the problem seemed to have passed.

Then she recalled the flying images and hope surged through her. Was this a sign that her memory would fully return? If the pain and dizziness came with every new memory, she welcomed it. Something a little less dramatic would've been equally welcome, but whatever it took.

If the episode signaled a serious medical condition, then she'd deal with that in Denver, too. Right now she had a trip to prepare for and good-bye notes to write.

As she reached for the doorknob, the dizziness assailed her again. Sofie dropped to the floor and closed her eyes, waiting to see what secrets would reveal themselves this time.

The livery was near Miss Lottie's, meaning Luke had to walk right past the Taylor house on his way. He passed by the front of the house, knowing Graham's room was at the rear. Still, seeing the house reminded him he had to hurry.

He hadn't ridden a horse since age eleven, when he'd spent the summer at camp. Still, he remembered enough about the basics to believe he could pull this off, and he'd lead Sofie's horse if necessary. Gentle and dependable would meet their needs well.

He pulled open the door and entered the dim interior, noting a set of wide double doors open at the rear, where the old man who ran the livery was mucking out stalls. Luke zeroed in on him and headed in that direction.

"Well, Lucifer, you're actin' like a colt again."

The sound of Sam's voice brought Luke to a halt halfway down the row of stalls. Though Luke didn't want a witness to his travel plans, he reminded himself that in this time, he wasn't an escaped convict.

Con-priest was more like it.

He looked at the black stallion Sam was grooming. The marshal talked to the giant beast as if it were human and understood every word.

The animal's eyes commanded Luke's attention. They glittered with mischief as the horse snatched the brim of

Sam's Stetson between its teeth and flung the hat across the stable with a toss of its head. The horse whinnied as Sam chuckled and stomped after his hat.

Sam bent to retrieve his hat, meeting Luke's gaze as he straightened. "Well, guess you got to see Lucifer in action, eh?" The lawman chuckled again. "That horse is one helluva lot smarter'n most men I've known."

"I can see that." Luke only knew one thing for sure. He didn't want a horse anything like Lucifer. "Beautiful animal."

"Finest horse I've ever owned." Sam jammed his hat back on and jerked his head toward the stall. "C'mon over and meet Lucifer."

"Meet him?" Luke laughed and shrugged. The horse was aptly named, though Cujo would've worked, too. "Uh, sure. Why not?" Making nice with Lucifer would give Luke a chance to say good-bye to Sam.

"Mind your manners, Lucifer," Sam said as he slid in beside the horse. "We got company."

The horse thrust its muzzle toward Luke's clean shirt and nibbled, leaving behind remnants of horsey breakfast. "Uh, gee, nice to meet you, too." He couldn't take his gaze off the horse's eyes. Lucifer really seemed to understand everything. It was uncanny . . . and disconcerting.

Sam handed Luke his bandanna. "Sorry 'bout that." The lawman patted Lucifer's neck. "He's still pretty young, but damn smart."

"Yeah, I can see that." Luke dabbed horse mess off his shirt. "I'm glad I ran into you, Sam."

"What's on your mind?" The marshal slid a feed bag over the horse's muzzle—thank goodness—and stepped out of the stall, shutting the half-door behind him.

"Sofie and I are getting ready to leave for Denver," Luke said, deciding not to waste any time making up a story. "Snow will start soon and Roman said she could travel, so I figured we'd better get started."

Sam nodded and stroked his whiskered chin. "Yep, makes sense."

"I'm here to buy a couple of horses and we'll need supplies, too." Even as he spoke, Luke realized Sam was the perfect person to help him choose a couple of horses. Gentle horses.

"Henry's got a few in the paddock out back." Sam started walking that way without being invited.

"Does he now?" Luke cleared his throat and followed his mentor to the open doors at the rear.

"Henry, the Father here needs a couple of horses."

Henry had buried a son and almost lost another in the smallpox epidemic. Luke remembered the funeral, and he searched his mind for the other boy's name, relieved when it came to him. "Henry, how's Micah doing?"

The man grinned and spit tobacco juice into the corner. "Just fine, Father." He wiped his hand on his overalls, then thrust it toward Luke.

Without hesitation, Luke shook the man's hand and mumbled words of relief about Micah's continued recovery. And meant it. He'd really fallen into his role. *Scary.*

"So you need horses?" Henry leaned his pitchfork against the door frame and headed into the bright autumn sunshine. "Got me five decent ones here. Epidemic left a few horses without owners." Henry sighed. "Money we get for 'em will pay their keep, then the rest'll go to any family."

Sam shoved his hat back farther on his head, squinting into the sunlight at the horses in the far corner of the paddock. Two of them munched on hay, while another reached over the fence to pull mouthfuls of dried grass from the ground. The others stood staring at the humans.

"What if there ain't no family left?" Sam asked, directing his lawman's gaze on poor Henry.

The other man chuckled, unaffected by Sam's query. "Anythin' left is goin' to Doc Taylor, 'course."

"Good, good." Sam walked toward the nearest horse, running his hands over the animal expertly. "This one don't show much spirit."

"That's good." Luke approached the animal with a grin when Sam frowned at him. "I want gentle and dependable times two. Not spirit."

Chuckling, Henry went around to the front of the horse and lifted its lips back to expose its huge horsey teeth. "This here ain't no youngster, Father."

"I appreciate your honesty, Henry." Luke cleared his throat. "Frankly, I don't plan to keep the horses long after we reach Denver. I'll probably give them to the Church."

Luke made a mental note to make sure he did just that. No more lies. He'd find a church—any church—and donate the horses once he and Sofie were finished with them. After this journey, he and Sofie would be ready for a nice fast train.

Though Sofie might still be looking for an airport.

Guilt constricted his throat, but he forcibly banished it. The memory of Warden Graham's eyes peering through that hood knifed through Luke, reminding him to hurry. The day was half-gone already.

"This one look okay, Sam?"

"If you don't mind a horse with no spirit, she'll do." Sam turned to Henry. "Horse got a name?"

Henry nodded. " 'Course. This is Rosie. Everybody in Redemption knows everybody *and* their livestock."

"Rosie?" Sam spit toward the nearest fencepost. "Well, she looks sound, but that's 'bout it."

"That's all I want. I'll take that one."

He chose another equally docile creature named Sissy and let Sam haggle over price while Luke poured gold nuggets into Henry's outstretched hand.

"That'll include the tack," Sam said, rather than asked.

"Sure thing, Marshal." Henry placed the glittering nuggets on a scale, indicating he was accustomed to trading in gold, rather than regular currency. "Even throw in a sidesaddle for the lady."

Sam shot Luke a look. "Ridin' through the mountains is rough, Luke," he said. "I dunno what kind of experience Miss Sofie's got with sidesaddles, but I reckon ridin' astride'll be safer."

Luke knew if Sofie had any riding experience, it wouldn't have been in a sidesaddle. "Two regular saddles then. Thanks, Sam."

Sam also accompanied Luke to the dry goods, where they purchased blankets, something called hardtack, canned beans, jerky, and canteens. If not for Sam's experience, Luke might've ridden into the wilderness without the proper supplies.

Sofie trusted him—Luke couldn't let her down.

They walked the horses to the rear of the parsonage, where Sam and Luke shook hands. "Father, if you're ever in Ft. Smith, Arkansas, you look me and my missus up. Hear?"

The back door opened and Sofie stepped through. She eyed the horses warily, then smiled at Sam. "Thank you for everything, Marshal." She offered him her hand.

Sam looked at her strangely, then grinned and shook her hand. "Miss Dr. Sofie, it's been a pleasure meetin' you and Luke here."

"Thank you, Marshal, and thank you for helping Jenny and Shane."

"It's honest work." Still grinning, United States Marshal Sam Weathers took a step back and tipped his hat. "Godspeed, ma'am. You remember how I told you to find the pass, Luke?"

"I do, thanks."

Luke watched Sam walk away, then chuckled and looked at Sofie. "Who *was* that masked man?"

An expression of surprise and suspicion crossed her face,

but he watched her bring it under control. A dark cloud fell across her eyes.

Something had happened during his absence. Fear trickled through his veins. "Did . . . did you have any company while I was gone, Sofie?" He had to know. Could Warden Graham have walked over here and told Sofie everything? Of course he could have. Luke remembered the man walking without a limp earlier today.

"No, whatever gave you that idea?" Sofie turned and opened the door, but just stood there without entering for a few minutes. "By the way, there's no way I'm riding a horse in a dress. I'm borrowing a pair of your jeans and a shirt before we leave."

"Good idea."

She stepped through the door and turned to face him again. The smile she flashed was false.

Something was definitely wrong.

"I can't wait to get back to civilization and fast food," she said casually.

Too casually. *Oh, my God.* Had she remembered? Her laughter came too easily. Forced.

"I've had enough of antiquity to last me a lifetime," she said, still brandishing that fake smile. "If I never see another Victorian dress, it'll be too soon."

"Uh . . ." What could Luke say without playing his hand prematurely? Nothing. He was trapped until she played *her* cards. Sofie had obviously remembered something.

Enough to make her suspicious.

"Maybe we'll pass a McDonald's on the way," she said, as she closed the door behind her.

How much had she remembered? Everything? His breath caught in his throat. Did she know about him?

No, she couldn't know everything. Why would she have agreed to leave with him if she knew?

"McDonald's." Luke sighed, mustering his self-control. "I don't think they allow horses in the drive-thru," he muttered to the nearest horse, shock and uncertainty still ricocheting through his brain. In response, Rosie batted her big brown eyes at him and nudged his chest with her muzzle.

Leaving behind a trail of half-chewed oats.

Chapter Eighteen

Sofie remembered how to ride a horse. Sort of.

When she climbed into the saddle, she knew to grip the reins with one hand, sparing her injured shoulder. She remembered to pull the reins on only one side to make the horse turn, and to pull evenly on both sides to make it stop or slow.

She was on a roll. Now if she could just stay in the saddle . . .

By the time they reached the top of the first hill, Rosie was displaying much more vigor. "Looks like you have your hands full," Sofie said.

He shot her a sheepish grin over his shoulder. "Yeah, I've got my hands full here."

"I see that." Sofie turned and looked back over her shoulder. "Oh, look."

Luke stopped his horse beside hers and they both stared down the mountain. Nestled at the base of a snow-covered peak, the town of Redemption looked like a postcard fit for any Rocky Mountain vacationer to send home. Tears stung Sofie's eyes, and she dragged the back of her gloved hand across them.

"I'm going to miss them, too," Luke said, his voice low and sincere.

When he reached over to touch her arm, Sofie turned to face him. "I know." Guilt welled up within her when she saw the worry lines creasing his forehead. She hadn't meant to upset him with her flippant remarks earlier, but she knew he was hiding something, and she was determined to find out what.

"I'm glad you left notes for everybody." Rosie stepped sideways and Luke grabbed the reins again. "With your sore shoulder, it's a good thing you got Sissy instead of this rowdy old nag."

Despite all her suspicions, Sofie laughed. It felt so good and natural to laugh with Luke. Even though he was keeping secrets from her, she loved and trusted him. An oxymoron? Probably, but there it was. Sighing, she urged her horse into a slow walk along the trail behind Luke.

Mid-afternoon sun promised good traveling weather, at least for today. Sofie prayed they wouldn't get lost, and that the weather would hold until they reached Denver. After her flash of new memories this afternoon, she was more eager than ever to see Dr. Bowen. Maybe once she recovered all her memory, she could eliminate the nagging suspicions she had regarding Luke and his secrets.

Though they could never be lovers, they could be friends. Sighing, she urged Sissy over a fallen log. Disappointment threatened her resolve, but she blinked back her tears and cleared her throat.

Luke had chosen his life as a priest, and she had no right to question that. She loved him, and she'd simply have to restrain her feelings to friendship only.

Admiring the way his hair curled at the nape of his neck, she remembered the silky feel of it beneath her fingers. And with a flash of fire low in her body, she remembered the warmth of his lips on her flesh. Her breasts swelled and ached, longing to welcome him again.

So much for restraint.

Luke had strayed from his vows, but not completely. They'd both been under a lot of stress after the epidemic, especially with the threats hanging over Jenny and Shane. He hadn't touched her since that night, except as a concerned friend.

A friend—get it straight, Sofie.

Regret and disappointment merged with determination, and she lifted her chin. She would temper her obsession with this man, and she would recover her memory and get on with her life.

That was that.

The air cooled rapidly as the sun settled behind the highest peak to the west. Maneuvering their horses along the rocky trail became increasingly treacherous until they descended into a valley, where the terrain leveled somewhat. Luke paused and wiped his brow, glancing back at Sofie with a smile.

"So far, so good," he said. "We're supposed to find a stream along here that we should follow all the way down."

"As good as Triple A, I'm sure." Sofie returned his smile, determined to keep things friendly and easy between them.

Luke chuckled and looked up at the darkening sky. "We could've gone to Cripple Creek and caught either the stage or train down to Colorado Springs, but Henry said it would be faster to go to Denver on horseback."

A train. Sofie sighed wistfully. A little luxury would be welcome about now, but speed was more important.

"I'd like to find that stream before it gets any darker," he added.

That made sense. She prodded Sissy to follow when Luke started farther into the valley. Though the sky was still light, down here with the mortals, shadows gathered, making their surroundings more ominous with every step.

"What's that?" Luke brought his horse to a stop and cocked his head.

"What? I don't hear anything." Sofie fell silent when he raised his hand. After a moment, she heard something. "Is it water?"

Luke nodded and prodded Rosie toward the sound, with Sofie following closely. She didn't want to lose sight of Luke in the murky light.

"Right on schedule." Luke held back a branch until Sofie and her horse eased by and entered the clearing. "This stream and the sun will be our guide."

"Good." Sofie's butt was more than ready to part company with the saddle. "Pity it isn't a hot spring."

Groaning, Luke dismounted and held her reins as she did the same. "Yeah, I could use a soak myself."

The air grew frosty as Luke unsaddled the horses and hobbled them nearby. "I sure hope I did that right, or we'll wake up sans horses," he said, carrying a bundle of sticks to a flat area near the stream. A circle of charred stones indicated someone else had once camped in the clearing.

"You must've been a Boy Scout."

Luke glanced up, a guarded expression in his eyes. "Once upon a time," he said.

His secrets. Sofie watched until the fire was going well before glancing at the nearest clump of trees and shrubs. "I, uh, need to . . ."

He nodded and fed more wood to the blaze. "Don't go too far."

She had no intention of straying far. After taking care of business, she returned quickly to the fire's warmth. She couldn't bear to sit too soon, so she turned her backside toward the heat.

Luke chuckled, and she couldn't suppress her answering grin as he fumbled through their supplies. Within a few

moments, she smelled something cooking and turned back
to find a small iron kettle in the coals near the fire's base.

"If I'm doing this right, we'll have beans tonight."

Sofie smiled. Anything warm sounded good right now.
Shivering, she squatted down near the fire.

"Cold?" Luke walked away, then returned a moment
later with a blanket. He wrapped it around her shoulders,
letting his hands linger a moment, Sofie thought, before he
returned to tending the beans. And had his hand brushing
against her braided hair been accidental . . . or deliberate?

Stop it, Sofie.

She wanted to touch him desperately. As she watched
him move around the fire, stirring the beans and adding
wood to the fragrant blaze, her heart swelled with love and
longing. He was definitely a special man.

Of course, it took a special kind of man to dedicate his
life to God. The reminder of his vows made her throat
clog with unshed tears, and gut clench with guilt.

I love you, Luke.

And she would take her love for this man with her to the
grave. She knew that now. Regardless of what happened, or
where they went after reaching Denver, she would carry
her love for him in her heart forever.

Always.

He filled a tin plate with steaming beans and handed it
to her. "Careful, it's hot."

She took the plate and watched him serve himself, then
he sat on a rock beside her. "I think cowboys always drink
coffee, but I'm a wimp. It keeps me awake at night." He
spooned beans into his mouth, then turned toward her.
"But if you want some, I could—"

"No, water's fine." She lifted the tin cup to her lips and
took a long drink. "Thank you."

"My pleasure."

Sofie ate her beans in silence, then offered to rinse the
dishes in the stream, but he insisted on doing it himself.

"You're spoiling me," she argued.

"I know."

Those two little words poured over her like warm maple syrup. A shiver skittered down her spine, and she pulled the blanket closer as she watched him rinse the dishes in the stream then pack them away for the night.

"Sam said to hang our food in a tree away from where we sleep," he said, tossing a rope over a branch and tying their supplies to it.

Where we *sleep?* Sofie's breath caught and her pulse launched. *Houston, we have lift-off.*

Luke pulled the rope, hoisting their supplies into the air, high enough that no creatures would be able to reach it. "There. Even Big Foot couldn't reach that."

"Big Foot?" Sofie suddenly noticed the night sounds. An owl hooted, something else scurried along the ground just beyond the friendly circle of firelight. "Oh."

Chuckling, Luke fed more wood to the blaze. "I'll keep this going, Sofie," he promised. "Don't worry."

She knew the flames would keep wild animals away, so she relaxed somewhat. No, her greatest threat wasn't from wild animals, but from herself.

Because in her heart and soul, she couldn't deny that if Luke weren't a priest, she'd throw herself at him tonight. She'd give anything to feel his lips on hers, his gentle touch against her flesh.

His body buried deep inside hers.

Oh, God. She swallowed hard and let the blanket slip from her shoulders. Cold was definitely not her problem now.

"You okay?" He returned to her side, absently poking at the embers with a long stick. "Your shoulder hurting?"

"No, my shoulder's fine." She drew a deep, cleansing breath and released it very slowly. The distance to Denver suddenly seemed much farther.

"Good. I was afraid the night air would aggravate it."

Aggravated was a good word, but definitely didn't apply to her shoulder. Sofie squirmed slightly, trying to ignore the ever-tightening knot of desire low in her belly.

She must've been sexually active before her amnesia. Otherwise, how could she have such specific knowledge of what she was missing? What she wanted.

Now.

Closing her eyes, she visualized Luke covering her with his long, muscular body, pressing his hard erection against her soft, hungry—

Gasping, she lurched to her feet, leaving the blanket behind as she fled to the stream. Maybe a frigid mountain stream could douse the fervent flames in her body and heart. Luke was beside her in an instant.

He touched her.

No, don't do that. She couldn't stand it now. Not now. She'd snap if he kept touching her.

"Sofie?" He stepped in front of her and put both his hands on her, one on her upper arm and the other on her cheek. "You don't have a fever."

She shook her head. *Oh, yes . . . yes, I do.*

"What's wrong?" He stroked her cheek with the backs of his fingers, sending rivulets of desire cascading through her.

Sofie trembled and he wrapped his arms around her. "You *are* cold," he whispered against her hair. "Come on back to the fire."

I have a fire of my own. She trembled again as he rubbed her back, his hand roaming over her spine in slow, stimulating circles.

"Oh, Luke," she whispered, wanting to devour him on the spot. She felt like a nocturnal predator, preying on unsuspecting priests. "Please . . ."

"Please what?" His voice grew husky and he buried his face against the side of her neck, nuzzling her without

actually kissing. Everything he did could easily be miscon-
strued as totally innocent.

But Sofie couldn't forget that night on the floor of the
parsonage, when he'd branded her body and soul. Now
they stood beneath the stars, the silent night enveloping
them in a cocoon so private no one would ever know.

No one but them.

"Don't, please," she said, pulling away and returning
to the campfire.

She heard him follow, knew he paused mere inches
away, but she refused to look away from the bright orange
flames. Luke was far more dangerous than the most blis-
tering inferno.

"I'm sorry," he whispered. "So sorry."

Warden Carl Graham would see justice done. He didn't
care what happened to him in this bizarre place and time.
All that mattered was that he fulfill his destiny.

By carrying out Luke Nolan's execution.

Why else had he been spared from certain death? He
had a mission to complete, then he could die in peace.

Pulling the gray mask over his hideous face, he crossed
the small bedroom he still occupied in the Taylor house
and opened the door. Today he would see justice done at
last.

Physically, he felt strong enough to complete his duty,
though a nagging ache in his chest plagued him. He knew
it was his heart. At his last physical, the doctor had warned
him he had to retire and start taking it easy.

But none of that mattered now.

Forsaking his limp at long last, he went down the hall
to Dr. Taylor's office. With his strength returned, he would
now fulfill his mission, making his disguise—such as it
was—unnecessary. Wouldn't that old quack be shocked to
learn who Father Salazar really was? Without bothering to

knock, Graham opened the door and entered the doctor's office.

The white-haired physician looked up from the papers on his desk with an expression of surprise. His woolly eyebrows shot upward, then a smile split his face.

"Mr. Smith, it's good to see you up and about." Taylor rose and approached.

"Where's Nolan?" Graham asked in his raspy voice. "Where's he staying?"

Taylor's shock multiplied and his mouth fell open. "You can talk."

"Where's Nolan?"

Dr. Taylor shook his head and removed his spectacles. "Nolan? I don't know anyone by—" He snapped his fingers. "Oh, wait, there's someone by that name in Cripple Creek—owns a saloon, I think. Is that your name? Is this Nolan a relative of yours?"

"Not hardly." Graham moved closer. The thought of delaying his mission long enough to explain the priest's true identity was unthinkable, though he'd looked forward to it. "Where's the . . . priest and that doctor?"

His gaze narrowing, Dr. Taylor shook his head. "They left yesterday for—"

Fury boiled in Graham's gut and he swept his arm across Taylor's desk, scattering papers and ink across the floor. "Where'd they go?" A roar erupted from somewhere deep in his soul. "Where?"

Taylor looked at the mess, then marched to the outside door and opened it. "Get out of my home," he said in low, clipped tones. "I've done my duty by you, but you've overstayed your welcome in this house, and in Redemption."

Graham moved toward the open door, not caring if he had a roof over his head, food to eat, or a place to sleep. Nothing mattered except justice.

Nothing.

"Where?" He stopped in front of Dr. Taylor and lifted his chin, pinning the man with his gaze. "Tell me that . . . and I'll go."

Taylor was apparently weighing his options. After several moments, he said, "I don't know why you want them, but they went where you'll never find them. Now go."

Dora Fleming appeared in the doorway, her eyes wide with shock. "What's—?"

"Where'd the priest go?" Graham stepped into the doorway, glowering down at Dora. "Tell me."

"Don't tell him anything, Dora," Dr. Taylor called from behind Graham.

Ignoring the doctor, Graham stared intently into Dora's eyes. "Tell me."

"Denver."

Denver. Graham pushed past her and staggered into the street, aware of the door being slammed behind him. He didn't care about that—burning bridges was now a moot point.

Only justice.

He hadn't been outside except for the day they moved him from the school to Taylor's house. He wasn't a bit worried, though, because now that he knew Nolan had gone to Denver, he knew exactly where to find the bastard.

Warden Graham had made it his business over the years to learn everything he could about Luke Nolan and his family. Yes, he knew *exactly* where Nolan would run, and he would follow.

But first, he must prepare the execution chamber.

Luke opened his eyes to a gray shroud. Was he dead? If so, this certainly wasn't hell. Too damned cold.

After a few moments, his vision acclimated itself to the dull light of dawn, and he pushed to a sitting position. The temperature was easily twenty degrees colder than the previous day. They had to hurry to lower elevation before it started to snow.

How many days had it been since they left Redemption? He'd lost track after three. Still, he figured they shouldn't be too far from the pass that would take them down the Front Range and into the rolling foothills.

He sniffed the icy air and looked at the thick layer of clouds overhead. Without the sun's warmth and guidance, today's journey would be more difficult than he'd hoped.

"Sofie?" They wouldn't take time for breakfast this morning. "Sofie, we have to go now."

She stirred and stretched, pushing herself up onto one elbow. "Ugh."

"Ugh?" Luke chuckled as he retrieved their supplies from a nearby tree and started to saddle her horse. "I'm afraid winter's catching up with us, so we're going to skip breakfast and try to eat lunch where it's warmer."

"How about Howard Johnson's?" Grimacing, Sofie stood and ran her fingers through her wild mane of curls. "Holiday Inn?" She arched a brow when he laughed. "Super 8?"

As she disappeared into a clump of trees for some privacy, Luke's laughter ceased. Sofie must have remembered more. With every day that passed, she grew more vocal about the culture they'd left in the future. And her knowledge of semi-useless information would make her a natural in a game of Trivial Pursuit.

They were far enough from Redemption that he could tell her his plans to leave the church now, and ask her to marry him. She had to say yes. She had to.

But this morning, he couldn't take the time to propose. Getting her out of these mountains before snow fell took priority.

Tonight. Promising himself, he finished saddling the horses and freshened their canteens in the frigid stream.

The cold air stung his cheeks and wind howled down the mountain, right through his wool coat.

Zeke had said buffalo robes were the only way to keep warm in the mountains, but Luke had left too quickly to acquire such luxuries. He shuddered and fastened a canteen over each saddle horn just as Sofie reappeared.

"It's going to snow," she said, her eyes filled with worry. "I can feel it."

"Yeah, I know." Since necessity required they sleep in their coats and gloves, they were ready to go within a few minutes.

They couldn't talk above the wind, so Luke assured himself of Sofie's safety by periodically glancing back as they followed the trail along the stream. In some places, the ground gave way so suddenly, they had to circle into the woods, then back again to the stream. Without the sun, he had no other guide.

He looked back at Sofie again when snow started to fall. The narrow opening in her muffler allowed him to see the expression in her eyes. Fear and worry.

Ditto.

The rocky terrain hindered their progress, but Luke decided to push ahead until they had to stop. Sofie obviously shared his urgency, and never uttered a word of protest as the snow grew heavier and started to stick.

After Rosie almost lost her footing, Luke realized they had to slow their pace even more. *Damn.* He could barely see ten feet ahead.

Reminded of the day he'd carried Sofie into an abandoned mine to hide from a storm, he wished they could find such shelter now. Squinting, he explored the surrounding terrain, praying for a miracle. Would God listen to a fake priest? All Luke could do was try.

Please, God, for Sofie . . .

He heard her shout and icy shards of fear lashed through

him. Bringing Rosie to a stop, he turned to see her pointing across the stream.

Luke looked where she pointed, making out a shadowy shape through the blur of white. Too large to be a man, he realized after a moment that it was a small cabin.

Thank you.

He motioned with his hand that they should cross the shallow stream. Halfway across, the wind took on a different pitch. No, not the wind.

Sofie's scream.

As if in slow motion, he watched her horse stumble and pitch Sofie into the icy water. Luke vaulted from the saddle and rushed to her side.

By the time he reached her, she was completely submerged. He pulled her soaked body from the water and lifted her into his arms, pulling the muffler away from her face enough to see her closed eyes. She was unconscious, but breathing.

She had to be all right. "Stay with me, Sofie," he whispered against the howling wind.

Staggering from the water and up the opposite bank, Luke was vaguely aware of the horses standing nose to tail. He spied a dugout or something built into the side of the mountain beside the cabin. The stupid beasts didn't have sense to take cover on their own, but he'd tend them later. Sofie came first.

The abandoned cabin was small and square, but sound. Luke pushed the door open with his shoulder. It only opened partway, forcing him to squeeze through with his burden.

So cold. He had to get her warm and dry.

Snow filtered between the logs, where the chinking had crumbled away. The back of the cabin must have been built against the mountain, because it wasn't as drafty.

Spotting a bed, Luke realized that the cabin was too clean to have been empty long. With any luck, he'd also find a few supplies, and he'd leave some gold to repay their absent host. Some warm quilts lay neatly folded on a shelf above the bed. This was a sure sign their luck was about to improve. *I hope.*

He peeled the soggy gloves, muffler, hat, and coat from Sofie and dropped them to the floor. She was so pale and still, but he knew she wasn't dead. He would've felt it and known the moment she left him.

He pulled off her sodden shoes and socks, then removed his jeans from her slim hips. She moaned in protest as he slid the wet shirt from her shoulders. "Atta girl, Sofie," he said, blinking back the tears of relief that burned his eyes. "Talk to me."

Even her underthings were soaked. He hesitated for only a moment, then removed them, too. Now wasn't the time to permit his hungry gaze to feast. He clutched her to him fiercely, his love pouring from his heart and into hers.

"I love you, Sofie," he whispered fiercely. "Don't die, baby. Don't die."

After wrapping her in one quilt and piling two more on top of her, Luke left her on the bunk and went to the stone hearth. A lantern sat on the mantel. "Let there be light," he muttered, fishing the small tin of precious matches from deep in his coat pocket.

With the lantern's light, he found the firebox filled with enough wood to last them a few days. The dry wood caught fast, and soon bright orange flames devoured it, filling the tiny cabin with much needed warmth.

Rubbing his hands together, he crossed the room to check on Sofie. Pulling back a corner of the quilt, he found her beautiful green eyes staring up at him.

"You're awake." He sat on the edge of the bunk and stroked damp curls back from her face. "How do you feel?"

"Head hurts." Her voice trembled, and he tucked the quilts around her more snugly. "Again."

"I'm just glad you're all right." He sighed, then cleared his throat. "Nothing else hurts?"

"I don't think so, but I'm sleepy." He watched her look around. "Is this heaven?"

Chuckling, he found and squeezed her hand through the quilt. "I think it's just this side of it."

"Still snowing?"

"Yes, which reminds me . . ." Luke stood, but remained close to the bunk, leaning down to study her face as he spoke. "I have to check on the horses and get our supplies."

"Be careful."

He nodded. "Listen, Sofie, if anything happens to me out there—"

"Don't talk that way." She tried to sit up, but he pressed her back against the quilt. "Don't, Luke. Promise me."

"I'll be careful."

"Okay, but you're still wet."

"I'm going to get a lot wetter." He studied her for a few moments, mustering his courage. "When I get back, there's something important I have to tell you."

She stared in silence for a few minutes. "I'm not going anywhere."

"Good. I'll be right back."

Luke wrapped his muffler around his neck and across his face again, and made sure his ears were covered. He pulled on his slightly damp gloves and glanced back at Sofie before he went out into the blizzard.

The blast of cold hurt. There was no other word to describe it. He pulled the door shut quickly behind him, then ducked his head into the wind, trying to see the horses. Feeling his way along the side of the cabin, he finally saw them only a few feet from the dugout.

So much for horse sense. He grabbed the reins, and Rosie and Sissy both gave him looks that said, "In your dreams, buster. We're staying put."

After much tugging and cussing, he finally managed to drag the stupid beasts out of the storm. Of course, if horses were really smart they wouldn't let humans ride them. Luke should be grateful for their stupidity. Later maybe.

The quiet of the dugout was awesome. It was much better insulated than the leaky cabin, but he wouldn't trade the bed and fireplace for anything.

He unsaddled the horses and gave them both a generous portion of feed. Then he filled the empty trough in the corner with snow, hoping it would melt enough to provide the animals with water until the storm passed.

Sofie'd been right. This was heaven. Comparatively speaking. They had a decent amount of food, shelter, heat . . .

And each other. It was time to set the course for the rest of his life.

Chapter Nineteen

The vertigo Sofie'd suffered before slammed into her again with a vengeance. Her stomach heaved, and if there'd been anything in it, she knew it wouldn't have stayed down long.

Images spun through her head, sharper and clearer than ever before. A different flash of memory flooded her brain with pictures—a man in a hospital bed. In her heart, she knew the young man was someone she loved and cared about, but her vision wouldn't let her see his face clearly.

Tears stung her closed eyes, but the dizziness subsided, leaving her spent and shaken. She heard the door open, and a blast of cold air swirled through the cabin. *Luke.*

"Sofie, what's wrong?" Luke gently shook her shoulder. "Wake up."

Furious with her inability to remember, she lurched from beneath the quilts and lashed out at her only friend. Luke was keeping secrets. He knew things that could help her end this madness. She struck blindly with her fist until he grabbed and held her wrists.

Tears streamed down her face and her body convulsed. "Tell me, damn you," she said. "Tell me."

The expression of helplessness in his eyes was too much. Sofie sagged against him, letting him support her weight. Sobs tore from her heart, from her soul, from her shattered memories. "Please, t-tell me."

His arms went around her, and she felt as if a great weight had been lifted from her. Her sobs ceased and her tears subsided, as his warmth penetrated her bones and offered comfort. The rough wool of his coat teased her chilled flesh.

Her naked flesh.

Of course, he'd obviously undressed her himself, so she had nothing left to hide.

Nothing except her heart.

"What is it you want me to tell you, Sofie?" he asked, his voice gentle and seductive. "You know I'd never hurt you. Don't you?"

Sofie nodded against his shoulder, the rough fabric abrading her cheek. "I . . . I want to know everything you know about me." She lifted her face and looked up at him. "You *must* know something. Otherwise, why were we together that morning? Please, please don't lie to me."

"Sofie . . ." Luke sighed, bringing his hand up to stroke her hair. "I have so much to tell you."

The fire's heat and his embrace chased away the chill. "I'm listening."

"All right."

She rested her head against his shoulder again, slipping her arms around his waist. Desire made her feel warm and languid. She wanted him now more than ever, but she needed to concentrate on getting answers to her questions.

He cleared his throat and stroked her hair, now completely free of its tight braid. "Aren't you cold?" His voice sounded strained.

"My clothes are wet. Remember?" Reluctantly, she slid

from the protective circle of his embrace and pulled a quilt from the bed. She should be ashamed, parading around nude in front of a priest, but a wicked part of her loved the way his gray eyes smoldered as he watched her wrap the quilt around her body. "There, is that better?"

Clearing his throat again, he removed his coat, hat, and boots, then carried the wet items over and spread them out before the fire with hers. Sofie loved watching him. His movements were spare and precise, and well-toned muscles rippled enticingly beneath his shirt. For a priest, he was one fine hunk of man.

Focus on the questions, Sofie. Trying to ignore the coil of longing that settled low in her belly, she drew a deep breath. Luke was ready to provide answers, but she had to put her questions into words. Intelligible words. She could do this.

Preparing for the inquisition, she climbed onto the bunk and folded her legs, covering herself completely with the warm quilt. He returned and sat on the edge of the bed, his smile warm and his eyes stormy. Yes, he definitely knew something.

"I put some snow in a kettle over the fire to heat." He sighed, appearing resigned. "All right, ask your questions, then I'm going to fix us something to eat. I'm starved."

She kept the quilt tucked around her while she turned to face him. She wanted to watch his eyes. His beautiful eyes . . .

"What happened? Who am I?" There, that was pretty specific. "And why do I remember things that don't exist here? I can tell you understand some of those things, too. *Please,* Luke?"

"I . . ." He rubbed his eyes, then looked up to meet her gaze again. A muscle twitched in his jaw. "Well, I don't think Plan A is going to work after all." He gave a cynical laugh.

"Plan A?" Sofie's heart thudded against her ribs. She knew something important was about to happen. "What?"

"Are you sure you're ready for this?"

She nodded, praying she wouldn't regret it later. "Go ahead."

"Something crazy happened that morning." He shook his head. "I . . . I don't know exactly how this happened, but somehow those explosions . . ."

"Somehow those explosions *what?*"

His expression grew somber as he met and held her gaze. "Sofie, those explosions threw us back in time over a hundred years."

She laughed. It was a crazy kind of laugh, sort of like something from *The Bride of Frankenstein.* After a moment, her laughter died. As crazy as it sounded, wasn't this the only explanation? Wasn't that why Redemption had seemed trapped in the past?

Because *they* were trapped in the past?

"I . . . I don't understand," she said, her voice sounding much calmer than she'd expected. "You're saying we're both from the future?"

"Yes." Luke sighed. "Instead of dying in that explosion, we were thrown back in time."

"Together." Sofie's throat clogged with unshed tears as the enormity of their situation struck her full force. "We should've died, but we were spared for some reason."

"Some would say divine intervention." He reached out to stroke her cheek with the backs of his fingers. "Sofie, you're so beautiful."

She swallowed hard, knowing there was more he hadn't said. "You really don't know my name?"

"No, but I wish I did." He tugged at his collar and rubbed the back of his neck. "Someone told me you were a doctor, but we weren't formally introduced."

"I see." She tilted her head to one side. "Where were we? What was happening there?"

"A, uh, an electrical experiment. Government stuff."
He gave a nervous chuckle. Too nervous.

"A medical procedure?" She watched his changing
expression, knowing he still hadn't told her everything.
"Luke, I remember seeing you in a hospital gown. Tell
me."

His face paled and he dropped his hand to his side.
"Just an experiment. I really don't know much more than
that."

Tears stung her eyes and she shook her head. "You're
still keeping something from me, Luke." Her voice cracked
and she wondered why and how she'd fallen in love with
this man. How could she, when he continued to withhold
critical information? "Tell me."

His face reddened beneath a few days' growth of beard,
and the expression in his eyes was haunted. "Sofie . . ."

She rose onto her knees and faced him, gritting her
teeth as anger warred with the love she still felt for this
beautiful, lying man. "Tell me."

"I'm not a priest, Sofie. Never was."

Her blood roared through her veins and pounded in
her head. "You're . . ."

"Not a priest."

Shock spiraled through her. "Not a priest?"

"Never was," he repeated.

She stared at him, watching the expression in his eyes
carefully. He was telling the truth. "I don't understand."

He sighed and shook his head slowly. "How could you?"

"Why, Luke?" Dumbfounded, she watched a light flare
in his eyes as his gaze drifted down the front of her, as
if he could see right through the patchwork quilt. Her
confusion made way for the hunger she'd struggled to
keep buried all these weeks. The full meaning of his confession, and all its implications, hit her suddenly and without
mercy.

The man she'd been lusting after and fallen madly in

love with wasn't a priest? They were two *consenting* adults thrown back in time together, with no sacred vows standing between them . . . "Really not a priest?" Her mouth went dry and the flush of desire swept through her.

"Really not." He gave her a boyish grin, then reached out to cup her cheek again.

Her other questions could wait. After weeks of self-denial, her physical needs were cutting in line. No more waiting. She knew what she wanted, what he wanted, and now there was no reason not to . . .

With trembling hands, she opened the front edges of the quilt covering her aching breasts, enjoying how his smoky eyes darkened from gray to obsidian. A smile tugged at the corners of her mouth and she let the quilt fall from her shoulders.

She loved the way his gaze caressed her bare flesh. Her nipples hardened beneath his scrutiny, aching for his touch. And his mouth. Oh, she definitely remembered his mouth. Her breathing quickened and the emptiness within her became unbearable.

"Well, then . . ." She bit her lower lip, then ran her tongue over it slowly. Sensuously.

His soft intake of breath assured her he understood her unspoken invitation. How could he *not?* Like a bow drawn too tight, her body quivered in anticipation.

Slowly, he trailed his fingers from her cheek, down the column of her throat, to the curve of her shoulder. He rose onto his knees to face her, placing his hands on her shoulders. "Sofie, do you understand what you're doing to me?"

She nodded. "I don't know what kind of woman I am—was," she said, violent need rocketing through her. "Naughty or nice, all I know is what I want—what I need. *Now.*"

"Now?"

"Luke, do I have to draw you a picture?" She pulled

his hand from her shoulder and dragged it to her bare breast. "An X-rated picture?"

His gaze drifted down the length of her, then back to her face. "You're sure?"

"Now, Luke." Her voice fell to a husky whisper. "Now."

Her nipple was burning a hole in Luke's palm. Something snapped inside him. Desire, love, relief? Yes, everything hit him at once. The woman offering herself to him was much more than a hot, naked babe sending out an invitation.

This was Sofie—the woman he loved.

Even in the dimness, her eyes were wide but not frightened. She lifted her lips to his in offering, and he was lost. With a guttural growl, he hauled her firmly against him in a single powerful tug.

Lightning flared between them, hot and thick, crackling with an intensity that stole his breath. He took her mouth gently at first, but she made it clear that gentleness was not what she wanted. Or needed.

That suited him fine. The fire flared too hot and out of control. Their only defense against the blaze was to let it *burn*.

Lips, tongues, teeth, nothing held back, Luke took and gave in turn. That urgent, commanding kiss was the catalyst that broke the dam of reserve for them both. Suddenly they were all hands and mouths, touching, stroking, tugging at his remaining clothing.

Naked and panting, he pulled back to gaze into her eyes, drowning in their blue brilliance. Savage need spiked from her and into him, urging him to take her without preamble.

"Now, Luke," she urged, seeming to read his thoughts. "Now."

Just like the night he'd awakened her from that erotic

dream, she knew exactly what words would drive him over the precipice. Yes, he'd take her now. He had no choice and she obviously shared his urgency. Raw need slammed into him with a violence that stunned him.

Naked and breathless, they faced each other, waiting for the other to make the next move.

Then she nearly killed him.

Reaching between them, she took his erection in both hands. Like a shotgun with both barrels cocked, he nearly exploded on contact. Of course, Sofie had no way of knowing how long it had been for him . . . how little sexual experience he really had.

Feel your way, Nolan. He could do this. On the job training was the only way to fly. *For every action, there should be a reaction,* or something like that.

She'd touched him right where it counted, so now it was his turn. Cupping her bottom in his hands, he lifted her up and against him, savoring the gasp of shock and pleasure that erupted from her.

"Please," she whispered, her tone almost pleading.

Her arms slipped around his neck and she kissed him again as he dipped his hand between her legs. She was hot and ready, and she jerked her mouth away from his, arching her neck backward.

She moaned a sultry, sexual sound and wrapped her legs around his hips. Desperate, he answered her primitive growl with one of his own as he lowered her to the bunk. As agile as a gymnast, she shifted her legs from his hips to his waist, pulling him closer.

He froze over her, his throbbing tip against her warm, moist folds. She was hot, and he knew she'd be tight. A shudder of longing rippled through him, but—one more time—he searched her face for reassurance. Her eyes were wide, glazed with passion, begging for release.

"Come home, Luke," she said.

And he did.

He thrust into her. Powerfully. She pressed her cheek against his sweaty shoulder, urging him on with words that would've shocked the good citizens of Redemption. Her words and moans floated around him in an erotic cloud as he drove into her again and again.

She contracted around him in primal hunger and need—her nails raked his shoulders. Hot, so hot. She met him, drew from him, demanded all he could give, arching and writhing against him and with him.

Like a vise, she swallowed his full length and cried out in completion. Luke strained and exploded within her, culminating their mutual need.

Home at last.

Mere inches from his lips, Sofie savored his expression for her future memories. They stayed like this, staring and panting, for what seemed like forever. The only sounds she heard were the howls of the wind outside and the slowing thunder of their heartbeats.

He lifted his upper body from her, though he remained buried inside her. She wriggled slightly against him, smiling when he winced.

Gazing down at her, he said, "I love you, Sofie." Simply. Clearly.

Exhilaration shot through her. *He's not a priest and he loves me.* "I love you, too. So much . . ." A tear spilled from the corner of her eye and he kissed it away.

All the weeks of denial and guilt were gone forever. Now she could love and be loved. Nothing else mattered. All that mattered was his gentleness stirring the fire in her heart and soul, and—at long last—her body.

"Sofie." His whisper caressed her cheek as he lowered his lips to hers.

A moan rumbled from deep in her throat as her insides sprang to life all over again. His mouth was silky yet demanding—filled with promise. Luke broke their kiss and gazed into her eyes again. His pupils were huge, obliterating all but a thin ring of silver around their black centers.

"I want you," she said.

"Again?" He chuckled, waggling his eyebrows.

"Always."

He pulled her more tightly against him, flaunting his renewed ability to satisfy them both yet again. Lowering his mouth to hers, his tongue converged with hers in a primitive and unmistakable reproduction of what their bodies had just experienced.

On fire, she was at the brink of losing conscious thought yet again. She'd hungered for this—denial was futile. Ever since that night on the parlor floor, she'd dreamed of completion, of consummation, of victory.

And once tasted, she knew she'd never get enough of this man.

He raised up to stare down at her again. Her heart thundered in synch with her libido as candid hunger and desire flared in his smoky eyes. Even that brief moment of tranquility was imbued with sinful yearning. Wild, fundamental human need.

This was much more than just great sex. Love fueled her, drove her, weakened her, yet empowered her at the same time.

Sweeping her lips with the tip of her tongue, she gave him a lingering smile. She rested her cheek against his shoulder, cherishing the texture of his skin. "Make love to me—with me—again. Now."

"I think now is your favorite word. Woman, you make me crazy." He nuzzled the side of her neck, driving her mad as he traced slow, lazy circles. "I love you so much it scares the hell out of me."

"Good. Hold that thought." She smiled a secret smile against his warm skin. *He loves me.* Joy swept through her all over again, leaving her agog for a few breathless moments. They were companion time-travelers, spirit-mates.

This was their destiny.

"Wait right here."

He climbed off her and ran across the room, returning with the kettle of melted snow and a rag. Her gaze feasted on every delicious inch of him as he dampened the rag with steaming water. After setting the kettle aside, he bathed her very gently with the warm rag. The texture of the soft cloth against her skin drove her mad with desire.

Then she took the rag from him and returned the favor, savoring the feel of the warm dampness skimming over his skin. She paid special attention to certain areas of his anatomy.

Growling, he tossed the rag to the rough wood floor and playfully shoved her down to the bunk again. As he covered her again, she glanced between them at his aroused state. Her insides clenched as she contemplated the feel of him buried deep inside her again.

Her physical need was powerful, but even that paled beside the love she felt for this man. She'd been prepared to carry that love to her grave, without ever touching him or being touched by him.

This was nothing less than a miracle. Tears filled her eyes. Yes, physical love fueled by spiritual love was truly a miracle.

She had it all.

Moaning, Luke kissed her, plundering and seeking. But just as quickly, he abandoned her mouth for new territory.

He definitely didn't need her to draw him a picture.

She groaned as his lips blazed a path down her throat

to the slope of her shoulder, sketching warm, wet circles. He bent down and kissed her just beside her swollen breast.

"I've dreamed of kissing your butterfly," he muttered.

Sofie laughed softly, then gasped as he made his dream come true. With his tongue, he outlined the shape of her tattoo, gradually easing his way up the curve of her breast.

Her entire body grew heavy and boneless as he lingered over her for a few profoundly erotic moments. She thrust her hips against his, urging him to take her.

"You are an impatient wench," he murmured against her flesh.

"Only for you."

He gave her a roguish grin, then dipped his head to her breast. Coaxing her nipple deeply into his mouth, he suckled until she thought she'd die from the want of more. Watching him augmented her desire and reminded her of the miracle of their love.

He cupped her breasts in his hands, sharing himself between them. She lost herself to rising need, lacing her fingers through the dark curls at his nape, savoring the conflicting textures of this man she loved.

Brushing his tongue across her tender flesh, he glanced up at her. The hunger shimmering in his eyes made Sofie simply dissolve in a puddle of love and need.

She wanted to touch him . . . taste him. Fair was fair, after all. Very gently but firmly, she pressed his shoulder. Releasing her, he gave her a questioning glance.

"My turn," she whispered.

Her wicked smile should've warned Luke he was about to face his Waterloo. She nudged until he was flat on his back, then she slithered over him.

Life could be worse.

He wanted and needed her more than anything or anyone he'd known in any century. Nothing could be better than being stranded in a blizzard with Sofie. Nothing.

She kissed and nibbled his lower lip, then moved lower to linger over his chest and nipples. He hadn't realized his nipples could be so sensitive as she nipped and licked until he groaned in full surrender. She maneuvered her legs between his as the tips of her breasts tantalized the skin of his abdomen.

He reached for her, wanting to bring her back to his mouth, where he could kiss and be kissed, taste and be tasted. Eluding him, she kissed his thighs and the base of his engorged sex. Scattering punishing kisses where he'd never expected to be kissed, she paused just when he thought he couldn't take anymore. "Sofie . . ."

He wove his fingers through her hair and didn't breathe. He didn't dare. His inexperience was showing, and right now he didn't want to lose control. Wincing when he knew he couldn't take another moment of her delicious torture, he shifted away. "No . . . more."

Though he *desperately* wanted to experience what she'd been about to deliver, the time wasn't right. This was all too new and explosive for him. Later . . .

He grabbed her hips and maneuvered her astride him. She hesitated, and the anticipation almost killed him. This was something he'd only read about in magazines and had believed he wouldn't live to experience firsthand.

"Don't torture me, baby."

She lowered herself onto him. "So . . . big."

"Mmm." He cradled her hips and buried himself, watching her shocked expression. "So *tight.*"

She moved against him, her eyes glittering with wicked promise. "So *right,*" she whispered.

Yes, right. Only a miracle had brought them to this. No doubt remained in his mind that he and Sofie were meant to be. This was bigger than both of them.

She fastened herself around him, clutched him deep

inside, and angled her hips just right. Wanting to watch her, Luke kept his gaze on her face.

She moved against him and he drove upward to meet her. Her hair fell in loose, sexy curls. And her breasts . . . He reached up to fill his hands with them, encouraged by her astonished gasp and sudden contraction.

"Mmm." He urged her forward, then tasted her tawny nipples. Sweet. So sweet . . . She throbbed around him and he nearly exploded then and there.

But he wouldn't go alone. Rolling her nipples between his thumbs and forefingers, he watched her as she propelled her pelvis against him. The veins in her neck became distended and her head lolled backward. The sight and feel of her riding him, her beautiful breasts filling his hands, her head thrown back in ecstasy . . .

They came together. Straining and groaning, sharing and pulsing, she slumped against him, delivering delicate kisses along the side of his neck. Luke stroked her back, holding her to him in awe.

She was his. Nothing stood between them except his conscience and the truth. *Damn the truth.* Instead of telling her he was leaving the priesthood, he'd told her he'd never been a priest. More true than the latter, but still a lie of omission. She still didn't know who he really was.

Or *why* he'd been masquerading as a priest.

But when he'd returned to the cabin and found her so upset . . . Plus, in all honesty, he realized that knowing they were fellow time-travelers created an invisible bond between them. And Luke wanted—needed—to bind her to him in every conceivable way.

Before she learned the whole truth.

Guilt, as potent and toxic as the day he'd learned of Grandpa's death, threatened to pollute something pure and beautiful. His gut knotted and burned. Lying to the woman he loved was lower than low.

She was obviously regaining bits and pieces of her memory. He couldn't bear to see her look at him as a murderer. Though he knew he was innocent, she wouldn't.

Unless, maybe, he told her first. Somehow, some way, he had to eventually tell Sofie the truth. Soon.

All of it.

Chapter Twenty

Sunlight glaring off snow without the protection of sunglasses was not fun. Sofie pulled her hat lower over her eyes as she followed Luke down the pass. The snow was melting faster than it had fallen, exposing patches of bare ground.

Every time she thought about the fact that she and Luke were from another century, she shook her head. Maybe, if she ever remembered her family name, she could find her ancestors. But what would she tell them? To say their situation was bizarre would be an incredible understatement.

Just ahead, the earth seemed to vanish, but after all the miles they'd traveled, Sofie knew it meant another downward slope. She hoped this one didn't have as many switchbacks as the last.

Luke brought Rosie to a halt and glanced back over his shoulder with a wide grin. "Look," he said.

Sofie edged her horse close to his and gazed down at

the vast plain before them. Far in the distance, she saw a city. "Denver?"

Luke nodded. "If I'm not mistaken, in our time, this will be called Lookout Mountain. Maybe it already is."

"Gee, wonder why." She answered Luke's grin with one of her own. "How long will it take us to get down there?"

He shrugged. "I've given up judging distances via horseback, but I hope within a day."

A barrage of emotions bombarded Sofie. Looking down on the city of Denver triggered no memories for her, though she felt certain she'd been there many times. "Was Denver your home, Luke?" She really knew little about this man she loved.

He tensed and cleared his throat. "Yes, it's home." Gazing down the pass at the massive plain, he sighed. "At least, it was."

Sofie reached for his hand, and he brought hers to his lips, kissing it fiercely. After a moment, he lowered it, but kept it in his grip.

"I have something to tell you," he said quietly, then turned to face her with a haunted expression. "I . . . I was convicted of a crime I didn't commit, Sofie."

She sensed he needed to tell her about this, though she knew in her heart it wouldn't—couldn't—change her feelings for him. "I'm listening."

"I went to prison for eleven years." He shook his head and rubbed the back of his neck. "But I want you to know I was really innocent. Do you believe me?"

Sofie squeezed his hand. "Yes, I do." She smiled up at him. "I love you, Luke Sa—"

"Not Salazar." He shrugged, but the haunted expression remained. "Nolan. My last name is Nolan."

Something else occurred to her and she studied his eyes. "You haven't told me why you were pretending to be a priest, Luke." She rolled her eyes and laughed softly. "I can't imagine why anyone would."

"I'm getting to that." He patted Rosie's neck absently. "I guess you could say I ran a little farther than I'd planned."

Realization slammed into Sofie. "Whoa, are you saying you were still in prison when—"

"Yes." He met her gaze, his eyes glittering with anger and something more. Fear? "After those explosions, I realized—thought—everybody else was dead. Father Salazar was, and I needed clothes, so . . ."

"I see." Sofie swallowed the lump in her throat. She'd been more than ready to accept that Luke had a criminal record, and that he'd been wrongfully convicted. But he was also an escaped convict.

"Sofie, if you'd been in prison for eleven years for a crime you didn't commit," he said carefully, "and you found yourself in a position to just walk away . . ."

"Yeah, I see your point." She leaned over and kissed him. As she straightened, she caressed his cheek with her gloved hand. "I love you, Luke, and you're safe here. What's past—or future—can't hurt you anymore."

"I sure hope you're right." He sighed again, then seemed to gain control of his emotions. As he flashed her a grin, he appeared years younger. "Thank you for loving me, and for believing me."

"My pleasure." And it was. She looked toward Denver again. "Guess we'd better get moving."

"One more thing." He took her hand again and gazed intently into her eyes. "Sofie, I couldn't ask you this before telling you who I am, but now . . ."

Her heart did a somersault. "I'm listening."

"Will you marry me when we get to Denver?"

Tears filled her eyes and spilled down her cheeks. "Yes," she whispered. "I'll marry you."

They kissed again, and Sofie wished they could spread a blanket out on a dry patch of ground to seal their engagement. Making love with Luke Sa—*Nolan* every day of her life would be heaven. No doubt about it.

"I have one more question, though," she said as they parted. "Why didn't you drop your disguise after you learned we'd been thrown back in time?"

His eyes hardened again and she regretted pushing the point so soon. It could have waited. "Never mind," she said, "we can discuss this later."

"No, now." He looked into the distance beyond her, at something she suspected only he could see. "The shame." He turned his gaze on her again. "I didn't want to feel ashamed of something I didn't do ever again."

She studied his expression for several moments, knowing in her heart that he meant exactly what he'd said. "Yes, I understand." She kissed him again, then straightened in her saddle. "Your sense of honor is one of the things I love most about you."

He waggled his eyebrows at her. "Oh, I thought it was . . ."

Leaning closer, he whispered something in her ear that would've given Mrs. Taylor heart failure. Sofie's pulse quickened and her breath froze. Heat suffused her body and she squirmed in her saddle.

She maneuvered her hand beneath the edge of his coat and cupped the hard, impressive evidence of his desire. "That, too, big guy."

His gaze raked her, though she knew he couldn't see anything through her bulky coat and baggy jeans. "Later, I'm going to hold you down and kiss every inch of you."

Hunger oozed through her body as she rubbed her palm along the hard ridge beneath his jeans. "Every . . . inch?"

"Yeah." His voice sounded hoarse. "Every gorgeous inch."

"Pity we have to wait." Slowly, seductively, she used her thumb to trace circles around the hot, throbbing tip of his erection. "Hmm . . . ?"

"The sun's warm," he whispered against her lips. "Isn't it about lunch time?"

"Let's skip lunch and get right to dessert."
"Oh, God."

Luke no longer felt like a liar, though he still hadn't told her the nature of his alleged crime, or the fact that he was being executed when they'd been thrown back in time. He knew she would ask eventually, and he would tell her the truth.

No more lies. He was finished with lies.

As they neared Denver, his tension mounted. He knew that the building that housed, or would house, his grandfather's shoe repair shop already existed. Something tugged at his subconscious, and he couldn't stop thinking about how much he'd wanted Grandpa's respect. Instead, the old man had died ashamed of his only heir.

But Luke had to concentrate on the here and now, such as it was. He had a new life ahead, and a woman who loved him. He was about to get married.

Denver was far different from the city he remembered, but much of it was still familiar to Luke. The energy and vitality—the heart of the city—were already present. A stab of homesickness shot through him as they rode through town.

First, they visited the assayer's office and he cashed in the gold nuggets the citizens of Redemption had given them. Then they found a hotel near the area that would one day be known as the 16th Street Mall.

Two blocks from his grandfather's shoe repair shop. Four blocks from the Victorian house where he'd been raised. The sight of the beginnings of the State Capital jarred him. Though still under construction, the skeleton of the dome and the building itself was yet another reminder of his grandparents and his childhood.

And his shame.

After they checked into the hotel and cleaned up, Luke

left to buy a dress for Sofie and some decent clothes for himself. Wedding clothes. His internal radar dragged him over two blocks, where he stood and stared at the brownstone that would one day belong to his grandfather.

From the outside, it looked very much as he remembered, though it now boasted a bright orange awning. Tears burned his eyes and scalded his throat, then he noticed the store was a millinery shop and dressmaker. He could probably find Sofie something nice there, and manage to satisfy his own curiosity at the same time.

After crossing the cobblestone street, he mustered his self-control and pushed open the door. Displays of hats, lace collars, and gloves filled the front room, and a large open book occupied a table between two wing-backed chairs. Gaslights glowed from ceiling and wall fixtures.

He looked at the back wall, noting its brick construction, and a wave of nostalgia blasted through him. Grandpa had torn the bricks off that wall and replaced it with gleaming wood paneling and a multitude of shelves. Luke remembered helping the old man tear down the bricks himself with a hammer and chisel. It had been tedious work, but laboring beside Grandpa had been one of Luke's favorite boyhood activities. How he'd loved that old man . . .

"May I help you, sir?"

Clearing his throat, Luke forced his attention to the well-dressed woman. "Yes." She wore a white, lace-trimmed blouse buttoned nearly to her chin. Her hair was pulled into a bun or something at the back of her head, and a decorative comb held one side. A brooch at the front of her blouse was her only jewelry.

Was this how Sofie should dress? The dresses she'd borrowed from Dora had been much more practical, but this was Denver, not Redemption. For the wedding, he decided, she needed something frilly.

"Are you looking for a gift, sir?"

"Yes, a wedding gift." He looked around the store at all the frills. "Do you have any dresses?"

"You mean ready-made dresses, sir?" She appeared scandalized.

"Well, yeah, the wedding's today." Luke chuckled. What would she think if he told her he and Sofie were already sharing a hotel room? "Something I can buy and walk out the door with."

"Only some samples." She hoisted her chin up a notch or two.

Snob. "Well, my fiancée is about, er . . ." He looked the woman up and down. "She's about your size, only a little bigger right, uh, here." He held his hands cupped out in front of his chest.

The woman gasped, and he dropped his hands to his sides. "Sorry, ma'am," he muttered, realizing immediately that he'd just committed a major social blunder. In any century. Heat flooded his face, but he pushed onward. "Would any of your samples fit someone that size?"

She gave a stiff nod and disappeared into the back room, where Grandpa would one day keep fragrant pieces of leather, tools, and supplies. Luke wondered what was back there now. Probably lace and stuff.

"Here we are." The woman returned with three dresses draped over her arm. She hung them from hooks along the brick wall and stood back. "If we had time to take measurements, I'm sure I could create something lovely for your young lady."

"Yes, I'm sure you could, but we're in a hurry." Luke heard her gasp, but decided to ignore it. Let the woman think whatever she wanted. Well, considering how intimate he and Sofie had been the last few days, she could be pregnant. The thought made him smile, which shocked him even more.

"Do any of these meet your approval, sir?" the woman asked stiffly.

Forcing his attention back to choosing Sofie's wedding dress, Luke zeroed in on something soft and blue—the color of Sofie's eyes. "I like this one."

"That's a traveling suit, sir."

"Oh, well, she'll need one of those, too." He wasn't wealthy, but he had quite a bit of money after cashing in his gold. One dress was a myriad of checks, which he ruled out immediately, and the third one was glittering gold, obviously meant for a party. Even he could tell the neckline was cut very low, and the waistline tightly fitted.

"This one." He pointed at the gold. "I'll take this one now, then bring her back to try on the blue one tomorrow, if that's all right."

The clerk nodded, open approval showing in her eyes and surprising Luke. "You must love her very much."

"More than my life." Luke instantly changed his opinion of the sales clerk.

"Your fiancée is a very fortunate young lady."

"Nah, I'm the lucky one." He smiled and asked the woman to throw in any underthings Sofie might need, too.

Blushing, the clerk boxed everything for him, and he asked her where to find clothes for himself. As he left, he glanced back over his shoulder at the brick wall. He could actually see himself standing there as a young boy of about nine, right beside Grandpa.

Why did that one small event from his childhood haunt him so? At any rate, he was glad he had an excuse to return to the store. He smiled, realizing he could tell Sofie why the building was important to him.

Yes, he was the lucky one in this deal. Not only was he going to marry a woman he loved, but she was the only person in the world who would understand his memories of events that hadn't happened yet.

The air outside was crisp but the sunshine brilliant. He had no idea of the date, but they were definitely well into October now. Too late to travel west by covered wagon, but maybe there was a train across the southwest. He knew there was one through Wyoming by this time. Or they could go south and catch a boat to California, though that would mean traveling around South America. He had no idea whether or not the Panama Canal had been built yet.

Strike that idea. The thought of being confined on board a ship for months sounded awful. Especially after eleven years in prison . . .

Determined to put that experience to rest once and for all, Luke drew a deep breath. He had clothes to buy, and he needed to find a church. Any church.

Guilt threatened his resolve again. No, not any church. He wasn't quite ready to enter a Catholic church. Besides, all the rules and rituals required for a Catholic ceremony would take time. If there was one thing Luke didn't want to do again, it was wait.

Within an hour, he returned to the hotel with his arms laden with packages. He and Sofie had an appointment with a Methodist minister later in the afternoon.

If he had a Big Mac and a large order of fries for both of them, life would be perfect.

Sofie giggled when Luke insisted on carrying her across the threshold after their wedding. She didn't care that the hotel clerk had looked at them with disapproval when Luke asked for a bottle of champagne to celebrate their wedding.

Nothing mattered except the man who now held her in his arms. Nothing at all.

He lowered her to her feet slowly, letting her body slide along the front of his. This was their wedding night. Her head swam with the delicious possibilities.

His mouth captured hers and Sofie relished his unique, compelling flavor. The kiss was bottomless, wet, savage. The best kind.

His lips left hers to venture down her throat, and she was vaguely aware of him kicking the door shut behind them. A trail of fire in its wake, his mouth tarried at the swell of her breasts above the daringly cut gold dress.

Her breasts swelled and ached in anticipation. Boldly, she inched her hand downward, thrilled to find him swollen, too. Ready.

"God, Sofie, I—"

A knock at the door made them groan in unison, then Sofie sighed and said, "The champagne."

"Damn stupid idea of mine. You stay right here and hold that thought."

"Why, what thought might that be, sir?" She batted her lashes innocently.

"Mmm, I've always wondered what it would be like to ravish a, uh, proper young lady."

"Oh, my. Did you say ravish, sir?" She batted her lashes again, giggling when the impatient waiter pounded on the door again, more loudly than before.

Luke released her and threw open the door. The waiter brought in two bottles of champagne, opened one and filled two glasses. Luke tipped him, then ushered him out and closed the door.

He handed her a glass, then took one for himself. "You know something?"

"What?" He was so close she could smell the tangy substance the barber must have put on his skin, and the musky male scent that was Luke's alone.

"I've never tasted champagne before."

A moment of regret threatened her happiness, but she dismissed it. "And I don't remember tasting it before, so this will be a first for us both."

"Here's to us . . . and to our future together." Luke tapped his glass gently against hers. It made a melodic ringing sound as he linked his arm through hers and raised his glass to his lips, while she did the same.

She took a long drink of the cold, bubbly liquor. "Mmm."

"Mmm," he echoed, his gaze on her over the rim of his glass. "It's very good, but I've tasted one thing I like even better."

"Dr. Pepper?"

Luke threw his head back and laughed, spilling his glass of champagne down the front of her exposed cleavage. "You're so romantic, Sofie," he teased, looking at her. "Hmm, shame to waste good champagne."

Before she realized what he intended, his warm tongue was following the cool droplets of spilled champagne along the curve of her breast. He dipped his fingers into his glass and sprinkled more champagne across her flesh.

Breathlessly, Sofie watched him repeat his earlier behavior, licking and sucking sparkling droplets of champagne off her skin. She eyed the bottles sitting on the table, wicked thoughts dancing through her mind. "Luke?"

"Hmm?"

She touched her finger to his lips and summoned her sultriest voice, "Unhook me, lose the monkey suit, then bring that champagne to *bed*."

His eyes bulged, but he nodded vigorously. She slipped from his embrace, then turned so he could release the endless row of hooks at the back of her dress. That he kissed every millimeter of skin as he exposed it was an unexpected perk. By the time she stood before him wearing nothing but a corset, her breasts protruding high and round above it, she was already dangerously aroused.

She watched him nearly tear off his suit and fling it over the back of a chair. Her gaze gravitated to his proud manhood, jutting out from a nest of dark curls. He was big and hard.

And hers.

The expression in his eyes was filled with promises, and Sofie knew he would—and could—keep every one.

"Unlace this thing?" She turned her back to him, surprised to feel his hands on the bare cheeks of her butt instead.

"Later," he whispered, urging her to face him again. He leaned back to gaze down at her approvingly. "Got a whip stashed anywhere?"

"Luke!" She giggled, reaching down between them to hold his solid erection in both hands. "I don't think we'll need one. Do you?"

He shook his head. "More champagne?" Reaching to the side, he grabbed the open bottle off the end table. With a wicked smile, he pressed his thumb over the opening and gave the bottle a gentle shake.

Then he sprayed her.

Sofie gasped in shock as the cold liquid splattered across her bare breasts. Her nipples hardened instantly and her surprise turned to something much more powerful than humor.

Suspiciously nonchalant, he took her hand and pulled her toward the bed, the open—and far from empty—bottle in tow. Chuckling, he nudged her playfully into bed and placed the bottle on the nightstand.

Sofie giggled, but as she witnessed the transformation in his eyes, her laughter dissolved into a gasp. He put one knee on the bed, hovering over her in the well-lit room. His gaze raked her, and she took the opportunity to study him thoroughly as well.

She couldn't bear to look and not touch, so she reached for him, but he grabbed her hand. "No way, wife. I'm in charge now." He gently but firmly gripped her wrists and pressed them to her sides as he climbed over her.

"Wife?" She could barely breathe as his heady scent and her own desire gripped her.

"I like the sound of that." He nuzzled her neck, just below her earlobe, then kissed and nipped his way downward, stopping to lick champagne off her flesh along the way. "Wife," he murmured against her tattoo.

Naked and wanting, she treasured each touch of his lips, each swipe of his warm tongue against her bare skin. She felt foreign and exotic, detached from her physical being, yet acutely conscious of every rising need that charged through her.

Her insides trembled, and she grew increasingly aware of the emptiness Luke would soon fill. She craved this coupling even more desperately than before. After all, this was their wedding night.

She watched in awe as he tasted her, kneading her supple flesh just above the corset. Her nipples stood proud and ready, looking as if she'd applied blusher to make them more prominent. But the mere thought of Luke's mouth made them tingle and grow with need.

"Mine," he murmured against her flesh, drawing her nipple deeply into his mouth.

"Yes, always." Moaning, she arched against his wonderful mouth and secured her hands behind his neck. She cherished each caress of his tongue, each gentle pull of his lips against her breast.

Her body wept for him as he left her breast and kissed his way downward. Eager to feel him inside her, Sofie tightened her grip on him, but he quickly shifted himself between her quivering thighs.

Instinct told her his intentions, though she had no way of knowing whether or not she'd ever experienced this delicious torture before. This was madness. Sweet, delicious madness.

She shivered, but definitely not from cold, as he kissed the slope of her hip and placed his hands beneath her bottom. He held her securely, tipping her toward him as he kissed his way lower. Molten heat concentrated between her legs as she anticipated his touch.

Then, wondrously, he tasted her, slowly and gently.

She'd weathered some intensely erotic dreams these past few weeks, but she'd never even imagined anything this wild and wicked.

Fever consumed her. She heard an odd, low sound—her own purr of pleasure. This was primal. Ruthless.

Spectacular.

She immersed her fingers in his short curls as she climbed higher and higher. Nothing existed except his possession, his mouth, and her need.

He was all-powerful. Merciless. His tongue possessed her, his hands held her hostage. Her hips arched ever upward. Ever closer. She shattered into a billion dazzling fragments as completion swept through her.

Then he kissed her thighs again and maneuvered himself upward, cradling her breasts in his skillful hands. Something wet sprinkled across her breasts, and she realized it was the champagne again, but now she welcomed the cold droplets, because she knew what would follow.

No longer gentle, he nursed at her breasts like an infant, pressing them together to sample each in turn. "Sweet," he murmured, tugging and suckling, driving her to the brink of madness.

She was on edge, near the fringes yet again. He hadn't let her come down far and she was ready for more. Gently, he rolled her onto her side and released the laces, slipping the corset from her sweat-slick torso. She moaned as more droplets of champagne touched her skin, followed immediately by his warm, wet mouth.

"Now, Luke," she breathed, unable to form coherent thoughts, let alone speech. She only wanted and needed, and knew he could end her misery.

His mouth took hers again as he covered her with his hot, hard body and stroked her tongue with his. Then she felt his heated arousal tantalizing the tender folds of her vagina. She was ready—so ready. His first hard plunge made her cry out in victory.

"Yes." She wrapped her legs around his waist, inviting him even more deeply into her starving body. Hot and hungry, she fused herself to him. A moan rumbled from deep in her throat as he retreated, then returned again. And again.

And again.

He murmured words of endearment as his delicious torture went on and on, pushing her higher and higher, to spiral out of control. Each thrust grew more forceful than the one before, more demanding. He reached for her legs and draped them over his shoulders as he continued to possess her.

Hard. Fast. Deep.

She crossed into a shadowy dimension of delight and pleasure where nothing else mattered. Every movement exposed a piercing new pinnacle, a more luscious layer than before. She opened her eyes, but the light faded, then returned even brighter.

Deep and sure, he came into her again and again. She was brainless, primed for every stroke of his body, answering his quest with several small orgasms which built and snowballed into one continuous, achingly divine moment.

He filled her with himself—branded her, made her his in every way. Sofie held him deep inside, never wanting to let him go.

He kissed her deeply, breathlessly, then eased his weight to her side, gathering her against him. She curled onto her hip with her back against him, cherishing the tender kisses he bestowed on her bare shoulder.

"I love you, Mrs. Nolan," he whispered, his warm breath tickling the fine hairs at her nape.

She stretched and rolled onto her back, gazing into his beautiful eyes. "I love you, too, Mr. Nolan." She stroked his cheek with her thumb, praying their love would always be like this. Perfect and strong. Yes, time would temper their love to steel.

She smiled, remembering the remaining champagne. Reaching for the open bottle, she raised up on one elbow and pressed him to the mattress with her free hand.

"What . . . do you think you're doing?" he asked, looking warily at the bottle.

Sofie tilted the bottle and took a long pull of bubbly liquid. "Thirsty?"

Before he could answer, she emptied the bottle.

Right between his legs.

Graham startled awake at the sound of a trolley rattling down the street. His shoulder ached from lying on the cold cobblestones, and his stomach burned from too little food and too much rotgut whiskey. He kicked the empty bottle at his feet and staggered toward the end of the alley.

The murderer and his bride were up there in a nice soft bed, while he slept in the gutter. He clenched his fist and shook it at the building as the city of Denver came awake.

He knew in his gut that Nolan would do something stupid today, and Graham would be ready. Everything was prepared and waiting. It was just a matter of time now.

The ache in his chest sharpened again, but he massaged it until it passed. He didn't give a damn what happened to him, as long as he finished his job first.

He'd remain in the shadows until the right moment came. And he knew it would.

After all, justice always prevailed.

Chapter Twenty-One

Pushing aside the 1891 version of *The Denver Post*, Luke watched Sofie button the front of one of Dora's baggy dresses. He took a sip of coffee, leaning back in his chair.

"I thought you left all those things in Redemption." He smiled at her answering scowl. "Oh, yeah. I forgot, you aren't a morning person."

She walked over to him and smiled before delivering a pseudo-throat culture with her lips and tongue. "On the contrary, husband," she whispered, reaching between his legs. "That's not what you were saying about an hour ago."

"Touché." He loved her open sexuality. The thought gave him pause, then he chuckled to himself as she returned to dressing for the day.

"What's so funny?"

"I was just thinking what a modern, liberated woman you are." He watched a line crease her brow as she looked up at him from tying her hiking boots. The delicate slippers that matched her wedding gown wouldn't work for everyday. Besides, he loved those beat-up hiking boots. They were her.

"Well, I guess doctors have to be liberated." She shook her head. "I still don't see how I could be a doctor and not remember something about it, though. I guess Dr. Bowen will be able to help me with that, too."

Luke's blood turned to ice. Swallowing the stomach acid that rose in his throat, he stood and walked over to sit beside her on the bed. "Sofie, you still plan to see him?"

"Of course." She patted his hand. "Don't you want to know who you're married to?"

"I know everything I need to." That frigging guilt surged through him again. What right did he have to deny her the chance for memories like those he treasured from his own childhood? The answer came simply and swiftly. None. "Okay, then. I'll ask the desk clerk if she knows how to reach him. We can phone for an appointment."

"Oh, that's right, they do have telephones now." She grinned.

"You're a real nineties' kinda gal." He grinned as she stuck her tongue out at him, struggling not to succumb to his recollection of her tongue and half a bottle of champagne.

"Very funny."

Jarred from thoughts of real lovemaking that had been more erotic than anything his imagination could have conjured, Luke cleared his throat. "How would you like to take a walk down my Memory Lane this morning?"

"I'd like that."

At least taking her to try on the traveling suit would postpone her seeing Dr. Bowen a little longer. Luke realized now he would have to accept the inevitable. Sofie would at least try to recover from her amnesia, and he had no right to stand in her way. In fact, he owed her the truth. Eventually.

"Memory Lane, Luke. Remember?"

"Yeah." He proceeded to tell her about his grandparents, about growing up in Denver in their old Victorian house, and helping his grandpa at the shoe repair shop. He even told her about the brick wall that had fascinated him yesterday.

"You mean"—she squeezed his hand—"you bought my wedding dress in that same building? Luke, that's so special. Thank you."

"Yeah." He shrugged. "I couldn't resist going in and looking around, and since they had what I needed . . ."

"I've been thinking about something."

"Uh-oh, this sounds serious."

Sofie punched him lightly on the arm. "Hey, I am serious, buster."

"Okay, I'll be good."

"That'll be the day." She smiled, then grew sober again. "This time-travel business . . ."

"Oh, that."

"Yes, that." Sighing, she put her chin in her hand and stared at him as she spoke. "If we're here now, will we exist when we originally existed?"

Luke chuckled. "When I first learned what had happened, I spent at least a week trying to figure out all the paradoxes of this." He shook his head. "I just don't know, Sofie."

"Well, assuming we'll still be born at the place and time we were originally born . . ."

"I think I need a drink."

"Last night you had enough champagne to hold you a while, I think."

"Mmm, look who's talking." He cupped her breast in his hand and brushed his thumb across its peak through her dress. "Fine vintage."

"The best and don't you forget it." Sofie grabbed his face and kissed him fast and hard, then pulled his hand away from her breast. "If you don't stop that, we'll never get to our walk down Memory Lane."

"So?"

"Get a grip on your hormones and pay attention," she said. "I'm trying to be brilliant here."

"You're always brilliant."

"Anyway, if we aren't born at the place and time we originally were, then how can we be here now?"

"I'm not going there." He laughed and draped his arm across her shoulders. "That's too complicated and completely unanswerable."

"Yeah, I suppose, but . . ."

"But what?"

She straightened and looked at Luke, her expression deadly sober. "Is there some way you could leave a message or sign for yourself?"

"I . . . don't know." Luke's stomach did a somersault and he straightened. "If not for myself, then maybe for Grandpa."

Sofie put her palm to his cheek very gently. "I see the pain in your eyes and feel it in my heart when you talk about him, Luke."

"Yeah." It hurt like hell whenever he remembered the note from Grandpa, still tucked in the back of Father Salazar's Bible. Rising, he went to the leather pouch he'd removed from the priest's dead body the morning of the explosion.

Sofie remained seated on the bed, watching him, and he loved her all the more for granting him this moment's privacy. He looked at the note, the crucifix with Father Salazar's initials etched into its back, and the well-worn Bible Luke had used to perform a bogus wedding ceremony and dozens of funerals.

After several moments, he looked up at Sofie and sighed. "If there's any way to change what happened, to prevent the circumstances that sent me to prison and caused Grandpa's shame . . .''

"You have to do it." Sofie stood and walked partway across the room. "I'll do anything I can to help."

He nodded. "I need paper and a pen. Ink, I suppose. I don't think ballpoints have been invented." He wrapped the Bible in paper and tied it with ribbon, then carried it with the other items to the small desk near the window. "I suppose this is worth a shot."

Luke wrote three letters on the hotel's stationery. One to his grandfather, which included the note in Grandpa's own hand in the same envelope. All he told the old man was how much he loved him, that he'd been innocent of the murder, and that all he ever wanted was to make his grandparents proud.

Instead of a fancy symbol, he used his thumbprint to press the warm wax into place, remembering when he'd been arrested and booked for murder.

Unjustly.

The second letter was to himself, telling him to be good. Basically. The third letter was one he had to write even more than the other two. He addressed it to the liquor store clerk who'd died that night Luke's world had fallen apart. If he could convince that man not to go to work that fateful night . . .

Maybe these letters could perform another miracle, if they fell into the right hands at the right time. An image of him and Grandpa tearing down that brick wall flashed through his mind again, and he suddenly knew where to hide everything.

His heart collided with his ribs as the woman he loved fidgeted around the room, obviously trying to stay out of his way. He loved her so much it hurt sometimes, but it was a pain he never wanted to be without.

Now all he needed was a way to prevent his shame.

"Ready?" he asked.

Sofie nodded, obviously understanding the significance of what he was about to do. "I guess we're off to change history then."

"I sure as hell hope so." He looked down at the letters and Bible tied together with a ribbon. The crucifix would go, too, he decided.

Sofie tapped his shoulder and held something silver before his eyes. "This, too, please."

"Why?"

"I don't know. I just want our things to go through history together. I mean, what if . . ." Sofie touched his arm. "What if these letters change things so much that this—that *we* don't happen?"

He stared at her for several minutes, unable to believe such a horrible thing was possible. Gathering her against his chest, he held her silently for several minutes, then lifted her chin so he could watch her eyes.

"We're meant to be, Sofie," he said, and meant it. "In any time, any place, any lifetime."

She smiled, though tears appeared in her eyes. "Yes, I believe that."

"I cherish you." He brushed his thumb along her eyebrow. "Never forget that."

"I won't, Luke." Tears slid down her cheeks, and he captured one on the tip of his finger. "I won't."

He held her tear to the light streaming through the window behind him. "I love you," he whispered, then kissed her very gently. Straightening, he searched her expression. "Promise me, Sofie, that no matter what happens, you'll remember we're meant to be. We belong to each other. Always."

Sofie kept the secret of her dizzy spells and memory flashes to herself as they walked the short distance to the millinery shop. Luke didn't need to hear her problems right now. He had enough to worry about.

She'd remembered more apparently unrelated instances during the night. Maybe it had been the champagne, or perhaps it was because she felt safe and loved now. Who knew? But for some reason her memory was beginning to return.

Whoever she was, whatever she remembered about herself, she didn't want it to interfere with her marriage. She loved Luke desperately, and she couldn't bear for anything to come between them.

She wouldn't *let* anything come between them.

They stood together on the sidewalk, looking through the window of the building his family would one day own. She memorized the appearance of it, including the bright orange awning under which they now stood. The color distinguished this building from all the others.

"All right, so while you have the shopkeeper busy helping you with the suit, I'll hunt for a loose brick."

Luke seemed nervous, but that was understandable. "Can I be 007?" she asked, trying to take the edge off his anxiety.

"No, your voice isn't low enough." He gave her a quick peck on the cheek. "Let's go."

A bell rang as they opened the door, and Sofie admired all the interesting hats on display. After a moment, a woman appeared from the back room, wearing a beautiful navy dress with white lace at the collar.

"Ah, I see you're back for the fitting." The woman introduced herself to Sofie, then showed her to the dressing room.

Sofie admired the blue velvet traveling suit. Black braid trimmed the cuffs, waist, and collar, and the buttons were covered with more blue velvet. She tried on the jacket and skirt, admiring the way the color looked with her eyes.

"I can see why your husband chose this color for you,"

the woman said. "Lovely, and it fits as if it were made for you."

"Yes, I guess it does." She furrowed her brow, realizing she needed to buy Luke a little more time. "Do you think it's too snug across the bust—er, bosom?" Heat flooded her face. At least she hadn't said "boobs."

"Not at all." The clerk laughed and tugged at the hem of the jacket in back. "The buttons don't pull apart in front, nor does it pucker across your back."

"True." Sofie appeared to scrutinize the fit with a critical eye, turning and prancing in front of the mirror, though her thoughts were in the other room with Luke. "You said it's a traveling suit?"

"Yes, your husband thought you would be needing one." The shopkeeper leaned closer and whispered, "A surprise honeymoon, maybe?"

Sofie shrugged, remembering Luke's reaction this morning when she'd mentioned Dr. Bowen. Had he really believed she wouldn't go see the doctor who might help restore her memory? That made no sense.

"He's very handsome."

"Who?" Sofie furrowed her brow, then met the shopkeeper's shocked expression in the mirror. "Oh, you mean Luke—my husband. Yes, he's very handsome."

"You're still a nervous bride, I think." The woman tugged and adjusted the jacket, and looked at the hem of the skirt. "The skirt is a mite long, I think, but some good high-button boots should do the trick."

"Do you think so?" Sofie half-turned to check the hem, though her mind was on her husband. She was far from a nervous bride. On the contrary, she was a very eager bride. She had no idea what her past had been like, or how much experience she'd had with men and sex, but she definitely knew her way around in bed.

Thinking of the champagne she and Luke had licked

off each other's skin last night made her warm all over. She tugged at the close collar of the jacket.

"Is it too tight there?" the woman asked.

"No, it's fine." Sofie managed a weak smile, but the image of the champagne she'd poured over Luke intruded on her thoughts. Had she really done that to him?

Oh, yes.

"I'll pin the hem, then this should be ready for you by Friday."

Sofie nodded, mumbling something affirmative, then reached for the top button of the jacket just as the curtain opened behind them. In the mirror, she stared at the figure looming there.

Mr. Smith.

The shopkeeper whirled around just as Smith's fist came down hard on the side of her head. Sofie opened her mouth to scream, but Mr. Smith grabbed her arm and jerked her hard against him, clamping his hand over her mouth.

She bit down hard as he slammed her against the wall. Her head rang from the impact, but she tried to focus on the man. Why was he here? What did he want?

Mr. Smith dropped a folded piece of paper on the floor beside the unconscious shopkeeper, then he hauled Sofie through the curtain and out into the street. Where was Luke? Dizziness crashed into her.

"My niece is ill," Mr. Smith said in a raspy whisper to the gawking onlookers. "Make way . . ."

Then the world went black.

Luke took great care in replacing the brick he'd found on the back side of the wall. The hollow behind it was just the right size for the Bible and letters. Maybe it was another sign. A good one.

There he went again, seeing some kind of special sign

in everything that happened. Well, considering how happy he was with his new wife . . .

Smiling to himself, he returned to the front room of the shop and waited for Sofie to come out of the dressing room. They were taking an awfully long time. That probably meant the suit required alterations.

Luke flipped through the book on the end table, growing bored with the sketches of Victorian coats and dresses, but finding his interest piqued somewhat by the corset section. Of course, all these models wore more than just a corset.

With a flash of fire to his groin, he remembered the way Sofie had looked standing in front of him wearing nothing but that corset. Man, oh, man, the way her breasts had been pushed up and out, just waiting for him to come along and . . .

He shifted uncomfortably in the chair, planning exactly what he would do to his wife once they were back at the hotel. With growing impatience, he tossed the book back onto the table. What was taking them so long? He stood and paced the room, from the front window to the rear wall, then back again. Finally, he went to the dressing room curtain and cleared his throat.

"Sofie?" No response. He knocked on the wall beside the curtain. "Sofie?"

Still nothing.

A low moan wafted through the closed curtain, reminding Luke of that morning in the execution chamber, when he'd first heard Sofie's cry for help. Terror tore through him and he jerked aside the curtain.

The shopkeeper was on the floor, the side of her face badly bruised. Luke knelt beside her and helped her to a sitting position. "Where's Sofie?" he asked, looking around the small room frantically. "Where's my wife?"

"I . . . I don't know." The woman pressed her hand to the side of her face and head. "He hit me."

"Who hit you?" Luke's pulse roared and his palms turned sweaty. "Where's my wife?"

She looked around the dressing room, her eyes wide and frightened. "Good heavens, he must've taken her!"

Gritting his teeth, Luke's gaze fell on the folded slip of paper on the floor beside the woman. "What's this?" His voice shook.

But before he actually retrieved the piece of paper, before he opened it and read the words, before he allowed his sense of reason to argue the facts, he knew. His vision blurred as he tried and failed to read the words.

The woman took it from his trembling hand and rubbed her eyes, then read it aloud: *"Your chair awaits."*

Luke took the note from the clerk's hand and helped her to her feet, though all he wanted was to run out the door after the woman he loved. Sofie. His wife.

"The cash box is still here," the clerk said from behind the counter. "I don't think anything's been stolen."

"Only my wife."

"We don't know that for certain."

"I know it." Luke looked at the door, then back to the woman. "You all right?"

"I'm fine." She looked at him thoughtfully. "I'd better call the police. They'll want to talk to you."

Luke shook his head, stuffing the note into his pocket. "They can't help me."

"But what about your wife?"

Luke handed a roll of bills to the clerk. "For the traveling suit."

"That isn't necessary."

"Yes, it is." He dropped it on the counter when she didn't take it from him.

"Don't you want to tell the police about your wife?" she asked again. "Do you know the man who left the note?"

"I'm the only one who can help her." He blinked and

headed toward the door. Nothing mattered except saving her. Not even his precious freedom.

He retrieved Rosie from the hotel livery and stopped for minimal supplies and something else he swore he'd never own. A gun. Graham didn't have much of a head start, but he had one. The chances of Luke running across them in the wilderness were slim at best. Even so, he prodded Rosie to the fastest pace he dared, wishing now he had Sam's Lucifer.

He knew exactly where the bastard was taking Sofie. Though Luke didn't have a map or road signs to follow, he knew he could ride straight to that damned mountain blindfolded.

He knew it in his gut, because he was riding to his own death.

My chair awaits.

Chapter Twenty-Two

Sofie recognized the terrain before they actually reached the mountain. At first, she thought Smith was taking her back to Redemption, but he headed farther north, toward the cave where their adventure through time had begun.

Why? The man hadn't spoken to her during their several days of travel, except to hiss orders in his surreal voice. Even when she'd begged him to tell her why he'd kidnapped her and who he was, he'd refused to answer.

She knew in her heart that this man was after Luke. She had no idea why, but she was determined to protect her husband, no matter what.

When they reached the familiar mountain, Smith dragged her into the cave. A powerful stench slammed into her as Sofie stared at the high ceiling, the broken steel beams, light fixtures dangling by their cords. She knew only one thing for certain. This place was much more than merely a cave.

"Who are you?" she asked again as he dragged her through the debris toward a door at the rear.

"Justice," he hissed.

The guy had superhuman strength, fueled by his madness, no doubt. "Let me go." She jerked her arm, but his iron grip held fast. "Why are you doing this?"

He remained silent until they reached the door, where he dragged her through and slammed it behind them. They were in complete darkness, but it didn't smell as bad in here. Her captor's breathing sounded hollow and amplified in the confined space. She felt so vulnerable here in the dark with a madman. A tremor of pure terror replaced her anger. Did he intend to rape her?

He struck a match and lit a lantern. The room was filled with controls and gadgets—all broken and useless—and a computer sat in the corner. The entire mountain must've traveled back in time with them. Eerie.

Luke had said they were conducting some kind of electrical experiment that morning. He'd still been a prisoner then . . .

The dizziness assaulted her again and she fell to her knees, clutching her head. Something exploded in her left temple as images soared past her mind's eye. She squeezed her eyes shut, trying to decipher the flying pictures.

She saw Luke, bald and wearing the hospital gown. He looked terrified. And she saw herself trying to convince a man wearing a dark suit to listen to her, believe her, pay attention to her. Why?

Her usual nausea came and she drew great gulps of foul air, ignoring her captor's movements. She saw the suited man's eyes clearly now, glittering with a deranged and evil light. Hideous, terrifying eyes.

Familiar eyes.

"Oh, my God," she whispered, forcing her eyes open to stare at the hooded man. "You're from the future, too." She pushed to her feet, grabbing the edge of a broken desk to steady her. "You were here that morning."

"So the *doctor* remembers." Venom tinged his words.

"You caused this. Prevented justice. Killed innocent people."

"Others?" Sofie's throat and eyes burned from the stench as she stared at him.

Smith shrugged. "You don't recognize the stench of rotting flesh, *doctor*?" His gaze intensified. "God works in mysterious ways. He spared only me to do His will."

There were dead bodies here. Sofie's stomach lurched and she broke into a cold sweat. She swallowed hard, struggling for control. Yes, dead bodies.

But she had to focus on here and *now*. On survival. "Who *are* you?" God, if she ever needed to remember, it was now. "Why are you doing this?"

Raspy, demonic laughter filled the room, but he stopped after a moment, seized by a violent fit of coughing. No longer dizzy, Sofie bolted for the door. His hand snaked out and grabbed a brutal fistful of her hair.

"Damn you, let me go." She spun around, punching and slapping, clawing at his hood. The back of his hand smashed into her face and flung her to the floor.

"*See* what you did?" He yanked off the hood.

Struggling to her feet, Sofie stared in horror. The man's scars were grotesque, his mouth twisted into a permanent snarl. If he weren't so vile and cruel, she would've chastised herself for her reaction. When she'd dressed his burns back in Redemption, she had no idea . . .

"Who are you?" she whispered, biting back her rising terror. "Why are you doing this?"

"Carlton V. Graham," he said, leaning against the closed door and holding his chest. "Warden of this *brand-new* federal penitentiary." He barked a derisive laugh. "Dispensing justice one . . . last . . . time."

Sofie shook her head, trying to sort through the man's crazy explanation. "This mountain was a prison and you were the warden?"

"I *am* the warden." Continuing to rub his chest with

one gloved hand, he pulled the hood in place again with the other. "The first, the last . . . and the only warden."

Okay, so the guy had a motive for his demented behavior, but he was obsessed. "I still don't understand why you're trying to hurt me."

"*You* caused this." He held his hands toward her, palms up. "You and your terrorist friends."

"Terrorist?" Sofie pressed down on the top of her head, trying to remember more. "No, I'm a doctor."

"Think so?" Obviously struggling to regain control of his rage, he picked up a length of rope and told her to turn around.

Sofie weighed her options. There was only one exit, and The Incredible Hulk wasn't about to let her leave. Would Luke know where she'd gone, or would he believe she'd left him?

The mere thought of hurting him brought tears to her eyes, but she blinked them back. She would not show weakness.

"You still haven't told me why you kidnapped me," she said, holding her head high. "Why?"

"He'll come for you."

"Oh, God." Sofie swallowed hard, hope and fear mingling into a new, undefinable emotion. Luke *would* come for her. "I remember, you left a note."

"Of course." Graham pushed her shoulder until she turned her back to him, then he tied her wrists together. "Nolan will come soon."

"Don't hurt him." No longer able to hold back her tears, they spilled silently down her cheeks in scalding streams. "Please, don't hurt him."

"Your lover is a murderer."

"No." Sofie turned quickly to face the man. "No, he can't be a murderer. Besides, he was inno—"

"He *claims* innocence." Graham grabbed Sofie's upper

arms in a bruising grip. "Nolan was found with the prover-bial smoking gun. He was guilty all right."

"No." Her gentle Luke would never kill anyone. She couldn't accept that. "You're mistaken."

"So *you* say." Graham released her arms and moved to the door, turning to face her again with his hand on the doorknob. "For eleven years, I waited to see justice done. Eleven years . . ."

"He was waiting for justice, too," Sofie whispered. *"Real* justice."

"I postponed my retirement to see Nolan fry."

Fry? Sofie swayed, trying to understand. Realization made her stagger. She looked at Graham, finally compre-hending where they were, and what the so-called electrical experiment had really been. "Oh, my God."

Graham clenched his fist, staring beyond her at some-thing only he could see. "Six times, he was granted a last-minute stay of execution." He met her gaze again. "Much more mercy than he showed his victim."

"Luke is innocent." Sofie's voice caught in her throat, but she refused to shed more tears. "He's innocent."

"Guilty." The warden shook his fist upward. "And I *will* carry out his sentence. It's my duty."

"Just let us go." Sofie cleared her throat. "It's 1891. Nobody cares."

"I care."

"Please, don't—"

"Do you remember how he looked that morning?" The maniacal gleam in Graham's eyes intensified. "They shaved all the hair off his body and head, then restrained him in the chair."

The warden's words coincided with Sofie's fractured memories. Her stomach lurched as she remembered the terror in Luke's eyes. "I remember," she whispered. "My God, I remember."

"This prison was high-tech all the way." Graham looked around and sighed. "You and your friends ruined it all."

"What friends?" She drew a deep breath, wishing she could use her hands to push her hair out of her eyes. "You keep blaming me for this, but I'm—"

"Responsible for this injustice." The warden's voice fell to a whisper. "Terrorist."

"I don't understand." Tears burned her eyes again. "I just don't understand."

"Justice is all that matters." He opened the door, looking back over his shoulder once more. "You don't need to understand anything but that."

He reached behind himself and grabbed the lantern, then left her in total darkness.

She bowed her head. "Please, don't let Luke come after me."

Less than half a mile from the execution chamber, Rosie went on strike. Luke begged, pleaded, coaxed, and he even smacked her on the rump, but the horse refused to budge.

She was old and he'd pushed her too far, too fast, too hard. He took the gun and what supplies he could carry, and continued up the mountain on foot.

To Sofie. She had to be all right. Had to . . .

"Well, I'll be gol-durned," a familiar voice called from just ahead.

Luke looked up and saw the beautiful, gnarled face of Zeke Judson. The hillbilly grinned and started toward Luke.

"I didn't figger on seein' you in these parts again, *Padre.*"

Luke didn't have time to explain everything now, so he cut to the critical stuff. Sofie. "Zeke, am I glad to see you!"

"Somethin's wrong." Zeke's expression grew solemn. "Where's Miss Dr. Sofie?"

"She's been kidnapped." That was true. "Remember Smith?"

"The burned fella?"

"Right." Luke drew a deep breath, then plunged ahead. "He followed us to Denver and kidnapped Sofie. Said he was taking her back to where we were in that explosion."

"When her head got bunged up."

"Yeah."

"Why?" Zeke scratched his head.

Luke stared into Zeke's rheumy eyes. "Because he wants to kill me. He's using her to lure me there."

"What in tarnation . . . ?" Zeke gave a brief nod. "Show me where." He held his shotgun in both hands.

Luke pointed up the mountain. "At the top." He looked around. "Are you alone?"

"Me 'n Ab was huntin', an' I been tryin' to talk him outta gittin' hitched." Zeke aimed his thumb over his shoulder. "I'll fetch him."

"All right, but I can't wait. I'll meet you in the cave at the top of this mountain." Luke grabbed Zeke's arm. "Thank you."

Zeke gave a quick nod, then jogged away to find Ab.

Luke had help now. With renewed determination, he continued up the mountain. Realizing Graham would be waiting for him, he moved into the trees, constantly watching the granite wall that shielded the execution chamber.

And the chair.

He tried not to remember the searing jolts of electricity plundering through his body. He tried not to remember the terror of being restrained in that chair, knowing he was about to die.

He tried . . . but failed.

Finally, the granite wall where he and Sofie had emerged that morning appeared. Still unaccustomed to the weight of a gun in his hand, Luke tightened his grip. The last time he'd held a gun was the night his life had been destroyed.

If necessary, he would use this gun. And if he had to die to save Sofie, so be it.

Graham wanted justice. *I'll give the bastard justice.*

He ducked behind a tree near the opening and looked back down the mountain. No sign of Zeke and Ab yet. Something white floated by. Snow. The flakes multiplied quickly, and the wind whipped them into a frenzy.

Looking down the mountain again, Luke realized the sudden storm would delay Zeke and Ab, and possibly prevent them from finding the mountain at all. *Damn.* Then Luke glanced toward the opening again, realizing the snow would also make him more difficult to see.

He slid the saddlebags from his shoulder and left them beside a tree, then checked to make sure the gun was loaded. It was.

Walking boldly through the blinding snow, Luke faced his two greatest fears.

The electric chair and losing Sofie.

The former was acceptable, but only if it prevented the latter.

He pressed his back against the icy granite, inching his way along it toward the opening. Memories of the last time he'd been here threatened to interfere. He'd never seen a more beautiful dawn than that one, but tomorrow's would be even more beautiful.

With Sofie.

He squeezed through the opening and held his breath. The stench of decomposing bodies hit him like a missile. His execution chamber had become a time-traveling tomb.

Swallowing his nausea, he flattened himself against the inner wall. The chamber was almost completely dark, and he waited for his heart to slow to a reasonable pace.

Lantern light suddenly appeared across the wide chamber, drawing Luke's gaze.

Sofie.

Tied to a chair with a gag over her mouth, she sat there staring at him. She shook her head violently, her eyes wide with fear.

Where was—

Something heavy slammed into Luke's skull. He struggled to remain standing, to hold on to the gun, but the floor rushed toward him.

Strong arms grabbed him from behind and the gun fell with a loud clatter. Luke blinked, trying to focus and reach for it, but a booted foot shot out from behind him and kicked the gun across the cement floor.

"Justice."

That grating voice jerked Luke back from the dark, welcoming void which called to him. He couldn't pass out now.

"Sofie," he whispered.

The warden chuckled. "Your chair awaits."

Luke was so weak he could barely move. His head swam and his gut heaved.

"Look, Nolan, there it is." The warden dragged Luke toward the center of the chamber. "Open your eyes, you filthy murderer, and *look.*"

Luke heard Sofie trying to shout through her gag, and he looked at her again. She was so close, but he couldn't wrench himself free of the warden's death grip.

"No, look *there.*" Graham grabbed Luke's head and aimed it toward something shiny.

The chair.

Firewood had been carefully arranged around the chair. So Graham had made a few modifications for Luke's execution. Steel didn't burn, but flesh did. His flesh.

Luke drew a deep breath and pulled one arm free. He twisted and fought, but Graham flung him to the ground and came down on him with his knee.

"Let her go." Luke would do anything to save the woman he loved. Anything.

"She's a terrorist."

That made no sense. Luke shook his head and looked up at the hooded monster. "Free Sofie . . . and I'll do it." *Come on, Zeke.*

Something heavy fell near the entrance. The ceiling was coming down. Luke looked up at the broken beams and crumbling rock.

Graham appeared to weigh his options, then moved his knee from Luke's chest. As he stood, he pulled a gun from his pocket. "In the chair."

"You'll free Sofie?"

"Get in the chair."

Luke had no options. Again. Graham had a gun and he held Sofie prisoner. Defeated, Luke turned to face the chair.

Sofie screamed through her gag, but he didn't permit himself to look at her now. The moment he touched the icy metal, Luke's body filled with the heat of electrocution all over again. He felt the pain as if the volts were raging through him at this very moment.

God help us.

Swallowing his fear as much as possible, he dropped into the chair and looked up at Sofie. She was frantically trying to get free.

"Don't . . . watch, Sofie," he said, still staring at her, even as Graham wrapped rope around the chair and Luke and tied it.

Once Luke's arms and torso were secure, the warden tied Luke's ankles to the chair as well. Then the bastard walked away and released Sofie from the chair. She leapt up and hurried toward Luke, her hands still tied behind her back and her mouth gagged.

"Terrorist," Graham shouted from behind her, shoving her into Luke's lap.

"No!" Luke's roar echoed through the chamber, and another shower of stones and steel beams fell from the ceiling. "Let Sofie go."

"Terrorist," Graham repeated as he tied Sofie to the chair with Luke. "Burn with the murderer."

Luke met Sofie's terrified gaze. She sat sideways in his lap, and her arms and shoulders were securely tied to the chair. The gag prevented her from talking.

He craned his neck to reach her mouth with his, using his teeth to pull the gag away. She gulped air into her lungs.

"Luke, I remember," she said breathlessly. "I remember why I was here that morning."

Graham walked around the chair, igniting the firewood in several places. *Hurry, Zeke.*

"I love you, Sofie," Luke whispered. "I'm so sorry."

"I'm not a doctor."

"Terrorist," Graham muttered.

"I came here to stop your execution and an activist group helped me get inside the prison. In here." A tear trickled down her face. "They said I looked like the doctor who was scheduled to attend the execution. They grabbed her and I took her place. I didn't know they planned to bomb the prison."

"Liar." Graham struck another match and dropped it to the outer circle of wood, obviously wanting to prolong his pleasure.

"Sadistic bastard."

"Luke, listen to me," Sofie pleaded. "I don't want to die without telling you the truth."

And, barring a miracle, they would die. "Go on." Smoke thickened and curled around them, spiraling toward the high ceiling of the chamber. "Tell me, Sofie."

"My brother . . ." She bit her lower lip. "He died the night before your execution. He was shot by the police after a robbery."

"I'm listening." Luke concentrated on her voice, on her face, and shut out the choking smoke and approaching death. They were bound so tightly, nothing could save them from the flames.

"Ricky, my brother—"

"Ricky?" Luke's head roared. "My God."

"Yes, as he was dying, he told me about the liquor store clerk," she said quickly. "And about you."

Luke gazed into her eyes. "Your brother?"

Sofie nodded. "He was a wild boy, always in trouble, and . . ." She coughed in the thickening smoke. "But before he died, he begged me to stop your ex . . . execution."

Luke wanted to hold her. He wanted to wrap his arms around her. "Thank you for telling me." His throat burned from the smoke and they both coughed. "I love you, Sofie, no matter what. None of this is your fault."

"I tried to stop them." Her voice dripped acid. "I was up all night, trying to reach congressmen, judges, lawyers, the governor." She coughed again. "I even called the White House."

"You did?" He rested his head against her chest, feeling her chin on top of his head. They couldn't hold each other while they died, but they were together. Still, he wished there were some way to free her from this nightmare. She didn't deserve this.

Neither of them did.

More sections of rock and steel tumbled from the ceiling. Luke tried to see through the smoke, spotting Graham near the entrance. The creep stood there staring.

Sofie lifted her head to look down at Luke's face. "Kiss me."

He met her lips, pouring all his love into it. If only he could set her free . . .

As the flames grew hotter, a commotion erupted near the entrance. Luke and Sofie both turned to watch Zeke and Ab rush in and struggle with Graham.

More of the ceiling came down, then a low buzz commenced in the chair. A familiar sensation. "My God."

Though he felt no pain, he recognized the unholy *zing* of the electric chair.

Another section of ceiling fell. "Cave-in," Zeke yelled. "We gotta save 'em."

"Can't, Zeke," Ab called over the falling debris. "God forgive us."

Luke saw Ab forcing Graham through the entrance. "You're gonna hang, Smith."

Zeke looked back over his shoulder and looked up. "I'm comin' for you, *Padre*," he called just as a huge section of ceiling and rock fell, blocking the entrance forever. Luke prayed Zeke had escaped before it was too late.

Then the flames grew and the impossible electrical current intensified. Luke lifted his face to his wife and met her lips again.

One last time.

Chapter Twenty-Three

Denver, Colorado—Present Day

Sofie Danzano pulled her Volkswagen into a parking place across the street from the brownstone with the bright orange awning. Her heart hammered into her ribs and her palms grew sweaty against the steering wheel.

With trembling fingers, she reached for the magazine article again. The caption under the photograph gave the street address. This was definitely the right place.

But was it *the* place?

She combed her fingers through her hair and used the rearview mirror to freshen her lipstick. She'd waited all her life for this day. Maybe she was nuts, but she had to know once and for all.

Climbing from the car, she slung the straps of her leather backpack over her shoulder and slammed the door. She stood there for several moments, still holding the magazine in her hand.

Memories of the dreams that had plagued her since

puberty flooded her mind. Dreams she wasn't sure were dreams at all, where she'd stood on this street and had visited that building. She'd been raised in Pueblo, not Denver, but this place haunted her for a reason. She'd been here before. She knew it in her heart and soul.

Reincarnation? Maybe. All she knew was the street lawyer in the magazine article *was* Luke Nolan.

Her Luke. Her *husband* in another place. Another time. "Welcome to the 'Twilight Zone.'" She almost never read magazines—what medical student had the time?—but being stranded for two hours in DIA while the airline found her luggage, she'd had nothing better to do.

Fate had led her to this particular issue of this particular magazine. She didn't doubt that for a minute.

She was scheduled to begin her residency here in Denver next month, but she had a few free weeks to investigate this mystery. Turning the page, she looked at the man's photo again. He had long, wavy hair pulled into a ponytail. Though the hair bore no resemblance to the man in her dreams, the face was his.

And the name.

He was an attorney—a street lawyer. The article told of his altruism and endless hours of community service. Yes, this sounded like something her Luke would've done, if he'd had the chance.

Filled with determination, she stuffed the magazine into her backpack and removed her sunglasses, dropping them into her pocket. She wanted to see his expression when he saw her for the first time. Again.

This was nuts. She was nuts. But she had to know. She'd never been able to have a serious relationship, because she felt connected—married?—to Luke Nolan. A man she'd never actually met.

Or had she?

The door squeaked and a bell jingled as she stepped inside. For a moment, she was mentally transported back to 1891, when she'd last visited this place. But it looked different now. A glass case filled with shoe paraphernalia and a modern cash register occupied one side of the front room. The dressing room where she'd been kidnapped by that maniac had a door on it instead of a curtain.

But it was still the same place.

The bricks were gone from the back wall, too. Did that mean—

"Ah, it's a beautiful morning." An elderly gentleman walked into the room, smiling. "May I help you?"

"Yes, I hope so." She swallowed hard. Was this Luke's grandfather, alive and healthy? She put out her hand. "My name is Sofie Dan—"

"Sofie?" The man's eyes widened. "Sofie? Tell me, how do you spell it?"

Smiling, she answered. Once upon a time, Luke had asked her that same question.

"Amazing." His smile was wide and welcoming. "My wife and I, we believe in miracles."

A shiver skittered down her spine. "Miracles?"

"Yes, miracles." His expression became intense as he stared at her. "I'm Albert Nolan."

"I . . . I guessed. I'm pleased to meet you, Mr. Nolan." Sofie opened her backpack and showed him the article. "I'm looking for—"

"My grandson, of course." He winked. "His office is through the door in the back room and up the stairs."

It's almost as if he expected me. Sofie stared at Mr. Nolan for several moments. "Do you . . . know why I'm here?"

"Go talk to Luke, darlin'." He chuckled quietly. "Sure took your time about getting here. Wait 'til I tell his grandmother. She'll be thrilled."

Stunned, Sofie tucked the magazine under her arm and went into the back of the store. She opened the door that led to a tall, narrow staircase and climbed to the second floor.

An open window at the top of the stairs provided a gentle breeze, and she paused for a moment to cool off and gather her wits. She half-expected to awaken and learn she'd fallen into an episode of "X-Files."

She proceeded down the narrow hallway. The door at the end stood open, and the breeze from behind her flowed past her and into the room ahead.

He had his back to her. The dark, wavy ponytail made her doubt again that this could be the same short-haired man she'd fallen in love with and married in 1891.

She almost changed her mind as she stood frozen there in the doorway. A glass display case caught her eye and she took a few steps over to glance into it. Procrastinating.

But her heart almost stopped as she focused on the case's contents. There in the case were the Bible and crucifix she remembered. Before she could look at the other objects, she heard the chair squeak behind her.

As she turned to face him, her head swam and her heart made an illegal U-turn in her chest. His eyes widened and he removed his small, wire-rimmed glasses as he rose slowly from his chair. "Sofie," he whispered, dropping the glasses onto his desk. "Sofie."

Her eyes stung with tears as he walked around the desk and stood in front of her. This was her Luke. All her doubts fled as she gazed into his beautiful gray eyes. This man had been her husband. She knew it in her heart and in her soul.

"Luke?" Her voice cracked and tears streamed down her face. So much for mascara. "You . . . remember me? Know me?"

"My God, I can't believe it's really you." He drew a deep breath, then released it shakily. "I'm so glad you're here."

She nodded and turned to look in the case again. "I recognize the Bible and crucifix." When she looked at him again, he smiled. He stood so close she could feel him, smell him, almost touch him.

The urge to throw herself into his arms was almost overwhelming, but she held herself back. No need to scare him away now that she'd finally found him.

"I . . . I don't understand any of this," she said quietly, facing him again. He stood so close to her. The special energy that always flowed between them was still present, as it had been in the past and in her dreams. "Was it another lifetime?"

He shook his head. "I don't know exactly." Tilting his head to one side, he smiled again. "All I know is that when Grandpa and I tore the bricks out downstairs, we found these things with three letters." He shook his head and chuckled. "They're in my handwriting, and there was a note in his."

"I remember," she said, transfixed.

He held her gaze with his. "And I remember the night before."

"Our wedding night." Heat flooded Sofie's face and she averted her gaze.

Silence stretched between them, then Luke opened the glass case and removed a small, silver object. "Do you remember this?"

He handed the item to her, and Sofie turned it over in her hand. "Yes." She smiled and held the tarnished silver closer. "My ID bracelet. No wonder your grandfather asked me how to spell my name."

"You keep that," he said. "It's yours."

Uncomfortable again, Sofie shook her head. "I'd like all these things to stay together, if it's all right with you."

"Sofie, I . . ." He sighed and shook his head, obviously as confused as she.

"I . . . I've always wondered what happened to Jenny and Shane and everybody in Redemption."

His eyes brightened. "Just a minute." He retrieved a wooden box from the glass case and opened it, gingerly removing an old, leather-bound book. "Look."

"Miss Dr. Sofie?" A new flood of tears blurred her vision, and her hands trembled as she traced the engraved words with the tip of her finger. "I can't quite make out the author's name. Who . . . ?"

Carefully, he opened the book and showed her the title page. "Jennifer Latimer Hill," he said. "It was published in 1928."

"Jenny." She blinked back her tears until her vision cleared. "Have you read it?"

"Many times." He smiled. "Read the dedication, Sofie."

She cleared her throat as he turned another brittle page. *"For Dr. Sofie and Father Salazar, wherever you are: Thank you."* Overcome by tears, Sofie heard but didn't see Luke put the book back in its case for safekeeping.

"It *really* happened," she whispered, drying her eyes with the back of her hand.

"Yes, I know it did."

The passion in his tone prompted her to look up, and his expression sliced through her tissue-thin veneer. He looked at her with hunger, desperation . . . and love.

"Luke," she whispered, "I've dreamed of you for so long."

"And I you." He brought his hand to her cheek. "I didn't understand the significance of all this stuff for years, but as I grew older . . ."

"I know. The dreams started." Sofie shivered as he gently stroked her cheek. "It really, really happened, didn't it?"

"Yes. I *believe.*" He nodded and brought his other hand to her face as well. "Sofie, I've waited for you and prayed for this moment."

A sob tore from her throat and tears slipped unheeded down her cheeks. "So have I, Luke."

"I didn't know your last name," he confessed, still cupping her face gently in his large hands. "Or where to search for you."

"Danzano. My last name is Danzano. And I couldn't remember exactly where this building was." If only he'd continue touching her forever. "I'm from Pueblo, so I don't know my way around Denver very well."

"How . . . ?"

She remembered the magazine article, but when she reached for it, he removed his hands from her face, leaving her bereft and shaken. Summoning her sense of reason, she handed him the article. "When I saw the orange awning and read the address, I had to see for myself."

"Thank God you did. I begged Grandpa to add the orange awning about ten years ago, because I hoped it would help you find me." He set the magazine on his desk and put his hands on her cheeks again.

Yes.

"I know it's crazy, Sofie, but . . ." He kissed her so gently, she thought at first she'd imagined it. His gaze held hers captive, smoldering just as she remembered. "I love you. I've always loved you. And I've waited for you."

"Oh, God, Luke." Dropping her backpack, she threw her arms around his neck and clung to him, absorbing his essence and energy. "I love you, too."

He laughed quietly, then tilted her chin and kissed her again, and this time there was no room for doubt. Leaving her breathless, he kept his arms around her. His hooded gaze made it clear he felt everything she did.

"We love each other, but we just met," she whispered, still stunned that all this was true. Really true. "I've never been able to . . . to be with another man, because of my memories of you. I felt as if . . ."

He nodded. "I know." He brushed the backs of his fingers along her cheekbone, then delicately traced the outline of her upper lip. "We'll have to get to know each other again, I suppose, in this time."

She nodded, swallowing the lump in her throat. "Yes, I'd like that."

"But I want you to know, I expect us to get married again, and I'm going to ask the real Father Salazar to perform the ceremony."

"Yes, definitely yes." God, this was crazy, but she meant every word, and she knew he did, too. "I love all this hair." She reached behind him and tugged his ponytail.

"Big improvement, I'm sure."

She grinned and he kissed her again, hungrily. Desire stormed through her. This was Luke. Her Luke. Her husband once upon a time.

And he would be her husband again.

After breaking the kiss, he held her in his arms as their hearts thudded in unison. "Do you remember what I said to you just before we brought the letters here, Sofie?"

She nodded against his shoulder. "I'll always remember." Leaning back slightly, she looked intently into his eyes. "You said, 'Promise me, that no matter what happens, you'll remember we're meant to be. We belong to each other. Always.' "

"Yes, always." His warm breath was a caress against her cheek. "Marry me, Sofie. I don't want to wait any longer."

She smiled, the insanity of marrying a virtual stranger was lost in her knowledge that they were meant to be. This was right.

Fate and destiny.

"Yes, Luke," she said. "On our anniversary?"

His grin widened. "That's only six weeks away, you know."

"I remember." She kissed him softly.

"But I'm not sure I can wait that long to, uh . . ."

Need, fierce and sure, shot through her. Her body trembled in his embrace, and she nodded. "Now."

"As I recall, that's one of your favorite words." His voice sounded husky as he led her into the hallway. "Let's keep it in your vocabulary."

"I like the word more, too."

He groaned, leading her down the hall to another door. "This is my apartment."

"Convenient." His uncompromising acceptance of her—of *them*—was incredible, and it validated everything she'd carried in her heart for so long. Her insides trembled with longing, her heart swelled with love, and her mind reeled in helpless acceptance.

They walked into his apartment. It was clean and sparsely furnished with beautiful antiques.

He stopped just inside, closing the door behind them. Holding her hand, he gazed intently into her eyes. Perhaps she should feel cheap and brazen, but she didn't. In her heart, she knew she'd been with him before in *every* sense of the word.

With an encouraging smile, he said, "I have one question before . . ."

She wanted him so desperately, she could barely breathe. "Does it involve champagne?"

"Mmm, no, but I'll get some." He tilted his head to one side, devouring her with his gaze. "Do you still have the tattoo?"

Smiling, she reached for the hem of her sweater and pulled it over her head. "See for yourself."

And he did.

Epilogue

Sofie turned to the last page of *Miss Dr. Sofie,* cherishing the new copy Luke had made for her seven years ago as a wedding gift. The copyright had long since expired, and she knew the words written by Jenny Latimer couldn't possibly mean as much to anyone else as they did to her and Luke.

Their unborn baby chose that moment to turn a somersault against her bladder, and she placed a protective hand over her swollen belly. A larger, darker hand covered hers, and she looked up to meet her husband's gaze.

"Only two more months until little Sam—"

"Or Jenny."

"Or Jenny." Luke knelt beside her chair and pointed to the book. "Read to me."

Sofie smiled and turned her attention to the printed words, knowing which part her husband wanted to hear.

"Author's Note: This story is true, based on my own memories of living in Redemption, Colorado. Dr. and Mrs. Roman Taylor remained citizens of Redemption until their deaths in 1909 and

1911, respectively. Dora Fleming married Sheriff Ab Johnson, and Zeke Judson disappeared and was never heard from again. Mr. Smith was a man filled with hatred, though no one ever knew why. He refused to talk even when they hanged him for the murders of Father Salazar and Dr. Sofie. My brother Shane went to college and became a Texas Ranger, then later a United States Marshal. Marshal Sam Weathers was killed in 1896 by an unknown assailant on the banks of the Verdigris in Indian Territory. And I married Franklin Hill, a rancher in East Texas, where I live to this day with my husband and our three children: Sofie, Luke, and Sam.

"When I get to Heaven, I want to thank Miss Dr. Sofie and Father Salazar for all they did for the little girl they barely knew in 1891."

A tear slipped down Sofie's cheek and Luke captured it with his fingertip. "I love you, Miss Dr. Sofie."

"I love you, too," she whispered, her voice catching in her throat. After a moment, she drew a steadying breath. "But that's *Mrs.* Dr. Sofie, and don't you forget it, *Padre.*"

Dear Readers:

While cleaning out an old file cabinet—something I do every couple of decades—I ran across some notes from a speech I made in college for a political-science project. The topic was the death penalty, and one of the articles I'd saved involved a young man who survived the electric chair. The emotional impact of his story struck me all over again, and before I knew it Luke Nolan introduced himself to my muse and *Another Dawn* was born.

Sofie and Luke prove what many of us already know—that love can and does shatter the boundaries of time. With a love as destined as theirs, anything is possible.

I hope you enjoyed *Another Dawn*. I love to hear from readers. Write to me at:

P.O. Box 1196
Monument, CO 80132-1196

Or visit my home page on the WorldWide Web for information at http://www.debstover.com/.

May all your days include a bit of magic.

Deb Stover

BOOK YOUR PLACE ON OUR WEBSITE AND MAKE THE READING CONNECTION!

We've created a customized website just for our very special readers, where you can get the inside scoop on everything that's going on with Zebra, Pinnacle and Kensington books.

When you come online, you'll have the exciting opportunity to:

- View covers of upcoming books
- Read sample chapters
- Learn about our future publishing schedule (listed by publication month *and author*)
- Find out when your favorite authors will be visiting a city near you
- Search for and order backlist books from our online catalog
- Check out author bios and background information
- Send e-mail to your favorite authors
- Meet the Kensington staff online
- Join us in weekly chats with authors, readers and other guests
- Get writing guidelines
- AND MUCH MORE!

**Visit our website at
http://www.zebrabooks.com**

ROMANCE FROM JO BEVERLY

DANGEROUS JOY   (0-8217-5129-8, $5.99)

FORBIDDEN   (0-8217-4488-7, $4.99)

THE SHATTERED ROSE   (0-8217-5310-X, $5.99)

TEMPTING FORTUNE   (0-8217-4858-0, $4.99)

ROMANCE FROM JANELLE TAYLOR

ANYTHING FOR LOVE   (0-8217-4992-7, $5.99)

DESTINY MINE   (0-8217-5185-9, $5.99)

CHASE THE WIND   (0-8217-4740-1, $5.99)

MIDNIGHT SECRETS   (0-8217-5280-4, $5.99)

MOONBEAMS AND MAGIC   (0-8217-0184-4, $5.99)

SWEET SAVAGE HEART   (0-8217-5276-6, $5.99)

ROMANCE FROM FERN MICHAELS

DEAR EMILY   (0-8217-4952-8, $5.99)

WISH LIST   (0-8217-5228-6, $6.99)

AND IN HARDCOVER:

VEGAS RICH   (1-57566-057-1, $25.00)

YOU WON'T WANT TO READ
JUST ONE—KATHERINE STONE

ROOMMATES (0-8217-5206-5, $6.99/$7.99)
No one could have prepared Carrie for the monumental
changes she would face when she met her new circle of friends
at Stanford University. Once their lives intertwined and became
woven into the tapestry of the times, they would never be the
same.

TWINS (0-8217-5207-3, $6.99/$7.99)
Brook and Melanie Chandler were so different, it was hard to
believe they were sisters. One was a dark, serious, ambitious
New York attorney; the other, a golden, glamourous, sophisti-
cated supermodel. But they were more than sisters—they were
twins and more alike than even they knew . . .

THE CARLTON CLUB (0-8217-5204-9, $6.99/$7.99)
It was the place to see and be seen, the only place to be. And
for those who frequented the playground of the very rich, it
was a way of life. Mark, Kathleen, Leslie and Janet—they
worked together, played together, and loved together, all behind
exclusive gates of the *Carlton Club*.